Angel of Song

Book Three in the Master of Illusion Series

Anne Rouen

First published 2015 by StoneHut Publishing
PO Box 116, Manilla NSW 2346

**National Library of Australia Cataloguing-in-Publication
entry:**

Angel of song / Anne Rouen ; editor, Felicity Matthews.

ISBN: 9780992403621 (paperback)
Opera—France—Paris—Fiction.
Sopranos (Singers)—France—Paris—Fiction.
Women in war—France—Fiction.
War stories.
Matthews, Felicity, editor.
A823.4

Cover Images:
'WW1 British Soldier' — Copyright: Johncairns — via
iStockphoto LP
'Beautiful angel among golden dust'— Copyright: Konradbak —
via Dreamstime

Editing & Cover Design by Web Etch Design and Editing

Printed by CreateSpace, An Amazon.com Company
Also available on Kindle and other online stores

DEDICATION

Angel of Song is dedicated to the memory of my adored grandfather who served on the Western Front with his unit, the 3rd Australian Field Bakery, from 1916 until the end of the war. He left for France a Master Baker and came home in 1919 a pâtissier *sans pareil*. He appears in the pages of this book as Jack.

PROLOGUE

4 December 1929

'All right, all right,' called the publisher. 'I am coming. There's no need to break the doorknocker.'

'Apologies, Monsieur, it's cold out here. Special delivery. Sorry about the lateness of the hour.'

'Another manuscript by this anonymous author?'

'*Oui*, Monsieur. She said you did not need to know her name.'

'She? *Une femme?*'

'Yes, Monsieur.'

'Ah ... She is not worried about remuneration?'

'No, Monsieur, she said not. She said that she has learnt that there are things that money cannot buy. For her, the writing of it—the journey, you understand—was worth more than any monetary recompense.'

'Indeed?'

'But she did say one more thing, Monsieur. She said this is the last manuscript, and when you have finished it, you will know who she is ...'

The publisher laughed. 'Not want recompense, indeed!'

He signed for the package, glancing down at the title.

'Book Three: Angel of Song.'

In spite of himself, he could not resist. Tearing off the wrapping, he settled down to read.

CHAPTER ONE ~ UNDERCURRENTS

Nine am, 21 September 1913

Last evening we were all so happy, so contented with our lot. Yet, this morning, Angel is distressed. And I am at a loss to know why.

'*Sacré mille* …' The marquis du Bois, reading his paper over morning coffee, started and frowned, concentrating on a small segment hidden away at the bottom of the page. He put down his cup with a crash. '*Mon Dieu!*' he breathed, returning to the segment, perusing it with even greater concentration. 'Why have I not seen this coming? But then, have I not? Have I not, indeed?' His troubled eyes went to the pile of correspondence littering the table.

His protégée, pausing before the mirror in the hall to adjust her hat to a slightly more dashing angle, swept up the skirts of her riding habit and ran lightly to put her head around the door of the salon.

'You are not riding with us, this morning, Angelpapa?' she asked, eyeing him doubtfully, since he was still in his dressing-gown.

He lay the paper aside, his expression lightening as his

gaze rested on the young woman he was pleased to think of as his daughter. 'I think not. Not this morning, my angel. Tomorrow, perhaps? You are looking remarkably fresh after your night of dissipation.'

Angelique flew over to his wheeled chair to put her arms around him and drop a kiss on his brow. 'Thank you, thank you, thank you—Oh, a thousand, thousand thank yous—for my ball, last night! It was wonderful! It was … Oh, it was … beyond description!'

'It was my very great pleasure, my darling.' He eyed her flushed cheeks and shining eyes, quizzically. 'I suppose this, er … enthusiastic response means that I will soon be receiving a visit of ceremony from a certain *distinguished* young gentleman?'

She made a parrying gesture, murmuring, 'I do not know. But,' her voice strengthened, 'I loved my dance with the marquis du Bois! Did you enjoy it, Angelpapa?' She whirled around with an invisible partner, humming the tune of the *Emperor Waltz*.

'Of a certainty, all nine, no, ten steps of it. Indeed, it made my night, my dear.'

She smiled delightfully. 'You see, I told you that you could do it: that I would make you dance with me!'

'So you did, my dear, so you did. And is there anything else you wish to tell me?'

She presented an innocent face. 'But, I do not know what you mean!'

'Is that so?' he drawled. 'Well it does not matter.'

'Oh,' she went on, 'it was all such fun, last night! I know Mama cannot speak, but I am sure she enjoyed herself. Did you have fun, Angelpapa?'

He thought of himself sitting beside Katarina—she who could no longer speak or show expression, he who could hardly walk—watching the others dance: Madame Dupont and the duc de Belvoir, the comte de Villefontaine and the duchesse, Angelique and the young marquis de Beaulieu. And then, Angelique had come, insisting he dance with her while her partner sat with her mother. They were pitifully few, the steps he could now manage. Yet, just a few months ago, he had taught her to waltz himself.

He smiled wryly. 'Fun,' he mused. 'I would not have put it in quite that way myself. Let us just say that I found it delightful, most entertaining ... But fun?' He cast up his eyes. 'The fatuous expressions favoured by the youth of today!'

She tossed her head. 'Oh, *passé de mode*! You are not usually so old-fashioned, Angelpapa!'

There was a glint in his eye. 'If events play out as I expect they will, you may discover just how *démodé* I can be, my dear child.'

'Oh, suitors!' She giggled. 'I danced with so many! But whatever you say, I think we all enjoyed ourselves. Did you see my papa waltzing with the duchesse de Belvoir? Did they not make such an elegant couple?'

'The duchesse and the comte are both very accomplished dancers,' he agreed. 'They received many compliments on their stylish waltzing.'

'Papa said that he liked dancing with her very much. He said that, besides being a good dancer, she is a very gracious lady. Etienne told me afterwards that his mother, too, enjoyed herself.'

'Indeed?' he murmured. 'One does not have to ask whether or not the marquis de Beaulieu enjoyed his night ...'

His lips lifted a little at one corner as she coloured, feverishly changing the subject.

'Godmama is a wonderfully graceful dancer, is she not? I had no idea—I have never seen her dance before—well, only the steps to demonstrate to her ballet students, of course; but I have never seen her waltz.'

'No, she does not usually dance, but *du vrai*, she has not lost the lightness and gaiety she had as a ballerina.'

'Tell me about her when she was a ballerina. You knew her then, Angelpapa?'

'Yes, indeed. I watched all her performances.'

'But when did you meet her?'

'So many questions, Petite! Why now?'

She shrugged. 'I did not think to ask you before, and whenever I asked Godmama, she turned it off. But I do want to know. Please?'

'Oh, very well. When we were children, she rescued me, homeless and nameless, from a street in Paris and took me home to her opera house. I suppose I was about nine—she a little older. Will that do?'

'But you are the marquis du Bois! How could you have been homeless and nameless on a Paris street? Oh ...' She pouted. 'You are making up a tale for me!'

'No, no, I would not do that, but it is a long story, Petite. I will tell you another day. Your godmama rescued me, and before he died, Monsieur Dupont made me promise to take care of her. One way or another, she has been with me ever since; although, I think of late, it is more that she takes care of me. Back then, because I had no name, I became known as Angel ——'

'Because of the way you sing!'

He smiled. 'Perhaps it was my saintly disposition? However it was, we both thought it amazing when, out of your own spirit as a little girl, you began to call me Angelpapa—even though you had never heard that name. But I thought you wanted to know about Madame Dupont, my dear?'

'I do! Oh, I do! She will never talk about her young life, but I have heard her students whispering amongst themselves. She was a famous ballerina, was she not? A prima donna, even?'

'Indeed, she was. She had many admirers. They called her "La Belle". She was very, very special, indeed. But then,' his knuckles whitened on the chair arms, 'her career was cut tragically short.'

'May I know what happened, Angelpapa?'

He looked beyond her at a scene that she knew was

working powerfully on his emotions. She could not know that he was weighing up the horror of the tale side-by-side with the fact that Angelique should know that, out there in the world she was about to enter, there were those who would wish to harm her.

'I will tell you. You are old enough to know, now. However, it is privileged information, and you must never mention it to Madame Dupont or anyone else, Petite. She cannot speak of it. It is too painful for her. I will only tell you on that condition.'

'Of course, I would not do that! But I have always wondered …'

'Very well. Elise Gordonnier was seventeen ——'

'My age,' she breathed.

'When she was attacked outside the Opéra Français by a homicidal maniac who lay in wait for her.'

'Oh, no! Oh poor, poor Godmama! How terrible!' She felt physically ill.

'Steady, Child. I should have known this would be too much for you to bear.'

'No, please tell me! I will be all right.'

'Are you sure you can you cope with it?'

She nodded.

After looking at her closely, he continued, 'The police knew about him, but he was a royal prince and, therefore, thought to be above the law.'

'Do you mean that someone could have stopped him and did not?'

'There are different rules for those with power and those without,' he confirmed. 'Many were afraid of him, for he had always murdered his victims.'

'Are you saying that if someone is powerful enough, they can get away with anything?' She was horrified.

'That is why you must be careful, Petite; why I have decided to tell you this harrowing tale. Your career will put you in the path of many different types of people. Amongst them are those we must avoid for, sadly, the law will not always support us.'

'But, if he murdered ... How, then, did Godmama survive?'

'Ah, that is where her fortune changed: her life was saved at the last second by the great conductor, Monsieur Dupont, returning with his orchestra from a soiree. However, she was so badly injured that she could never dance at that level again. It was after this that she married Monsieur Dupont.' He looked down at his hands. 'The prince was later found dead beside the Seine.'

A little chill feathered up the back of her neck. Somehow, she knew that this man, whom she loved more than anyone, had meted out his own justice: in his own way, in his own time. She said quickly, to dispel the sickening visions he had conjured up, 'But she is all right now, isn't she? Godmama, I mean? She said she enjoyed her evening!'

He nodded. 'Yes, dancing with the duc. The gossips would have had a merry old time had not the comte stepped in when he did.'

'To dance with the duchesse, you mean?' she asked, thoughtful for a moment. 'I saw Godmama last night waltzing with the duc de Belvoir: he held her as if she were ... Oh, a precious, precious *objet d'art*; she looked so happy. I have never seen her look like that. They danced as if they were in love. Oh ...' She put a hand to her mouth. 'I am sorry, Angelpapa! My tongue runs away with me!'

He spoke under his breath. She could hardly hear him. 'So! My astute angel has seen what others may well have noticed; though, I did my best to defuse it.'

'Pardon?'

'You were quite right, Petite,' he answered. 'The duc has been in love with her for many years, since long before he met the duchesse.' He smiled. 'It was hardly a secret that he was, perhaps, her most devoted follower. Madame Dupont is probably the only one who did not know it. It was a wonder that she did not make the connection: but no, it was a complete surprise to her since he worshipped from afar, as the saying is. Of course, once her career was over, she isolated herself from all that. He has been remarkably constant for so little encouragement. But you see, once the spark of true love has been ignited, it cannot be quenched. It is there forever.'

'So, he was in love with her before she married Monsieur Dupont?'

'Oh, yes, before that, too.'

'But why, then, did they not marry?'

'A duc has obligations, my child. He is not free to marry whom he wishes. In many ways, he has power; but in others, he is a slave. *Noblesse oblige*,' he murmured. 'Some take it seriously.'

'But what about the duchesse?'

'There can be no doubt that the duchesse knows all about it, my dear. She would have known when she married him that he was in love, and with whom,' said the marquis. His lip quirking at one corner, he added in dry tones, 'It was blindingly obvious to those of us with even the smallest powers of observation, *je vous assure*. And knowing him, he would have told her, if only to prevent her finding out some other way. It was her choice to marry, and in my estimation, she has accepted it. Nothing has come of it, after all. Madame Dupont and the duc are both honourable people. The duchesse, like all women of her class, has been brought up not to expect marriage to be a love match. No, in such circles it is more likely to be regarded as an "asset match".'

Shocked by his cynicism, she exclaimed, 'But, Angelpapa, may not a duc marry one whom he loves?'

'Oh, certainly, my dear, but only if he falls in love with a lady of his own class.'

'Is that why you have never married?'

'I am not a duc, Petite,' his voice deepened.

He was not looking at her, but in a blinding flash, she realised something she had known subconsciously all her life.

'It is because … You love my mama, do you not? I know that you do!' *How could I say such a thing?* She wondered, almost fainting with fear. Clinging to the edge of the table, she sank into the nearest chair. Her lips framed words she could not speak; an apology she could not utter, for this she had to know.

He frowned over her bent head, alive to her distress. Impetuous and wilful she may be, but Angelique was not usually insensitive in this fashion. Once, too, he would have torn to shreds the author of such a question, but he was not the same man; and this was his own little angel. And yet … He did not want to bare his heart to her, or anyone. 'Enough of these indelicate questions,' he replied, forcing himself to return a light answer. 'Too much prying is not good for the young. There are some things in life that are beyond mere words.' But he could see that she needed the truth.

Taking her hand and holding it, he said simply, 'I love you both, my dear.'

'Angelpapa …' She hesitated. 'I cannot remember a time in my life when you were not with me. Since I was a little girl, I have always felt surrounded by your love. I have always loved you more than anyone. My papa, even.'

'We are being very serious, this morning, Petite. It must be the result of our late night. Too much euphoria brings about the opposite state of melancholia to approximately the same degree, I find.' Sensing that she was not to be fobbed off, that something deep inside her was driving her, he added, 'Many years ago, when you were a very small child, I made my pledge to your mother that you would be to me as my daughter; that I would cherish you and nurture you, developing your great singing talent as if you were my own. Even though, to my eternal regret, you are not my own flesh and blood, you are, without question, the daughter of my spirit. Does that answer you, my angel?'

'Yes, thank you,' she whispered. Then, emotion-charged words tumbled out, 'I could not live without you, Angelpapa!'

'Do not talk in that fashion, Angelique.' He spoke almost roughly. 'Look at me—at how much I have failed in health in the last few months!' His mouth twisted. 'Soon, my dear, regrettable though I find it, you will have to learn to live without me.'

'No! No! Do not say that! I cannot! I cannot!' Real distress darkened her eyes. Hysteria was not far from the surface.

He saw, and comforted her, caressing her cheek. 'Come, my child! Let us not talk about it now. We must not spoil the memory of your ball. Do not forget that we have both your first season and your first tour to think about.' He made an immediate, irrevocable decision: 'And I am determined to go with you on that!'

Instantly, her misery turned to joy. 'Did I hear you say that you are coming with me on my tour?'

'Indeed!'

'Truly? Oh, Angelpapa, that is wonderful! Oh, I cannot, cannot believe it!' Then, seeking reassurance, she added, '*Vraiment?*'

'Yes, really.' He spoke calming words. 'Of course, my child, most certainly, I will be with you. You have my word. So, now, there is no more need to worry, *hein*? That is my good angel.' Lifting her chin with a finger, he added, 'The morning is too good for my beautiful debutante to be indoors in this melancholy mood. You must go along for your ride. Etienne and his sister will think you are not coming. I will see you in the music room upon your return; we must work on the songs for your tour. Wrap up your throat well!' he commanded, as an afterthought.

'Of course, Angelpapa!' She showed him her neatly tied stock.

'Off you go, then, my child. I will come with you tomorrow.'

She embraced her guardian once more before she left; her beautiful amethyst eyes swimming in tears. He watched her disappear behind the doorpost and sat, staring at nothing, a muscle working in his jaw. She was his golden child, and his heart went out to her. So brilliant, so talented and, yet, so fragile: all her life she had had to be protected and nurtured beyond any normal consideration, perhaps because of the circumstances surrounding her birth. Who, other than himself and Madame Dupont, could realise that? Who, when he was gone, would be able to look after her? Etienne loved her, he knew, but would he have the understanding and inner strength and stability to support her in the way her delicate spirit required?

Frowning, he returned to his paper. He was still frowning over it when, a little later, Madame Dupont entered the room. Once again, he lay it aside.

'Ah, Madame, good morning.'

'Good morning, Monsieur. You are unwell this morning?' she asked a trifle anxiously, since he had forgone his usual morning ride. For, even though his illness forced him to use a wheeled chair much of the time, he was still a competent rider, able to sit tall and athletic on his horse; a form of exercise he embraced daily. 'Tired after your night out?'

'Something like that, Madame. I wish you to send for Monsieur Merignac, if you please.'

'Now, Monsieur? But ... he will be rehearsing his orchestra.'

'I know, but this is too important to wait.'

Something had visibly upset him.

'Something in the paper, my dear?' She eyed the broadsheet apprehensively.

'Here, take it with you. See for yourself. But send for the conductor, at once!'

'Yes, Monsieur, it shall be done right away,' she murmured, enquiring, as usual, 'More coffee?'

He shook his head. 'Later, perhaps, but only if

Monsieur Merignac feels himself to be in need of refreshment.'

As soon as she had carried out his request—no—order, she searched the paper for whatever it was that had set him off.

She was left baffled. King Constantine sneaking into Paris in the late afternoon. And not a bit of wonder: The Greek King's unfortunate comments on the recent Balkan Wars had not endeared him to Paris. But she already knew Angel's estimation of him: a spent force, unloved by his people. Besides, the Balkan Wars were over.

Pilot Adolphe Pégoud performed a *boucle à boucle* in a Blériot XI. Nothing there: Angel would have been pleased by that, having had his own input into some of these aeroplanes, following their progress with intense interest; for of late, aircraft design had become quite a passion with him. But, flying in loops? The thought made her queasy.

Seventeen people killed in a bridge collapse at Villeneuve-Loubet. *Oh, poor things!* It was probably due to the dreadful spate of wet weather they were having, and regrettably, there would probably be more such incidences if it did not abate. She stopped a minute. Was that the trouble: that it was one of his bridges? No, it simply would not happen! She thought carefully. No—definitely no bridge of his design had been constructed at Villeneuve— any of the Villeneuves! No, it was not that.

The usual ructions in the French parliament. Nothing new, there. It happened with monotonous regularity. What, then? Not this, surely? A small paragraph tucked away at the bottom of the page announced that the German parliament, later in the year, was expected to send a military mission consisting of a few specialist officers to Sirkeci Station. *Where on earth is that?* She went to the globe and began to turn it on its axis. *Oh, here we are: on the straits between the Aegean and the Black Sea—oh, yes, Turkey.* What was there to upset one about that? It was half a world away, and the Kaiser had probably built it for them, anyway. Besides, if the Germans wanted to spend money in Turkey, how could it possibly affect France? Especially since, as everyone knew, the Ottoman Empire was on its last gasp. *Crows after carrion,* she thought disdainfully, folding the paper.

She was troubled. Perhaps the illness of the marquis was beginning to cause him to develop anxiety, as well as progressively limiting his movement?

The butler moved into her line of vision.

'Yes, Henri?'

'Monsieur Merignac has arrived, Madame. He is waiting in the morning room.'

'Take him through to the salon, Henri. Monsieur le marquis wishes to see him.'

'Very good, Madame.'

She noticed, with compassion, that the butler was limping. He, too, was growing old, and his work was getting too much for him. She shook her head. One would have to be brave to mention the matter to him. Best to let him be the judge of when he was ready for retirement!

Of course, since the marquis had moved into her wing of the mansion, Henri's workload had become lighter. Her salon had become, to all intents and purposes, the studio, office and recreational area of the marquis. It was a bright, welcoming room and kept him under her eye.

The marquis had had a lift installed to the first floor, where he had his design studio proper, his bedchamber and that of his man, the new music room and several guest chambers. She and Angelique had moved to the second floor into the renovated student dormitory: now a set of feminine and very pretty boudoirs and sitting rooms. On the top floor were the old music room and her studio, vast and empty, where she still went every morning to practice at the barre before starting her day.

§

'Ah, Maestro, well met!' The marquis shook the conductor's hand. 'Sit down, Monsieur, *s'il vous plaît*. It would please me if you could call to mind the Handel Oratorio *Messiah*, in which Angelique made her solo debut at the Opéra Magique.'

'But of course, Monsieur.' The conductor bowed. 'How could I forget? *Mon Dieu*! The reviewers went wild that night, about you both!' he recalled with enthusiasm.

'You are too kind, Monsieur,' murmured the marquis. 'On that night, there was a party including the Archduke and Duchess of Austria-Hungary and a group of young royals purporting to be an envoy from Kaiser Wilhelm II of Germany. And afterwards there was the rumour of a secret meeting between representatives of our two countries; I believe you said. Was there an outcome to this misguided event? If, indeed, it occurred.'

'Oh, yes, it occurred, Monsieur.'

'And the outcome, hmm?' He frowned intently.

'Why, if I remember rightly, it was just as you predicted, Monsieur. Our generals walked out. About halfway through, as you said they would. The matter was, as I understand it, left unresolved.'

'Given the combination of Germanic diplomacy and Gallic sensibility, it was a foregone conclusion, *mon brave*,' he murmured. 'And you do not know any details of the subject of this aborted discussion?'

'Monsieur, we were sworn to secrecy!' The conductor's bird-like gaze met his. 'But of course, as owners of the theatre, you and Madame Dupont are privy to any information given to me,' he amended hastily. 'Or any other of your staff, for that matter.' He eyed his employer a little apprehensively, for even in his wheeled chair, but a shell of the man he once was, he still radiated an indefinable air of menace.

The steely gaze of the marquis softened a little, and the conductor went on, 'Unfortunately, I cannot help you in this regard, Monsieur, since I was with my orchestra.' He hesitated. 'You feel the subject of this meeting may be important? To France?'

The marquis replied fretfully, as if talking to himself, 'The Kaiser—so arrogant and aggressive—the countries of Europe in an arms race: all strutting and posturing. Tension, everywhere …'

'It is true what you say, Monsieur. But is it not merely the rattling of sabres?' He shrugged. 'It has been going on for years.'

'As you say, Maestro. But it will only require one of these pompous mountebanks to feel that his *amour-propre* has been offended …'

The conductor took in the enormity of his words.

'Oh, God forbid, Monsieur! God forbid!'

'I tell you, Maestro, they are only waiting for a trigger they can pull without censure!'

'But what are you saying, Monsieur? Who will pull what trigger?' Madame Dupont had come in unnoticed.

'As usual, Madame, you have put your finger on it,' replied the marquis. '*Du vrai*, you could stick a pin in a map of Europe, blindfolded, and not be far from the answer! Take these, for example.' He held up the sheaf of letters, showering them back onto the table. 'All these requests: Can I help improve the design of battleships? They all want their dreadnought—or preferably, something bigger and better. Huh!' he added bitterly.

'Can I bend my mind to aircraft to make them faster, more deadly, fly higher? Am I not already doing enough in that direction?' he demanded, waving a complicated aerodynamic design.

'Is there a way to make bigger guns, faster gun carriages, more explosive ammunition?

'Can the internal-combustion engine—infernal, rackety contraption that it is—be made stronger, more efficient, more reliable? Strangely enough, they do not ask for it to be made quieter! There is no end to the madness, Madame!' He calmed his voice, but his eyes flashed. 'Nor, it would seem, European man's desire to wreak the maximum in death and destruction on his fellows. And when I tell you that it is not just France asking for these things, but potential enemies as well as allies … And now, today, I read that German Military personnel are about to be placed at southern Russia's only gateway to the world,' he said finally, 'I tell you, I do not like it. No, I do not! And Russia will not like it, either!'

His words fell into an electric silence, eventually broken by the conductor.

'There is much in what you say, Monsieur. I have not thought … I have not looked at it like that, before.' He cleared his throat. 'It has occurred to me that our theatre manager, Gaston, may know what went on at the meeting of which you speak. He organised the catering. I apprehend he served the refreshments himself. To preserve discretion, you understand.'

'I see. Thank you, Maestro.'

The conductor, politely refusing Madame Dupont's offer of coffee, bowed himself out with a creased brow.

A brooding silence descended over the room, unbroken until the marquis snapped out, 'Send for your dog, Madame. I must have speech with him.'

'But, Monsieur …' she began.

'Oh, enough, Madame! I am not in the mood to argue. We are both old men now, hopefully with more wisdom than in the past. I can hardly be a danger to him, like this!'

'No, Monsieur.'

'Besides, you will speak to him first and explain to him that he must tell me all he knows.'

She was stung into protest. 'And that will be enough for Gaston to break his secret oath?'

'Of course it will, Madame. I do not call him your dog for nothing. We both know the lengths to which he has gone for you in the past, will go for you now and, no doubt, in the future – until he dies, probably. He may have married Mathilde—for convenience, *sans doute*—but I know where his heart lies.'

'Companionship. It was for companionship. He asked for my approval, and I gave it.'

'Hmph, *cela va sans dire*. Otherwise, he would not have done it. When you bring him in, stay in the room with us to encourage him, in the event that he is not inclined to co-operate.'

'Yes, Monsieur,' she replied, leaving the room. It would take all her considerable diplomacy to reconcile Gaston to the demands that were about to be made on him.

The marquis sighed, flicking his correspondence with a disparaging finger. Once, he, too, had been bent on destruction. But he had learnt. Why could not these fools see what they were about to unleash on the world? God's world—he could now acknowledge.

§

'Thank you for coming, Monsieur,' the marquis du Bois said formally, surveying his theatre manager in a manner that the latter found extremely offensive.

Gaston bowed stiffly. 'It is my pleasure, Monsieur. How may I serve you?'

'If Madame Dupont has carried out my request, you know very well how you may serve me,' he responded in steely tones.

Gaston remained silent.

There was a hint of the implacable about Gaston. He had always been like that—stolid, immovable. Madame Dupont was reminded of the eternal philosophical question about the irresistible force meeting the immovable object, and since she did not want to find out the answer here in her salon, she said, 'Gaston, please, you promised me ...'

'Yes, Madame.' Gaston spoke woodenly. He had meant to do as Madame had asked of him, but as soon as he got in front of this arrogant swine (of an aristo), his hackles went up, as always.

'Well, Monsieur?' There was a faint threat in the hated voice. His eyes went miserably from one to the other, and since Madame Dupont was beginning to look distressed, he capitulated.

'You will not like it, Monsieur,' he warned.

'You may leave me to be the judge of that, if you please. Go on, man!'

'It defies belief, Monsieur, but ——' He caught the other's eye. 'When the Kaiser's delegation and ours had finished their pleasantries and general discussion, they shut me out of the room, Monsieur, but—you know your cupboard—the secret one?'

'Yes, yes, of course I know it! Will you get on with it!'

'Yes, Monsieur. By that time I felt that something was going on that was not right, so I went back through the passage in the wall and hid there, in that cupboard, so that I could listen.' His face had gone a dull red. Incredibly, the man felt shame in admitting to this behaviour.

'There is nothing to be ashamed of, Gaston. You obviously had a very good reason for doing what you did.' Madame Dupont spoke gently. 'You have done this for France. You would do more than that for your country, would you not?'

'Indeed, Madame.' The words were simply spoken, but both of those watching knew that, if necessary, he would die for her—stolidly, silently—just as he had always protected Madame Dupont.

'And you heard ... what?' she prompted, knowing he would find it easier to tell all this to her, rather than the marquis.

'I heard a terrible thing, Madame. A terrible thing! It is no wonder our generals walked out.' Sweat had broken out on the manager's brow.

'May God give me strength!' breathed the marquis, turning his eyes to heaven. 'And save me from fools like this!' he shouted, bringing his fist down on the table with a whack.

Madame Dupont jumped and glanced imploringly at the theatre manager.

Keeping his eyes on her, he went on in a whisper, 'The Kaiser's men, they told our generals to break our alliance with Mother Russia. They said if Russia objected, Germany would defend us. They said if we would not join an alliance with Germany, we must declare neutrality. They said ...' He was almost sobbing. 'That they would give us one year to decide. That is when the generals walked out, Madame.'

'*Mon Dieu*!' The marquis was white.

'But that is not the worst, Madame! I heard them talking amongst themselves afterwards, about what they would like to do to our generals, and what they will do to them and to France when—when, Madame, not if!—they conquer us. They said they are ready, that they have the troops, the guns, the war machines waiting for the call. They talked of secret weapons. They said they cannot be beaten.'

The eyes of the marquis were twin sapphire points. 'And what did you do then? After you had heard this ... slanderous scuttlebutt?'

'Do? What do you mean, Monsieur? What could I do?'

'You said they mentioned secret weapons. What secret weapons?'

'They did not say what they were, Monsieur.'

'You told the generals what you had heard?'

'No, Monsieur.'

'And why did you not?'

'But, Monsieur, how could I? The generals had already gone, and I was sworn to secrecy. Who could I have told?'

'My God, Madame!' roared the marquis. 'Get this idiot out of my sight before I do something I regret!'

'Come, Gaston, you have done well. Monsieur le marquis does not mean ... We are very grateful to you, my friend!' She shepherded him out, ignoring the hissing sigh behind her.

When she came back, the marquis was writing furiously, cursing now and again at the spluttering of his pen.

'You are distressed by such news, and no wonder. I do not know what to think, myself.' She watched his nib jam and break. 'May I do that for you, my dear?'

'No, Madame ... Oh, here, then. I am sending a communication to General Joffre. Before nightfall, I am determined to have an answer to all this!'

Taking a new pen and a fresh sheet of paper, she copied the missive as he dictated and sent it off. Within the hour, the general's aide arrived, remaining closeted with him for some time. As soon as he had gone, Madame Dupont went back into the room.

He answered her question before she asked it. 'It would seem, Madame, that there is not much urgency, after all. Apparently, when the generals sent to the Kaiser to find the meaning of this outrage, he back-pedalled considerably. As well he might! He swore that he knew nothing of this scandalous ultimatum; that the delegation was unauthorised by him; and that it was a group of unruly minor royals endeavouring, amongst other things, to overthrow him, as well as to provoke vulnerable states into a declaration of war. It sounds unlikely, but it appears that the Kaiser's ambassador apologised for them, or more likely, threatened reprisals on them.' He dropped his eyes, playing idly with the fringe of the tablecloth. 'Do you know, Madame, I do not think either of these things is the real truth. I believe it lies somewhere between. I think the Kaiser did send an envoy, but with instructions to sound out France's position, diplomatically. These crass fools have revealed his hand before he was ready to show it. It would appear that, according to our own Military Intelligence, the threats were merely posturing, and there is no immediate danger of war.'

His lip lifted wryly. 'Most of its would-be instigators

wish first to bring in their harvests unmolested, and no-one wants to consider such activities in the depths of winter. Most understandable, I am sure. So ...' He shrugged. 'Perhaps we can shelve it, for now. Perhaps I overreacted, after all.'

Madame Dupont nodded. It was what she had thought herself.

'Oh, and by the way ...'

'Yes, Monsieur?'

'This morning, in a fit of madness ... It is all I can put it down to,' he smiled ruefully, 'I told Angelique that I would accompany her on her first tour.'

'But, my dear Angel ——' In moments of stress, though it was strictly forbidden, Madame Dupont was prone to revert to his childhood name.

'I know, I know ... It will have to be restricted to a tour of Europe, and not the world tour she has been offered. Monsieur Merignac and the Orchestra Magique will still travel with us, of course, but the world tour can come later—when she is more experienced and no longer needs me. In truth, I do not see myself travelling by ship.'

'No, indeed!' She found it hard to envision him travelling anywhere, by any means.

'I shall sing with her, of course.'

'But, Monsieur, you have not thought!' She was aghast. 'Can you do it?'

'A good question, my dear, a good question. I will try for two duets at each performance: one at the beginning; one at the end.' He looked her over. 'That is not a very encouraging expression, Madame.'

'No, Monsieur.'

'I have promised Angelique ...'

How she dreaded those four words, usually the prelude to great suffering on his part. 'I see. There is nothing more to be said then, is there?'

'I knew you would see it that way, Madame. The poor little one: she needs me. After this first tour, I am convinced she will be able to do without me. But for now, no. It is clear that she must have my support. Now, I must go and organise our music, before she returns from her ride. I can leave our itinerary to you?'

'Of course, my dear.'

She wheeled him to the lift, discussing various preliminary aspects of the proposed abbreviated tour without, she hoped, revealing too many of her misgivings about the whole thing.

CHAPTER TWO ~ MORNING RIDE

Ten thirty am, 21 September 1913

It is so nice to look out the window and see Angelique riding off with her friends. My secret wish is that the young gentleman riding beside her will be in her life forever. He is quite a favourite with me, a proper man for a jeune fille of whom I am so proud. And his younger sister, Elise, such a sweet young girl.

The elegant young lady and gentleman, waiting with the groom and the horses, looked up from their conversation.

'At last!' cried the young lady, joyfully. 'I thought you were never coming!'

The young gentleman regarded appreciatively the beautiful creature flying down the steps with hoydenish abandon.

'Good morning, Mademoiselle,' he said, the formal greeting belying the warm glow in his golden-hazel eyes. 'Your steed awaits you.'

'Etienne, Elise …' She was breathless, tears forgotten. 'I am sorry to have kept you waiting.'

'Not at all. We have only just arrived, have we not, Elise?'

'Oh … oh, yes, of course! But a few minutes, my dear.'

'Liars.' She laughed, her cheeks delightfully flushed. 'But I do love you for your tact and kindness.' She kissed Elise and gave Etienne her hands, shyly avoiding his glance.

The groom, disapprovingly observing the colour in her cheeks and her fluttering manner, placed the reins over her horse's neck, holding them for her as the young marquis threw her lightly into the saddle and turned to help his sister. It looked like the marquis du Bois wasn't riding this morning. That meant that he would have to go in his stead.

Fast, that's what they were, the young people of today. It wouldn't have been countenanced in his day, young people riding out without proper supervision. The marquis should have been with them to keep an eye on Mademoiselle Angelique. A proper handful she was and always had been, ever since a child. He smiled, remembering her battles with her pony. It was hard to say which of them had been more determined: he to stay in the stable yard or she to go out; although, they had usually managed a compromise, with a little help from himself or the marquis.

To be sure, she was an excitable filly, very hot at hand and liable to go off into hysterics at the drop of a hat. He patted his pocket to make sure he had the little bottle of smelling salts, which the marquis had decreed one of them must carry whenever they rode out with her. Highly strung, that's what she was, and easily out of control unless the marquis du Bois was there to keep her calm. And yet, she looked like an angel, sang like one, too; and in his opinion, rode like a goddess—though perhaps he was biased. Yet, critically watching her sensitive handling of her reins as she took them from him, he did not think so. A little frown creased his forehead. He hoped there would be no contretemps on this outing. Temperament, that was her downside; and he did not feel confident to deal with it. He felt strongly that the marquis should be here. Strange it was, the way he could quell her with a glance under his brows and a quiet endearment: and the only one who could, by what he had heard around the household and seen for himself. Even Madame Dupont, who could, without saying a word, make the worst bully slink away, had had trouble with her until the marquis had taken a hand.

He shook his head. This young marquis had got himself a job of work; that was certain. Deftly shortening the stirrups, he mounted his employer's horse, following at a discreet distance.

The young marquis de Beaulieu, listening with indulgent amusement to the inconsequential chatter of his companions, was content to ride beside the glorious creature who had taken his heart with one glance from those incredible amethyst eyes. Of course, the conversation was all about the ball last night at which, for the first time, he had partnered Angelique. Dreamily, he remembered the feel of her in his arms. She was passionate, vibrant, adorable. He wanted that passion for himself, even though he knew he must share her, metaphysically speaking, with thousands of her followers.

Quiet, patient, his nature was to protect; and Angelique, willowy and fragile, aroused all of those instincts in his calm breast. The son and heir of a man who governed wisely from a long line of philanthropic ducs; he was imbued with the urge to take care of those less able to take care of themselves.

'Oh, look! Who in the world is this coming?'

He heard the little throb in his sister's voice and looked hard at the approaching horseman. One of the de Villefontaine boys; that was certain. They were like peas in a pod. He knew Elise was hoping it would be Philippe.

He addressed Angelique: 'It is your brother, Luc.'

'Oh.' Of her three brothers, Luc was the one she least understood, the one who openly showed aggression to her.

Philippe, she loved, for he was kind and gentle like her papa; and Christian was like a big soft cushion, without deep convictions, but warm and generous, withal. But of Luc, she was afraid; for he seemed to harbour a deep-seated animosity that was never far from the surface, and she never knew when some seemingly innocent remark would set it off.

Elise, admirably concealing her disappointment, invited him to join their party; and since the road was wide, they rode four abreast. She engaged him in jocular conversation, which, nothing loth, he returned.

'I should go back soon,' Angelique spoke in a nervous aside to Etienne. 'Angelpapa will be expecting me for my lesson. I do not like to keep him waiting.'

'Oh no, surely, not yet!' cried Elise. 'We have hardly started our ride! Anyway, I have always been curious. Why do you call him Angelpapa? The marquis du Bois, I mean?'

'I don't know. I have never known him by any other name. Godmama said I named him that when I was very small: too young to remember, I'm afraid.'

'Godmama?' trilled Elise. 'I have often wanted to ask you … and I can because we are all but family, are we not? Why, when you have a perfectly good mother and father of your own, were you reared by Madame Dupont and the marquis du Bois?' The indiscreet question momentarily dislocated the symphony of the horses' hooves.

Both Angelique and Luc flushed vividly.

'Elise!' warned the young marquis. 'You have gone beyond the line with your ill-bred curiosity.'

'No,' said Luc. 'No, she hasn't. Why should she not know? After all, as she says, we are almost family … Tell them, dearest sister,' he added, with heavy sarcasm. 'Etienne needs to know what he has let himself in for. Tell them why you live with Madame Dupont and the marquis instead of the comte and comtesse de Villefontaine, and your three big brothers!'

'I do not know what you mean, Luc! You know that I

was too young for Papa to send me away to school, as he did you boys when Mama became ill, so he left me with Angelpapa for my singing lessons, and Godmama for my ballet and other schooling.' Angelique spoke breathlessly; her colour fluctuating in a way that would have warned the groom had he been closer.

'Hah! A manifestly whitewashed version, if ever I heard it!' jeered her brother. 'I will tell you why!'

'Please, Luc ———'

'Angelique has always been precious, going off into hysterics if she cannot have her way, crying night and day for her "Angelpapa" when our father brought our mother home to us. We were sent away to school, but that was not good enough for my little sister, was it, eh? Of course, when it became clear that Godmama and the marquis were spoiling her rotten, Papa tried to send her away to school; but she ran away.'

'Please, Luc, I could not stand it without ———'

'"My Angelpapa",' he mimicked. 'Don't we know it! When she was sent back, she set up such a screech that they put her in isolation—where she spent her time drawing opprobrious caricatures of her teachers on the walls—including a most reprehensible likeness of the headmistress in a compromising situation with the dancing master!'

At this, a little glimmer of amusement dispelled the frown in the eyes of the young marquis. 'What? Kissing the dancing master, was she? Well, good for Angelique!'

'Well, she was! I saw them!' cried Angelique, close to tears.

'Yes, and recorded it for all to see! Well done, Sister!' Luc bowed exaggeratedly over the pommel.

'It wasn't my fault! They had forgotten I was in the detention room, and I had to hide when they came in. Afterwards, I was there for such a long time alone that I became bored and drew them on the wall. There was no slate or paper,' she explained.

'Evidently,' continued Luc, as if she had not spoken, 'it must have struck a chord, for she was expelled. Even Godmama despaired of her. Didn't she, dearest *Ange*?' He smiled evilly. 'And there you have it, Monsieur. If you still wish to offer for my sister …?'

'No-o-oh!' moaned Angelique in mortification, one gloved hand to her mouth.

'Then, I have to warn you that the only one who can control her is her precious Angelpapa!' He rounded on her ferociously. 'And that is Mama's mare you are riding! Is there no end to you?'

'Stop it, Luc! Stop it! Please, do not! You know Mama gave her to me when I grew too tall for my pony!'

'Enough! That is enough!' snapped the young marquis, but Luc had gone too far to stop now.

'We were all happy until you came along,' he cried viciously. 'It is your fault our mother is like she is! Your fault! I wish you had never been born!'

'No!' Angelique, sobs choking in her throat, spun her mare on her haunches and galloped back the way they had come.

Etienne, turning his head to shout instructions to the groom and finding himself addressing his rapidly diminishing back, said evenly to Luc, 'How dare you treat your sister in that fashion! What do you think the marquis du Bois will have to say when he hears about it?'

'Oh, the marquis!' He gestured disparagingly, giving an ugly laugh. 'I am not worried by him! The marquis du Bois has shot his bolt!'

'I would not be too sure about that if I were you.'

'Why? What can he do in his wheeled chair? Run over me?'

'He can do several things,' replied the other, quietly. 'One of which is to authorise me to do it for him. And now, while I rescue *your* sister, you will escort *my* sister home, taking the greatest care of her. For, if she does not arrive safely, I will forget that I am a gentleman and give you the thrashing you deserve. Be thankful that I do not have the time to do it now.' And he, too, turned and galloped back the way they had come.

Looking her companion over with shocked eyes, Elise rode on without comment, leaving Luc to follow, equally a prey to shame—a slow-burning jealousy and an uneasy conviction that this time it was he who had gone beyond the line.

Elise, herself, battling to hold back tears of mortification and distress, was horrified at the storm precipitated by her ill-considered question—asked out of a kind of lighthearted naivety. She had been deeply shocked by the hatred and aggression displayed by Luc and knew she deserved the homily that would presently be delivered by her brother. Ignorance, she knew, was no excuse. But there had been nothing in her own relationship with her brother that could have prepared her for Luc's attitude to his own beautiful sister.

Oh, poor dear Angelique. If only Etienne finds her safe, she prayed silently, *I will never be so doltish again.* That stupid, stupid question—if only she could have snatched it back! Oh, if only it had been Philippe and not Luc who had come riding down the road. Philippe, in whom she cherished an innocent maiden's dream. An unbiddable tear rolled down her cheek. As soon as was possible, she would abjectly apologise to her dearest friend; and never, ever, ever, again would she ask stupid questions.

CHAPTER THREE ~ SUITORS

Midnight, 21 September 1913

In the twenty-four hours since Angelique's debut, we have been inundated by suitors. And Angel has treated them to such a display of temperament that already he has a reputation as a tyrant! Perhaps in the long run, it will be a good thing. Poor Angel, I know that he wants the same one I want. Justin and I have tried to protect both him and Angelique from the unsuitable ones, but now and again, one slips through. I'm not sure whom I feel sorriest for: Angel or the Suitors!

The groom, leading Angelique's horse beside his own in a quiet walk, was deeply troubled. God knows what would have happened if he had not been able to catch her. Thank God the marquis kept fast horses and he was riding his own big gelding. She would have galloped blindly in any direction until … who knew? At best, maybe her mare would have taken her home. At worst? … Well, it did not do to dwell on it.

'Be easy, Mademoiselle,' he had soothed when he had ranged alongside her wildly galloping horse and taken hold of her rein. 'Slow down, Petite. There, there.'

At this point, it was not clear to Angelique whether he was addressing her or her mare; but he had taught her to ride as a little girl, and she was used to obeying his instructions. Without thinking, she slowed to a walk, allowing him to control both horses.

'*Eh bien*, Mademoiselle,' he murmured, 'you are safe now.' He took the bottle of smelling salts from his pocket, endeavouring to hold it under her nose. 'Breathe, Mademoiselle, breathe! Come, now. That is right. Calm, calm, Mademoiselle.' He spoke soothingly, as he would to a frightened horse. Yet, he knew he was not really getting through to her.

He supposed he would have to take her home, but shuddered at the thought of the reaction of the marquis when he saw her like this. The young marquis had shouted something at him when he had gone after her, but he had not heard it. Ah, here he was, coming now. Let him explain this contretemps to that old fire-eater: the marquis du Bois!

'Breathe, Mademoiselle,' he instructed. 'Again, Mademoiselle. That is right. Here is your young gentleman, coming now.'

The marquis de Beaulieu, having slowed his horse to an easy canter when he had come in sight of them, pulled up, surveying the distressed damsel on her sweating mount. 'Oh, my dear one, you must not let yourself be upset by such a *bêtise*. It is but a tempest in a teacup. Not worth all this angst. Of a certainty, your brutish brother deserves a flogging!' He turned to the groom. 'My thanks to you, Jean, you did well to catch her. But we cannot continue like this. The marquis du Bois will have us horsewhipped if we bring Mademoiselle home in the vapours!'

'Indeed, Monsieur!' said the groom, handing him the smelling salts. 'Just what I was thinking myself.'

'Walk the horses for us, if you please, while I take Mademoiselle for a quiet stroll in the garden here. When she has composed herself, you may escort us home. It will not hurt her mare to be walked quietly, either,' he added, noting the heaving flanks and foaming neck. 'A bran mash later, I should think.'

The groom nodded, taking his reins as he dismounted and stood by Angelique's stirrup. Common sense: that was what was required here; and this young marquis seemed to possess it in abundance.

'Come, my sweet,' he said gently. 'Let me help you down. We will go for a walk in this delightful garden, and you shall tell me all about it.'

Angelique, still breathing irregularly, calmed at once, sliding down into his arms. Supporting her tenderly, he held the smelling salts under her nose, while she clung to him as if to a lifeline.

As they walked away, the groom, seeing her respond to this gentle treatment, stared after them, a dawning respect in his eyes. Mayhap the marquis du Bois was not the only one who could handle her, after all.

Continuing to speak soothingly until Angelique's breathing calmed, Etienne took the little bottle from her hand and put it in his pocket. He had a fair idea now why the groom had it ready and resolved to always carry a bottle himself. 'Tell me about it, my love,' he said, holding her hand between both of his. 'Tell me why there is this clash of spirits with your brother. I apprehend he is closest to you in age?'

'Yes,' she nodded. And there, walking amongst the trees and shrubs, the whole halting story came out. Here and there, he asked a question when something she said puzzled him; but in the main, he just listened. As a first-time auditor, he was aware of two things: the first, just how sad a story it really was; and the second, her utter dependence on and unconditional love for the marquis du Bois.

At the end of the story, she had calmed so much that he judged he could take her home, so he turned about, retracing their steps. 'This, what you are telling me here, really boils down to sibling rivalry,' he told her. 'Your brother resents you because the attention he had been used to was suddenly removed with the illness of your mother at your birth. He is punishing you for it by treating you in this fashion. But do not worry, my sweet, I will not allow it to occur again: that you may be sure of!' He smiled down at her.

'They say I must not get so upset by such things—that I have excessive sensibility. They say it so ... accusingly.'

'Of course you become upset. You are sensitive; your nerves are easily put on end. You would not have such wonderful rapport with your audiences if you did not have this extra sensibility, my sweet.'

She leaned against him, taking strength from him. Incredibly, knowing all her faults, he still wanted to be with her. She raised her eyes to his. 'You understand,' she said. 'You understand.' *Like Angelpapa.* 'And you do not ... mind?'

'Of course I understand, my love. I mind only that others have been permitted to upset you. It is my desire to protect you from the arrows and unpleasantries of life, so that you may get on with charming all our hearts out with your glorious voice. That is your destiny.'

'Oh, Etienne ...' Her lips quivered into a tremulous smile. 'You are so good to me.'

'Nonsense, my angel. I am happy to see you smile. Mayhap that is my destiny: to make the beautiful Angel of Song smile.' He put his hand over his heart in a comically exaggerated gesture.

'Oh, Monsieur!' she chided. 'Do you think to make a joke of such a serious matter?'

'No, my dear one. I swear on my life that I have never been more serious.' The intensity of his gaze made her heart give a queer bump, but he said merely, 'And now we must get you home before the marquis du Bois decides to put me in his sights, for by now you will surely be late for your music lesson, my dear one!'

§

The marquis, out of his wheeled chair, was standing by the piano, sorting music. Arrested by the sound of running footsteps, he looked up, eyes narrowing as Angelique rushed into the room, and he saw her blotched complexion.

'Angelique?'

'Oh, Angelpapa!' She flung herself into his arms, beginning to sob again; her face pressed against his coat.

Over her head, his outraged eyes met those of the younger man just entering the room. 'Monsieur?' The question thrummed with menace.

The marquis de Beaulieu stood his ground, meeting his gaze with a rueful smile. He appeared to have no difficulty in sustaining the fiery glare and spoke with his usual gentle calm: 'I do apologise for returning Mademoiselle Angelique to you in this state, Monsieur. I assure you, it will not happen again. I was not aware of certain, er ... family difficulties. Next time I will know what steps to take to prevent it.'

'Oh ... Luc!' The marquis relaxed, turning his attention to his drooping pupil. 'Have I not told you, Petite, to ignore that boorish brother of yours?'

'Yes, Angelpapa.'

'He is jealous of you, merely.'

'Yes, Etienne said that.'

'He is trying to get under your skin: hurt you with his nasty remarks.'

'Yes, Etienne said that, also.'

'Indeed?' He shot a dry glance at her companion. '*Alors*, I am relieved to find that Etienne appears to be a young man of such eminently good sense!' He turned to the marquis de Beaulieu, holding out his hand. 'I am indebted to you, Monsieur. No doubt you will wish to assure yourself of the safe return of your sister. Angelique must have her singing lesson now, but if you like to return in one hour, you may join us for luncheon.'

'Thank you, Monsieur. I will avail myself of your kind invitation,' he replied, adding with a twinkle, 'although, I have no doubt of the wellbeing of my sister.'

The marquis, looking after him, thoughtfully stroked his chin. Perhaps he would do, after all.

'*Eh bien*, my angel,' he said, striking a note on the keyboard. 'Let us begin with our scales.'

§

It was as they were finishing their lesson that the comte de Villefontaine walked in, unannounced.

'Papa! I am so happy to see you!'

'Indeed, my dear. And how is my beautiful daughter today?'

'Well, indeed, Papa. Etienne is coming to lunch.'

The comte's eyes questioned the marquis, who nodded slightly. 'Ah, a fine young man,' said the comte with satisfaction, kissing his daughter and shaking the other man's hand.

Angelique, excusing herself, went off to change out of her riding habit.

As she left the room, the marquis enquired: 'Katarina is well this morning?'

'My wife is as well as can be expected, Monsieur.' There was a faint emphasis on the comte's first word.

'You do not think the evening was too much for her?' asked the marquis, somewhat anxiously, disregarding the inflection.

'Oh, no, no, Monsieur, nothing like that.' The comte relented. 'Oh, no, no. Indeed, she gave me to understand that she enjoyed the outing tremendously.'

'Indeed?' murmured the marquis. 'I am very happy to hear it.' Adding reflectively, 'But not so happy, Monsieur, to have heard something else.'

'Indeed not! It is what I have come to see you about:

this nasty temper of Luc's. I do not know where he gets it from.'

'Certainly not his mother.'

'No, Monsieur. As you say,' replied the comte without expression. 'He is sorry he hurt his sister, Monsieur, but it appears that he blames her for his mother's illness.'

The marquis snorted. 'Ridiculous! It is ridiculous to blame an innocent child for the sins of others!'

There was a short silence. The comte swallowed and looked out the window while the other continued, 'Luc should not have been sent away to school so young. You should have got a good woman to look after him—let him see his mother, at least. You neglected your children, Monsieur. Madame Dupont tried to tell you!'

The comte made a gesture of misery. 'Monsieur, you are right. Often have I regretted ... But at the time, I thought it best to keep them away from her.' He wrung his hands. 'You *know* what she was like!'

'Indeed, I do! And the redeeming thing about you is that you did not, in any way, neglect her.' He fell silent, regarding him sympathetically. 'But rehashing the past will not solve the dilemma that has reached an impasse today.' Receiving no answer, he added, 'This situation cannot go on, you know. Angelique is fragile; she cannot take this sort of attack and then go out and perform onstage. You know how easily she goes to pieces—how little it takes to send her nerves and emotions spiralling out of control. If the marquis de Beaulieu had not brought her back to me ——' He restrained himself with an effort.

'I know, Monsieur, I know. But what can I do? They are bound to meet occasionally.' Xavier had always had difficulty with the discipline of his children, ranging from laxity with his boys to ineptitude with his daughter.

The marquis studied his worried, honest face. The man was speaking the truth. '*Eh bien*, Monsieur, since you do not know, I will tell you what you will do.' The quiet tones of the marquis brooked no opposition. 'You will buy him a commission and send him to Morocco.'

'An officer in the Foreign Legion? Oh, I do not know!' Xavier was wavering, as usual.

'Do you not? But I do! You will find it is what he has always wanted but has been afraid that you will not allow him to go.'

'It is true that he has asked permission to join the cavalry and also to travel abroad. But he is young. I was not sure he was ready.'

'Indeed, Monsieur, there can be no doubt,' replied the marquis, smoothly. 'You will make him this offer, and we shall all be happy.'

The indecisive nature of the comte did not allow him to be certain of the underlying threat he thought he heard in the other's voice. Before he could make up his mind, the marquis added abruptly, 'You had better stay to luncheon with us, if you've nothing better to do. You may further your acquaintance with Angelique's beau. I expect Madame Dupont will wish to see you.'

The comte accepted this graceless invitation, and they made their way to the dining room.

'Xavier, my dear ... Welcome!' Madame Dupont hurried to greet him.

'I hope I have not inconvenienced you, Madame.'

'Of course not! There is always room at my dining table for you, Monsieur.'

'Thank you, Madame. You are very good.'

'Katarina did not feel up to coming with you today?'

'She is with her modiste, choosing some hats.' He grimaced slightly. 'I thought I should leave her with it.'

'Very wise,' commented the marquis, waving a careless hand. 'I leave all that sort of thing to Madame Dupont.'

'Katarina has a great fashion sense, Monsieur.' She turned to the comte. 'What Monsieur le marquis does not realise is that I always give her the final say in any apparel I choose for Angelique or myself.'

The comte looked gratified. 'You could not do better.'

'No, indeed! A little more of this excellent chicken casserole, Monsieur?'

'Etienne would like some, Godmama.' Angelique, having recovered her complexion, eyes brimful of laughter, silently dared him to deny it.

'Thank you, Madame.' He sent Angelique a look of agonised reproach, which was intercepted by Madame Dupont.

'Here you are, Monsieur. And I will pass you this delicious herb omelette for Angelique. She must have some more of that. Our chef has made it especially for her.' She smiled at them both.

'Touché, my sweet,' murmured the marquis de Beaulieu to his love as they struggled with their extra portions. 'Madame Dupont is *femme formidable*, is she not? Finely, has she called your bluff!' He raised his eyes respectfully as the comte addressed him, replying attentively.

Madame Dupont was very pleased to see such good manners in a young gentleman. Even in love as he was, he did not forget to pay attention to his other table companions. Indeed, she admitted to herself, he was a favourite of hers; for he had very much the warmth and dignity of his father, the duc de Belvoir.

After *déjeuner*, the young marquis accompanied the comte to his club; Madame Dupont took Angelique to view the results of her mother's appointment with the modiste; and the marquis retired to his design table in a bright corner of Madame Dupont's salon where, some little while later, he was apologetically disturbed by his butler.

'Yes? What is it, Henri?' The marquis looked up from his work.

'A young man has called, Monsieur, to see you. I apprehend it concerns Mademoiselle Angelique.'

'Not another one!' The marquis cast up his eyes. 'But of course, why else do we have visitors? How many, now, is it that have come asking to pay their addresses: twenty

… thirty?'

'Oh, at the very least, Monsieur!' He did not tell him of the numerous hopefuls he had skilfully dissuaded. Only the most persistent of them ever got as far as the marquis. 'The card tray in the hall is overflowing! And the bouquets!' He shrugged up his shoulders. 'After Madame Dupont has filled the house with them, she can send the rest over to the Académie Mirage to the students.'

The marquis nodded. Madame Dupont may have given up her ballet teaching, but she still kept a good eye on her School of Ballet, now under the aegis of her best student, Jeanne, a retired prima donna, and the new wife of Monsieur Merignac. He stopped, remembering how the maestro had broken his news to him:

'I am about to embrace the married state myself, Monsieur.'

'Eh?'

'You are surprised, Monsieur? So am I.' The conductor's lean cheeks were red. 'You see, I have never found anyone I could love more than my music. So, I never married. But then I met Jeanne. Of course, she was far too young. I mean, what would she want with a *vieillard* like me? But incredibly, she did. You see me a happy man, Monsieur.'

'If you mean to tell me that you found someone you love more than your music, then all I can say is ——'

'Not more, Monsieur. I cannot, *cannot*, say that. It is an impossibility for me, you understand. But I do not love my music more than her, you see?'

'It is a very fine point, but I think so. Jeanne is the first woman you have loved as much as your music?'

'Exactly so! I am a man who has everything, *hein*?'

The marquis frowned, recalling the joy radiating from his person, and his own dry response, 'A fortunate circumstance, Maestro. Be sure to cherish it …'

A muscle jerked in his cheek. He put down his slide rule with a snap. 'I suppose I had better see this young man. But we shall have to put a stop to this constant stream of suitors. It is beyond the pale!'

'Yes, Monsieur.' The butler showed in the hapless youth and retired.

The marquis rounded on him savagely: 'Yes? What do you want?'

'Er ... er,' stammered the poor young man, his eyes following the progress of a large black and white cat that unfurled itself from the depths of an armchair and strategically left the room. He had to suppress a sudden, irrational desire to follow the creature.

'Come on, out with it! I am a busy man. I have no time for these piddling interruptions!'

Monsieur de Nouailles haltingly made known his desires.

The marquis tapped his pencil on the desk. 'Have you the means to support my ward, Monsieur?'

'Yes, Monsieur. I think so,' confidently replied the suitor. 'I am tolerably well-heeled. I can send my man of business if ——'

Ruthlessly interrupting him, the marquis questioned further, 'Have you any idea how expensive it is to keep her in gowns for her singing engagements? Or how much it costs to maintain an entourage on tour?'

'But she wouldn't ——' began the dismayed young man.

'Wouldn't what?' His eyes were hard as diamonds.

'She wouldn't have to tour as Madame de Nouailles, Monsieur. She would have charge of her own establishment: a substantial mansion. I would not allow my wife to sing on a stage,' he added, 'like a common entertainer.'

'Enough! I have heard enough! Common entertainer? How dare you! You have not the faintest idea! No, you may not! It is an affront, Monsieur!' The enraged blue gaze held him paralysed while it pierced him through. 'I have had enough of the lot of you! Mademoiselle de

Villefontaine is otherwise engaged and will remain so! Have I made myself clear? She will not see any of you!'

'No, Monsieur. I mean, yes, Monsieur, er ...' He flinched at the brutal tones.

The marquis rang the bell. 'This interview is over. Do not call again. Ah, Henri, *à la bonne heure*! Show this gentleman out, if you please.'

Shepherding Monsieur de Nouailles out into the hall, Henri sympathetically helped him into his coat, handing him his hat and cane. 'I wish you a good day, Monsieur.'

'A good day? After what I have just been through? Oh, you must be joking, Monsieur! I suppose there is nothing left for me to do except blow my brains out, or throw myself into the Seine ...'

Obviously a young gentleman lacking in imagination, thought Henri. Since Mademoiselle's debut, he had heard many inventive ideas of self-disposal from disappointed suitors, including jumping off the Eiffel Tower, the Arc de Triomphe, the Ponte Vecchio (one Italian hopeful) and the cliffs of Normandy.

'Oh, no, Monsieur! Truly, many have come on the same quest as you. I will tell you,' the butler leaned closer, '*you* are one of the lucky ones!'

'You mean ...?'

'You are able to walk out of here, are you not?'

The would-be suitor started emerging from his misery for a moment. Had he not heard somewhere that the marquis du Bois had a murderous temper? Just what was this butler trying to impart to him?

The butler, holding his eyes significantly, certainly seemed to be trying to convey some sort of message. 'I cannot tell you what I have seen, Monsieur,' intoned Henri, portentously.

'Truly?' faltered the suitor, feeling his hair stand on end in growing horror as the butler's impassive face relaxed for a second, and he briefly closed one eye.

'*Mon Dieu!*' Monsieur de Nouailles at last got the

implication. Clutching his hat and cane, he stammered his thanks as the butler saw him off the doorstep. With every step he took, the demeanour of the marquis grew more evil: his speech imbued with such menace that, by the time he shared the memory of its horror with his friends, it had assumed terrifying proportions.

With a white countenance, he whispered a garbled account of his conversation with the butler, passed on by his friends to their acquaintances. Thus the rumours started—embellished according to the imagination of each *raconteur*—until the marquis (conveniently forgetting his past) would not have recognised himself in the Machiavellian character described by Angelique's disappointed suitors; although, he would have obtained a peculiar satisfaction in the depiction, hugely enjoying his reputation.

Returning to the salon, Henri picked up a book from the floor, placing it within reach of his employer.

'Thank you. You have seen off our young musketeer?' He added with satisfaction, 'I think I have discouraged that one!'

'Oh, indeed, Monsieur,' replied the butler. 'I do not think he will darken our door again.' Turning away, he permitted himself a glimmer of a smile.

If the legend grew amongst Angelique's disappointed suitors that the marquis was an evil ogre who kept his beautiful, golden-haired angel locked away from the world—constrained, as it were, between the music room and the concert hall—then it was equally apparent that while they fantasised about her rescue, in reality, none dared to cross the threshold of the hôtel du Bois, leaving its occupants in relative peace.

But there were those who moved in the privileged circles of the duc and duchesse de Belvoir who could have told of one who the marquis du Bois was pleased to approve. The trouble was that he had not yet made a declaration that the marquis could use to forbid any further aspirants to Angelique's hand.

CHAPTER FOUR ~ THE ROYAL TRAIN

28 September 1913

I am so busy organising Angelique's tour, holding dinners and soirees, accompanying Angelique to all the balls and festive occasions for a girl's first season. It is a great coup to have secured the Royal Train for our tour! Of course, I adore the excitement, the business of it, but what Angel has asked of me, above and beyond this, is unbelievable. If he wasn't so obviously distressed, I would refuse.

The hôtel du Bois, once more buzzing with excitement and activity, welcomed couturières, modistes, tailleurs, coiffeurs and others as the day drew closer for Angelique's first tour.

The marquis himself, fighting failing health, was still determined to accompany her, even though the travelling presented great difficulties.

'Monsieur! A coup!' Madame Dupont entered the room with an even lighter step than usual, a happy lilt in her voice. 'The authorities are letting us have the use of the Royal Train for our tour. That will simplify matters greatly. It will be much more comfortable for you to travel,

Monsieur. What do you think of that?'

He smiled. 'The Chief of the Railways is very taken with Angelique. He wants her to sing in his hometown, Nice. Of course, he knows she will not go if I am not with her; so by a stroke of the pen, he assures himself of her presence. It is amazing the doors that are opened by an angel, is it not, Madame?'

'Indeed, Monsieur, and I for one am very grateful! It makes matters so much easier!' She had been so worried about travel arrangements for the marquis that she was uncharacteristically expansive. Throwing wide her arms, she declared, 'Oh, I could kiss the general!'

'I would not advise it, Madame. You do not think that you are possibly being a little precipitate in your transports? You have yet to make his acquaintance. Are you not afraid of being considered just a tiny bit forward?' His eyes held a mischievous expression she had not seen for years.

'Oh, Monsieur!' What outrageous statement would he make next? She had long ago given up protesting at the sometimes indelicate remarks with which he regaled her. Even so, she was stunned by his next utterance.

'And while I am about it, I may as well remind you that I do not think you should be kissing any ducs, either.'

'That warning is ... unnecessary, Monsieur,' she replied in a suffocated voice.

'Is it?' queried the marquis, a gleam in his eye. 'I am not so sure about that. Not after what I saw at Angelique's ball.'

She put her hands up to her face, whispering, 'Oh, I told him it was unwise for us to dance together.'

'Oh, you did, did you? And what did he say to that?'

'He agreed that it would be unwise. Then he said that wisdom was for later.'

'I agree with him,' said the marquis, unexpectedly. 'Quite right. You were happy, were you not, waltzing with him?'

She put up her chin. Did he really expect her to answer such a question? To reply, *oh, yes, Monsieur,* like a child asked whether she had liked a sweetmeat?

'Sometimes, Monsieur, I think it is an outrage,' she said reflectively, 'the things that you say to me.'

'I know, Madame.' He had the grace to look slightly ashamed. 'You are so calm, so kind, so patient. Sometimes I give in to my baser self, just to needle you; to disturb that tranquil surface you always present to the world.'

Unruffled, she replied, 'I may be wrong, Monsieur, but I seem to remember that you decided to send Luc to the Foreign Legion for just such an impulse, did you not?'

'Indeed, I stand corrected, my dear. I suppose I could apply, but … do you think they would accept me?'

She pretended to consider. 'No, Monsieur. Once, perhaps.'

'Oh, cruel!' He sat back, regarding her with fond amusement. 'Come, Madame, I will not tease you any longer. But this I will say in all sincerity: You deserve a little happiness, my dear. Neither of us has found much of it, one way and another. Our life's desires unfulfilled, so to speak. If for ten minutes, you were happy, who can find fault with that? The duchesse was not hurt by it.'

'No, Monsieur, as you say.' Her grey-green eyes held a troubled expression.

He let it go. 'Now to more pressing matters. What have you done in regard to stage costume for Angelique?'

'As we agreed, she will be dressed all in white. Always. But of course, there will be different styles; various fabrics; also the detail will be varied with gold, silver or crystal decoration. The couturière is renowned for it.

'Yes,' he approved. 'She must be all in white: the details of which I will leave to you, and when we sing our duet, I will be all in black.'

'With a white shirt, Monsieur, and your cravat: in matching fabric to her dress; and your pocket handkerchief; with the same detail, only smaller, of course.

It is Katarina's idea.'

He inclined his head. 'Whatever you say, my dear. What about day wear when she is not performing?'

'Monsieur, that is another coup! The House of Lanvin, who is making her gowns, wishes to design her entire wardrobe!'

'Jeanne Lanvin … hmm! She is a good woman. It is a pity she divorced old di Pietro. Did you know that their daughter sings? She has potential, too, and much dedication. I think she will make an opera singer if she continues to practise the way she has been doing, the little Marguerite. Not to be compared with Angelique, of course, but she is very good.' Looking up sharply, he added, 'You are satisfied with the standard of the couture?'

'Yes, indeed, Monsieur. But you are behind the times. She remarried years ago. Madame Melet, I mean Lanvin, does such beautiful work. Her gowns are avant-garde, Monsieur, such perfect detail and decoration: their skirts fall so beautifully. Her *robes de style*, so exquisite!'

'Indeed, Madame? And what does Katarina think?'

'She wears them herself.'

'Very well. Let her do it.' With a little gesture, he dismissed perhaps the greatest fashion house of the day. Why would Lanvin not want to dress Angelique? Any astute designer would know that, with her fame and figure, she could quite well be the greatest advertisement for their fashions that they could possibly achieve.

'In truth, I do not mind who designs her gowns, Madame, as long as it is not that Chanel woman. Not only do I think her designs unfeminine and unsuitable for Angelique, I find her conduct bold and unbecoming. Calling herself Coco! I put it to you: is that or is that not a frivolous name?' He shook his head. 'How does she expect to convince us she is a serious designer?'

'I believe she was named Coco because of a song she used to sing.'

'Oh, she *sings*, does she? Perhaps I would call it

something else!' He snorted. 'At least I have been spared that enlightening experience! And as for her latest inappropriate concoction—I will not grace it with the word "design" … "la marinière" does she not call it? *Outré*!' he added in scathing condemnation. 'And if we are going to speculate about her name, Madame, from what I have heard—on her own admission, mind—it is more likely to be a shortened form of cocotte!'

'Oh, no, Monsieur! It is true that her designs at the moment would not suit Angelique, but they are simple and understated. She is a little ahead of her time, that is all,' said Madame Dupont, who sometimes yearned for simplicity in dress, adding soothingly, 'She is an eccentric, merely; and she may perhaps, on occasion, seem a little abrasive.'

His eyes were cynical. 'You are prone to understatement yourself, Madame,' he murmured, his eyes and body language telling her much more than his words. 'We will have to limit this tour to France and Italy, my dear.'

'Indeed, Monsieur, I think it is a good idea for both of you. The first tour, particularly, will be very stressful for Angelique.'

'I was about to discuss this aspect with you, Madame. I would like the marquis de Beaulieu to accompany us. I fear that performing at night will render me bedfast during the day. Angelique must have someone to take care of her at those times.'

'Of course, Monsieur, do not agitate yourself. The marquis de Beaulieu will be happy to accompany us. Indeed, he has already asked for Angelique's itinerary so that he may meet us in every city. I have told him that, subject to your approval, there will be a berth on our train for him.'

'Well done, Madame!' He became thoughtful. 'What do you think of them together? I have been waiting for him to ask either myself or her father for her hand. But so far, he has been silent. He is most attentive: appears to be devoted to her. I was certain ... What do you think, Madame? Have I not backed a winner here?'

She read his anxiety. If the young marquis did not come up to scratch, or if for some reason, Angelique's affection waned, who would she have in the world? And Angelique was needy; they both knew that. Angel had already chosen him to care for her when he, himself, succumbed to his illness. 'My dear, I would not disturb myself if I were you. They are both very young. They must get to know each other before making such a decision. I think they will make a match of it, yes. But you must have patience, *mon ami*. I believe they are in love, but only time will tell. Angelique is not a fool, and he is a most attractive young man.'

'Well, of course, my dear,' he countered smoothly, picking up a certain note in her voice, 'you would think that. He is the image of his father, is he not?' He raised both hands in surrender. 'Peace, Madame! Do not look at me like that! I apologise!' He was silent a minute, then, 'My dear, have you thought that we may meet up with your daughter? We will be at La Scala, you know ...'

Madame Dupont shook her head sadly. 'I do not think she will see me, Monsieur.'

'Surely, after all this time, she will be willing to let bygones be bygones!' He shrugged. 'We can hope that she has at last grown up and forgotten her childish spite and ... vindictive jealousy against me.'

'I do not think so, Monsieur. If you do, you do not know my daughter. Cèline does not forgive.'

'But you will try, Madame?'

'Oh, yes. When we reach Milan, I shall offer her the olive branch. Whether or not she slaps me with it, we shall see.'

'You know, as well as being wrong, it was very foolish of her to treat you in this way. She does not know what she has missed. It is her loss, my dear.'

'That is a very nice thing that you have said to me, my friend. I thank you.'

'*Pas du tout*, Madame. *Pas du tout!* It is but the truth. Is that the time? I must go to the music room. Angelique will be waiting for me.'

'Here she is now.' Madame Dupont's finely tuned ear heard the hasty steps as Angelique, catching up her skirts, took the stairs two at a time. She shook her head. 'She will always be a hoyden.'

'No, Madame.' The face of the marquis was stern. 'She will always have spirit and energy, *joie de vivre!* An infectious enthusiasm for life! It is in part what makes her so special. Angelique cannot be categorised.' He wagged an admonitory forefinger. 'You must not forget it.'

'No, Monsieur,' she agreed, wheeling him to the lift. 'But when she behaves in that fashion, perhaps I feel that my training has been lacking.'

'Pah!' he snorted. 'She has everything required to fit her for life. You will see.'

'I would agree with you, my dear, except for the fragility of her nerves.'

'That is why she must be looked after most carefully; why she must be nurtured and supported. For in all that she does, she expends so much of herself that she has nothing to fall back on. Poor little angel. It is her nature, my dear. No amount of training can cater to that. We can only prepare her as much as we can, and then provide the support she needs.' He thought a little, before adding, 'I am confident that, between us, we have done all that is possible to make her ready for this tour, at least.'

Angelique met them, pulling aside the grille at the top of the stairs as the lift arrived, greeting them as if she had not seen them for months. Madame Dupont smiled. That was Angelique. She took a moment to listen to the heavenly voices warming up before she went back to organising the details of the tour.

The Royal Train! She danced a couple of steps. *But, the*

Royal Train! Oh, it was an answer to a prayer, for now she would not have to worry about hotel accommodation that would allow for the wheeled chair of the marquis.

They had decided to go by train because of the difficulties of travel for him. He had flatly refused the offer of a motor lorry—noisy, smelly, no!—besides being notorious for breakdowns. Witness how many of them rolled into town daily behind the triumphant forms of a couple of large draught horses and their smirking drivers ... And these days, a horse-drawn carriage was far too slow, as well as out of the question for the wheeled chair. But there had still remained the problem of his accommodation until the Chief of the Railways had heard about it. Now, at every town, the luxuriously appointed carriages would be shunted onto their own platform. The Royal Train had everything: kitchen, dining room, sitting rooms, bed chambers—completely self-contained, absolute luxury! Everywhere they stopped, they would only need to arrange transport from the platform to the recital venue.

She sat down to write to each of the organisers, apprising them.

'Madame! Attend to me, if you please!' The marquis was being wheeled back into the room by his pupil.

This was not promising. A music lesson usually guaranteed her peace for at least an hour, if not longer.

'What is it, Monsieur? Is something wrong?'

'Madame, have you sent out those letters you were writing, yet?'

'No, Monsieur. I have just begun.'

'Oh, good! Angelique reminded me just now. She is having an attack of nerves, are you not, Petite? Madame, you must write to each opera house, informing them that I require a box directly in front of centrestage. Angelique must be able to see me the minute she walks out. Then, if she becomes nervous, she will keep her attention on me.'

'Of course, Monsieur, I have already done so. Also,

that her dressing-room must be able to be easily accessed by a wheeled chair, as must yours. I am now writing to cancel our accommodation, since we have our own luxurious mobile hotel.' She kissed her fingers. 'Thanks to the Chief of the Railways.'

'*Eh bien*, we will not go into that again.' The marquis glanced at Angelique. 'You see, my dear, it is as I told you. Madame Dupont has everything under control. There is nothing to worry about.' He turned back to Madame Dupont. 'She has been so worried that she cannot breathe, and consequently, her voice has lost its power. We are not having a good morning, are we, Petite?'

'Your deportment and your breathing, dear child!' Madame Dupont tapped the back of her hand under her chin. 'It is important for the wellbeing of your nerves, as well as your singing.' She observed her more closely. The child was paler than usual and languid in her movements, unheard of for Angelique. She was either sick, or ——

'Excuse us for a moment, Monsieur. We will meet you in the music room, directly. Come, my dear, up to your bed chamber,' she said, leaving the marquis at the top of the lift and accompanying Angelique up the next flight of stairs into her boudoir. 'Allow me to check your corset, my child ... Ah, as I thought, it is far too tight. No wonder you do not have the breath to sing. After you ran up the stairs the way you did, you must have very nearly fainted.'

'Indeed, Godmama, I did feel unusually faint, but I sat down until the lift arrived and I recovered. But then, the more I tried to sing, the more I could not catch my breath. It frightened me, Godmama!'

'Naturally, my dear. It is a new experience for you. But you must not allow Amèlie to tighten your laces so much.'

'But, Godmama ...'

'I know it is the fashion, my dear, to have an hourglass figure. But this look is not for you.' She regarded the sylph-like profile, which so far, appeared to be sending a large number of her male followers mad with desire. 'Who knows but what you will start a fashion of your own and tall, slender women will be in vogue: to the distress of every other well-cushioned damsel.'

Privately, she blamed the fashion periodicals for their exaggerated depictions of the female form. 'You are not missing anything, my dear. These young ladies with voluptuous figures become sadly over-fleshed in middle age. You are like your aunt, the comtesse de la Roche-Carillac, and your mother, who have kept their slender figures. You will live to be thankful for this, I promise you.

'You cannot compromise your singing, my dear. You must have moderation in all things, including the lacing of your corsets. Tomorrow I will speak to the corsetiere, to see if we cannot devise a garment that will allow your rib cage to expand when you draw in your breath. You do not need a corset, in any event. A nice camisole would do.'

'Oh, please, Godmama, it will be a scandal if I do not wear them!'

'Very well, but they must not be tight,' she replied, deftly remedying the situation. 'Breathe deeply now. Is that better?'

'Oh, much better, thank you, Godmama!' Angelique took a few more breaths, miraculously recovering her colour and her energy, dancing around the room.

'Monsieur le marquis has probably run out of patience by now, my dear.'

'Oh, yes! I am coming, Angelpapa!' she called, hugging Madame Dupont. 'Thank you, Godmama!'

Madame Dupont, turning away to ring the bell for her maid, thankfully did not see the unmaidenly way she slid down the banister and ran into the music room.

Shortly afterwards, having threatened Amèlie with the direst of fates should she tighten Mademoiselle's corsets to such an extreme degree again, she stopped outside the music room. Judging by the positive remarks punctuating each of the glorious notes, certainly not lacking in power, Angelique's difficulties had now been overcome. Smiling, she went back to her letters.

§

'Angelique does not lunch with us?' The marquis surveyed the empty expanse of the dining table.

'No, Monsieur. The duchesse has taken her shopping with Elise to purchase shoes and gloves to go with their new gowns, and they are lunching in town. She will be back in good time to rest before our soiree this evening.'

Madame Dupont seated herself on his right and offered him a platter of roast duckling and vegetables.

'Thank you, Madame,' he said, presenting his plate. 'I was in despair earlier, but I must congratulate you. Whatever it was that was ailing Angelique, you seem to have speedily resolved the problem. Her voice has never been better. What was her trouble, *hein*?'

She kept her eyes on the serving spoon. 'Oh, young girls, Monsieur ... She just needed a little breathing space, that is all.'

'Ah ...' He turned his attention to his meal. Then his head snapped up. 'What? You do not mean literally?' He began to laugh.

'All the young girls aspire to the figure of Mademoiselle de Mirabeau, the statuesque beauty who has taken the eye of the young vicomte de Villefontaine,' she explained. 'Much to the chagrin of the other young debutantes, including poor little Elise de Beaulieu, who is quietly heartbroken.'

He snorted, 'That over-fleshed milkmaid! I do not know why Philippe finds her so attractive. She will not fit through the door by the time she is forty. I told him so, too.'

'Oh, Monsieur! You did not!'

'I speak nothing but the truth, Madame.'

'Indeed.' Her eyes reproached him.

'Come, Madame. Someone had to warn the poor

fellow. Do you think his father would have done so?'

'Most emphatically not, Monsieur!'

He made a comprehensive gesture. '*Eh bien,* there you are, then.' He smiled ruefully. 'Our poor, misguided little angel. It is a swan aspiring to be a fat turkey poult, is it not? And I thought it was nerves! It is a good thing you were astute enough to see it, my dear.'

Madame Dupont's dimple peeped out. 'You see, Monsieur, I had one advantage that you did not possess. I had the advantage of knowing that a certain garment promising, well ... frank impossibilities, was delivered yesterday afternoon to Angelique's boudoir.'

'Madame, is it not amazing that society cannot be content with the simple charm and freshness of these young *demoiselles* without seeking to contort them into artificial forms with painted countenances: when youth has an inimitable beauty of its own? It is about the only thing upon which I agree with Poiret; although, he is another whose fashions I do not approve.' He folded up his table napkin. 'Life is full of conundrums, Madame. The older I become, the more it puzzles me.'

'Indeed, Monsieur.' Madame Dupont waved the coffeepot.

'No thank you, my dear. I have had elegant sufficiency. A very succulent dish.'

'I will tell the chef, Monsieur.'

His eyes softened as they followed her dainty form out of the room. She was kind, motherly, practical; beautiful in her own way; the Madonna personified. Wise, too. Where would he have been without her this morning: or any other morning, for that matter? Only once had he ever found her judgement to be wrong.

For the thousandth time, he cursed the fates that had led him to fall in love where he had and not with his loyal friend; for if he was not mistaken, that had been behind the promise Monsieur Dupont had wrung out of him all those years ago—to take care of her after he was gone. Of course, there was no guarantee that she would have had him either; although, it would have been a practical solution for both of them.

He knew certain crass individuals thought she was his mistress. It was acceptable to take a mistress—be one, too, if one was *une femme*—for they were accepted in society. Many men and women of his acquaintance made no secret of an *affaire de cœur* once their marital duty was done and an heir secured (although, behind their backs, they attracted a certain amount of sly comment). But he would not dally where he did not love, and he had only loved one: one whom he could not have, and because he could not have her, his title would die with him; his inheritance dispersed.

He shrugged; his thoughts returning to Madame Dupont and affairs of the heart. A virtuous woman and a law unto herself; she had, as a young ballerina, refused many such offers from very highly placed peers. Continuing to remain aloof after the death of Monsieur Dupont, she'd immersed herself in the theatre and her ballet school. His intuition told him that she had refused another such offer from the duc de Belvoir, though it did not stop her blushing like an adolescent whenever she met him. And the duc was just as obvious.

His lip curled. *What a pair we are, she and I,* he thought. But he knew Madame Dupont. He would bet his last *sou* that she would keep on refusing any more such offers: the duchesse and himself being her prime reasons. He knew her soft heart would not allow her to hurt the duchesse, and she would never abandon him. With Katarina out of reach and needing to present his people with an heir, he'd tried to ask her to marry him, several times. He just … could not do it.

And Katarina? It always hurt him to think of her. An exquisite agony. Having once made her go to Xavier due to his circumstances, when these had changed he had tried to reclaim her: driven by a passion that consumed him and threatened all of them. By the time he'd learnt the reason for her refusal, having greeted Madame Dupont's attempted explanation with homicidal fury, he'd already made a (fortunately) unsuccessful attempt on her life and then his own.

His hopes were further dashed by his own subsequent debilitating illness and the dreadful complication that had struck down Katarina on the birth of her daughter, so mentally disabling her that it had taken both he and Madame Dupont to support Xavier in taking care of her. To see his love an empty shell—unreachable, unable to speak and knowing no-one—was a blow from which he could not have recovered had it not been for Angelique, her little child, whose unconditional love and total dependence on him for her very existence had given him something to live for.

And then, more than five years later, a miracle: witnessed first by Madame Dupont, and then himself. Katarina, although remaining without speech or expression, was able to communicate her thoughts with pencil and paper. She'd come back to them.

Through it all, his love for her had never waned, becoming stronger, if anything. It proved what he had always instinctively known: love is forever. How he writhed within that fate dictated that he love in vain; that his love was to remain unfulfilled. In this life, at any rate.

He sighed, rolling his chair over to his design table. Within a few minutes, he was immersed in his latest project: a futuristic armoured vehicle with multi-directional firepower, capable of negotiating difficult terrain. For his inner voice told him that in Berlin, that holy city of science and learning, the engineers of the Kaiser were developing something remarkably similar.

Taking a break, his eye fell on the latest letter from count von Zeppelin, asking advice on the problem of the dreadful explosions that had so far destroyed most of the prototypes of his airship. He and the count had corresponded regularly over its design. A frown creased his brow. Provided they could fly high enough to avoid gunfire, airships could be used for warfare. And since he had become uneasy over Germany's activities, he now regretted advising count von Zeppelin to replace the hydrogen gas he used with one of the inert gases, perhaps helium.

At the soiree tonight, he would speak to General de Langue about the possibility of France developing an airship based on his own design. The words 'military surveillance' would attain a whole new meaning, possibly even a means of keeping the peace in these troubled times.

§

The guests, chattering happily, always enjoyed a soiree at the hôtel du Bois. Madame Dupont was a grand hostess, and the voices of the marquis and Angelique ensured a quality event. Tonight they had sung a delightful duet as a finale to the several performances of ballads and poetry by their musical and literary guests.

Mindful of past experiences, Madame Dupont had put the marquis on his honour not to hypnotise the guests or in any other way sabotage the occasion; and so far, all was running smoothly. Just now, from his wheeled chair, he was speaking with several of his learned engineering friends, with a passing glance now and again for his ward. Angelique was holding court with a group of young people; the young marquis standing back a little, seemingly content to admire her.

Then she saw three very late arrivals, General de Langue and two of his contemporaries, approach the marquis. A little frown came into her eyes as she watched these military gentlemen go off to the library with him. But how rude! They had not even had the courtesy to make an apology for their lateness. Just what was going on here? It looked as though they had not come for the soiree after all, but specifically to speak with the marquis. And here he was: leaving his guests. And he had promised!

Her thoughts registered real alarm as, a short while later, the three generals bowed rigidly to her, icily bidding her goodnight. Looking up, she saw the marquis, white of face and hollow-eyed, beckoning furiously. She followed him into the library.

'A pox upon these stupid fools of generals, Madame!' he raged. 'They are still buried somewhere in the last century. I cannot—*cannot*—convince them! And so: I have made my decision, difficult though it is.' He took a deep breath. 'I require you, Madame, to take my airship design, together with all my correspondence from count von Zeppelin, and deliver them confidentially to the King of England.'

She stared at him. 'The King of England? You do not mean ... personally, Monsieur?'

'Yes, Madame—you in person—to the King in person. There must be no whisper of what is going forward until you are with the King. You are the only one I trust to do this, my dear.'

'Oh, but —— Surely, there are others you can trust?'

He shook his head. 'There may be others I can trust, I do not know, and if I choose wrongly ...? *Eh bien*, it could be the Dreyfus Affair all over again. There are those who would wish to bring down the marquis du Bois—and any hint of treason would be the perfect way to do it. But I know that I can trust you. It is a fine point, but you see the difference, do you not?'

'Indeed.' She nodded. 'Oh, it was so wrong what was done to Dreyfus! An innocent man incarcerated all those years!'

'Oh, indeed, Madame, a gross miscarriage of justice, and all because of the lying testimony of the real perpetrator: even though the evidence was all on his side. It was a shameless case of anti-Semitism.'

'But what are you saying, Monsieur? You are not a Jew.'

He curled his lip. 'No, but prejudice is prejudice. Do

you think I do not know how it rankles with some of these nobles to accept among their peers one who first came to their notice as a showman?'

'But a most superior and talented showman,' said Madame Dupont with a smile, adding succinctly, 'and just as well born as any of them!'

'Madame Dupont,' he jeered, 'always the optimist. Oh, a curse upon these useless limbs!' he added, thumping his fists down on the arms of his wheeled chair.

'Be calm, Monsieur. Of course I will deliver them! Gaston will escort me. He and I are old adventurers.'

'No, Madame.' He shook his head. 'You will not obtain an audience with the King with Gaston as your escort. I was thinking of someone more … influential.'

'No, Monsieur! Oh, no!' Horrified, she realised his intention.

'I will speak to him. Do not have the vapours, Madame!' he said unfairly. 'This is for France … France; our beautiful France who is too short-sighted to see for herself what is needed. I do not want Germany to have the advantage over us, should the worst come to the worst. England, our ally, will be wise enough to put this design into practice.'

Endeavouring to suppress the chaotic thoughts that rendered her mute, she left him to return to their guests; the most distinguished of whom, a short while later, received a discreetly delivered note.

§

Later, relaxing over their customary hot chocolate, the marquis told Madame Dupont of his machinations. 'The duc de Belvoir has come up with a plan, Madame. He will arrange for Angelique to sing privately for the English King and Queen, supposedly on royal command. The duc and the marquis de Beaulieu will escort you both to England. The duchesse, being a loyal French woman of understanding will, at the last minute, be indisposed. It will be natural for her daughter to stay with her in Calais to look after her until your return. You will ostensibly go as Angelique's chaperone.'

'Ostensibly? *Bien sûr,* she will need one, Monsieur.'

'Indeed, and therefore no suspicion of what is really going forward will arise. The duc is some sort of cousin to the English Royal Family. He will have no difficulty in obtaining an audience with King George, who is an avid stamp collector. The duc will make it known to him that the marquis du Bois wishes to make a gift of a very rare stamp to complete a part of his collection. Fortunately, courtesy of my late father, I have such a stamp in my possession.

'I have told the duc that, since I will not trust this valuable item to anyone else, my envoy, Madame Dupont must be the one who presents this very rare stamp to His Majesty.'

'And what did Monsieur le duc think about the eccentricity of this whim of yours, Monsieur?' Her tone was dry.

'He did not say, my dear.' He gave her a bland look. 'When you present the King with the package containing the stamp—with my compliments,' he regarded her seriously, 'then, and only then, will you tell him what else is contained within it. Even the duc does not know of my intentions. It will stay that way, *hein?*'

'Of course, *mon ami,* do not disturb yourself. But,' she added thoughtfully, 'Monsieur le duc is an intelligent man. He will know that all this is not just about a stamp.'

'Indubitably, my dear, but being a man of sensitivity and discretion, he will not ask.'

'You do not feel any awkwardness in asking the duc to perform this service for you?'

He sent her an impatient glance. 'Madame, he will be only too pleased to escort you to England.'

'There are difficulties, Monsieur,' she replied, twisting

her fingers.

'I know it is an imposition, my dear. I would not ask it of you were it not important.'

'I know ... but I do not understand your reasons for involving Angelique in all this. Explain to me, please, if you will: what exactly is her role?'

'I have taught Angelique a new song. She believes it contains a secret message for His Majesty, but in reality,' he shrugged, 'she is your chaperone, my dear.'

She was speechless, beginning to rise to her feet.

'Stay, Madame, I have not yet finished.'

'*That* is a pity, Monsieur.' She sat back, meeting his eyes censoriously.

'As I have said, Angelique will perform for the King and Queen privately, and at a meeting afterwards, you will then present the King with the package containing the stamp and the documents. The next day, you will return to Paris, taking up the duchesse and her daughter in Calais on the way. Thus, on your return, the newspapers will only report on the rumour of Angelique's royal command performance, remaining in complete ignorance of what really happened at a private supper later. Directly upon your return, we will embark on our tour.'

'Very well, Monsieur. When does all this secret business set forward?'

'As soon as the duc can arrange an audience with the King. He is hopeful that it may be as soon as next week. He is quite a favourite with the King, who has often stopped by his château to break his journey on his many trips around the Empire. The climate seems to help with a lung condition he appears to be developing lately. The sunny summers of Provence are very beautiful to those who live most of their lives under cloud, my dear.

'He and the duc are very good friends despite the gap in their ages; their only difference being, I gather, that while the duc is a conservationist, he is hard put to prevent the King from shooting anything that moves in his forest.

I believe that, early in the morning before they go shooting, the duc sends the children of his servants out to play with their dogs in the wood for an hour or so, thus frightening off the game and limiting the carnage. But that is for your ears only, my dear!'

CHAPTER FIVE ~ A ROYAL COMMISSION

5 October 1913

I really do not know what Angel is about to send me on this wild goose chase. I know he is terribly upset, and I feel I have no choice. But to be so close to the one I love and must deny will be torture in the extreme. And I do not know what I must be expected to say to a King. Or, more importantly, what he will say to me!

The deck was bucketing and the gangway creaking as the travellers boarded the yacht commissioned by the marquis to take them across the Channel to England.

'Ah, this will be a rough crossing,' said the duc. 'I hope you ladies will not be seasick.'

Both vehemently negated this suggestion, then Madame Dupont lurched against the rail of the gangway, all but losing her footing.

'Take care, Madame!' The duc, a solicitous arm about her, helped her gain the deck.

'Thank you, Monsieur,' she murmured, disengaging herself hurriedly, her cheeks hot. *How ridiculous*, she chided herself. *You are not seventeen any longer. Perhaps Angel is right: I do need a chaperone.*

The crossing, though rough as predicted, was fast due to the brisk wind, and both ladies, while feeling rather ragged, were thankfully not ill.

A motor car was waiting to take them to London: the chauffeur to stay with them until they returned to Dover for the trip back to Calais. At the Savoy they ate, rested and dressed in their court finery; the duc and his son presenting very fine gentlemanly figures, attracting envious attention as they escorted their ladies: Angelique in a white floating Lanvin gown, and Madame Dupont in her customary black, relieved by Lanvin's exquisite detail in grey and silver.

In the royal apartments, Madame Dupont was making her curtsy to the King. Bowing over her hand, he said, 'How do you do, Madame Dupont? It is a very great pleasure to make your acquaintance. I saw you dance once, Madame. I was only very young, but I have never forgotten it. I do not forget a face, ever. And even if I did, I could not forget your beauty when you graced the stage at the Opéra Français with your marvellous interpretation of *Giselle.* Georges took me to see you. We share a name, you know. Teaching me about the arts, he said.' The King smiled, meeting the duc's eyes fleetingly over her head. 'It was a wonderful experience, Madame.'

Murmuring her usual deprecating reply, she exchanged a few conventional words with him before he turned to Etienne and Angelique. Madame Dupont now awaited the pleasure of Her Majesty; the duc ready to present her.

'You have not brought your duchesse, Monsieur?' The Queen's cool gaze passed over his companion.

'No, Your Majesty, I left the duchesse indisposed in Calais. My daughter, Elise, stayed with her. They are desolated not to be here with us.'

'Oh, what a shame! I hope she will soon improve.' Her eyes strayed imperceptibly to Madame Dupont.

'Your Majesty, may I make known to you Madame

Dupont, who has brought the gift, of which I wrote, for His Majesty; and of course has now to chaperone Mademoiselle de Villefontaine in place of the duchesse.'

Madame Dupont curtsied, Her Majesty graciously inclining her head. 'I am sorry that I did not see you dance, Madame,' she said after conventional preliminaries, 'but I have heard of your prowess as a ballerina.'

You have seen *Pavlova*, Ma'am?' said the duc. 'She is not a more beautiful dancer than La Belle.'

'Indeed?' she replied warmly. 'Then I regret even more that I did not see you dance, Madame. Tell me: what do you think of Nijinsky? Would you have wished to dance with him?'

'Oh, indeed, Ma'am, he is a most elegant—a superlative—dancer.'

'And the latest ballet that all the uproar is about? This *Rite of Spring*? What is your opinion of that?'

'I am sorry, Ma'am. I have not seen it, but I have heard it was a little controversial. Perhaps he is a better dancer than choreographer.'

The Queen nodded. 'Perhaps so.' She turned back to the duc, who was the bearer of fond messages from the duchesse for her.

Angelique, presented to both Their Majesties and complimented on her seraphic beauty, looked shyly towards the duc.

'Mademoiselle Angelique has a special song composed by the marquis du Bois for Your Majesties,' explained the duc. 'She wishes to sing it for you. At your convenience, of course.'

The King, after asking if she needed accompaniment, which she declined, showed them into a drawing room where they all sat. 'We will be pleased to hear you now, my dear young lady,' he said.

Amazed that she did not feel nervous, for the King, indeed, was a calming, benevolent presence, she sang superbly: her bell-like tones needing no musical accompaniment. It was as the marquis had told her it would be: just like a family gathering.

His Majesty praised her performance. 'Awe-inspiring, my dear Mademoiselle. Quite awe-inspiring, is she not?'

'Absolutely beautiful, my dear young lady, most excellent phrasing,' the Queen affirmed. 'And to sing like that, with no music: exquisite.'

'The composition, too, reveals the hand of a Master,' added the King.

Angelique, assuming from this remark that the King had indeed understood the message from the marquis purported to be in the song, was content.

'You must bring her back, duc, to sing with an orchestra in our Royal Albert Hall,' commanded His Majesty, addressing her kindly, 'You would like that, my dear? Of course ...' He added, twinkling at the duc, 'We have acceded to your wishes, Monsieur, for an informal, private supper. Indeed, it is no trial, for we have been surrounded by protocol for weeks. It will be relaxing to catch up with you and your dear son and further our acquaintance with these two lovely ladies you have brought to us from France.'

The Queen, satisfied that no impropriety had accompanied the non-appearance of the duchesse, was disposed to be regally gracious to her guests.

Madame Dupont, herself, was impressed with King George V and Queen Mary; though, at first, she had found the Queen's manner a little cold and formal. *Very English*, she thought, feeling as though, perhaps, they disapproved of her.

Nothing could be further from the truth. The duc, who knew his cousins well, could have told her that both the King and Queen were very drawn to her quiet dignity and unconscious native charm.

Strange, he thought, *La Belle is not a royal, yet in personal dignity, she has much in common with our hosts.*

Indeed, her peasant ancestry had caused the distress he

had always felt at being unable to marry her. And then, when he had decided to burn his boats and marry her after her rape—by his own cousin, God forbid!—he had not been able to find her until she had surfaced, already married to Monsieur Dupont. His most trusted servant having betrayed him by denying knowledge of her whereabouts. Lying to him to prevent scandal.

Then, and only then, had he looked for a suitable wife amongst his own class; for he worshipped the little ballerina so much that he would not offer her a *carte blanche*. That had only come after her near death at the hands of that intemperate thug, the marquis du Bois.

Admittedly, she had crossed him during a moment of blind rage. Admittedly, believing he had killed her, he had tried to kill himself. The most sensible thing he could have done: it was a thousand pities he had not succeeded! The duc felt a rising anger whenever he thought of it. Admittedly, too, he had never tried it again, but it was this that had driven the duc to overcome his principles and offer Madame Dupont his protection; and he still did not know if he were glad or sorry she had refused him.

At a cosy, informal supper (according to the monarch), the King unbent towards his guests, engaging them warmly in conversation. Madame Dupont noticed that he seemed to have a knack of finding a subject of interest to the person with whom he conversed. She discovered that, though regally formal, her bosom positively littered with precious jewels, the Queen was a loving wife and mother, saying at the end of supper, 'And now I must beg you all to excuse me, for I must say goodnight to my children. I have been a trifle anxious about Prince John. He has not been well today, and he will not sleep until he sees me. His Majesty will take you to view his stamp collection, and when the latest treasure has been safely mounted,' she smiled kindly, 'he will bring you to my sitting room where we shall have our tea.'

They all rose as the Queen left, escorted to the door by

the duc; the King offering his arm to Madame Dupont.

'Come this way, Mesdames et Messieurs, we shall view this precious stamp in my study.'

Madame Dupont, unable to speak privately to the King in front of the others, extracted the smaller envelope containing the stamp from a flat package in the specially made concealed pocket in her skirt. Things were not going to plan. She could only hope for a later opportunity.

At a table under a bright light, the King examined his newest treasure. 'Impeccable, Madame,' he said at last, putting down his magnifying glass. 'I have not seen one finer. I am greatly indebted to the marquis du Bois. Let us place it just here in this display cabinet with its fellows.' He moved away as he spoke.

Now. Here was her chance. With the others studying a part of the display on the opposite side of the room, Madame Dupont, explaining the remaining contents of the package, handed it over.

For a moment, the King stood rigid, then placing the envelope in the inner pocket of his coat, he said, 'Madame, I am greatly overwhelmed by the magnanimity of this gift. I send my eternal gratitude to the marquis du Bois. Please assure him that, given we are able to develop it as he says, it will not only be used for England, but indeed if the situation should arise, to protect our dear friend and ally, France.'

'Tomorrow,' he patted his pocket, 'these precious documents shall be given to my top-ranking designer in the Royal Engineers. Indeed, I thank you, dear Madame. I shall not write to the marquis du Bois, as was my intention, since it will not be wise; but you will tell him I shall treasure both of these remarkable gifts, even though one of them must never be mentioned. Indeed, when it appears, it will of necessity be thought a British design. It is truly a gift beyond price.' His face crinkled with warmth, transforming him from a stiff and formal monarch to what he really was: a kind, approachable gentleman.

After tea, graciously dispensed by Her Majesty, the duc met the King's questioning glance with a slight affirmative nod.

'We must reluctantly excuse our guests, my dear,' the monarch told his Queen. 'They will have to leave us now if they are going to catch the tide.'

§

Later, on the yacht, Etienne declared that he and Angelique would take a turn around the deck before retiring. Madame Dupont stood holding onto the gunwale, watching the bright trail of moonlight on the water. She shivered. Why did water always look so evil at night? So black and oily, so sinister?

Beside her, the duc put his hand over hers. 'You are cold, *ma chère?*'

'No, Monsieur, it is just …'

'I know … the sea at night. I feel the same way about it.' His clasp was warm. He drew her arm through his. 'Shall we follow the example of the young people and take a stroll on the deck, Ma Belle? Fortunately, the Channel is calmer this time.'

They followed the young couple who were conversing animatedly, the moonlight illuminating their happy profiles.

The duc spoke softly, 'Ma Belle, I know that whatever tonight was about was very important to the marquis du Bois. No ——' he stopped her as she was about to speak. 'I do not want to know what it was. Only that you have successfully completed your mission. Have you done so, my dear?'

'Indeed, Monsieur.'

'*Bien.* That is all I wanted to know.'

'Thank you for making it possible.'

'*De rien*, Ma Belle, my reward is your company. And how did you find Their Majesties? A charming and obliging couple, do you not think?' he asked, adding humorously, 'once one has pierced the Queen's armour of formality, of course!'

'They were very gracious, Monsieur. They appreciated Angelique, too. She was in good voice, was she not?'

'In very good voice, Ma Belle. She will have to come to England on tour, you know. The King wishes the English people to share in the beauty of her singing.'

'He is a good man.' Madame Dupont thought about the warmth and genuine good will expressed by Their Majesties at their leave taking.

'Very true, my dear. Yes, he is a wise and moderate ruler. Very loyal. The highest of principles! The British are lucky to have a monarch so devoted to their interests. You may also have noticed that he has the common touch: the ability to commune with a person at his or her own level. It is a gift that makes him revered by his people. The Queen also; though, she is more reserved.'

'Indeed, Monsieur, the Queen sets the fashion trends in England—a sure sign of her popularity. You know the King well, Monsieur? One can see you have a great rapport with him.' She did not add: *you have the same attitude to your people.*

He smiled. 'I have known him all his life, Ma Belle. We have been friends a long time. He was a lonely young boy, and I took him under my wing. He was not then first in line to the throne, you see, but since he has become King, I do not see him very often.' He sighed and patted her hand. 'It will soon be dawn, Ma Belle; our time together is almost up.

'Etienne, *écoute-moi*! Madame Dupont must take Angelique to their cabin. Five more minutes only to make your goodbyes.'

'*Bien*, Papa,' came the reply.

The duc walked with her a little way, then stopped. 'Ma Belle ...' He took her hands, pressing them to his lips. 'My love.'

'No …' Her protest was but a sigh. There were dangers in this: the darkest hour of the night, when the will was at its most vulnerable.

'You are right, my cherished one. Though I wish it could be otherwise, tonight or rather, this morning, wisdom must prevail. I will always treasure the memory of this unexpected time we have been able to spend together.'

'*Moi aussi*, Monsieur,' she whispered, though in reality, she had to steel herself against the pain of it; for until the duc had made known his feelings for her so many years after falling in love with her, she had not realised that there could be a joy—a spiritual ecstasy—in the touch of a certain man, or that she would long for this touch with all her being, marvelling that for most of her life she had been, as it were, a sleeper.

With the exception of her childhood friend, Angel, and the fatherly Monsieur Dupont, she had held herself aloof from all men; for her first physical encounter with a man had been so brutal, so traumatic a rape, that she had walled up the horror of it in a little dark place at the bottom of her soul and immersed herself in the care of others. An eternal mother, she had not known that her life was unfulfilled until the duc had given her a glimpse of what she had been missing.

She remembered how, at first, awakening night after night from the same dreadful dream, she had gone back to sleep in the comforting haven of Monsieur Dupont's embrace. For the short three years of their marriage, he had always been there for her, gathering her in his arms when she had cried out at night.

Kind and loving, Monsieur Dupont had explained to her that his great age prevented him from being the kind of husband she should have; and if she wished, she could discreetly take a lover. She understood that in marrying her, he had saved her life and given her and the tiny seed within her an honoured name; and more, she knew he loved her. Thus, she had innocently replied, 'No,

Monsieur, if you do not want me, I shall not bother with anyone.'

And he had laughed softly, 'Not want you? Oh, my dear!' and had held her gently, adjuring her to go to sleep as he had her safe. And, just as she had always believed everything he said to her when she was a little girl, she had believed him and slept. He had loved both her and her daughter in a gentle, wholesome way that had helped to heal her emotional wounds, treating the child as his own. And then she had lost him.

Together they had cared for their turbulent protégé, Angel: Monsieur Dupont encouraging and developing his great genius; the first to recognise his amazing talent as a composer. When he died, she had continued this care as a sacred duty. For, not only had she promised Monsieur Dupont, but Angel aroused all her motherly compassion, developing a bond of friendship that set her on the roller-coaster ride that almost ended her life: pitying him for his terrible affliction, terrified of his intemperate rages and worshipping his genius in all but equal degrees, she had done her best for him. Yet her daughter Cèline, whom she loved, had jealously plotted against him. *No! Too painful to think about!*

If only ... These were words she very seldom allowed to enter her vocabulary, self-pitying and unproductive as she felt they were. But sometimes, as now, she yearned for the kind of love that the duc—a caring, sensitive man—had offered.

No matter that the duchesse already knew when she married him that he loved another. Loving another was not a sin: doing something about it was! Thus, their hands tied, in consideration of her own responsibilities and sensitive to his, she had refused him and continued to do so. For both of them. It was hard—only *le bon Dieu* knew— but she would never leave the marquis du Bois. He had never been able to manage without her. How could she desert him now, when he needed her more than ever?

The duc picked up her hand, pressing it to his lips. '*À bientôt*, my adored one.'

'Goodnight, dearest Georges.' Her fingers clung to his for just a second before she turned away to accompany Angelique to their cabin below.

CHAPTER SIX ~ FIRST TOUR

21 October 1913

Italy, beautiful Italy. So far, the tour is going perfectly, better than anyone has a right to expect. My heart pounds at the thought of seeing my daughter, since I know I must be prepared for rejection. Because I know in my heart, she will not see me, even though Angel has said that I must be prepared to meet her here in La Scala.

Madame Dupont left the marquis in a quiet corridor contemplating an advertisement for Angelique's recital, while she went to find out what she could about her daughter. It was well done and he approved, but rolled his chair back in the shadows at the slamming of a door and approaching footsteps, smiling a little as a rotund figure came into view and halted, transfixed, before the poster.

'*Bella diva d'oro!*' cried Signor Morelli, kissing his pudgy fingers and gesturing widely. 'I will sing with her, this beautiful golden diva!'

'Oh, you think so, do you, Signor? Well, I may have something to say about that!' said a savage voice from behind him. 'What have you done with Cèline?'

The Italian tenor swung around, a ludicrous expression on his face as he surveyed the grim-looking man in the wheeled chair. 'Signor? I do not understand. Who are you to ask me such a question as that?'

'You do not know me, Signor?' The marquis, speaking softly, kept his predatory gaze on him. 'Strange: because I know you—Alberto Morelli!'

The once soulful liquid eyes, now almost hidden by rolls of fat, grew large. He made an expressive Italian gesture of incomprehension.

'Ah, but you do know me, Signor,' continued the soft voice. 'Cast your mind back to a time when you were the understudy to the tenor at the Opéra Parisien.'

'Yes, Signor?' His puzzlement grew.

'And you often came to the Opéra Français to court the daughter of Madame Dupont, did you not?'

'Indeed, Signor, but I cannot ...'

'*Bien sûr*, you knew me, Signor!' The marquis' eyes quizzed him, wickedly. 'Can you not place me?'

'No, Signor ...' stammered the tenor, discomfited. ''I am afraid ... I regret ...'

'Just as I expected,' purred his inquisitor. 'And yet, how relieved I am to hear it from your lips.'

'Signor? Pardon? But you confuse me.'

'*Eh bien* ...' The marquis curled his lip.

The tenor, rendered inarticulate by his sinister amusement, could only stare helplessly. Then he looked beyond him; his expression absurd with surprise and relief: 'Madame Dupont!'

'Alberto! Is it you? I did not recognise you. But where is Cèline? She is not with you?' Madame Dupont's surprise was edged with anxiety.

'But ... Did you not receive my letter, Madame? No? Strange! Well, er ... Cèline has left me.' He sounded aggrieved. 'She said I was too fat, too self, er ... not enough, er ...'

'Yes, yes,' said the marquis hurriedly, 'we understand!

But where is she now?'

He shrugged disconsolately. 'She ran away to America with a tall, slim baritone.'

'America is a very big country, Signor,' said the marquis, dryly. 'Where in America?'

'I do not know, Signor … Wait a moment, I think I remember her saying she wanted to dance on a wide road. I think that was what she said … wide or broad. They have them in America, you know, not little narrow winding streets like we have here in Europe; although, why she cannot be satisfied with a perfectly good stage …?'

'Broadway.'

'Pardon, Signor?'

'It is not a street, you cretin! Oh, it does not matter!' The marquis turned to Madame Dupont. 'She has gone to New York, Madame, to dance on Broadway. She is obviously a *succès fou*. I am sorry, my dear, if you want to see her, you will have to wait until Angelique tours America.'

The mention of Angelique reignited the Italian tenor. 'It is a sign! A sign, Signor! But I will sing with her, this Golden Diva! Oh, yes, yes, yes, yes, yes!' He kissed his fingers repeatedly.

'Oh no, you will not!' said the marquis, sternly. 'Your voice is too light for her.'

'How dare you, Signor!' The tenor was scandalised. 'I have a good voice!'

'Indeed, Signor, you have a very good voice. You would not otherwise sing at La Scala.' Madame Dupont tried to calm what she could see was becoming an incendiary situation.

'Agreed, Madame. He has a very good voice, yes.' The marquis turned to the tenor. 'You think that Mademoiselle Angelique has a good voice, Signor?'

'Oh, Signor … The purity of her notes! The perfection of her phrasing!' he gasped, gesticulating wildly. 'To die for, Signor! To die for!'

'Very true,' agreed the marquis, watching him cynically.

'Oh surely, Signor … Oh certainly, nothing could be more true than this that you have said. Indeed, she has a very good voice.'

'No she has not, you ———' His eyes met those of Madame Dupont. With a supreme effort, he abandoned the demeaning epithet, beginning again, 'She does not have a *good* voice. She has a great—a magnificent voice! Have you any idea, Signor, what happens when a merely good voice stands up beside a great voice?'

The tenor's face registered consternation.

'Precisely, Signor. Indeed, you may not realise it, but the beauty of your notes and, in a word, the excellence of your technique hides from your audience the fact that your voice lacks power. Think about what they will hear if you sing with one who, I tell you, not only has all your good points and more, but also amazing power. You see? They will not hear you, *mon brave*; they will hear only Angelique! And they will remember it, Signor! They will remember it. And your reputation will be lowered. Indeed, I am doing you a favour.' He smiled unpleasantly. 'In any case, you may be assured of this, Signor: I am the one who will sing with her!'

Signor Morelli, purple in the face and rendered speechless by this scathing attack, bowed stiffly to Madame Dupont and waddled off to his dressing-room where he relieved his feelings in the violent slamming of the door.

Madame Dupont and the marquis, both struck by the comical aspect of the outraged vanity expressed in the tenor's rigid back as he strutted away, were valiantly trying to stifle their laughter.

'Poor Cèline … *Du vrai*, one can hardly blame her, Madame,' said the marquis between gasps. 'He was an attractive young man, but … Oh dear!'

We are being unkind, she thought, feeling sympathy for the man, especially since her daughter had discarded him.

But … it was funny!

'It will be a miracle if he does not go off in an apoplexy after what you have just said to him, Monsieur,' she observed severely, wheeling him away. 'Not but what you are right, of course!'

Would her daughter have accepted her olive branch? Probably not, given her previous behaviour and thwarted attempts to expose Angel. Madame Dupont sighed. Perhaps they would never know. She could not tell whether the fluttering in her breast was disappointment or relief, for *au fond*, she had been sure her daughter would reject her. The feeling had grown stronger throughout the tour, and the closer they came to Milan, the worse it had become.

They had left the duc and duchesse in Paris directly after the performance at the Opéra Magique, Etienne and Elise travelling with them. The marquis had decreed that all Angelique's tours were to begin and end there, and this first was a grand occasion for the great, the legendary marquis du Bois—in a past life the Master of Illusion—to sing with his pupil, the exciting new diva, Mademoiselle de Villefontaine, ecstatically acclaimed as the Angel of Song: and no-one wanted to miss such a rare treat.

The pattern beginning here was repeated at every venue. First, the marquis and Angelique appeared onstage together in a duet. Then, during the recital performed by the Orchestra Magique and Monsieur Merignac, the marquis would be taken to a box directly in Angelique's line of sight, from which place he encouraged her, conducting and mouthing the words during each of her arias, returning to the stage to perform with her the last song as a duet.

So far, the tour had been a sellout success through all of France and selected venues in Italy, including the recently purchased French Embassy in Rome, the beautiful Palazzo Farnese, and now it was almost over. Milan, Nice and a special performance for the duc at Belvoir village were the last stops before going home to Paris for a final performance at the Opéra Magique.

Despite his difficulties, the marquis had managed to sing with his customary magnificence; although, he was now becoming quite tired.

Back at the Royal Train, they were lunching after their morning visit to La Scala.

'I am sorry we did not find your daughter, Madame.'

'Thank you, *mon ami*. It is kind of you, after ...'

'*De rien!* Water under the bridge. She must be a great success, my dear. It is not just anybody who gets to dance on Broadway, you know.'

'I know, Monsieur, but I could wish she had been just a little more faithful to her wedding vows. Even if ...' Her eyes were sad.

'Cèline always had her eye to the main chance, my dear, you know that. She backed the wrong horse when she chose Alberto and was too proud to tell you. She has decided to change jockeys midstream and will now try her luck in America. She will do well. I would not worry. Not everyone has your principles, my dear. One only lives once!'

'Horses, Monsieur, it is horses.'

'What?'

'Your metaphor.'

'Oh? Oh yes, of course ...' He shrugged. 'Well, if you do not wish to discuss it ——'

'No! No! Oh no-o-o!'

Angelique! Their eyes met in alarm. Madame Dupont got up from the table and hurried to investigate. There were no more distressed sounds, and in a short while, she was back to answer his unspoken query.

'Angelique was very upset about the young English suffragette ...'

'Suffragette? Oh yes, I know. Continue, Madame.'

'The one who threw herself under the horse of King George V at the Epsom Derby ... and was trampled to death.'

He frowned. 'But surely, this regrettable incident took place some time ago now?'

'Yes, Monsieur, it was last summer—well before her debut—but Angelique has only just heard about it. You remember that we agreed to keep it from her, knowing how sensitive she is? Unfortunately, while sightseeing in the city, they met up with some English tourists who began discussing the problems the suffragettes are causing in England. Blocking the roadways and chaining themselves to the palace gates and other such disruptive activities. Very militant, I hear. Since these activities have their roots in this very sad affair, the conversation naturally got round to it. Angelique was distressed for the girl herself, the dear King and the poor horse who would not have meant to harm her. Etienne thought it best to bring her away from them so that she might forget about it. But she cannot get it out of her mind and remembered it just as they were coming in to lunch, and so was upset all over again.'

'Oh the poor little one ... So soft-hearted! How is she? She has not become too agitated?'

'No, no. Etienne was able to calm her. He is good for her, Monsieur.'

'Indeed.' He paused. 'Where are they now?'

'Etienne decided to take the girls out to lunch, instead, to sample the Milanese cuisine. He thinks it will help to take their minds off it. I have told him that if he sees any more English tourists, to avoid them at all costs; and that he must have Angelique back to rest by half past two, at the latest. We cannot have her disturbed by any more talk of these young English women protesters before the recital.'

'Indeed, my dear, I think you have spoken wisely. These poor misguided *jeunes filles*—to do such a thing!' He shook his head. 'Thank God we have equality of the sexes in France, Madame. There is no need for any of our young *demoiselles* to take such a desperate course of action.'

Madame Dupont looked at him, opened her mouth and closed it again.

'You are very quiet, Madame.'

'I have not heard of any woman in France having been given the vote, Monsieur.'

'That is because there is no need for it, Madame. Any good French woman can advise her husband how to vote.'

'That is a canard.' But she smiled.

'*Les femmes*, they have so many things on their minds, so many household duties,' he murmured, watching her through half-closed eyes. 'So much so, that it is feared by certain gentlemen of my acquaintance that they will not be able to cope with having the vote. They are afraid that their delicate sensibilities will not be able to withstand the worry of making decisions like that, on top of everything else that occupies their minds, such as apparel, shopping, etc. What do you say, Madame? Can they cope with the vote?'

Preserving her countenance, she replied, 'I think so, Monsieur.' He was not getting a rise out of her today. Besides, she knew his mockery was aimed at the members of his own sex and was secretly hoping that she would see through it and share the joke. But it was a serious matter! Who was to blame? Men or women, for this belief? Was it not the devious 'power behind the throne' attitude adopted by the fairest of the fair sex to keep men believing that women were poor, frail little creatures, unable to make up their minds; unable to exist without men; when in reality …?

'They are also worried that you might choose a candidate for the wrong reasons, such as their looks or their charm.'

'Are they really?' Madame Dupont looked amused. 'Well, it could be an improvement,' she said demurely, 'when one thinks about it.'

His smile was tired. 'Will you call Charles for me, my

dear? If I am to sing in this cursed place, I must go and rest. How many more recitals are there?'

'After this? Only three, Monsieur.'

'It is very interesting, that,' he remarked thoughtfully.

'What is that, Monsieur?'

'The way that you say "only" ...'

His valet appeared in the doorway.

'Ah, Charles. In a good hour! Take me away, at once! Madame Dupont has been greatly depressing me.'

Refilling her coffee cup, she sat on at the table, listening to the gently courteous tones of the valet as he replied to his employer. A slight frown creased her brow. His sense of humour may be unimpaired, but it was becoming very difficult for the marquis to sustain his performances. And to have gone with her to look for Cèline this morning had depleted his precious energy even more.

She went to find Amèlie and make sure their evening costumes were ready. Her gown was in black paillette silk, trimmed with silver lace edging, bugle beading and finished with a silk ribbon waistband. There were tassels on the handkerchief points of the three-quarter length skirt of the bodice jacket. She'd had trouble deciding between that and a charmeuse-satin softly falling tunic overdress with embroidered hem and bodice, and a broad silk waistband—the underskirt of black silk.

Holding Angelique's gown up to the light, she nodded approvingly. Perfect. Yes, Amèlie was looking after her wardrobe well. This model was in ivory Japanese silk, the bodice daintily gathered at the shoulders into a set of tiny jewelled buckles, the front inset with lace and pin-tucked silk across the neckline, gathered into a cunningly wrought silk ribbon waistband decorated with a larger jewelled buckle. This same touch was repeated in the elegantly draped skirt, held together below the knee by a similar buckle, swirling effectively and glittering when she moved.

She checked that the shirt, cravat and handkerchief set

out for the marquis were the correct match for Angelique's chosen gown, the tiepin being in the shape of a jewelled buckle, before returning to her own compartment to rest.

Detouring to speak to Charles, who shared her anxiety over him, he replied in answer to her question, 'He is asleep at the moment, Madame, but I agree with you. He does seem to be rapidly losing what little strength he has left.' The valet's eyes were worried.

'You have been giving him his tonic?'

'Yes, Madame. And the tisanes recommended by Professor Lejeune; also the fresh fruits, the green vegetables, the succulent meats and fresh fish in the diet, Madame, the chef is very particular. We are doing everything we can to help him.'

'I know, *mon brave*, and it is appreciated. Perhaps if you were not, who knows, he may not still have been with us by now.'

'No, Madame.' The valet grew pale at the thought.

'Do not wake him until the last moment tonight, Charles. He will need the extra rest. Angelique can warm up her voice with me, for a start. If he is in his dressing-room fifteen minutes before curtain, it will be enough.'

'But, Madame ...'

'Do not worry, Charles. I will take the responsibility for it. You may tell him it was by my order.'

'*Merci*, Madame.' Charles bowed.

In the end, it did not come down to a question of blame; for the marquis awoke naturally in plenty of time, and all went as planned.

Some thoughtful person had decorated their box with small gold statues of Greek gods, including Atlas, Achilles and a slightly tipsy-looking Eros—the young Elise pointing this out with much merriment.

'Hush, my dear sister,' chided Etienne fondly, 'you will bring down the wrath of the house upon our heads if you giggle in this fashion in the best box of the great La Scala.'

'Oh, don't, Etienne, you will set me off again,' she

begged.

'Sit down, you two, before we are thrown out!' commanded Madame Dupont, hiding a smile. 'One on either side of me. Leave that space beside me for the wheeled chair of the marquis ... so! The curtain is about to rise.' Then her eye fell on the offending god. The child was quite right, he did look shockingly cast away. No wonder these old gods had died out, lost face or whatever. She smiled at the chastened pair as they silently obeyed her, eyes brimming with laughter, becoming serious as they waited in growing tension for the curtain to rise.

CHAPTER SEVEN ~ GOLDEN DIVA

Evening, 21 October 1913

*So far, it has been the most wonderful tour, and Angelique has
not disappointed us; my fears of the pressure of performing being
too much for her sensitive spirit having fortunately come to nothing.
In fact, she has performed spectacularly. Du vrai, she is the
embodiment of us all, having the refined, elegant features of the de
Villefontaines, Katarina's voice—only better—because she has
more need to sing and strive to improve. She has the spirit and
relentless pursuit of excellence of the marquis, and she has her
elegance of bearing, poise and control from the ballet I taught her,
since I largely brought her up. Why did I need to worry? Angel is
coping better than I feared, and Angelique's success is just
incroyable. My meeting with my daughter must be postponed until
she returns from her tour of America, so that allows me breathing
space to compose myself for her reception of me. So many surprises.
Are there any more, I wonder?*

The marquis sat on a magnificent throne: gilded, high-
backed and upholstered in red velvet, raised to put his
head at a comparable level to Angelique's. She stood with
him on the ornate stage; a hand resting on the carved arm

of the chair.

Their first duet, the haunting *Canzone de Katarina*, went well; for the audience was educated and appreciative of technical excellence. At the end of the song, they gave the performance a standing ovation, yelling, whistling and stamping. Madame Dupont noticed that they were a very interactive audience, having, on occasion when a voice had not come up to their expectation, hurled overripe tomatoes at their fallen idols. Or so she had heard. Perhaps it was an exaggeration, but whatever the truth of it, there seemed little likelihood of it happening tonight.

The Orchestra Magique began to play a new instrumental composition by the marquis, composed especially for the people of Milan, as Monsieur Merignac grandly explained beforehand.

Overwhelmed, the patrons were listening attentively as the marquis was wheeled silently to the box by a couple of strong men who made easy work of the stairs.

'I may have to stay here with these Greek gods, Madame,' he whispered, looking about him. 'For, burly porters notwithstanding, I think I have gone my length tonight.'

'Rest here awhile, Monsieur,' she replied in soothing undertones. 'Angelique's voice will soon renew your strength.'

'Dear Madame Dupont, the eternal optimist!'

The new composition was duly rewarded, all the people touched that a piece of music had been specially written for them and that no-one else had heard it before.

There was a breathless hiatus, and Angelique stood onstage.

'*Bella diva d'oro!*' shouted a man below them: a chant taken up by the entire house.

Angelique smiled, thanked them, focused her attention on the marquis and began her aria. From the first chord, Madame Dupont felt his concentration shift, his sagging frame grow more upright, as the power of her voice—the beautiful light and shade, the perfect shaping of each note—inspired them all. Intently, he followed every phrase with her until the last note.

'Perfect, my angel,' he breathed. 'Was she not, Madame?'

'Indeed! Wonderful!' she affirmed. Already he was regaining some of his energy. By the time he was needed for the final duet, she felt he would be up to it. The crowd roared and chanted. The marquis laughed in triumph.

But where was Angelique? She had left the stage, but why? Etienne rose and quietly went out the door. Then, she was in the box with them, Etienne holding her hands.

'Dear child, what has happened?' The marquis tried to rise out of his chair and failed. 'Why are you not onstage?'

Madame Dupont, observing her anxiously, was relieved. Angelique did not look as if she were in a panic.

'It is all right, Angelpapa. I am to have a little break. Signor Morelli wants to perform his most famous aria, *E lucevan le stelle* from *Tosca*, for his public. He was so insistent that I said he could have this spot, and I would take a break. What will I do, Angelpapa? Shall I leave out the second aria?'

'No, sing that one. You will leave out the next one. The second aria, it is your best one. Sit down with Etienne, Petite. You would like some refreshment?'

Shaking her head, she went over to her seat.

'I shall speak to these organisers over this, Madame!' said the marquis in a violent undervoice: his face a white mask.

Signor Morelli stood on the stage amidst wild applause. He was theirs: their own tenor. And he would be singing after these two foreigners. Wonderful as they were, they were still foreigners. They awaited eagerly the excellence to which they were accustomed.

He opened his mouth, his high notes pure and beautiful, his phrasing immaculate, as always, but something was wrong! His auditors shifted in their seats, puzzlement and disappointment written clearly on their faces. Signor Morelli did not sound the same as usual. Something was lacking in his voice. There was a silence—a smattering of applause. The tenor turned away, mortified.

'The fool,' commented the marquis, unemotionally. 'He was warned.'

Angelique returned to the stage, enthralling the audience with her best aria, thus exacerbating Signor Morelli's discomfiture even further; the marquis again following every note until her last solo. When the porters came back for him, under the cover of the furious stamping and the chant of *'bella diva d'oro!'*, he was easily able to take his seat on the great throne and sing with her the magical duet *Éternité d'amour* from *Le Perdu*, Madame Dupont's own Opera Ballet.

Madame Dupont sighed. *He has done it!* And the performance had been so polished. No-one could have known from his effortless vocalisation his fears that he would not be able to complete the recital. Two glorious voices: even La Scala, whose walls were saturated with glorious voices, was astounded by them. She felt sorry for Signor Morelli, but she agreed with the marquis: only a fool would put himself up for scrutiny alongside a voice like Angelique's. The Italian tenor's foolish vanity had driven him to take a step damaging to his career. She supposed that she could understand her daughter, even if she could not condone her actions.

§

There were a few days to rest before the performance at Nice, which went without a hitch. Then they travelled on, pulling into the siding at Belvoir Village early in the morning for a special matinée recital for the duc's people.

Today was their Feast Day: the day when they all dressed up in their finery and went to a banquet provided by the duc; for every year, at the end of harvest, all partook of the riches of the duc's estate—the fruits of their labour—as the duc put it. They all took their picnic baskets, as the duc had decreed that they must be able to take home their supper and a good bottle of wine, because no-one would cook this evening. Today was a celebration, *bien sûr*, and no-one was to work!

As a highlight of this celebration, the duc had invited the best voices in France to sing for them: France's newest sensation, their golden Angel of Song, and her teacher, the marquis du Bois. They were to give a recital just for them, for *alors*, were they not the duc's own people? And therefore special?

They crowded the platform, waving the French flag and chanting a welcome, escorting them across the square to the steps of the village hall. Nowhere had they received a warmer or more touching welcome; nowhere were they to enjoy singing more than with these good, simple folk who were earthy and loyal.

They passed long tables crammed with the produce of Belvoir, ready for the rush after the recital, arriving in the entrance foyer of the hall where the duc and duchesse awaited them.

Turning away from the duc who had kept her chatting for a few minutes about their tour, Madame Dupont was left alone with the duchesse. She smiled warmly, in expectation of her usual genial chat, and was rocked by the rigidity of the taller woman's features: the bleak expression in the normally friendly light eyes.

'Madame Dupont!' The duchesse looked her up and down, adding enviously, 'You have kept your figure so well, I do not know how you do it.' She glanced down at her own expanding profile. 'It seems that every day my waistline increases so that I keep on having to have my gowns altered. Do, please tell me: what is your secret, Madame?'

'You are very kind to say so, Madame, but I do not think I have a secret. I do not know, perhaps it is the dance exercises,' she replied, hiding her astonishment at the manner of the duchesse, who would not normally speak in such a personal fashion, let alone employ it as a greeting.

'You still dance, Madame?' The duchesse surprised her even more. *What an inapposite question!*

'No, oh, no,' she replied, puzzled. 'Just the limbering exercises every morning that help me start my day; that we have spoken of before. You don't remember, Madame? In truth, I have been doing them since I was about six years old. The habits of childhood die hard, you know,' she added, in an attempt to lighten the atmosphere.

'And is that how you have been able to hold onto my husband's heart all these years, Madame?' enquired the duchesse, in a hard little voice.

There was the space of a heartbeat.

'Madame?' Madame Dupont was taken aback. The duchesse sounded so tense and brittle, so unlike herself.

'I am sorry,' whispered the duchesse, taking refuge in her handkerchief. 'I do not know what has come over me lately.'

Do you not? I do! Madame Dupont, feeling sympathy for her, took her arm, steering her into the privacy of the cloakroom. 'There, there, do not distress yourself, Madame, I pray you. The duc is a romantic—an idealist— we both know that. *Tiens*, Madame, have I not heard you joke many times about having a heartless husband? Him having given it away before he met you? Perhaps he did once, long ago, fall in love with a young ballerina and romantically believe, as young men are wont, that he could never love another; but that young woman is dead, Madame. Please, I beg of you, do not let a ghost destroy your happiness.'

Seeing that the duchesse would not be comforted, Madame Dupont continued gently: 'You say he has not given you his heart, Madame—that is as may be. In truth, I think you have more of it than you know.' Then, beginning to despair as the duchesse wept on, 'Oh, Madame ... Why dwell on such a topic? Would it not be better to think upon all that he has given you, rather than the one thing that you fear he has not? Do you not share many wonderful interests: your two beautiful children; a deep, unbreakable friendship; the hearts of your people? You are lucky, for unlike many of his peers, he does not keep a mistress or indulge in *affaires de cœur*.'

The duchesse reared her head. Madame Dupont, reading the look, put up a hand.

'No, Madame, most emphatically not! *Je vous assure*, there has not been and—*non sera!*—there will not be! Before *le bon Dieu*, I swear it! So, think about it, Madame. If it is as you say, which of us has the most? Madame la duchesse with everything except (you say) his heart, but having, notwithstanding, his name, his children, his home, his living presence every day? Or Madame Dupont, having only an absent heart, which honour decrees she may not touch?'

She had not chosen to fall in love with the duc, and there was still that in her which believed what she had said to the duchesse: the duc had fallen in love with a young ballerina, a girl who no longer existed. It was just that the duc, when he looked at her, could only see the ballerina; she was sure of it.

His devotion to her had many aspects, aroused many emotions, but there was a caveat: the duchesse must not be hurt by it, and there was every indication here and now that she was. The duchesse had reached an age where one felt less than attractive, and small things were apt to grow out of all proportion.

Small comfort that she knew when she married him that he was in love with the young ballerina, Elise Gordonnier. But for over twenty years, he had kept his distance, sending flowers anonymously and attending all the performances under her direction, choosing to remain aloof, but keeping a vicarious eye to her. That was until the summer he had invited them to Belvoir. Still, she had no inkling of his feelings for her until he had—out of the blue—offered her his protection after the marquis had strangled her and departed, leaving her for dead. The duc, seeing he had offended her by his offer, had then made known to her his devotion for her, wanting to keep her with him. Of course, she had refused him, honour demanding it. And was it not the truth? Did not the duchesse have all the things that she, Madame Dupont, did not?

'Think about it, Madame,' she urged the duchesse. 'And now,' Madame Dupont resumed her brisk manner, 'as to the problems you are suffering today, I will give you a herbal recipe that you will have made up into a tea. Drinking one cup a day will relieve your symptoms substantially, and the balance of your mind will soon be restored. The weight increase should be reduced, and if you take a brisk walk every day in your most excellent garden, you will soon be your slender self again.' She touched her hand. 'Madame, *écoute-moi*! I will ask you one more question. Answer it truthfully, if not to me, then to yourself. It is this: if the duc had not told you of his circumstances all those years ago, giving you the choice of whether or not to marry him, would you have known from his manner towards you that he loved another?'

The duchesse, tears at last abated, all her attention on her shredded handkerchief, shook her head. 'No, Madame.'

'*Eh bien*,' said Madame Dupont, gently. 'And now, we must take our seats, for the recital is about to begin. After you, Madame.'

The duc stood on the stage with the orchestra behind him, holding up a hand for silence. 'My dear people, I am delighted to welcome you all here today.'

A great cheer arose, acknowledged charmingly. Madame Dupont saw that he knew and loved his people. There was no question that his sentiments were not fully reciprocated.

'It is my greatest pleasure to present to you our own French Angel of Song, Mademoiselle Angelique de Villefontaine, and her teacher, Monsieur le marquis du Bois.'

The applause reached deafening proportions. Angelique walked onto the stage beside the wheeled chair of the marquis, brought in by no less a personage than the heir of their duc. There was a gasp: these guests of their *seigneur* were indeed honoured. The people accorded their presence with even greater enthusiasm.

The marquis de Beaulieu and the duc bowed to the performers and the audience, taking their seats near the stage with the duchesse, Elise and Madame Dupont.

There followed a performance so inspired that it had to be heard to be believed, for the atmosphere was so charged with joy and goodwill that it sparked back onto the singers, igniting them. Madame Dupont could only marvel that, out of all the great cities and houses they had visited, their most inspiring performance had been in a small village hall before an unsophisticated audience of simple village folk.

Afterwards, the marquis endeared himself to the children by taking coins from behind their ears and from under their collars, only to present them again amid great hilarity. Madame Dupont once more found herself astounded by him.

At the end of the festivities, the duc invited them to the château for dinner.

'No, Monsieur,' replied the marquis, his eyes on Madame Dupont. 'Let us return your hospitality by entertaining you Right Royally in the dining car of our train.'

The duc turned to his wife. 'Shall we dine in the Royal Train, Madame?'

'If you wish, Monsieur,' she replied colourlessly.

The duc, looking closely at the duchesse, took her

hand. 'You are not well, my dear? I have been a little worried about you lately. You have not seemed yourself.'

'It is nothing, Monsieur. Just a slight headache. Madame Dupont has given me a recipe for a tisane to cure it.'

'Ah, that is very kind. Thank you, Madame.'

'*De rien*, Monsieur! I am sure Madame la duchesse will be much revived if she takes the tisane and a short rest before dinner.' Her gaze was just slightly reproachful, for she felt that he could have supported the duchesse more and perhaps reassured her after their visit to the King. And now, to do the right thing, he should excuse himself and take his wife home, giving her a little of his undivided attention. But no:

'Elise, my dear, take your mama home and see that she has this tisane. I will be along later when I have spoken to all my people. Then, we will return to the Royal Train for dinner.'

Madame Dupont turned her head away. Even the duc, a sensitive man, had failed to perceive the needs of his wife. For the first time, she compared him unfavourably with the marquis, who never failed in his perspicacity. Whether he treated this knowledge with cruelty or kindness—ah, that was another matter! At least the duc could be acquitted of deliberate cruelty—in her heart, she knew this—if not the usual male blindness.

Watching the warm, generous charm he had for his people, dismissing them to their homes in a way that made them feel anything but dismissed, she felt perhaps she had judged him too harshly, and today had been an exception. Thinking about the story told to her by the head gardener on her previous visit to Belvoir, she could see that the destinies of this people and their duc were inextricably intertwined. Little known though it was, the people of Belvoir had walled themselves up in the château with the duc of their time during the infamous period of the Revolution and protected him with their very lives: the walls of the château, as they had since medieval times, standing fast against attack. For they took the view that he was their duc, and it was up to them to decide his fate; and if they were satisfied with his behaviour, no Parisian rabble were going to trample his blood under their feet, *bien sûr*, or feed him to Madame la guillotine! He was to die in God's own time and be placed in the vault beside his ancestors or else, to a man and woman, they would all die with him! Pondering this, Madame Dupont saw that this duc, like this ancestor before him, drew the love and loyalty of his people in a way that could not be easily understood.

She jumped as the marquis wheeled his chair up beside her. 'Oh, Monsieur, you startled me! I am sorry; I have been wool-gathering.'

'So I see, Madame.'

'Have you seen Angelique, Monsieur?'

'Etienne has taken his mother and sister up to the château, and Angelique has accompanied them.' He paused, before adding in a gruff warning: 'You should have a care, Madame.'

She shrugged. Trust him to have perceived that which the duc had not. 'Perhaps you can hypnotise him, Monsieur?' she suggested crisply. 'What about that? Convince him that he loves only his wife. Why not?'

'You know the answer to that, my dear. If it were possible, do you think I would not have already done it?'

When she did not reply, he mused, 'Hmm, it is an interesting concept that: all men loving only their wives.' Adding at his driest, 'Would we die of boredom, I wonder? No gossip, no canards, no exciting conquest to look forward to at a ball; nothing to exercise the mind at a soiree, *hein*?' His smile was tinged with irony. 'And now, if we are finished talking nonsense, may I prevail upon you to either help me over these cursed cobblestones, or call Charles to attend me?'

'Of course, *mon ami*,' she replied, wheeling him towards

the platform. 'I must speak with the chef about our extra dinner guests. We do not want him to throw a temperament, which he might do if I do not give him time to prepare for them.'

The chef, however, far from throwing a temperament, managed to produce a regal feast of eleven courses, beginning with a clear consommé and ending with coffee, cheese, fruit and delicate sweet pastries.

They were served canapés in the ornate sitting room next to the dining car. The duc looked around nostalgically. 'It is a long time since I have been in this carriage,' he said to the marquis.

'It is very comfortable, Monsieur. We were fortunate to get it.'

'Indeed, so I heard.' Glancing at him significantly, the duc lowered his voice: 'I have also heard that the Chief of the Railways is very popular with *les femmes*—and they are very popular with him.'

'So I understand, Monsieur,' replied the marquis quietly. 'Do not worry; it shall be taken into account.'

They joined the others in chatting about the events of the day.

The duchesse requested the cloakroom, and Madame Dupont escorted her. 'It is just here, Madame. Madame?' The duchesse seemed to be having trouble with her breathing, so Madame Dupont gave her the smelling salts. 'You are unwell, Madame?'

'No, no. It is just … that I am overcome by the thought of what I said to you earlier. Will you forget it, Madame? I cannot believe that I spoke to you like that. Of course, I know that you have not … do not …' She stopped, embarrassed.

'Do not give it another thought, Madame, I beg of you. You have tried the tisane?'

'Oh, yes, yes I did. It has helped me greatly. But of course, when I realised the enormity of …'

'*De rien*, Madame! It is over. Continue to take the tea

and leave the past where it lies, I beg of you. When you are ready, come and join us for hors d'oeuvres.'

As Madame Dupont was about to enter the sitting room, the duc was asking them jocularly if they had the Mona Lisa safe on the train with them.

'No, Monsieur,' replied the marquis. 'Why do you ask? She has not been found overnight?'

'No, sadly not, Monsieur, but my people have confirmed the whisper that she was taken into Italy by the thief. All art dealers in the country have been told to be on the lookout for her.'

'Indeed, one wonders at the mentality of the thief,' marvelled the marquis. 'How would such a treasure not be recognised? In truth, it is its own security; for it truly is priceless, as the thief will find out when he tries to sell it.'

'How long has she been missing, now?'

'Oh, I don't know ... How long, Madame?'

'Oh, at least two years, I think. Her place in the Louvre looks so empty, does it not?'

'I predict she will soon be returned,' pronounced the marquis. 'I doubt if thieves are noted for their patience and—especially this one—certainly not intelligence. Moreover, if the duc's people are hearing whispers, it must be about to surface.'

The duc nodded. 'So I think,' he confirmed, adding as the duchesse entered: 'Ah, there you are, my dear. I was about to send a search party for you, thinking that you may have taken a wrong turn! You are not ill?'

'Oh, no. Thank you, dear child.' She smiled at Angelique, accepting the glass and pastry she was offered. 'I think I am a little hungry ...'

'We shall go in to dine in about five minutes, Madame,' said Madame Dupont. 'If that is of any help to you?'

'I think I shall survive until then, Madame. Just ...' she replied, biting into a savoury vol-au-vent. 'Oh, exquisite, I must send my chef to visit yours: this sauce is *aux anges*, my dear.'

Madame Dupont rendered up silent thanks. The duchesse sounded exactly as she used to.

It was a memorable dinner. The young people sparkled, and the duchesse, restored to her former self, conversed with her usual amusing warmth and grace. The duc, participating fondly, reminisced with great tact, exchanging humorous anecdotes with the marquis, and discussing new trends in the arts and ballet with the authority of a connoisseur.

Madame Dupont, seated between Etienne and Elise at the foot of the table, was able to relax; for it would seem that the duc had finally realised what had been ailing the duchesse and was doing his best to treat her with considerate attention. His apparent indifference to Madame Dupont was only that, but at least he had the grace to try.

She could see that the marquis was enjoying the conversation, for his dry humour was fired by the ready wit of the duc and his son, and spirits were high.

When the party broke up and the marquis thanked them for coming, Madame Dupont was staggered to hear him say that he did not know when he had enjoyed an evening more, complimenting the duchesse on her delightful children and her superior understanding.

The duc kissed Madame Dupont's hand. 'Thank you, Madame,' he said. 'I am in your debt.'

'For what, Monsieur?'

'For showing me where I was remiss.'

'*De rien*!' she murmured, meeting his warm regard. 'I am only glad that you have seen it, Monsieur.'

CHAPTER EIGHT ~ SOCIETY BELLE

10 January 1914

Angel has not taken the tour very well, after all. As soon as it was over in November, he seemed to collapse with exhaustion: bedridden over Christmas and New Year, with no apparent turn for the better. It is very worrying for us all. And now the State has asked a great favour of him. I know he will not be able to do it.

'Monsieur,' said Madame Dupont softly, 'are you awake, *mon cher*?'

'Eh? Oh, what is it, Madame?' The marquis, yawned, rubbing his forehead. In the weeks since they had returned from their tour, his health had failed markedly. He appeared desperately tired and slept most of the time on the day bed in the salon.

'The secretary of the President is here with a letter from him. Are you able to see him?'

'Give me five minutes to wake up, Madame, then send him in. Perhaps if I have a sip of coffee?'

'Here, Monsieur, I have it with me.' She set the tray on the table, handing him a cup. Coffee was the only thing that seemed to revive him, and he looked for it often.

'Here you are … Careful, now. What does the President want with you, Monsieur?'

'Who knows, Madame? One thing is certain: it will not be a new anthem for France!'

'No, Monsieur!' She was shocked. 'You would not do it anyway.'

'Of course not, my dear,' he agreed. 'I can see that I am not the only one of us here who is not fully awake!' He indicated the cat curled up on his feet. 'Will you take Voltaire to the kitchen? He doesn't like Monsieur Lebrocq.'

Madame Dupont scooped up the cat, clicking her tongue. Angel had always had an affinity for cats, and since his illness, the kitchen cat, bearing a striking likeness to Cheval, his magician's cat, had seemed to adopt him.

§

It was about half an hour before the secretary stood up to take his leave: 'May I tell the President that he has your co-operation, Monsieur?'

'I have some reservations. You see my problem, do you not?' He spread wide his arms. 'Tell President Poincaré that I shall give him my answer tomorrow. I am aware of the urgency of the matter, but weighed beside the safety of Mademoiselle de Villefontaine …' He shrugged. 'The State visit he speaks of will not present a problem, but as for the rest, I must satisfy myself of certain criteria—my answer tomorrow, Monsieur.' He held out his hand.

Henri, having shown out the official visitor, re-entered the room. 'Monsieur Merignac is here, Monsieur.' He observed him anxiously. 'Shall I tell him to come back another time?'

'No, no. Bring him in. He is the very man I need … In a good hour, Monsieur Merignac. I was about to send a message to you.'

'The royal visit, Monsieur?' asked his visitor, shaking

his hand.

'Oh, if that were all, Monsieur, if that were all! But you came for a reason, Maestro?'

'Yes, Monsieur. The government has asked us at the Opéra Magique to put on some special entertainment for the King and Queen of Denmark on their State visit in May. They have, in particular, requested the duet from *Le Perdu*. I do not know how you are placed …?'

'Behold me …'

'Indeed, Monsieur. I am sorry.'

'Having said that—there is no reason why Angelique cannot sing for them. Indeed, I have had a request from the President for just such a performance. Why do you not see if you can book the Italian tenor Caruso—he is making no small stir about the place, and he would be able to sing with Angelique.'

'Oh, indeed, Monsieur, one of the few. We have tried to book him, but he is very much sought after.'

'Understandably, he is a very fine tenor. Oh, well … Do your best. She can sing a solo if she has to.'

Monsieur Merignac waited. The marquis had intimated that there was something else.

'How are you situated, Maestro, in regard to availability? Is your orchestra able to go on tour—say— immediately after this State visit?'

'Why not, Monsieur? The Opéra Magique can invite other orchestras to perform while we are away. What do you have in mind?'

'The Kaiser has had the infernal cheek to invite Angelique to sing at the Schönbrunn in Vienna for the Archduke and Duchess of Austria-Hungary, and the Kaiser himself, of course. He has heard of her singing for the English Royal Family in their palace and demands to hear her himself.'

'Ah, Monsieur!' The conductor threw up his hands.

'Indeed, I am reluctant to let her go into that viper's nest—and most certainly will not allow it if you and your orchestra cannot accompany her. On the other hand, the President is making noises about our own French Angel of Song being an arbiter of peace between our countries, saying it is essential that we extend the hand of cordiality to avoid offending him.'

'To soothe the savage breast, Monsieur?' The conductor smiled knowingly.

'That *belliqueux* ... I do not think it will work, and I am afraid to send her, in case of trouble. I cannot go myself, like this.' Frustration and misery contorted his features into a grimace.

'Me and my orchestra, Monsieur, we will take the greatest care of her that we possibly can. But I have a suggestion: instead of jumping at the command of the Kaiser, why do we not announce a Royal Tour of Europe? Beginning at the Opéra Magique with the King and Queen of Denmark, going to Belgium, Luxembourg, Holland, for their royals; on to Vienna for the Kaiser; then, say, to St Petersburg for the Tsar and finally to London for the English King?'

'You may have something there, Maestro,' agreed the marquis. 'As long as you are with her, I feel that I must agree to the pressure being brought to bear on me by the President. Though, how she can possibly succeed where diplomatic missions would appear to be failing, I do not see. Barbarians do not appreciate beauty, Monsieur.'

'Oh, Monsieur, everyone appreciates the voice of Mademoiselle Angelique. If perhaps in the heart of the blackest villain, there is a tiny spark of light, be assured that our Angel of Song will search it out and find it,' proclaimed the conductor, waxing lyrical.

'Very well,' sighed the marquis. 'I will allow it. But if you see trouble, I give you leave to cancel the tour and bring her home.' He was suddenly white and still, eyes closed.

'Monsieur? Monsieur?' The conductor rose in panic.

The blue gaze refocused. 'Thank you, Maestro.

Madame Dupont will arrange your itinerary.' His voice slurred slightly. 'Take care of my angel,' he murmured.

'Pardon, Monsieur?' Failing to receive an answer, he looked again at the grey-white countenance and ran to the door. 'Madame! Madame Dupont!' He called to the butler: 'Get Madame Dupont, quickly!'

Suddenly she was in front of him, running into the salon. *No! No!* She screamed silently, seeing the white, smooth mask of his face. As she put a hand over his heart, his came up and covered it.

'Too tired,' he mumbled, letting it slide away.

She passed a comforting touch over his forehead. *'C'est bien*, Angel, my dear. Sleep now.'

Turning to the conductor, she said, 'The tour, it was too much for him, Monsieur Merignac. He has nearly killed himself, singing in every city ...' He must rest now. He gets so tired like this. We must get used to it ... not panic.' She smiled wryly.

'I know, Madame. He gave me a shock. I am sorry to have frightened you like that.'

'It does not matter. You have something on your mind, Monsieur?'

'Yes, Madame.' He gave her an outline of the conversation, adding apologetically: 'He has said that you will arrange the itinerary for us, Madame.'

'Of course, Monsieur.' She walked away with him, discussing the various aspects of the proposed tour.

§

The unsuspecting object of this unprecedented royal focus was, at this moment, abandoning herself to the pleasures of society in a way which would have been instantly forbidden by the marquis, had he not been too ill to notice, and would have alerted Madame Dupont, had she not abdicated her chaperonage to the duchesse in order to nurse him. Consequently, something that could have been easily nipped in the bud grew very rapidly to fruition.

Fêted by all, Angelique had become brittle and sophisticated, plunging herself into any madcap entertainment that offered; the frowns of jealous mothers of daughters only spurring her on. Presenting the very picture of the fashionable, uncaring young modern, she partied on into the night, rising early to go riding in the brisk morning air, often not even going to bed between exchanging her evening gown for her riding habit. But this was also bad, for it brought home to her that the marquis could no longer ride with her.

Angelique, panic-stricken at the illness of her Angelpapa and hearing over and over in her head when she lay down to rest, his voice saying: 'Soon, my dear, regrettable though I find it, you will have to learn to live without me', only went to bed when exhaustion drove her there, cramming her pillow into her mouth so that none would hear her screaming over and over again, 'No! No! Do not take my Angelpapa. How will I live without him?'

And then things got worse, for as well as hearing the refrain, 'without me, without me, without me', frightening voices shouted at her: 'You will die without him. You will die without him. Why do you not kill yourself now and get it over? Get it over! Get it over!' At this point, leaping up, she would fling herself into her riding habit and slip out to the stables. If no-one was around, Jean, the groom, would escort her. She did not pause to ask why it was that, at whatever impossible hour of the morning, the marquis de Beaulieu and his sister always met her somewhere along the way, returning home with her: Elise ensuring she was safely in her room in the care of her maid, making appointments for later in the morning to go with her to the various wonders that enlivened the days of their social set.

The marquis du Bois, too ill to give her lessons, had wrung a promise from Madame Dupont to supervise her voice exercises daily, before sinking back into a semi-coma. Of course, this frightened Angelique even more, but Madame Dupont, playing the piano for her to practise her scales and worried over the ill-health of the marquis, failed to notice that his pupil always stood with her back to the light, so she would not see her face. Then, when Angelique was told of her impending tour, well ... that really set the seal on it.

Partying even more frenziedly, she became more and more nervous and highly strung: dropping things and bursting into tears if she was startled; suddenly rounding on Etienne, and just as suddenly becoming remorseful and lovingly repentant; and always, at the back of her mind were the insidious voices clamouring at her to kill herself.

The young marquis, bewildered by this kaleidoscopic range of emotions, tried to keep himself a buffer between his beloved and those seeking to exploit her fragile condition. Society, as it was at the moment, presented deep pitfalls to the heedless, the young and the innocent. Keeping his counsel, he took his own steps to limit the damage; and of this, the marquis du Bois would have approved.

Quietly, calmly, he observed what was needed and took as many precautions as he could, including the accompaniment of Angelique at all times by himself or his sister and, whenever he could fit it in, daily practice of his oriental martial arts. He frowned on waiters who refilled her glass, making clear his requirements to the extent that all knew that if Mademoiselle Angelique had her glass filled more than twice, it must be with sparkling water or lemonade; and more, when they served her wine, that the glass be no more than half-filled, and if possible, the wine attenuated with water.

To Angelique and those in society, he was a kind and gentle young man, courteous, charming and sweet-tempered; and the servants who obeyed his instructions were generously rewarded. But those who broke his rules found themselves confronted by a cold and determined man, one who made it dangerously clear that he would go to any lengths to protect his loved one.

Servants and others, paid well to ensure that Mademoiselle Angelique did not succumb to the effects of alcohol, were all the more ready to notify him of drug traffickers and other such predators, so that even the most discreet of sellers of 'dreams and damnation' invited into society by some poor, addicted hostess, more often than not, found himself out on the street with no recollection of what had happened to him; the homeless finishing the job the marquis had started, quickly stripping him of clothing and valuables, thereby adding insult to injury. The gendarmes, miraculously appearing on the scene (too late to see what had happened, of course), would arrest him for vagrancy and indecent exposure, deaf and blind to any representations on his part, and immediately cast him into prison.

Because the young marquis had a way with servants (for no amount of *douceur* could buy their respect), they began to form a bond with him; a secret society, as it were, for the protection of their Angel of Song. In every house, he had a set of spies eager to report to him on what was going forward.

Day after day, aided by his sister and his secret army, he battled the destruction in Angelique's soul, despairing for her sanity, but conversely, loving her even more for the fact that he felt he was losing her.

Madame Dupont, coming upon her one morning as she came in from her ride, was horrified at her appearance. Angelique, brushing off her anxious enquiry, told her: 'It is nothing, Godmama. I was out late last night, that is all. I must hurry to change. Etienne and Elise are taking me to lunch and then on to the *Montagnes Russes* this afternoon.' She smiled brilliantly. 'It is all such fun, Godmama!'

Madame Dupont, feeling that her smile resembled nothing so much as a grimace, was troubled by her wan appearance. Not wanting to disturb the marquis, she conferred with Etienne who told her:

'This has all happened since we came back from our tour, Madame. She was fine until the marquis du Bois became so ill. I do what I can, but I cannot reach her. I try my best, Madame, but it is no use. She has changed towards me. Unbelievably! I do not know ...'

She was moved to pity by the misery in his eyes. 'Softly, *mon brave*, she loves you, do not doubt it; but she has always depended so much for her wellbeing on the marquis du Bois that this is very hard for her: for you both.'

'Madame, I understand that she is frightened for the marquis and that this is what drives her to behave in this fashion—to overdo—but others think that she is hard *and* society is beginning to whisper that she is fast.'

She stood back and considered him. 'And you, dear boy, do you care for the whispers of society? Or what others think?'

'No, Madame. I only care that Angelique is destroying herself. And that I, despite all my efforts, have not the power to stop it.'

His expression, young and vulnerable, wrung her heart. 'Do not blame yourself, my dear. Angelique is Angelique. There is only one who may be able to reach her. But tell me this: has what you have seen of her so far, made you think again about her ...?' Madame Dupont stopped. She could not ask a young man who had not committed himself such a question, could she?

'Madame, I do not care for all these things, except for the fact that it is tearing her apart. I love her and will always love her. She is divine! I only want to care for her, protect her, make her happy.'

'*Eh bien*, my son,' Madame Dupont put a hand on his arm. 'You are a good and faithful young man. Have patience, and you shall have your reward. I will speak with the marquis du Bois. It is the only thing left to do, but I will have to wait until he improves a little. He is showing signs: his colour is better, and he rests more comfortably. Do you think you can carry on a little longer, *mon cher*?'

'As long as it takes, Madame, as long as it takes,' he confirmed. 'I am determined upon that.'

Madame Dupont—faced with the same devotion she had seen in his father, the marquis and the comte—was almost moved to tears. She made a sympathetic sound and patted his hand. 'Angelique does not know how fortunate she is, my dear. But take heart, for she will. She will! By the way, where is she now?'

'She and Elise have some fashion business, upstairs. I thought I might wait for them here if it is convenient, Madame?'

'Of course, my dear, you will be very comfortable here in the library—not likely to be disturbed.' Her smile indicated that she knew very well a period of quiet would be welcome to him, especially since he knew Angelique was safe with his sister; for Elise, sweet and gentle like her mother, was also protective of her beautiful friend. 'And now, I must go to the marquis. He must have his cordial and a light meal, if he will take it. Do not fret, *mon cher*, all will yet be well.'

She left the young marquis to settle down in a comfortable armchair and wait for his sister and his love who were closeted with the couturière from Lanvin: *Les femmes*, they took hours to decide on their raiment. Soon he was asleep, having taken to catnapping where he could.

§

'Are you awake, Monsieur? I must give you your medicine. Can you take a little nourishment, do you think? It has gone noon.'

The marquis du Bois looked around at her. Puzzled, he picked up a fold of the bedcover. 'Madame, how long have I been like this?' he asked, swallowing the cordial with a shudder. 'Urgh! Disgusting! Can something that tastes like this really be beneficial?'

'I am assured it is so, my dear. Besides, is it not de rigueur for medicines to be vile?'

'Perhaps. I have not found any that negate your theory.' He put a hand on her arm. 'How long?'

'Oh, about two weeks, Monsieur.'

'Two weeks? Oh, no ...' He struggled to a sitting position. 'Angelique: she must have her lessons!'

'She has been practising her scales, my dear. Do you not remember?'

'Oh yes, vaguely. But now she must have some real lessons.'

'But, Monsieur, you have been very ill. Are you well enough?'

'I think so.' He sounded surprised that she should ask such a question. 'But, *du vrai*, I am famished!'

'Ah, how glad I am to hear you say that. I will bring you a tray.'

'Stay, Madame, help me into my wheeled chair, for I have a fancy to eat at the table.'

After doing prudent justice to a chicken consommé with croutons and a fluffy omelette, he accepted her offer of coffee.

'Are you feeling up to this, Monsieur? Or shall you have your coffee in your day bed?'

'No, no, Madame, this is a pleasant change. Fire away.'

'Monsieur?'

'I can read you, Madame. You have something on your mind. What is it, my dear?' Anxiety entered his voice. 'Is it Angelique?'

'You are right: it is Angelique. She is becoming very unstrung, and she will not rest, will take no notice of anyone. You know how she gets. You are the only one she will listen to. The young marquis is beside himself with worry, and she has been treating him in a very cavalier manner. I do not know if she means to test his love for her, but *du vrai*, that is what she has been doing. I am afraid that all this partying and lack of sleep will drive her into a nervous collapse,' she said, cursing herself for the bald way she had put it. But as she had learnt many years ago, one could not hide anything from the marquis.

He shrugged, though with a worried frown. 'It is no good telling me, Madame. I am a spent force now. However, I will speak to her and at least find out why. Send her to me when she comes in.'

§

'Angelpapa, you are sitting up! You are better? Oh, thank God. Thank God!' Angelique, overcome with joy, threw her arms about him.

'Be still, my angel. Let me look at you,' he commanded, holding her away and subjecting her to scrutiny. He could see why Madame Dupont was anxious about her. She was thin and restless. There were dark shadows under her eyes, and she had lost her fresh, dewy bloom of youth.

'My child,' he warned, 'you cannot burn the candle at both ends. There will be a reckoning one day.'

'Angelpapa! There is so much to do! So much to see! And when I come home and lie down on my bed, I am so wound up that I cannot sleep. That is why I get up to ride, for I cannot stand to lie there, thinking of things.'

'What things, my Angel?'

'Oh, just … things,' she replied vaguely, avoiding his eye; but he knew. Yes, he knew: for none knew better than he the demons that could tear a soul apart.

He did not pursue it, but said, 'You need a tisane to compose you when you come home. I will ask Madame to see to it. The herbs will help to calm your nerves for sleep. You will drink it, will you not? Even if it is not quite to your taste. For me?'

'Of course, Angelpapa. For you, anything!'

'*Bien*. Soon you will be yourself again, Petite. There is

nothing to fear. Now, call Madame Dupont, for we are going to have a music lesson; and I am not quite up to playing the piano yet. It is about time, is it not, that you had a little discipline in your life?'

'Oh, I love you, love you, love you!' *Do not leave me, Angelpapa!*

'Now, now, we must get on. Save all that for your beau. From what I have been hearing, you have been neglecting him.' But he was smiling.

'No, Angelpapa! I have not ——' She put a hand up to her mouth. Hadn't she, though? Had she not been taking him for granted, treating him offhandedly, just as Angelpapa had said? She knew she loved him. Oh, yes, she loved him. Yet, she did not know why his loving presence did not suffice to dispel her demons.

Thoughtfully, she wheeled her guardian to the lift, calling to Madame Dupont to come to play the piano for them as they passed her morning room.

Time went on. Perhaps Angelique improved a little, for it was as the marquis had said: she benefited by the discipline of the music lessons and his control over her spirits. But the dreams kept haunting her, and the voices went on. Though now she could say to them, 'Not yet! Not yet! Not while I still have my Angelpapa.'

The marquis du Bois, even *she* could see, was becoming more and more frail. Where was his great energy: his great spiritual power? Fear threatened once more to overwhelm her. *Do not leave me, Angelpapa!*

Then, one day, standing with the calendar in her hand, staring with horror at the imminent tour date, she collapsed completely into hysteria. Briefly revived by Madame Dupont, she went to the marquis on the day bed in the salon.

Sinking down onto the floor beside it, her dark amethyst eyes burning with distress, she moaned, 'Angelpapa, I cannot go on this tour! How can I go without you? Please, please, please come with me! I need you beside me when I sing!' She buried her face in the quilt.

The marquis, placing a hand on her head, stroked her tangled curls, regarding tenderly this mercurial, talented child who had become a sparkling accomplished diva— still with one driving need—to sing. But he saw only the impulsive, golden-haired child coming to him for comfort in her distress. 'Oh, my dear little angel, I am an old man, practically bedridden, I fear. With the best will in the world, I cannot come with you, let alone accompany you on the stage.'

She flung herself upon him, arms around his neck, sobbing: the one person in the world who could do so with impunity. He allowed it for a few minutes, then put her away from him, drying her tears with his handkerchief. 'There, my child, that is enough! Look at me.' He spoke with authority.

She obeyed, but with heartbreak in her eyes.

'Oh, my dear! Come, smile at your Angelpapa ... There!' He held her hands tightly. 'I cannot be with you in body, but I make you this promise, Angelique: You will give me your itinerary, and wherever you sing, anywhere in the world, I will be beside you. Do you understand? I will be there with you, as close as we are now.'

'Yes,' she said. 'It is your spirit that will be with me, supporting me, helping me to sing.'

'Indeed!' he affirmed, adding sotto voce: 'And the world will not be able to believe what it is hearing ... Meanwhile,' he spoke decisively, 'we must get you out of this social melee and take you on a holiday. Ring the bell and ask Henri to find Madame Dupont.'

'I will find her, Angelpapa.'

In a short while, she returned. 'Godmama is coming directly.'

'Madame, look at this child,' he said, when she entered. 'She cannot go on tour looking like this! Can we take her on a short holiday first, do you think?'

'Good idea, Monsieur.' She studied Angelique, taking in the signs of stress and nervous exhaustion. 'Two weeks at the seaside? We can do it if we have everything packed for her tour first, I think. The trouble will be keeping the crowds away from her once they have discovered where she is.'

'Hmph!' His worried glance again passed over his pupil. 'Have you been giving Angelique the tisanes, as I asked?'

Madame Dupont's clear gaze questioned her. 'Have I, Angelique?'

'Yes.' She turned repentantly to the marquis. 'I am sorry, Angelpapa, I have tried to drink them, as you asked, but I do not like them. They make me gag.'

'So: you have not been taking them. Then that explains it. I will give you another. And this one you *will* drink! Do you understand me? Listen to me, my child. I know the demons that have been beating on your heart—none better—for they are mine, too. This tisane will not make you gag; although, it will not be as efficacious, either. Madame will bring it, and you will drink it here in front of me every day before we sing. Trust me, Petite; it will have a beneficial influence on your spirits. My only fear is that there will not now be enough time for it to take effect before you have to leave on your tour.'

Madame Dupont went out to prepare the tisane and give the necessary orders to put all in train for their holiday, and for the packing to begin for Angelique's tour.

The marquis was very thoughtful, plucking at his quilt. 'You are in love with young de Beaulieu, are you not?' he asked slowly.

'Yes, Angelpapa.'

'Even though you do not always treat him as you should?'

'Angelpapa, I am sorry. I do not know what comes over me sometimes. But I really do love him.'

'*Bien.*' He nodded. 'It may be a good idea for you to become engaged before you leave on your tour.'

She hung her head. 'We are already engaged, Angelpapa.'

'Oh, is that so? And you did not think to tell me or your papa, or even, perhaps, *as a last resort*, ask our permission?'

She flushed at the irony in his voice. 'Angelpapa, we wanted to keep it unofficial until I return from my tour. Besides,' she added buoyantly, 'Papa likes him very much, and I already know that you approve!'

'Oh, indeed? You can read my mind now, can you?'

She smiled her lovely smile. 'Of course! Otherwise he would have received the same cavalier treatment that all my other gentleman callers have been subjected to, would he not?'

He narrowed his eyes. 'I think I have occasionally called you a minx, my child.'

'Angelpapa!'

'Come, then.' He relented at her shocked protest. 'Bring my wheeled chair to me, here: so! We had better sing, while I still can do it!'

'Yes, please!' She began to wheel him to the lift to take them to the music room.

Madame Dupont, entering the empty salon a few minutes later with a steaming cup, shrugged her shoulders, spun around and went out again.

§

Later in the day, standing before Angelique's guardian, the marquis de Beaulieu bowed courteously. '*Bonjour*, Monsieur. I understand you wished to see me? I hope this means that you are feeling better?'

'Do not worry about that, young man!' commanded the marquis du Bois. 'What are your intentions towards Angelique?'

'But, Monsieur, is it not obvious? I wish to marry her, of course.'

'Oh? It is obvious, is it?' replied the marquis; his voice edged with sarcasm. 'If that is the case, why then have you not had the grace to ask either her papa or me for her hand?'

'I beg your pardon, Monsieur,' he apologised. 'I have been ready to do so any time these past few months. But Angelique,' he shrugged. 'She wanted to wait until the Royal Tour is over. She wants to be able to concentrate on the enjoyable moments of a betrothal: the choosing of the ring, our betrothal party, the social engagements without the stress of ——' He broke off, adding eloquently, 'These things, they are important to *les femmes*, Monsieur. At least I tell myself that is the reason she delays; although, lately I have begun to wonder ...'

'Well,' said the marquis, waving a dismissive hand, 'I will leave all that to you and Angelique. What is concerning me at the moment is why she looks the way she does.'

'Monsieur, Madame Dupont and I have discussed this. We feel that she has been worrying over your illness.'

'Oh, the poor little one, indeed she has. But that is not all. In everything she does, she needs very much the support of a strong man. Are you that man, Monsieur?'

'Yes, Monsieur. As far as I am concerned, I am. But you must put this question to Angelique herself, for with her, there is only one. She is saying to me lately that she loves only the marquis du Bois!'

Observing the pain in his eyes, the marquis said quietly, 'She might well have said that—particularly if she was in a fit of pique—but that is not how I read the situation. No, not at all. *Au contraire!*' He regarded the young man sympathetically. 'She has had me for a long time, dear boy, and she has been used to depending on me. But you see, I can be of no help to her now. That is why I am looking to you to take care of her for me. But of course, it will take a little while for her to learn to rely on you. I have watched you, and I believe you have the strength of character, the patience and, yes, the love for her. It will come, my son, do not despair. Soon you will be the one she looks to. But I do not like the look of her. Could she, do you think, have had any contact with a certain white powder prized for its energising effect?'

'Cocaine, Monsieur? Oh no, I am certain I have nipped that in the bud.' He shook his head firmly. 'No, Monsieur. I have people in all the houses watching over her. Elise and I make sure she is never left alone. I am confident I can keep her safe from that. And any overindulgence in the alcohol. She is very susceptible to that. Only a very little is needed to send her over the roof. It is just that she is unused to it. But ...' He swallowed and looked away. 'There is no denying that at times there seems to be a melancholy come over her that none of us can shift.'

'I know it. Just be with her. That is all you can do at those times. And if possible, get her to sing. She must sing, you understand, for her wellbeing.'

'Yes, Monsieur, I understand. I will do all that you say.'

'Angelique, she needs so much more care than anyone else, and I am very tired,' fretted the invalid.

'Do not be anxious for her, Monsieur, for I shall take care of her.'

The marquis du Bois sat silent. Self-assured and without conceit, this quiet young man had impressed him from the outset: the perfect foil for Angelique's excitable temperament. Somehow, he had always known that he would be the one to take his place. Had chosen him, even, because of it. And what he had heard from his valet about the fates of several rips, roués and other undesirables at his hands had only strengthened this belief.

'*Eh bien*,' he said dryly, 'without even asking: you have my permission to marry her. *When* you can find the time to get around to it, of course!'

CHAPTER NINE ~ MORNING CALL

20 April 1914

There are many surprises in life and relationships. Sometimes we find that those we love have depths that not even our love can discern.

A few days later, the duc de Belvoir called, sending up his card, asking to have speech with Madame Dupont and Monsieur le marquis du Bois. Madame Dupont was a little surprised. The duc had never before paid them a morning call.

Admitted into Madame's salon, he greeted her fondly, 'Ma Belle, it is the greatest delight to meet you again. You are looking well, I see.'

'I, too, am enchanted to see you, Monsieur. You also look well,' she replied, a pink flush in her cheeks, allowing her hand to rest in his for a fraction longer than was strictly necessary.

'The marquis: he is not here?'

'He is giving Angelique a singing lesson. He will be here shortly, Monsieur. Will you not take a chair? I will ring for coffee.'

'I thank you, Madame.' He sat opposite her, placing a hand over hers. 'May I take this moment alone with you to make an apology, my dear?'

'But, Monsieur, whatever for?' she asked in considerable astonishment.

He sighed. 'The duchesse has confessed to me that she embarrassed you with an extraordinary outburst on the occasion of the recital at Belvoir Village. She is mortified and begs your forgiveness, my dear.'

'Oh! It was nothing!' Madame Dupont, opening her eyes, gestured dismissively. 'The duchesse has no need to apologise to me, Monsieur. Besides, she has already done so. It would be better if you did not know of it.'

'No, listen, Ma Belle, it is not just the duchesse.' He withdrew his hand. 'I know that stolen moments and clandestine meetings are not for such as we ... and I respect your decision in this matter. I hope you understand that only the extremity of your situation, as I then perceived it, forced my hand where you were concerned.' He regarded her earnestly. 'It was not an offer made lightly, Ma Belle, but once having made it ... I found it difficult to let go of the idea. I hope you understand, for I am afraid that, between us, the duchesse and I have made you uncomfortable. And that, my dear one, is the last thing I would wish for you.'

'I understand, Monsieur, there is no need to apologise. And no, I was not made uncomfortable by your offer. I was just ... surprised.' *And honoured and flattered and devastated.* 'The duchesse was not herself. She is not to be blamed. But you must not worry about me. The marquis did not mean to hurt me, you know, and he will not hurt me now. He has been very ill. You have guessed, I suppose, that he is Angel, the friend of my childhood? We have a long history together.'

He nodded. 'I guessed, the day we spoke of love at Belvoir. But it wasn't until I heard him sing with Angelique at the third performance of *Le Perdu* that I was certain of it. The opera ballet, you see, made the connection for me. For years I had wondered where I had heard him before. And then ... Pfft.' He snapped his fingers.

'I am sorry I did not tell you before, *mon cher*, but we had to keep his identity secret for many years. Xavier, in his jealousy, had falsely accused him over the accidents in the opera house; and I could not give him up to the gendarmes. But now, Xavier has accepted him and his help. He knows who he is, but he has mellowed, so it no longer matters. I could not have let him go to prison, Monsieur. I could not let such genius be lost to the world.'

'I know that your compassionate heart would not allow you to do such a thing, but I do not know how you stayed with him, my dear, after what he did to you.'

'He needs me, Monsieur.'

So do I. 'Ma Belle, you are so kind, so forgiving, so generous. Each minute I am able to spend with you, even as now, is a bright spot in a grey day, a tender spring flower in a bleak winter landscape.'

'That is very nice, Monsieur, you have a fine, poetic turn. Ah, but you are a romantic, *bien sûr*. But me, I must be practical. I am sorry to disappoint you, Monsieur.'

'Ma Belle, are you saying I must not come to see you like this?'

'It would be best, Monsieur, do you not think? We should keep on in the way we planned to go on; the way we must go on. Nothing has changed since we last spoke.'

'Oh, my dear, you break my heart all over again, but you are right. Yes.' He smiled ruefully. 'You know how to bring me down to earth, Ma Belle.'

'I have to, my dear, both of us.' *And yes, I do know how.* 'But tell me, the poor duchesse, worrying about such a thing, how is she? Etienne and Elise, I see them all the time, coming and going with Angelique; but since the illness of the marquis, I have not been able to go about in society. I am very grateful to her for chaperoning Angelique.'

'Apart from remorse for not conducting herself like a woman of breeding towards you, Madame, she is very well. Thanks to you, I have back my best friend, for whatever is in that tisane you gave her has been working well.'

'It contains herbs that restore the balance of the psyche, *mon cher.*' She took a deep breath. 'The duchesse loves you, and the fact that she thinks you do not love her has been playing on her mind of late.' There, she said it! She waited in trepidation for his reaction, for he could, on occasion, embrace a chilling hauteur.

'But, Ma Belle ...' He frowned, protesting mildly, 'I am very fond of the duchesse.'

'I know that, *mon cher,* but does she?'

He smiled ironically. 'Some of us are fated to love those we cannot have. She knows ... She has always known who has my heart. From the beginning, I have been honest with her.'

Madame Dupont thought about her conversation with the duchesse. 'Indeed, Monsieur. But I cannot help thinking, though it goes against my principles to say it, that in this case, honesty may not have been the best policy.'

His shoulders sagged. As a man of honour, he had done his best in a situation where the love of his life was now suggesting that perhaps his best was not enough. He had laid out the terms of his contract in a circle where a marriage proposal was most likely to be approached in the light of a business proposition, and the duchesse had accepted them. (Madame Dupont could have told him it was because she was in love with him). That their marriage had been to him (besides his duty) no more and no less than a deep and pleasant friendship—a comfortable robe he wore while he yearned over the unattainable—was entirely due to the warmth and devotion of his wife. And being a naturally considerate man, he had been perhaps even more solicitous and nurturing of her to try to compensate for the absence of his heart.

But Madame Dupont perceived something he did not.

He really did love his duchesse. He just did not know it. She shifted ground. 'Etienne and Elise, your beautiful children, Monsieur, they have been wonderfully supportive of Angelique.'

'I thank you, Madame. I am most glad to hear it.' The duc sat upright, looking momentarily pleased. 'It is in part what I wish to speak to you about. Etienne is, of course, deeply in love with Angelique.'

'It is reciprocated, Monsieur, do not doubt it.'

'Are you sure, Madame?' He frowned again. 'Etienne has been very doleful of late. He has been afraid that she is losing interest in him.'

'Oh, no, no, no, Monsieur. *Au contraire*! I do not know what she would do without him.'

'When I have seen her in society, these last few weeks, she has not seemed to be happy. She appears overstretched, fragile: very nervy. Fame has not been good for her, I think.'

'Monsieur, she is very attached to the marquis, and she has been afraid that he will die. This is what has been at the bottom of her actions; and I, too, have been very worried about her. Now that he is recovering, so will she.' She put out a hand to him, which he covered with his own. 'Do not doubt it, Monsieur. Angelique loves your son.'

'I am glad,' he said simply, eyes searching hers. 'There should be one happy ending out of all this, should there not, Mignonne?'

'Yes, Monsieur.' She blinked back tears. 'With all my heart, I hope there is.'

The arrival of the coffee gave her time to compose herself. Setting out the cups, she began to pour.

'We do not wait for Monsieur le marquis?'

'No, Monsieur. When he and Angelique are singing,' she shrugged, 'sometimes they get caught up.'

'Ah, artists at work, eh? I know, time means nothing to them.'

'Precisely, Monsieur. So, at least this way, we shall have

our coffee before it grows cold, and if necessary, I shall send for a fresh pot for the marquis.'

'Your practicality is ever a delight, Ma Belle.'

'And now, Monsieur, you must tell me all about the latest performance of *Les Ballets Russes*. Angelique told me your family took her to see it. What did you think of them, *mon cher*?'

She could not have picked a better topic. Immersed in a technical discussion of their favourite art form, they sat together chatting comfortably; two loving, self-controlled people, each secure in the company of the other.

This is how it could have been if … *No! Do not dare to think it!*

The door opened, and the marquis wheeled himself in. The duc rose to shake his hand. Madame Dupont poured him coffee that was still hot.

After a few pleasantries, the duc came down to business. 'Monsieur and Madame, my visit to you concerns Angelique, for it has come to my notice that she does not appear to be doing well. No doubt she is suffering from a mixture of fatigue and nervous fears over her imminent Royal Tour. This is as great a concern to you, I am sure, as it is to me.'

'Indeed, Monsieur!' Madame and the marquis spoke almost in unison.

'After discussion with my family, I have come to you with a suggestion. The duchesse and I, my son and daughter, Elise … By the way, did I tell you we named her after you, Madame?' he added, with a bow.

Madame Dupont blushed. The marquis raised an eyebrow.

The duc smiled. 'No doubt you are aware that Elise and Angelique have become fast friends?'

They signified their knowledge of this fact with the marquis saying, in some amusement, 'I would hazard a wager that we see more of your lovely daughter than you do, Duc!'

'And your delightful son!' added Madame Dupont with a smile.

'Ah,' said the duc. 'I do not doubt it! You could hardly see less! They do not spend much of their time at our hotel; let me tell you. Perhaps I should send over their respective maid and valet, should I not?'

'No, no,' disclaimed the marquis, 'we have not quite come to that point yet; I promise you.'

The duc brought them back to the discussion at hand. 'Well, as I was saying: we wish to accompany Angelique on what she calls her Royal Tour.' He held up one hand as the marquis made a move. 'It is time we took a holiday. I never did the grand tour, you know.'

No, thought the marquis, cynically. *You could not tear yourself away from the salle de danse ...*

'Angelique will be adequately chaperoned by the duchesse, as in fact, she has been these last few weeks. She will have Elise as company and will have the protection of my son's and my escort. I have come to assure you that, should you accept my suggestion, you need have no fears for her while she is on tour; for we shall keep her safe.' He spoke now to the marquis. 'I know what is worrying you, Monsieur, for it is the same thing that worries me, and I shall keep a weather eye. You have my word that, should the wind change or even become the slightest bit chilly, I shall bring her home to you, immediately.'

The marquis nodded. 'Indeed, Monsieur, I thank you.'

The duc continued, 'As you have no doubt realised, my son is in love with her, Monsieur. He will go with her, *sans doute*, but it will be more *comme il faut* if we go, too. It will show the world that, amongst other things, their union has our blessing.'

The marquis, unhappy about parting with Angelique (especially to such a grand seigneur as the duc), was inclined to be short. 'Indeed, Monsieur? A trifle previous, are you not?'

The duc studied him keenly. 'Perhaps it will look that

way, Monsieur. But I do not think so, and neither, I venture to say, do you,' he replied quietly. 'Indeed, it has been obvious to me since I first saw them together.'

'And to me,' said Madame Dupont. 'And to the marquis, also, has it not?' She turned to him, brows raised, not quite hiding her surprise at his denial; for Angelique had told her of his suggestion that she and Etienne should become engaged.

But the marquis, keeping his cards close to his chest, would admit nothing, merely returning her glance with an unreadable one of his own.

After a slightly uncomfortable pause, he said slowly to the duc, as if it pained him, 'I thank you, Monsieur. On reflection, I think it an excellent scheme. Madame Dupont and I will rest easier knowing that she has such a distinguished and, dare I say …' He bowed slightly. 'Formidable escort. I am grateful that she will not now have to face the kinds of problems I had envisaged because I could not be with her. And just so you know, Monsieur,' he added a trifle aggressively, 'I approve of your son as a suitor.'

'Indeed, Monsieur,' murmured Madame Dupont. 'How could it be otherwise?'

'I thank you, Madame and Monsieur.' The duc transferred his gaze from some far point. 'I assure you, my son will cherish her. But now I have another suggestion. If it is suitable to you, I shall take Angelique with me to Belvoir to recover her bloom. This she will do in the good country air with no disturbances and plenty of sleep at night.' He saw the marquis' face. 'This invitation is, of course, extended to you also, Monsieur and Madame: You will come with her? To spend the time with her before we leave? I beg that you will!'

'I regret, Monsieur, that I am not up to the journey,' replied the marquis. 'Indeed, I thank you, but I am desolated that I must decline your kind offer.'

'I am sorry to hear it, Monsieur. And you, Madame?

You will come with us?'

She met his eyes fleetingly. Dropping her own, she replied, 'I am sorry, Monsieur, but Monsieur le marquis has need of me. He is unwell. I could not leave him at this time.'

'Of course, Madame, as you wish. You can be sure we shall take care of her as our own.' Beneath the courteous reply, there was no sign of the intense disappointment he suffered.

'One moment, Monsieur, if you please. Angelique must have a say in this.' The marquis rang the bell and sent for her.

The duc greeted her warmly, and she responded in kind; but when she heard the proposal, she went to the marquis and knelt at his feet, clasping his hands.

'Angelpapa! No! I must not leave you before I have to!'

'My child ...' He stroked her cheek tenderly. 'Look at the state of you. You would not drink your tisanes, and now you see what has happened? We must be parted sooner than we wanted, because you would not obey me in that one small matter.'

'But, Angelpapa, I am taking them now. You know that I am!' she pleaded.

'I know, my angel, but it is too late. They have not had time to take effect.' He spoke very gently to her, 'So now, you must do as I say. Go with Monsieur le duc and rest before your tour. Before you go, I shall give you some times. At these times, you will sing. At the same time, you will concentrate hard until you visualise me standing beside you, singing with you. Understand this: You must not give up until you see me! Is that clear?'

'Yes, Angelpapa, I will do as you say. I will never disobey you again. I understand that you are preparing my spirit.' She winked away tears. 'And Monsieur le duc is going to look after my health.'

'Of a certainty, my dear child, the good country air of Provence will soon have the roses blooming in your cheeks again,' agreed the duc, smiling fondly at her.

The marquis, lowering his eyes, appeared to be frowning over a small spot on one wheel of his chair.

Agreeing to return in two days time with Elise, the duc took his leave.

'Let me walk you to the front door, Monsieur,' said Angelique, taking his arm. Looking up into his warm golden-hazel eyes, she exclaimed, 'Oh, you are so like Etienne! I mean, Etienne is so like you!'

The duc patted her hand. 'I know what you mean, my dear. All the de Beaulieus are alike. When you come to Belvoir, make sure my son shows you the portraits of our ancestors. I think you will perceive an uncanny likeness amongst the ducs de Belvoir.'

Once they were out of earshot, Madame Dupont turned to the marquis. 'That was a fine lot of say you gave her, *mon cher.*'

He shook his head. 'If I had, she would not have gone; and I doubt our ability to keep away the followers and give her the rest she needs at the seaside. In contrast, damn his noble hide, Monsieur le duc has only to lower the portcullis to keep them at bay. I would say that her beau will be greatly relieved for, I fear that by now, he is also suffering from exhaustion from trying to keep up with her.' He sent her a speaking look. 'As you told me, she has been leading him on a pretty dance, my dear. But … I must not repine too much, for this way, as she says, I have a chance to prepare her spirit.'

A little later, Angelique came back into the room, looking for the marquis.

'He has gone to rest, my dear. He said he will see you at dinner.'

'Monsieur le duc is coming for me the day after tomorrow, and I want to spend what time I can with Angelpapa.'

'I know, my dear, but he needs to rest now. You will see him at dinner.'

'I understand.' She was quiet a moment, then, 'The duc, Godmama, is he not a beautiful man?' *I can see why you love him.* 'I declare, if I was not in love with his son, I would fall for him; for I am more than half in love with him already!'

Madame Dupont smiled at her extravagance of speech, saying gently, 'He is a grand seigneur, my dear. You will be very well looked after; I am happy to say.'

'I know, Godmama, but he is not Angelpapa, is he?' she sighed.

'No, my dear. But you must remember the promise of the marquis: that you will feel his presence there beside you when you sing. The mind is very powerful. It can conquer the body. Remember that! If he says he will be beside you when you sing, you may believe it.'

'But how? How can that be, Godmama, when he is here, bound to his wheeled chair?'

'I do not know, my child. It is a great mystery. But I have had the experience before, of the *incroyable* power of his mind, and that is why I say: believe it!'

Looking into her eyes, she was satisfied that Angelique would accept her word, even if she did not quite understand.

CHAPTER TEN ~ THE SILVER CORD

28 April 1914

We so miss Angelique! The house is like a tomb without her. I wonder how she is getting on? One thing is certain: Angelique will not lack nurture at Belvoir with her prospective family. But will it suffice? And if not, will Angel's attempt at the long distance support of her spirit be the answer? I have no doubts about his ability, but since Angelique has not been tried, hers may be another matter.

Angelique had been gone for days and the house seemed desolate without her sparkling presence. Madame Dupont sighed and looked in on the marquis. He appeared to be sleeping, but she knew better; for in his hand he held Angelique's itinerary.

It was no use trying to disturb him, for he simply was not there. He was in the music room at Belvoir, singing with his pupil; and what is more, he would be with her every morning until Angelique returned to perform for the King and Queen of Denmark in three weeks time.

She and the marquis would sit in their usual box at the theatre. The marquis had not required that he be in full view of Angelique, for he wanted her to begin the tour as she meant to go on—visualising him standing beside her, singing with her—and not to look for him in the box, because a few days after that she would be off on the train to Bruxelles with her distinguished escort.

Madame Dupont sighed again. It would be even more draining for the marquis; he would need all his strength to support Angelique onstage. This projection of his spirit? The spirit wandering from the body? Astral travel, was it? Whatever it could be called, it was extremely exhausting for him; and little though she knew it, extremely hazardous. But as she had told the young diva, she had no doubt that he would do it; for in past years, he had demonstrated to her the almost unbelievable power of his mind. Uncomfortably so. Even, dangerously so!

She thought back on his ability to hypnotise entire audiences, easily making happen that which he willed, so that he could call Katarina onto the stage to sing with him at his behest—unremarked and unremembered—for he could erase it all from their memories with a snap of his fingers.

Feeling impelled to protect both him and the comtesse from discovery by some chance un-hypnotised witness, she had been the only one to stand up to him; and she still trembled when she recalled the frightening glow in his eyes just before she had been thrown bodily across the de Villefontaine box by his fury. And he had been on the stage! How many metres away?

Later in society, though he had largely given up his magic, it was not beyond him to occasionally hypnotise his hostess and fellow guests in order to make his escape from an evening he found particularly boring. And now, even though his physical strength was diminishing rapidly, conversely the strength of his spirit was becoming increasingly dominant.

Angelique, in the peace of the countryside away from the clamour that was Paris, slowly began to respond to the tranquil charm of Belvoir and its people. Exploring the château; strolling in the picture gallery, seeing the same, familiar face looking out of many of the portraits, just as she had been told; riding about the estate with the duc, Etienne and Elise; and most importantly, practising her singing daily, she achieved a modicum of serenity.

The latter was most productive of it for, concentrating hard as she sang, she was eventually able to visualise the marquis standing with her. At first, nothing happened; and when it did, she found it extremely difficult to maintain: but she persevered and was rewarded. As the days passed and her focus increased, she began to see him immediately; his presence soon becoming so real that if she reached out her hand she could touch him.

'Angelpapa,' she murmured, while waiting for the pianist Monsieur Merignac had sent with her to begin her scales. 'You are with me as you promised ...'

The days she enjoyed, spending time with Etienne who loved and protected her; chatting amongst the spring flowers in the garden with Elise, her best friend; and singing in the evenings to entertain them, basking in the warmth and fond regard of the duc and duchesse; all these things were balm to her spirit. But the nights ... Ah, they were a different matter! After Etienne had kissed her goodnight at her door and Elise had seen her safely tucked up in bed: then it started!

Her fears crowded in on her, suffocating her. And the voices! Ringing in her head, round and round, not allowing blessed sleep to come, telling her over and over to kill herself, for the marquis would not be with her long. She could throw herself off the tower, could she not? *Why not? Go on! That would be a quick end.* How hard it was to resist the strange compulsion to get out of bed and creep up the circular staircase to the battlement they had explored earlier on the roof of the tower, and then ... She held on for dear life to her bedsheet, winding it around herself, desperately trying to block them out. *I will not get up! I will not! I will not!*

Yes, the nights were to be endured, counting interminable hours until daylight when, paradoxically, the voices would be silenced and she would fall asleep, grasping just enough of the precious commodity to keep functioning. Then incredibly, out of her struggle to survive these insidious voices of the night, she found a way to silence them forever: when she heard the voice of the marquis saying 'without me' as a prelude to those other evil voices, she visualised his dear face; the wry twist to his lips; his fine, chiselled profile; the gleam in his sapphire-blue eyes; the love he had for her radiating from him, enveloping her in its warmth: she could feel it!

Yes, there he was, sitting in the chair by her pillow, so recently vacated by Elise, holding out a loving hand to her. '*Eh bien*, my angel, I am here.'

'Angelpapa!' she murmured. 'Oh, thank God! Please, never leave me.' And placing her hand in his, she slept: the voices quiet, at last.

After this night, there was a remarkable change in her. She grew more robust, confident, radiating a healthy glow; for every night, her guardian sat by her bed, watching over her, dispelling the voices, the fears: allowing her to sleep.

The duc, noticing it particularly, remarked in passing, 'Did I not tell you, dear child, that you would regain your sparkle here with us at Belvoir? And it has not been long. You will soon be yourself again, Petite.'

She returned his smile, thanking him. She could not tell him, or anyone, about her night terrors, or her solution to them. He simply would not understand, and perhaps think her *fou*. She thought it herself sometimes.

It was strange: she loved Papa, Mama and dear, practical Godmama, but they were none of them necessary to her existence—not like Angelpapa. She loved Etienne; he was a beautiful young man, and he made her heart bump deliciously at his touch and a certain expression in his eye. She knew she was becoming more and more dependent on his calm presence to sustain her, but was he necessary to her existence? 'Not like Angelpapa,' she whispered. 'Nobody is like Angelpapa.'

And yet, between them, in an uncanny alliance of the physical presence of the young marquis and the spiritual presence of the old, these two kept her safe from her demons; their nurturing presence allowing her to flourish in their love like a beautiful, delicate lily.

Meanwhile, at the hôtel du Bois, the marquis had reluctantly consented to the installation of a telephone; although, he complained that he could not get enough peace anyway, without becoming a slave to a technological nightmare. Madame Dupont, finding it both a blessing and a curse, noticed that he began to use it more and more to keep in touch with the outside world.

Like all new technology, it had its limitations, occasionally frustrating him to the point where he almost had it pinging off the table, so hard did he slam down the receiver into its cradle.

Unfortunately, there was not yet a connection to Belvoir, so there was no chance of him speaking to Angelique in any way other than the spirit.

§

Time passed, and Angelique returned to Paris.

The marquis du Bois, at their reunion, after he had extricated himself from her fervent embrace and wiped away her tears of joy, was elated by her healthy appearance and aura of wellbeing. '*Allons*, Petite, I want to hear you sing now. I can see we did the right thing by sending you away; hard though it was for us. Monsieur le duc has looked after you well. You have regained your bloom. No doubt you will be in fine voice, as you were developing at Belvoir.'

'It is a strange thing, Angelpapa, that even though you are here—I know you are here—your presence was just as real to me at Belvoir, when you were not with me.'

He turned from the piano. 'I was with you at Belvoir, Petite, just as I am now; never doubt it. The body, it is a dwelling place for the spirit ...' He looked down at his weakened limbs. 'Or a prison. Wherever you are, I will be with you; for I know how to pick the lock.' He did not add: *it is easy to leave the body when you know how. The trick is to be able to return.*

He struck the opening chords of her aria. 'Now, from the beginning ... *Con spirito, ma chère* ... *Eh bien, je demande* ... *Et alors, glissando* ... *Oui, très belle* ... *épatante* ...'

The week Angelique spent at home was a golden time, interrupted midway by the recital at the Opéra Magique for Their Majesties of Denmark.

'*Eh bien*, my angel,' said the marquis, waving her itinerary. 'We begin tonight: just as it was at Belvoir. Remember that when you visualise me, it is, *en effet*, your spirit calling to mine. Do not fear, I will always answer your call. Tonight is a testing ground for you. I do not want you to look for me in the box; you must see me beside you on the stage.'

Afterwards, he said to her, 'You did well, my angel. You saw me singing beside you?'

'Oh, yes, Angelpapa. Just like at Belvoir! Even though you were only up in the box, I could feel your presence on the stage.'

He put up a hand. 'Uh-uh!'

'Oh, I know ... You really were with me on the stage. Now I know you are there, I will be able to sing anywhere in the world and have you with me, will I not?'

'Of course, my darling, of course!' he reassured her. 'That is the purpose of it.'

§

The duc called to see the marquis when Madame Dupont was out with Angelique for some last minute alterations to her gowns: the young diva having regained a little weight. Good weight, as Madame Dupont was careful to inform her. 'We are just adjusting your gowns to what they were a few weeks ago, that is all.'

The duc had seemed to take Madame Dupont's words to heart, and now treated her with a punctilious formality that almost broke her heart—until she saw the warmth in his eyes when they rested on her. That had not changed. No, the duc, having made his apology, now avoided her company unless it was a formal and public situation. The only other thing that changed was that the flowers began arriving again. Sent anonymously, they had intrigued her for years: now she knew who it was who filled her salon with exotic blooms; messages of love written wordlessly in their glorious faces.

The marquis knew it, too, curling his lip; though, he did not comment. Greeting the duc now with becoming gratitude, he thanked him for his benevolence and careful nurturing of Angelique.

The duc was charmingly dismissive. '*De rien*, Monsieur! It was a great pleasure to see her return to health. I have to tell you that Their Majesties of Denmark were very impressed with the voice of our Golden Angel. Indeed, word has it that they regarded their evening at the Opéra Magique as the highlight of their State visit.'

'Indeed? *C'est bien*,' he replied, looking gratified.

'Angelique sang very well, I thought. Even better than I have ever heard her, as a matter of fact.'

The marquis nodded. 'Yes, her voice is maturing.'

'She is remarkably attached to you, Monsieur.'

'I know it.' He gave his crooked smile. 'But there is room in her life for others, Duc.'

'Of course. Do not worry; we shall take good care of her.'

'Indeed, I hold no fears as to that, Monsieur.' He had begun to like the duc, a gentleman of some weight, even though he had always resented his interest in Madame

Dupont.

'I will take my leave now. My fondest regards to Angelique and Madame Dupont. I shall see you in a few days. This is it, eh … Angel?' The golden-hazel eyes asked a friendly question. The duc was holding out his hand.

The marquis took it at once. 'Indeed … Georges,' he replied warmly. '*À bientôt.*'

The duc left, only to return in a time that seemed to the marquis and his pupil altogether too short.

For the rest of the week, Angelique could hardly bring herself to leave the marquis, spending most of her time by his day bed. Soon she would be gone. She held onto his promise that he would never leave her: that when her spirit called to him he would come.

Departure day arrived before they were ready, and she said her goodbyes to him in the house, trying her best to be secure in the knowledge that he would be with her.

'You have my itinerary, Angelpapa? So that you know where to go?'

'Indeed, my child. I have a copy in every room. Etienne and his family will take care of the practicalities, and I will be with you. All you will have to do is sing. That should not be too hard, eh?' He kissed her brow. 'Go with God, my angel.'

Madame Dupont and her parents saw her safely into the care of the ducal family and waved them off at the station.

Sitting alone in the carriage, tiring of watching the scenery, Angelique focused on the empty seat opposite. 'I am selfish, Angelpapa, I want you with me all the time.'

Etienne came in and sat down beside her. 'Hullo, my sweet. Daydreaming again? Your luggage is in your sleeping compartment next to Elise's. You are not nervous, my love?'

'No.' She smiled. 'That does not sound like me, does it?'

'It is well, my sweet.' He kissed her fingers, retaining

her hand in his, content to just be with her.

She looked again at the seat opposite. The marquis du Bois no longer sat there.

§

The first few weeks that Angelique was away proved to be a particularly volatile month in Paris, as the marquis, dividing his time between feverishly perusing the papers and lying in a comatose state while he supported Angelique on tour, remarked to Madame Dupont.

He became very interested in reports of experiments with radiotelephony exchanging messages between a Paris transmitter and receivers located at various distances up to two hundred kilometres from the capital. He knew the duc had funded some of this groundbreaking technology and had also begun to construct a powerful transmitter and receiver on the highest tower at Belvoir. It was encouraging that a radio ham in England had intercepted some of the messages.

And then, in the space of four tumultuous days, a government led by Alexander Ribot had been appointed and fallen.

'*Nom de Dieu,* Madame!' exclaimed the marquis. 'One would despair for the peace of Europe when even our own parliament resembles a war zone!'

And as if *le bon Dieu*, having had his name invoked, had perhaps endorsed this observation, two days later they endured the most violent storm that Madame Dupont had ever lived through. She had not personally heard of any deaths, but she was sure there would have been. Trees were down, roofs taken off, windows smashed, stormwater drains overflowing into houses. The hôtel du Bois survived—the gardens damaged but the house relatively unscathed. Madame Dupont and the servants kept busy mopping up torrents of water coming in through weakened window frames and under doors.

Into this damp environment, President Poincaré appointed the socialist René Viviani, Premier and Foreign Affairs Minister; the marquis wryly wondering how long the government would last this time.

Paradoxically, throughout all this political and natural upheaval, Paris continued to celebrate the bicentennial of that elixir of life: champagne.

There was nothing to suggest that 28 June, 1914, would be different to any other day of that summer, and indeed, the household of the marquis du Bois ran with its usual clockwork efficiency. Since Angelique was travelling between engagements, the marquis was able to rest; and it was only hindsight that marked the day as a flashpoint.

That night, nothing disturbed the sleep of the household of the marquis; and the ducal party, lulled by the rhythmic clackety-clack motion of their train, rested well.

The duc de Belvoir, uncharacteristically sleeping late, awoke to find the train standing still. Dressing leisurely, he ordered breakfast in his sleeping compartment and pulled up the blind to see where they were. Ah, Stuttgart! Overnight they had passed into Germany.

As the whistle blew and the train began to pull away, his glance idly swept the platform, focusing on a headline on a newsstand. On an exclamation, he got up and pulled the communication cord. Whatever he said was lost in the protesting scream of metal upon metal as the rapidly accelerating train suddenly locked on its brakes.

At about the same time as the duc, issuing succinct orders and parting with an inordinate number of gold coins, was gently overwhelming indignant rail staff with his manner and his largesse, the daily newspapers were being delivered to the hôtel du Bois, where they were placed routinely on a tray to be delivered to the marquis when he rang for his morning coffee.

'A refill, Monsieur?' asked Madame Dupont, entering with the inevitable coffeepot. The marquis, absorbed in his paper, did not seem to hear her.

'Monsieur?'

Slowly, he raised his head to stare at her, and she knew in that moment that the picture meeting his tortured gaze was too terrible to contemplate.

'Angel, my dear, what is it? What is wrong?' she gasped, abandoning the coffeepot and going to look over his shoulder.

A stark headline pronounced that the Archduke and Duchess of Austria-Hungary had been assassinated. Smaller print revealed that it had happened in Sarajevo, Bosnia, and that the assassin was the adolescent Serb Gavrilo Princip, steeped in terrorism by the Black Hand.

'Tut, tut, tut: so young to be a murderer,' murmured Madame Dupont distractedly, shocked at such a slaughter of Heads of State.

He turned his head to view her in forbidding silence. 'That would appear to be a moronic utterance, to say the least. Is that the only thing you can think of upon seeing a headline like that?' he demanded. 'My God, Madame, the whole world is about to erupt, and Angelique ... Angelique is over there in the middle of it! And I have no way ——'

'But, my dear, are you not overreacting a little? It is a terrible thing, yes. But it has happened in a relatively minor country.'

'Oh, it has, has it?'

'Yes, Monsieur. Austria- Hungary will declare war on Serbia and that will be that.'

'You think so, do you? *Du vrai*, I would like to have your simplistic approach to the matter! I tell you this, Madame, it may be a minor incident; although, I am sure Their Highnesses would not have thought so, but it is just the beginning of an avalanche that will engulf us all.' His hands clenched on the arms of his chair. 'Why did I not stick to my guns? Did I not know? Did I not see? I should have known those fools of generals would have got it all wrong! I should not have let Angelique go on tour! Where *are* they?'

'I am not sure ... somewhere in Germany, I think. They had finished in Holland and were travelling last night and today ——'

He interrupted: 'I remember now! Stuttgart. They would have left there earlier this morning. Where is that rail schedule?' He scrabbled amongst the papers littering the table. 'Here, you must use this to find out, Madame! Then send a wire telling her to return home immediately!'

'My dear, she is with the duc de Belvoir and his family. He said he would bring her home if danger threatened. How can I send such a wire to him?'

'You must, Madame! How do I know if he has seen the papers? Or would even put the same construct on it as I have?' he demanded, turning on her with biting sarcasm. 'Besides, you have only to call, and he will come running!'

Two spots of colour flared in her cheeks. 'Monsieur!'

'We have no time for this!' he declared. 'You must do as I say. Send a wire to Monsieur Merignac, ordering the orchestra home, and one to your tame duc to suspend his tour and bring Angelique back immediately. Tell him it is a matter of life and death! *That* should bring him.'

She stared.

'It is no lie, Madame! Can you not see the evil that is about to be unleashed on the world?'

'My dear, I do not understand. Why are you so disturbed over an assassination? These things, regrettable though they are,' she shrugged, 'they happen from time to time. You, yourself, Monsieur ...' She hesitated, delicately.

'Assassination, Madame? That is coming it a bit strong! I would have said that what I did was to administer justice—not to be compared to a cowardly attack by some canaille on a Head of State!'

'No,' she murmured. 'Not cowardly, never that, but he was the King's cousin, I believe.'

He sighed. 'This is not at all the same thing, Madame;

surely, you can see that! The prince who attacked you was a serial murderer. A madman! You were his only survivor. Have you forgotten the lengths to which we went to hide you from him? And you have suffered all your life, have you not?'

She did not answer.

His eyes were kind, as he said, 'Attend to me, Madame. How many other young people and perhaps you, yourself, again?—you know how hard he tried to find you!—would have become his victims had I not stopped him?' His nostrils pinched with distaste. 'Even me he lusted after ... *scélérat*! Well, Madame, he may have been above the law, but he was not above justice.'

She nodded. The time he spoke of was a horrifying black blur she could not contemplate. Only once had she allowed herself to think of it, to relive it in all its ghastly detail ...

'Of a truth, my dear,' he spoke gently, 'the removal of such evil from the earth cannot be compared to the political motives of a crazed assassin. But while the European monarchy welcomed my solution to that particular problem, they will be decimated by this. Remember that trigger I spoke of, Madame, that they were waiting for? Well, this is it!'

'But surely it will just mean a resumption of the Balkan Wars, will it not?'

'No, no, Madame. Think! Remember all the alliances, treaties, ententes dividing Europe? Germany will support Austria-Hungary; Russia has a treaty with Serbia; and if Germany is to go after Russia, she will have to turn her back to France. She cannot do that with impunity and, so, will have to wipe us off the slate first.'

'Our alliance with Russia! I did not think of that. But, Monsieur, have you forgotten how heavily fortified is our border with Germany? She will not be able to do it.'

'No.' Then, raising his head to stare at her, he exclaimed, 'Belgium! They will come through Belgium! But

…' He held up a finger. 'Britain has guaranteed her neutrality, and Britain has colonies around the globe.' He went white. 'It will involve the whole world, Madame! *Mon Dieu*! Send those cables at once and get her home before Europe erupts in a bloody mess!'

Eyeing him speechlessly, she hurried out.

In a few minutes, she was back. 'This telegram has just been delivered, Monsieur. It is for you.'

With shaking fingers, he tore open the envelope, reading it silently; his face white and set. 'It is from the duc de Belvoir,' he said quietly, handing it to her.

Hardly grasping its import, she scanned the contents:

Wind changed stop Very chilly stop Coming home at once

The marquis gripped her hand. 'Thank God, Madame! Oh, thank God that your duc is a man of intelligence!'

CHAPTER ELEVEN ~ DECLARATION OF WAR

3 August 1914

The world has changed forever. I cannot write more.

With the inevitability of some great clock winding down, events culminated in the repudiation of an ultimatum from Germany, and on the third of August, the resulting declaration of war. Angelique had been home for a month.

Paris could not believe it; although, such sapient gentlemen as the marquis and the duc were completely unsurprised. Angelique, though frightened, took refuge in her blind faith in her guardian and the damping common sense of Madame Dupont.

Etienne, handsome in his captain's uniform, rode off with his company to Verdun, silently breaking his heart over Angelique; his mind on their final meeting, for only God knew if he would ever see her again.

Angelique, hurling herself into his arms, had cried, 'Oh, Etienne, I am so afraid!'

'You must be brave, *Chérie*, we must all be brave. They are saying that it will not be for long—that the war will last a matter of weeks—a few months at the outset.'

'But you are going to the Front,' she wailed. 'I am afraid you will be ——'

'Hush, dear one, it is only Verdun. Douaumont is a great fortress, you know. I will be safe there. We shall quickly send the Kaiser about his business, and perhaps retrieve Alsace and Lorraine from his grasp: who knows?'

'Oh, I will miss you so much!'

'And I you, my love. Will you write to me every day?'

'Oh, yes! And you will write to me?'

'Every day, my angel.'

'Go with God, my dear love.' And she had kissed him in a way she never had before; a way that was to stay with him and comfort him in his dark days on the Front.

§

The duc, after hurried consultation with the War Ministry and the marquis, and a touching goodbye to Madame Dupont and Angelique, went back to Belvoir where he had set up at his command the most powerful radio transmitters and receivers ever invented.

'I do not like to leave Paris at this present time,' he said to the marquis before he left, 'but I believe that I can best serve our country by co-ordinating the gathering of intelligence for the Allies.

'My people always seem to know what is in the wind. It is a talent they have. I go home now to organise this talent to be useful to France. I shall send them out in parties, selling produce, you know, things like that, all over the country. Peasants going about their business will not be noticed particularly. Among them will be radio operatives who will transmit at prearranged places and times to receivers at the château. Important information will be immediately relayed to Paris and the Front. This is the best technology the modern world has to offer, and I shall make full use of it.

'What I did not tell you, and this is known only to the duc de Belvoir and the leaders of his people, is that there is a whole town inside the mountain beneath the château. There are secret entrances in the most unlikely of places. Moreover, unless you know exactly where to look, you will never find them; and because there is no direct link, as such, to the château above, there is little chance of its discovery should the château fall to the enemy. It is a bit like a maze, complicated by hidden doors and medieval mechanisms to make a quick end of those who trespass without knowledge or permission. Of course, this barbaric machinery is now mostly deactivated, but it can be reset if necessary. That is where you could help me, if you would?'

'But certainly, Monsieur, it goes without saying. If you would send me some drawings of the old devices, I could, perhaps, advise you on how to go about it.'

'*Merci*. I will do so.' The duc put an urgent hand on his companion's sleeve. 'If the war takes a turn for the worse and Paris is overrun, you must bring Madame Dupont and Angelique to Belvoir.'

The marquis smiled. 'I will send them if I have to, Monsieur, you may be sure of that. There is perhaps an underground palace in Paris that could be brought up to date, failing ability to travel. I will set my mind to both these tasks. We will then, tactically speaking, have all flanks covered. But, *eh bien*, we should not take such a pessimistic view just yet.'

§

As days went on, fortress after fortress fell on the borders of Belgium and France, and the shocking carnage became evident; the expression of the marquis grew grimmer, and Madame Dupont had a sinking feeling in the pit of her stomach. This was exacerbated by the dreadful news that Madame Aranova and Professor Lejeune had been amongst the casualties. A howitzer shell had killed them instantly, incinerating them in their vehicle as they travelled through Mons on their way back to the Aranov estate.

At first, there was only silence after the marquis, holding her hands, had passed on the terrible news to Madame Dupont. They had loved both Madame Aranova and Professor Lejeune. Madame Aranova had been like a mother to them, and Professor Lejeune a healing light.

And yet, they felt that they had lost something more than two people that they loved. Madame Aranova represented their last contact with their childhood: Madame Aranova, who had recognised in a little girl the exquisite talent of a great ballerina, who had seen the beauty of Angel and not his disfigurement. And Professor Lejeune, who had healed them both, rejuvenating them from the destruction of their lives. Both gentle, loving people: Their bodies had been destroyed by weapons of hate in a conflagration of evil. It seemed to be the ultimate injustice. Unspeakable. Obscene.

'At least they were together,' said Madame Dupont, at last, her voice choked with tears. 'But to die like that ...'

'They would not have felt anything,' said the marquis. He heaved a sigh. 'If it is any comfort.' And that was all that was said. There could be no funeral, and they mourned in silence, as each day brought forth new horrors to take the place of those that had passed.

'All this bloodshed, Monsieur. Horrific!' she murmured, one day.

'Madame, I am at my wit's end with these anachronistic generals. How many good young men will have to die before they realise these old-fashioned cavalry charges out of equally old-fashioned fortresses will not stand up to the German War Machine? Liège lasted twelve days: one day for each fort. One would think that would be the signal to them to rethink, but no: the bloodbath continues!'

'Indeed, Monsieur, as well as the dead, I have heard there are already so many wounded that there are not enough hospitals to treat them all.'

He shook his head. 'We shall have to do something better than this! We have aircraft now and tanks, if I can only convince the generals of how to use them. Get someone from the War Ministry on the telephone for me, Madame, if you please.'

'Yes, Monsieur.' She took a step, then turned. 'There is something we can do, Monsieur, something practical.'

'Yes?'

'We only use one wing of this house. Why do we not make the rest of it into a war hospital? There is a British group of women doctors and nurses with a foreign service willing to staff such places, if we cannot find enough French women to do it.'

'Very well, Madame, as you wish. You shall be in charge of it, but let us see if we cannot find enough nurses in Paris before we turn to foreign services, *hein*? Now, get me one of those generals on the telephone. I will try again to convince them.'

She listened to him speaking into the instrument. As usual, he wasted no time on tactful preliminaries:

'I have read of the latest bloodbath, General. What do you have to say to me? ... What do you mean: nothing? Have I not sent you extensive and detailed plans to improve your military battle strategy? Not that it would need much! *Du vrai*, even the veriest simpleton would be able to improve on it! ... Oh: you do not wish to discuss it over the telephone? What do you suggest? ... Very well ... *Bon. Bon.*

'Perhaps the generals will at last be willing to listen to me, Madame.' He eyed her, thoughtfully. 'They are sending me a secretary to assist me in delivering to them my designs and battle plans, and liaise between us. The telephone is a dangerous instrument, it seems: too many ears during wartime. This new secretary, he has been injured, invalided out, but he still feels he can be of use. He is an Australian. They are sending him because he studied engineering in Berlin before the war. Fortunately, he speaks several languages, including French.'

Shortly after this, a tall freckle-faced young man stood facing the marquis.

'So, you are my secretary,' said the marquis, observing him intently.

'Yes, Sir. Hugh Watson at your service.' He handed him a letter of introduction.

'Sit down, Monsieur.'

'Please call me Hugh, Sir. I was never one for ceremony. Hope you don't want me to kowtow and palaver ... not very good at that, Sir.'

Since the latter part of this speech was more or less incomprehensible to the marquis, he went on his gut instinct and said, 'No, indeed. Common sense and a little bit of engineering knowledge should cover it.'

'Good-o, Sir.'

'You are lame. Will this work be too much for you?'

'Not at all, Sir, slows me down a trifle if I have to walk too far. Other than that ...' He shrugged.

'Well, you will not have to walk. We have an automobile available, if you can abide the noise. I want you to take some documents to General de Langue for me. But first, you must meet Madame Dupont.'

All Madame Dupont's motherly compassion was aroused by the big, loose-limbed young man with the shy grin. Greeting him kindly, she asked, 'You were fighting in France, Monsieur?'

'Hugh, please. No, Madame.'

'How then did you end up here in Paris and not England ... Hugh?'

'Some French fishermen pulled me out of the Channel and brought me to Calais. I was in the hospital there until I recovered, but I did not want to go home with the war not won. There are plenty of my countrymen over here, so I offered my services to your Military Engineering, and the rest you know. A gammy leg will not prevent me doing office work.'

'No, indeed. You are very brave, Hugh.'

He blushed. 'No, Madame. The men in the trenches, they are the brave ones.'

'Very true,' said the marquis. 'But we can chat later. First, the documents.'

'Very good, Sir.' He turned to Madame Dupont, deferentially. 'It was a great pleasure to meet you, Madame. I hope we can chat later, as Monsieur le marquis has said.'

'Of course, we shall, Hugh, of course ... We will talk over dinner. I shall look forward to it.'

His eyes asked a startled question.

'Yes, of course you shall have your meals with us. If you work with us, you eat with us. Unless, of course, you have made other arrangements?'

'No, Madame, I thank you. It is very kind.'

'*Pas du tout.* I shall see you at dinner.' She smiled as he bowed and took his leave.

§

Madame Dupont and Angelique went to the main teaching hospital in Paris, explaining what they wanted. Then they went in turn to her School of Ballet, the Opéra Magique and their society friends. At the end of this, they had a trained skeleton staff and a large number of volunteers.

In a short while, the Hospital du Bois awaited its first ambulances from the field hospitals and clearing stations at the Front.

Even Madame Dupont, a woman of fortitude, felt her liver curl at the sight of these poor, mangled young men; and Angelique, collapsing into hysteria as the ambulance attendant changed a blood-soaked dressing on a slender young man in a captain's uniform, was administered treatment for shock by Matron.

Luckily for all of them, the marquis was not there to

witness Matron apply two sharp slaps to Angelique's face, thrusting her unresisting form into a chair. 'Listen to me, my girl. These young men have been through enough. The last thing they need is to see beautiful young women screaming and fainting with horror at the sight of them. You say you want to help? Very well, bandaging wounds may not be your strong point, but you sing, do you not? Hold their hand, speak comforting words, sing to them their favourite songs. That is how you can help. But ...' Her eyes ranged over the devastated, uncontrollably sobbing girl. 'If you cannot do that, stay away, for you are no use to anyone the way you are.

'Madame Dupont!' she called. 'Take Mademoiselle away and give her a shot of cognac and a strong cup of coffee. I hope the other volunteers you have mustered have stronger intestinal fortitude, or *du vrai*, I will have to spend more time attending to them than my patients!' She shook Angelique by the shoulder, urging her to her feet. 'Come on, Girl. Pull yourself together now. This is but the tip of the iceberg! Luckily, you are not at the Front— where you would have cause to carry on like that.' She looked up. 'Nurse! What have you got there? Where is your common sense! That is for another region, entirely! *This* is an ear syringe!'

Madame Dupont, taking advantage of this diversion, put her arm around Angelique and led her away.

'Oh, Godmama,' she wailed. 'I am so, so sorry. I thought one of them ... I was afraid ...'

'You thought it was Etienne? Oh, you poor child!'

'Oh, Godmama, what if he comes in like ... that?'

'I know, my darling, I know ... We must just pray and be strong.'

'Be strong? Just the thought ... Oh, those poor, poor soldiers! I did not know they would look like that. Oh, those poor, poor young men! It is too terrible! Too terrible ...' she finished in a despairing whisper, ceasing her sobs.

'It is understandable that you feel like that, my dear. It

is very difficult to have to see them that way. And with the added worry that it might be … someone we know. Never mind, you do not have to come here any more, if it is too upsetting for you.'

'But, yes, Godmama, I want to! Matron is right. It was very bad of me to add to their distress. I know what to expect now, and I shall not get upset like that again. Unless …' her voice quivered, but she went on resolutely, 'if they want someone to hold their hand and sing to them, then that is what I shall do.'

'Are you sure, my dear?' asked Madame Dupont, amazed at what she was hearing.

'Yes, I am sure. Now, I must ask Angelpapa how I may get the music of songs popular with the British soldiers, so that I may be able to sing something dear to them. I must learn them quickly.'

She was calm, determined, focused: a far cry from the pitiful shell that had been so unceremoniously dealt with by Matron in the hospital such a short time ago. Matron's treatment had certainly worked. Madame Dupont reflected on the many, many bouts of hysteria they had had to deal with over the years. No-one had thought to approach it in the brutal fashion adopted by Matron.

Mind you, thought Madame Dupont, *she might have had Angel to deal with straight after. And he may have been a trifle too much, even for a tough old bird like Matron!* 'Very well, as you wish, my dear. I shall return to the hospital, then,' she replied, leaving Angelique in the hall.

Later, rolling bandages, she thought about the war effort of the marquis; for apart from this hospital, he had made available his great resources to the Allies, including the château du Bois as a military headquarters, and all his designs and plans for aircraft, tanks, tank traps, barriers, machineguns, emergency bridges and pontoons for boggy ground—the latter becoming very necessary—for it just seemed to rain and rain, making life in the trenches even more miserable and fighting fraught with difficulty.

Les Boches can think themselves lucky he is not a young man, she thought, remembering his athleticism, and his uncanny ability to stalk and kill his victims soundlessly. *Of a certainty, he would have got amongst them!*

She could not know that in later wars, the Maquis and the Special Forces would employ his dark methods with devastating impact.

At this moment, he was working on a battle plan with his secretary. With a terrain map between them and tiny carved battle pieces, they played a complicated game: fighting mock battles; evolving strategies using aircraft, tanks and infantry to find a way to reduce the horrendous cost in lives. They took turns at being the enemy to ensure that no strategy they could think of was overlooked.

'Do you know, Hugh,' said the marquis, slowly, moving a battle piece. 'I do not think you have told me how you came to be picked up by a fishing boat in the Channel?'

'I was a gunner on an airship, Sir, spotting submarines. We were shot down. Blown out of the sky.'

'An airship? A British airship?'

'Yes, Sir. A prototype—experimental model.'

'Are you telling me they did not employ the helium instead of the hydrogen? After what I told them? No, you would not still be alive! What happened, *mon brave*?'

'A high flying aircraft got us in his sights. The skin of the airship was holed, and I took a bullet in the hip. It could be worse, Sir.' He smiled wryly.

'Indeed! Tell me your thoughts on the limitations of the airship for warfare.'

'Well, you see, Sir, the helium does not allow the airship to fly as high as the hydrogen. Winged aircraft are able to fly very high now, and faster— much faster—and they are, of course, more manoeuvrable.'

The marquis nodded slowly. 'Yes, I get the picture. And, of course, you were vulnerable as a gunner: lack of armour, for one thing.'

'Too right, Sir. I was on a gantry built out from the side

of the gondola—not much more than a couple of planks. I was stuck out like a wart on a wombat, so to speak.'

'Eh? Oh, one of your strange Australian animals. I see …' He was silent a minute. 'I do not think the airship can be developed for further use in this war. It may still be employed for surveillance, but not for active combat. We shall have to concentrate on winged aircraft. I think that is where the future of aviation lies.'

'Too right, Sir, you've got that right. It is a pity. The airship is a beautiful thing. Carries more passengers, too. Perhaps it will have a role in peacetime.'

'Perhaps. As long as the fools do not sacrifice safety for extra weight carrying capacity by using the volatile, lighter hydrogen instead of helium. The trouble is … it cannot be guaranteed.'

'No, Sir. Particularly if they think more money is to be made that way. That's your machinegun nest gone, Sir.'

'Was that not a little reckless, Hugh? See how you have left yourself open to counterattack from my tank regiment?'

'Oh, dear … My men! What a rotten general I am! I hope I am the enemy. Oh, I say, go easy with those tanks, Sir!'

'That has cut a swath through your infantry, Hugh,' said the marquis with satisfaction. 'I don't know how you are going to counter *that*.'

'I'm not, Sir. I shall have to withdraw and regroup. That was a good strategy. Shall we try again?'

'You're very optimistic, Hugh. You forget that I still have my infantry intact. I think you had better save what you can, admit defeat and fly the white flag!'

Eyeing the board ruefully, Hugh decided he was right. 'Yes, I think ——' He looked up and stopped, apparently stunned by the vision that met his eyes.

'Oh! I am sorry, Angelpapa. I did not mean to interrupt you.' Angelique, appearing in the doorway, stepped back in confusion.

'Come in, my dear. You have not yet met my secretary, Hugh.' He beckoned her in, rectifying this omission.

'How do you do, Hugh. You are from the War Office?'

'Yes, Mademoiselle.'

'And you are English?' she persevered.

'Australian.'

'Oh, Australian! Then perhaps you can help me, if Angelpapa permits?'

'What is it you need help with, my child?' queried the marquis, frowning slightly. 'Hugh is a very busy man.'

'Matron has told me that I may sing to the wounded soldiers in the hospital. Many of them are British, and I came to ask you how I can obtain the scores and lyrics of their favourite songs so that I may be able to sing them for them.'

The marquis turned to his secretary. 'Well, Hugh? Can you help?'

'By Jove, Mademoiselle, that is a wonderful idea. It may take me a little while to get them for you, but you shall have them, if I have to write them out myself!'

Thanking him with a blinding smile, she whirled out of the room, leaving it a duller place. Conscious of this, Hugh remarked to his employer, 'Your daughter is very beautiful, Sir.'

'Thank you, Hugh,' said the marquis, at his driest; Angelique's effect on his secretary not being lost on him. 'But she is the daughter of the comte de Villefontaine. I am her guardian, merely. One word: it will be better for all of us if you do not fall in love with her.'

'Oh, I say, fair go, Sir,' he protested, turning brick red. 'It would be easy to do,' he added quietly. 'But I already have a little girl in Calais. She nursed me when I was wounded. I think her beautiful, too. As a matter of fact, she looks a little like Madame Dupont must have when she was young ... But all these things must wait until we win this ghastly war.'

'Indeed,' replied the marquis, satisfied.

§

The duchesse and Elise came back to Paris to help Madame Dupont in the Hospital, fearfully aware that the next poor, broken young man to arrive in the ambulance might well be Etienne, one of his friends or one of Angelique's brothers.

Elise secretly worried about Philippe. But whatever happened, she would always hold in her heart the precious moments when he had taken her hands and said goodbye to her before going off to the Front. He had kissed them and then, daringly, her lips and asked her softly to add him to her prayers—just as if he had not, all the previous season, been amongst the crowd of worshippers dangling after a stately beauty. 'Of course,' she had replied, too tongue-tied to tell him that he was already there.

The marquis, making the first of his daily visits to the hospital to chat with and comfort the wounded, was horrified by some of the injuries, particularly those that disfigured their faces. 'Oh!' He turned his head away to hide his emotion. '*Du vrai*, Madame, the sight of some of these poor young men brings back some very bad memories for me, I can tell you. I cannot help but think that the person we need right now is Professor Lejeune. It is too bad that he is no longer with us.'

'Yes, indeed. These poor boys are in desperate need of his skills. It is such a pity that we cannot do anything for their disfigurements.'

'But, perhaps we can! He must have had students ... In fact, I know he did. When we go back, I shall set Hugh to search for them. He is good at that sort of thing. We must do something for these poor young men. Next time I come, I shall take some measurements of their faces with a view to making masks and artificial eyes for them to immediately improve their appearance. Also, I shall look into the making of artificial limbs. That is, if I do not run the gauntlet of that dragon of a matron,' he added, plucking moodily at the rug covering his knees.

'She is very good, Monsieur. She knows her job. I am sure if you would just take the time to explain to her what you are doing, she will approve.'

'Her approval is not necessary to me, Madame. She looks as though she only drinks vinegar and there is a permanent stench under her nose.'

Madame Dupont's heart sank at his uncompromising demeanour. 'She has a lot to contend with, Monsieur.'

Madame Dupont had a lot to contend with herself, trying to keep the peace between Matron and the marquis, who had struck sparks off each other upon their first encounter. Coming unannounced to inspect the new hospital on the eve of the arrival of its inmates, he had been impressed by the lines of neatly made beds with their fresh, clean linen. Even empty of nurses and patients, the wards had had an air of brisk efficiency and cleanliness. His hospital. He felt satisfaction that it looked the part.

'What are you doing here, Monsieur? You do not enter my hospital without permission from either me *or* the charge nurse.' The speaker, dressed in a dark grey bodice-jacket and skirt, was tall and gaunt with a narrow, desiccated face.

Swinging his wheeled chair around, he looked her over with disfavour. 'Ah, Madame Matron, is it not? Strange: I had the feeling it was *my* hospital.'

'No, Monsieur, let me disabuse you. It is my hospital and no-one—but no-one—enters without my permission. No matter who they are, Monsieur!'

He was not deaf to the challenge contained within the last statement. 'Indeed?' he replied bitterly, turning to leave. 'I put Madame Dupont in charge of this venture, and now I see what has come of it! Well, Madame Matron, it may be *your* hospital, as you say, but perhaps you will do well to remember that *your* hospital is in *my* house!'

Madame Dupont appeared noiselessly beside him. 'Ah, Monsieur, I have been looking everywhere for you!

General le Mesurier has called, and your secretary is out. Good morning, Matron. This is all looking very good!'

Once out in the hall, he said, 'I think you have made a mistake there, Madame. That woman cannot be good for the sick. She is a monster!'

'She is a matron, *mon cher*. They have to be like that. It is only a cover.' But she knew he would not be convinced.

Now, the best she could do was to try and arrange his daily visits while Matron was busy either instructing her nurses or supervising new arrivals, of which there were many. Of course, now that he had modified his wheeled chair and he was more or less independent, coming and going as he pleased, she would have to leave it to fate.

Madame Dupont did not even wish to contemplate the results of any further clashes of wills between these two domineering individuals, both formidable adversaries, accustomed to lesser mortals backing away.

Happily, aside from one or two memorable occasions, she was able to keep them far enough apart to preclude fireworks; although, every visit was a minefield, especially the time he discovered a middle-aged nurse surreptitiously drinking gin in the new operating theatre he had commissioned. Madame Dupont shuddered at the memory: Silently wheeling himself past the washstand, his outraged eyes taking in the slovenly creature raising the bottle to her lips; he grabbed the nearest thing to hand and hurled it at her. It hit the bottle, knocking it out of her hand and smashing both the bottle and the brand new porcelain ewer together on the pristine floor tiles, surprising a drunken exclamation from her.

'Get out of my house, you filthy, disgusting trollop!' he shouted, snatching up the matching bowl, which immediately plucked out of his hand by Matron, coming to a skid-stop beside him.

'Go on,' he roared. *'Fiche le camp!'*

'Oh,' said Matron, setting down the bowl out of his reach and drawing the back of one hand across her brow.

'How crude!'

'Squeamish are you, Matron?'

'Not at all. What is the meaning of this outrage, Monsieur?'

'I thought perhaps you might be able to tell me that.' His voice was deceptively quiet. 'Or rather, why I have found this filthy cow imbibing in my new operating theatre! *Nom de Dieu*, Matron! She is as drunk as a brewer's horse and with half the sensibility!' he exclaimed in disgust, observing the unkempt creature's mute distress at the loss of her only friend. 'I will not have her drinking mother's ruin or any other liquor in my house. *Eh bien*, look at her! She will be stealing the rubbing alcohol next, if she hasn't already done so. It does not say much for your management of this hospital, Matron, and you will explain to me why you have allowed it!'

Matron signed to the woman to leave. 'We are understaffed, Monsieur. I simply cannot get enough nurses to cope with the increasing numbers of patients arriving from the Front. Perhaps you do not realise that most of us here are too busy saving lives to watch a menial worker every minute of the day,' she finished, goaded into giving account of herself.

'You would be better off with no-one than that slattern.'

'That is all very well for you to say, Monsieur.' Matron tapped the floor with the toe of one boot. 'I haven't noticed you offering to empty the bedpans.'

'I beg your pardon, Matron?' The marquis looked down his nose at her.

'Well, Monsieur?' countered Matron, pursing her lips so that she looked more like a wrinkled prune than ever.

'Well of course not!' he replied after a moment of astonished silence. 'Do you take me for the chambermaid?'

Matron declined to answer: her expression anything but conciliating.

'Well, Matron?' he challenged, eyes flashing sapphire-blue.

Matron ground her teeth. 'I—cannot—spare—trained nurses for such menial tasks, Monsieur.'

'So, you employ this gin-swilling sow—for this—menial task?'

'Yes, Monsieur.'

'Well, it is all she is fit for, if that! It is far more likely that a home for hopeless inebriates would be the place for her. You knew that she drinks?'

Matron sighed in exasperation. 'As I have told you, Monsieur ——'

'You cannot spare trained nurses! But, Matron, she is a drunk! Are you going to tell me she is not clumsy? That she does not drop these ... bedpans?'

Matron shrugged. 'Sometimes, Monsieur.'

'So, that is why she smells,' he said with the air of one having made a pleasing discovery. 'So, *that* means that she is more hindrance than help?'

'Sometimes, Monsieur,' admitted Matron, as one who reluctantly tells the truth.

'Pah!' He viewed her with disapprobation. Matron, nothing loth, returned his stare unwinkingly.

Madame Dupont, who had heard the commotion and come running, a reluctant witness to this battle of the Titans, was finally noticed by the marquis, both combatants having been previously oblivious to her presence.

'You may send for your British nurses, Madame. Matron must have clean, sober, professional help. Even if it is only to empty the bedpans.'

'It is a very important consideration, Monsieur, but one of us can do that,' said Madame Dupont. 'It does not require much training, after all.'

'No, you will not!' he commanded, revolted by the suggestion. 'You will send for your British nurses, Madame—as many as Matron needs—*tout de suite*!'

'Of course, Monsieur,' she replied. 'But first, I will

clean up this mess. It is not good to leave broken glass and crockery lying about.'

'No!' he ordered, arresting her. 'Let Matron do it! She is the one who employed that *salope*!'

The opprobrious term caused Matron to bridle with fury and Madame Dupont to cast him a reproving glance. He cared nothing for the wrath of Matron, but Madame Dupont's reproach could tweak his conscience, and he momentarily subsided.

'Have no fear,' replied Matron, fiercely. 'I shall have your mess removed. I have tolerated your farmyard terms, but if you are going to employ the language of the gutter, it will not be in my hospital, Monsieur! You may take it elsewhere.' She cast him a look that would have done credit to a Gorgon. 'I'm sure I could not begin to think what it says about your upbringing!'

'My mess?' he roared, white around the lips. 'Gutter language? My God, Matron you have heard nothing yet!'

Madame Dupont, fearing that he was about to lay it down to Matron using who-knew-what foul language, put a calming hand on his shoulder. 'Come, Monsieur, let us return to our wing. This is not achieving anything, my dear. It is time for your tisane.'

'I will make you a tisane, Monsieur.' Matron had an odd glitter in her eye.

'No, thank you, Matron, you are far too busy. Besides, I want to wake up in the morning!'

'You go too far, Monsieur,' she warned, eyes snapping.

'Yes? You are leaving?'

'No, Monsieur. I am sorry to disappoint you.' Magnificent in her displeasure, she ignored him after this ironic retort, turning to his companion. 'Madame, I will have as many nurses as they can spare. Ten volunteers cannot be as much use to me as one trained nurse who knows her job. Good day to you.' Matron sailed off, wearing her slightly tattered dignity like battle armour.

'Oh, Monsieur! Could you not call a truce with Matron?

You know we cannot do without her,' said Madame Dupont, quietly despairing.

'Bah! *Cette femme*, she has not one minutiae of feminine softness in her soul! Let us go.'

At this present moment, they seemed destined to remain sworn adversaries.

However, when Matron saw the beautiful masks he fashioned and painted, exactly tailored to each individual face shape and skin colour, and the lifelike, artificial eyes made by the potter and the glass maker he brought with him, she was inclined to look upon him, if not with approval, at least with respect.

Angelique, taking to heart Matron's strictures, had obtained the scores of many of the British soldiers' favourite songs—courtesy of the secretary who had very quickly made good his word—and spent many days and evenings singing to them. The ones who were up to it sang along with her, worrying a little that Matron would 'fly into the devil's own passion and read us a sermon from hell', as expressed by one convalescent soldier. But there was no need for concern.

Matron not only looked tough, she was tough—but she was also a born nurse—and under her arid exterior, she hid her compassion for these poor young men whose dreams and lives had been shattered on the battlefield. Anything that would give them something to live for and look forward to was all right with her. And she, like very few, understood the healing powers of music. Another way in which she was like her natural enemy, the marquis du Bois.

Many a young man, having to come to terms with the realisation of one or both legs or an arm blown off or an empty eye socket and gaping facial wound, was immeasurably comforted on awakening to find a beautiful angel holding his hand and softly singing his favourite hymn.

The combined effects of good nursing, good

environment, hope and comfort made this the best hospital in terms of outcome for these unfortunate victims of war.

Then something happened that brought home to them the horror of this war in a way, which to Madame Dupont, recording it in her diary, was inconceivable.

CHAPTER TWELVE ~ THE WHITE WARD

23 April 1915

There can be no explanation; no excuse! For the extent of the inhumanity: the evil that has been visited on my countrymen and their allies. It is beyond belief!

On a day that began well but speedily assumed the proportions of a nightmare, Madame Dupont relayed a message to the marquis.

'Matron has asked to speak with you, *mon cher*.'

'What? I do not believe it! What can that witch of a woman possibly want with me?'

'I do not know, Monsieur, but it must be serious.' It went without saying: neither Matron nor the marquis willingly conversed with each other.

A slight frown came into his eyes. 'You are right, Madame. I feel uneasy about this. Let us go immediately to find out.'

At the emergency entrance, Matron was supervising a number of arrivals from the Front. 'Take these patients to the White Ward, Nurse.'

'Very good, Matron.'

The marquis looked on without a word. The White Ward was the ballroom. He had given it over with the proviso that it must only be used as a last resort.

As the patients were wheeled away one after another, there was a curious silence. Matron, herself, looking even more stern and uncompromising than usual, had her lips clamped together in a thin, straight line. Most of the new patients, their lips burnt and blistered, were blind with bandaged eyes; many wheezed and coughed or rattled, gasping for each painful breath as if it must be their last; some were silent, barely breathing at all; but each seemed to Madame Dupont to have a very low life force.

Matron, looking after them, turned as the marquis spoke: 'You wanted to see me, Matron? *Du vrai*, some of these poor young men will require prosthetics soon, *hein*?'

'No, Monsieur.' She shook her head. 'Those with a chance of survival have been sent elsewhere. All of these—without exception—will die.'

They stared at her in disbelief.

'It may be over hours, it may be over days or weeks, but the result will be the same. All that can be done is to make their last days as comfortable as possible—which will not be easy, or even, in some cases, attainable.' Her face might be a white, expressionless mask, but her eyes were alive with pain as she whispered, 'Oh, I do not know how there can be such wickedness in the world!'

Madame Dupont found her voice: 'But, Matron, what is it? Why do you say that they will all die? How can you know this?'

'This ungodly enemy, Madame! These poor men: Their lungs have been destroyed by a poison, so that even if they look untouched, as some of them do, they are hardly able to breathe enough to live, because the internal surfaces of the lungs weep so that they are literally drowning from within. And should any survive this initial stage, when suppuration starts, they will develop pneumonia and die of infection.'

'No!' She was aghast.

The marquis, who had been sitting with folded lips, finally spoke, 'Are you saying they have breathed in something from the air? A gas?'

'Yes, Monsieur. The Germans have released a poison gas over the battlefield. As the men charge, or as it drifts over the trenches, they breathe it in, burning out the delicate lining of their lungs. All the ones sent here have had too much of it and cannot recover. I know you did not want your ballroom used, but it is the only place big enough for them—and far enough away from the other patients.' She added grimly, 'It will not be for long.'

'It does not matter, Matron, do what you have to. But a gas to destroy the lungs? It is the most inhuman thing I have ever heard of!'

'It is a wicked death, Monsieur,' replied Matron. 'Designed by a fiend, without a doubt. Only a demon out of hell could have thought of such a thing.'

Madame Dupont was horrified. 'But, Matron, what are we to do?'

'After this first wave, Madame, there may not be too many serious cases, as I understand from the ambulance drivers, the troops have now been given simple strategies to counter such attacks until they can be issued with gasmasks. We must hope that it is so. But for now, these poor young men must be cared for, with their suffering eased as much as possible.' On these words, Matron hurried away, Madame Dupont staring after her. Had the tears blinding her own eyes been reflected in those of Matron?

The marquis touched her hand. '*Allons*, Madame, I must find Hugh and work out which gases these villains have been using. Perhaps we will be able to make up a chemical, which when released into the gas, will be able to neutralise it, rendering it harmless. The Kaiser deserves to be executed for this unspeakable crime. I would kill him myself if I could get up out of this chair! But, since I cannot, we must try and make this antidote, *tout de suite*. Come, there is much to do!'

She tried not to think of the shocking death sentence they had just witnessed. Hard as it was: life must go on.

§

The marquis spent long hours closeted with the best chemists in France. Hugh was kept very busy going to and from the War Office and liaising between eminent chemists, but however hard they worked and whatever antidote they put up to the generals in charge, they flatly said they could not have canisters of unknown gas polluting the skies and causing the Good-God-knew-what harm and that gasmasks would suffice.

The chemists threw up their hands and went home. The enraged marquis, despite numerous pleas from Hugh, threw the results of twenty-days hard work on the fire and was only saved from destroying several aerodynamically superior aircraft designs by the timely arrival of Angelique, who wanted to sing a new British song to them so that Hugh might be able to tell her whether she had got her pronunciation right.

The marquis, distracted from his purpose, calmed as he listened to her rendition of the popular *Daisy Bell*.

Both applauded at the end; Hugh saying, 'I would not change a thing, Mademoiselle. They will find your accent adorable.'

'Not too adorable, I hope,' said the marquis, with a warning glance.

'It will not do them any harm to fall a little bit in love with her, Sir. It will give them something to live for.' While he spoke, Hugh quickly gathered up the papers littering the desk, filing them carefully. What a setback it would have been to the progress of aviation to have lost them.

'Very well. Are you happy now, my dear?'

'Yes, thank you. I just wanted to make sure they will be able to understand my words, and Hugh says they will. So, I shall go and try them on the patients!'

'*Bien*, dear child. I will see you at dinner.'

Thankfully, no more terminally gassed patients arrived at the hospital; and after those first few terrible days, the ballroom remained empty. In a silent consensus, they all avoided the room; Madame Dupont feeling that they would never be able to hold another ball in it, for she would always see the ghosts of those unfortunate young men painfully gasping their lives away.

Slowly, the hospital went back to its usual routine, but one thing frustrated the marquis in his quest to help the disfigured. So far, Hugh had failed to track down a surgeon capable of the cosmetic surgery he envisioned. 'The doctors are all away at the Front ... the *many* Fronts,' he told him.

Then, one day, he came in breezily. 'I have found your doctor, Sir—in Scotland. Also I have contacted the WSWCC ...'

'The what?'

'The Women's Sick and Wounded Convoy Corps—it is a society of British women founded by a Mrs Stobart. They provide nurses, doctors; in fact, all personnel required to staff a hospital. I believe they are very good.'

'Oh.' He nodded. 'Continue.'

'Their foreign service is sending us a number of nurses. The doctor will travel with them.'

'You have the name of this doctor?'

'Yes, Sir, it is a Doctor Martin.'

'Martin ... Martin ... I am sure I remember a doctor of that name with Professor Lejeune. He was a very good young doctor. You have done well, Hugh. When do you expect them?'

'I have a note from Doctor Martin, here ... somewhere ... Ah, yes, here it is!'

The note was brief, merely stating that Doctor Martin

requested an interview with the marquis du Bois on the following Wednesday at ten o'clock in the morning and would attend at that time, if convenient.

'Very good, Hugh. I shall make sure that I am ready to receive him. Now, while you were out, the War Office telephoned. They want you over there to receive a dispatch.'

'Right-o, Sir. See you later.'

The marquis smiled as he limped away. He was amused by his secretary's accent and enjoyed his brisk no-nonsense attitude and quirky sense of humour. Hugh was a warrior, *bien sûr*, and a man of integrity. He was also a very intelligent engineer, and the marquis felt hopeful of their latest aircraft design: the one that Hugh had saved from the fire.

On Wednesday, the marquis, impatiently awaiting the arrival of the doctor, was disturbed by Henri opening the door. Beginning to announce a name, he stopped. Poor Henri, he had suddenly begun losing his short-term memory. 'Madame ... uh ... Madame ...'

The marquis beckoned her in. 'Come in, come in. You will have to be quick, Madame, I am expecting our new doctor at any minute.' He bent his gaze on her as if he would look right through into her brain. 'Wait a moment. You are the doctor?'

'Yes, Monsieur.'

'Professor Lejeune's student? Doctor Martin?'

'The same.'

A stunned silence reigned while he surveyed her. Dressed in a severely cut grey suit, short and trim like Madame Dupont, but built more solidly, she had straight red hair coiled neatly into a bun, fine Celtic features and a creamy complexion. Eyes the colour of the Atlantic looked directly into his. Like Madame Dupont, she was *femme formidable*. He approved with reservations: she had not yet passed his test.

'Come here, Doctor, examine my face. Tell me what

you find.'

She stepped forward. Sensitive fingers explored his features, lingering on areas under his hairline, in front of his ear, under his jaw and the fold of his eyelid. 'A long time ago now, Monsieur, you have had cosmetic surgery to the right side of your face. Around your ear, under your hairline and on your eyelid you have had skin grafts. You use a special emollient salve to keep your skin nourished, so that scarring is minimal. Because of the way in which Professor Lejeune has carried out this work, I believe your original injury to have been caused by a burn.'

'*Incroyable!*' he murmured. 'So, you know this work was carried out by Professor Lejeune, do you?'

'Yes.'

'But that is amazing! How do you know this?'

'It is easy to answer you, Monsieur. Quite simply, he was the only person who could have done it. More, he was the only person who could have made the evidence of his work invisible to the eye and all but the touch of a trained surgeon.'

'I see.' He was secretly impressed. 'You have a Scottish accent, do you not? What made you join Professor Lejeune, or he, from his position, to accept you?'

'Professor Lejeune was a pupil of Doctor Braid who was a Scot. In a complicated way, I am a relative of Doctor Braid. My father was also a physician and a colleague of Professor Lejeune, so I did not have the difficulty those of my sex usually have; and Professor Lejeune was only concerned with the ability of his student doctors, not their sex.'

'I can believe it. But when I was at Professor Lejeune's clinic, he had a student called Doctor Martin. Forgive me, Madame, *he* was a man.'

'Yes, Monsieur, he had already been with the professor for a number of years when I took up my study with him. That Doctor Martin later became my husband.'

'I see ... Where is he now?'

'I believe him to be working at a field hospital on the Russian Front. I am afraid I have not heard from him for … for quite some time.' Her face did not change, but her steady grey eyes blinked several times.

'Indeed? I am sorry. It is a regrettable war.' And on that deplorable understatement, he accompanied Doctor Martin to the hospital where she reviewed her prospective patients and was shown her new operating theatre: sterile and shining clean.

They were followed by Matron, who seemed to feel that the presence of a doctor in her hospital was a circumstance to be kept strictly under her eye.

'Oh, go away, Woman!' The marquis waved a dismissive hand. 'Have you not plenty to do? Doctor will call if she wants you. I can show her around. There is not the least need for you to be inconvenienced!'

'Well, really, Monsieur!' Matron looked to be about to nail him to the wall when her eyes encountered his. Arrested, she stared into them for a long moment. 'Certainly, Monsieur. If you are sure, Doctor?'

'Thank you, Matron. Monsieur le marquis knows this hospital well, I believe.'

Matron left without another word.

'You should come here more often when Matron is about, Monsieur,' said the soldier in the bed in front of them. 'That's the only time I've seen her without a word to say. And what is more, I enjoyed it!'

The marquis smiled. 'It is the only time, *mon brave*, I can assure you. I do not know what is different this time. How does she treat you as a patient?'

'Well … Between you and me, she is not such a dragon as she makes out. She is very kind when you are ill; but the more you heal, the more dragon-like she becomes.' He laughed. 'I have the feeling that as soon as you become well, you become an object of revulsion to her; but at the moment she is very good.'

'I am relieved to hear it. This is Doctor Martin. She

wishes to take a look at your injuries.'

§

Meanwhile, Henri, mortified at his devastating loss of memory, took several steps of his own, culminating in a requested interview with Madame Dupont. 'Madame, I have come to speak with you about my retirement. I regret to inform you that ... I am afraid I can no longer carry out my duties to the standard ... standard required in an establishment of this nature,' he told her; a break in his voice.

'Henri, I am very sorry to see you go. You have served the marquis du Bois very well, my friend, above and beyond the call of duty. You have helped me through many difficulties. I thank you more than words can say.'

'Indeed, Madame, we have had some interesting times, to be sure.' The butler smiled faintly. 'But you do not need to thank me. I have carried out no more than my duty.'

'Perhaps I see it a little differently to you, old friend. I regret that your cottage at the château is not available to you at present. Until it is, you will stay here with us in your rooms, of course.'

'Thank you, Madame, that is very kind. I understand that the château is needed by the military, but I shall go to my daughter at Versailles. You remember she married the head gardener there?'

'Indeed. That is most satisfactory for you, but we shall never find anybody to replace you, my friend.'

'Oh, yes, Madame, as we had envisaged, Justin is fully prepared to step into my shoes. I do not anticipate any disruption to the smooth running of the house.'

'I did not quite mean it like that. But I thought ... Has not Justin enlisted?'

'He was rejected, Madame,' he said, looking towards the door. 'Come in, Justin. I am just apprising Madame of your circumstances.'

Madame Dupont turned to greet the footman: a question in her eyes.

'Bunions, Madame,' he replied mournfully.

Recounting this conversation to the marquis over their late-night cup of chocolate, she added, 'So, we have a new butler. But when I told him, Monsieur, if he wished to wear slippers when his feet hurt that I would turn a blind eye, he seemed to be quite offended.'

'Well, of course he was, Madame! A butler in slippers? He would never live it down!' He laughed at her affectionately. 'But how *insensitive* of you, my dear!'

CHAPTER THIRTEEN ~ GUARDIAN BY PROXY

14 February 1916

Danger faces Angelique. And not just from the Enemy! We cannot let her go without her guardian, but Angel is too incapacitated to accompany her. Yet circumstances dictate that we cannot refuse. What shall we do? This is, perhaps, the greatest challenge to Angel's patriotism of all time! But then again, it is Saint Valentine's Day, so perhaps He will have something to say!

The Hospital du Bois began to get a reputation for surgical intervention. Soon, there was a waiting list for those requiring cosmetic surgery for horrifying facial injuries and those needing prosthetics.

'She is a jewel, a veritable jewel, a true disciple of Professor Lejeune,' said the marquis of Doctor Martin when the first results of her handiwork were unveiled. '*Eh bien*, my son, an artificial eye to match your own, and one would have to be very clever indeed to know that your injury had been more than a scratch!'

It also filtered out that there was a beautiful angel who came at night and sang to the patients, giving them hope and strength to carry on.

General de Langue, who had long had a predatory eye on the dewy beauty of Angelique, approached her guardian with a request. He had first been to her father who had flatly stated that he had ceded his authority over to her guardian, the marquis du Bois. The astounded general had then presented himself at the hôtel du Bois.

Fluently, he explained the difficulties of maintaining the health and morale of soldiers forced to fight for years in a debilitating conflict that had, at the outset, been confidently expected to last only a matter of weeks or months, at worst. Discussing the newest developments in a very frank and open manner, he seemed to be making an effort to drop his formality and appear on terms of intimacy with his host.

Finally, he revealed the true purpose of his visit. He had heard of the great work carried out in the hospital of the marquis.

'You are a true son of France, Monsieur. You have shown this by your actions. And your, er ... ward has also shown great patriotism, singing to these young soldiers. I have heard that she can make the difference between life and death for them. *Incroyable!*'

'Music is a powerful force, General. It is relevant to all aspects of life.'

'Oh, indeed, indeed! This is why I have come to you, Monsieur. Our troops need an elixir to dispel the depression over their spirits and renew them to greater efforts. The voice of Mademoiselle de Villefontaine is such an elixir.' He made a disarming gesture. 'I will be honest with you, Monsieur. We are in great danger of losing this war and being overrun by the enemy. It is crucial that you allow her to sing to our troops, and I have come to beg that you do so. Needless to say, she will be safe with me. I will not allow the slightest harm to come to the child. She will be given an apartment in our headquarters in Chantilly, the Grand Quartier Général, or GQG as we call it, and be driven to and from each venue accompanied by an armoured convoy. In fact, if you allow her to do this patriotic duty for France, I shall not let her out of my sight.' The general's persuasive voice went on in the same vein. According to him, the golden presence of Angelique amongst his troops was synonymous with winning the war.

Listening to him with an air of absent courtesy, the marquis du Bois was nevertheless tuned in with razor-sharp concentration. There was something about this general he distrusted. Oh, yes, now he remembered: a warning from the duc. Not that it was necessary, he could see for himself the way the man's eyes lingered on the trim figure of Madame Dupont when she came into the room.

'You remember General de Langue, do you not, Madame?' he asked, his own glittering wickedly. 'He is the one who procured the Royal Train for us before the war.'

'How do you do, General? Of course, I remember you. Indeed, once again, I thank you,' she responded, withdrawing her hand as quickly as possible from his; aware that the general, a fine looking man, was accustomed to being a success with the ladies.

'General de Langue has asked me to allow Angelique to sing to the troops ... under his protection, of course,' continued the marquis, in tones at odds with the glint in his eye. 'He feels they need her to boost their morale and keep them fighting for France.'

'Oh?' Her large orbs explored those of the general, watched with malicious amusement by the marquis as he shifted his gaze.

Ha! Just as I had thought! Madame Dupont had not lost her ability to discomfit gentlemen with lascivious intent. He defied one to sustain her penetrating regard! The marquis made his decision. 'I *will* allow Angelique to sing to the troops, General, since you have made such a good case for it.'

The general turned to him, eagerly. 'You will, Monsieur? Indeed, I thank you! France thanks you for your goodness in so doing!'

'Indeed, one feels it would be treasonable not to do so,' he murmured. 'But there is one condition that I will attach, General: one condition.'

'Yes?' The general's expression was benign, good-humoured.

'It is the only condition, but it must be met,' he warned.

The general smote his forehead. 'Of course, you must first assure yourself that Mademoiselle de Villefontaine is willing to do it! I may be able to help you there. Let me talk to her. Perhaps I can persuade her?'

'No, no, General: *pas du toute*. I know that Angelique wishes to do her patriotic duty. She is very willing to sing to the troops. No, no, it is not that.'

'Then tell it to me, Monsieur. I am sure that we can come to an arrangement. After all, we both want the same thing.'

Do we, indeed? Eh bien, let us see! 'I am happy to hear you say so, General,' responded the marquis, politely. 'Very well, in that case ... and I will have it in writing ...' He paused, continuing as the general affably inclined his head, '*Eh bien*, it is this: her fiancé, the marquis de Beaulieu, must be recalled from his post to accompany her as her escort.'

The general jumped as if he had been shot. 'But that is ridiculous, Monsieur. Ridiculous!' he spluttered. 'I do not know how I can do such a thing! You have no need to worry. I have already said that I will personally escort her. She will be safe with me.'

The marquis studied the handsome man who had been described by some as having 'the look of eagles', but he saw only a lecherous predator. '*Eh bien*, General,' he said, barely disguising his contempt. 'I have given you my condition. Take it or leave it.'

Madame Dupont broke the silence that fell after the general turned on his heel and walked out without another word. 'I do believe you are right not to trust the general, my dear. I do not wish to malign the character of the man, but I very much fear he has designs upon her virtue.'

'From what I have seen and heard,' he replied caustically, 'it would appear that he cannot look upon any reasonably personable woman without having designs upon her virtue, Madame.'

'You may be right,' she said. 'I am not comfortable with him, myself. He has such … caressing eyes.'

'Hmph!' The marquis vouchsafed no answer, but privately he agreed with her. However, since the word he would have chosen was 'disrobing' rather than 'caressing', a trifle indelicate for the ears of *les femmes*, he declined to comment. But that was not important: what was important was that he was about to circumvent the general's designs, whatever they may be—for now. He frowned. *What if the general had been speaking the truth, and Angelique was needed to redirect the course of the war?* He shrugged. The general had only to meet his condition, which in the light of his reaction, did not seem very likely. He sent for Hugh to carry precise instructions to his lawyer, just in case. Then, both he and Madame Dupont, busy with their respective war efforts, put it to the back of their minds and decided to wait upon events.

Not long after lunch, there was a commotion in the hall. They could hear hysterical screaming and sobbing.

'It is Angelique! Oh, *Dieu me sauve*! What has happened now?' Madame Dupont, heart pounding, ran to the door; the marquis wheeling himself frantically in her wake.

They could not quite believe the scene that met their eyes.

Etienne, in his bright captain's uniform, was supporting a fainting Angelique in his arms.

'*Bonjour*, Madame, Monsieur,' he said looking up with a wry smile. 'It will be all right in a moment, I think. Angelique, believing that I am dead, and that I am my … own ghost, has succumb to the shock. I suppose it must be a surprise for her to see me here.' He gazed at them, a puzzled expression in his eyes. 'It was for me, too. To be sent here, I mean.' Glancing down at his fair burden, he added, 'I would shake your hand, Monsieur, but …'

'No, no, I see you have your arms full at the moment,' replied the marquis. 'So! The general did accept my condition! I did not think he would the way he left us, and I heard no more from him. My apologies. I did not tell Angelique in case it did not happen. I did not want to raise her hopes, only to have them dashed down again; and now she has had a shock. Well,' he added indulgently, 'she will get over it. It is, after all, one of the better ones she is likely to have in this life.'

'With the greatest respect, Monsieur, I have not the faintest idea what you are talking about. It is as big a mystery as to why I have been recalled from Verdun,' replied Etienne, with as much exasperation in his voice as a man of even temperament could display.

'Did they not tell you, then?' asked the marquis, incredulously.

'No, Monsieur, they did not! I was at GQG in Chantilly, receiving orders to take back to Douaumont, when I was told my orders had been cancelled and I was to immediately travel to Paris, present myself at the hôtel du Bois and there await further instructions.'

'Indeed? Well, I can resolve that one for you, dear boy. You have been recalled from your post to escort Angelique when she goes to sing for the troops.'

Madame Dupont quietly moving to revive Angelique with the smelling salts, said to Etienne, 'I am very glad to see you, my dear. Bring Angelique into the salon now.'

Angelique turned her head, pushing away Madame Dupont's hand. 'Oh, Etienne, Etienne!' she cried. 'I cannot, *cannot* believe it! It is you! You are *really* here! Not dead! Not dead! Oh, thank God! Thank God!'

'Not dead, my angel, most emphatically not!' he replied, shepherding her towards the door. 'Come and sit down in the salon, *Chérie*. You have had a shock.'

They moved into the cheerful room where he seated

her on the sofa and sat beside her. Somewhat dazed and clinging tightly to his hand, she only half-listened to the marquis briefing him on his interview with General de Langue.

'The dog!' he murmured.

'Exactly so!' agreed the older man.

'But what do you mean?' asked Angelique, glancing from one to the other in bewilderment. 'I am perfectly ready to sing to the troops.'

'Of course, my angel,' replied the marquis, gently. 'Do not worry your head about it. The general is a very busy man. He will, perhaps, not always have the time to look to your comfort; whereas, Etienne will make it his priority.'

'Indeed, my love, your safety and wellbeing are paramount to those of us here in this room. It will be my greatest privilege to take care of you, *Chérie.*'

'Indeed, indeed!' agreed the marquis. 'Oh, dear God! Angelique!' This in mock revulsion as she showed signs of throwing herself into the arms of the young marquis, adding with a touch of amusement, 'I believe the rose garden to be quite deserted at the moment, my dear, and very possibly of a suitable temperature, too!'

'But it is raining, Angelpapa. *And* it is winter!' she cried, glancing around at their smiling faces. 'Oh, you are teasing me! It is just ...' she shrugged helplessly, the ready tears springing to her eyes.

Etienne tightened his hold on her hands, silently telling her that he did not mind her transports. In fact, if the truth be known, he longed for them. Unfortunately, under the eyes of Madame Dupont and the marquis, he was in no position to reassure her.

Madame Dupont, moving to her side, gave her a handkerchief, saying gently, 'Come, my dear child, your emotions are all over the place, and no wonder! But it will be better to restrict such perfectly understandable demonstrations of joy to more private moments. You do not want to embarrass Etienne, do you, *hein*? Now, you must come up to your room and rest. You will see your handsome escort at dinner. Do not forget that we are dining early tonight, so that you may sing to the convalescent soldiers at the Hôtel-Dieu de Paris—and we must not keep them up late.' She turned to Etienne with a sweet smile. 'Is not this an appropriate day for a reunion? You do not know what day it is, no?' She looked at each of them. 'It is Saint Valentine's Day.'

'Ah, Petite,' the marquis tweaked a golden curl, 'I did not mean to make game of you—on such a day, too. But go along now—you have had enough emotional upheaval for the moment.'

As always, she obeyed him, accompanying Madame Dupont without protest through the door held open by the young marquis.

'And when does Angelique go to sing for the troops, Monsieur?' asked Etienne, returning to the sofa after bowing out the ladies.

'I am waiting to hear. As I told you, I had no confirmation from the general that he would accept my condition. Your appearance was the first inkling that he had agreed to it. So, we wait now to find out where and when she begins her "tour of duty", and also for a certain piece of evidence of the good faith of the general.'

Etienne frowned. 'It bears his hallmark—General de Langue—does it not? No plans, nothing in writing, just makes up his mind suddenly and charges in like a rampaging bull, trampling over everyone until he gets what he wants. He doesn't let the odd scruple stand in his way, either.'

'I know it, my son, but that will be his downfall; for what he does not know is that you will stand in his way. It gives me great satisfaction to know that even over my dead body he will not have the power to fulfil his wicked desires!' He controlled his rising anger, dampened by a grim pleasure in the thwarting of the general's purpose.

§

The next morning, very early, the marquis sent for his deputy, captain, the marquis de Beaulieu. 'The itinerary has come, *mon fils*. I did not think it would be long, but *du vrai*, he has not given much notice, even for him. You will have to get a bustle on, for tonight Angelique will be required to sing for the Officers of the Realm at the Grand Quartier Général in the Palace of the Princes de Condé at Chantilly, where you will be quartered for the better part of the time. After that there is a list of dates,' he added, showing him the paper. 'But it says here the actual locations are to be kept secret until the last minute, to make the gatherings of the troops as safe as possible. I have no fault to find with that, but *mon Dieu*!' he predicted. 'The whole thing will be a scramble from start to finish. Fortunately, she has a few days at home here and there between engagements; so no doubt I shall see you both from time to time.'

The marquis de Beaulieu grasped at the most salient point.

'Did you say she will be singing for the officers tonight, Monsieur?' he questioned. 'General de Langue must be very anxious to begin. As you say: we shall have to get a move on!'

'Yes, he isn't wasting any time,' replied the marquis du Bois. 'But I have already given orders for two automobiles to be ready to leave at eleven o'clock, the second for the luggage and, er ... in case of a breakdown.' The marquis, maintaining his lack of faith in the internal-combustion engine, had not found anything about the latest vehicles to reassure him. 'Madame Dupont is supervising Angelique's packing, and I suppose your batman ...?'

'Yes, I will be ready, Monsieur. I have not much to pack. But why this mad rush on the general's part, do you think? And what about the way he went on about the troops? You would think he would start with them, would you not?'

'Oh …' He smiled cynically. 'Apparently the generals, having heard de Langue's claims, wish to see for themselves if her voice has the powers that have been attributed to it.'

'What a load of old kippers! I'll wager there isn't one of them who has not heard her sing at one time or another!'

The marquis was amused. 'Or that they have not rented a box at the Opéra Magique for at least one of her performances! But it should not be too taxing for her. I understand it is to be an informal soiree, just a few selected songs—nothing too strenuous. The real work begins tomorrow night when she sings for our troops.'

'Perhaps the officers, too, need inspiring to continue with this cursed war?'

'Indeed, my son, I think so. Things have been going very badly for us.' He straightened in his chair. 'But especially tonight—watch her well! And do not let yourself be browbeaten and ordered about by any of the generals. You are my proxy, and I have secured the promise of General de Langue. Not one of them is to be allowed an opportunity to impose on her,' he added grimly, 'tonight or any other!'

'Most certainly not!' agreed the young marquis. He studied his fingernails with casual interest. 'I wonder: shall I be facing a court martial by this time tomorrow, do you think?'

'No, my son, it will not come to that, nor will it be necessary for you to act tonight. You need just to be there: a witness for the prosecution, if you will. Do you think that I would trust that wily old fox, de Langue, one centimetre out of my sight? Or that I would allow you to face a general in the capacity of your rank as captain? *Non, bien sûr!*' he answered his own rhetorical question. 'I have taken the precaution of drawing up a legal document, which, when signed by the general, will allow you to take any steps you think are warranted to keep the person of my ward from harm. No matter who you have to act against, you will be legally exempt. Perhaps you did not notice my secretary, Hugh, in the hall yesterday? No, you were fully occupied! He had the document ready for signing upon your arrival. Of course, when he saw you, he took it straight around to the War Office as I had instructed. I have sent him off today to collect it, so he should soon be back with it.' He added with relish, 'Then we will see! For unless it is signed, the whole agreement is void. There will be no tour.'

The mind of the young marquis was still running on a single track. 'I am prepared to face a court martial, any number of them if I have to; but I do not know who will protect Angelique if I am found guilty of disobeying an order.'

'Indeed, my son,' smiled the marquis. 'But no general will be prepared to face what will be read out to the presiding judiciary if you do. I guarantee it, *mon fils*. There will be no court martial.'

At this moment, Hugh entered, bearing a scrolled document bound with ribbon and adorned with an official seal.

'There you are,' said the marquis, accepting it from Hugh and placing it in his hand. 'You, the marquis de Beaulieu—not Captain de Beaulieu, you understand—are now legally guardian of an angel, whenever she is out of my presence!'

'Thank you, Monsieur.' Etienne held it reverently.

The marquis, noting the intense satisfaction in his expression, was pleased. He had done all he could to keep his angel safe. Now it was up to God and the marquis de Beaulieu. Even if the worst happened and he faded out sooner than he expected, his innocent child would not become the plaything of any lecherous *roué* of a general— his document saw to that!

Once again, the marquis felt his gorge rise, a red mist blinding his eyes, at the thought of a notorious rakehell masquerading as a hero, using his position to defile an innocent flower: no doubt discarding her without compunction when he tired of her or she became inevitably *enceinte*. He pictured the general parading her as his mistress, flaunting her before his friends, miring her reputation, ruining her forever in the eyes of society.

This nauseating vision set his fingers itching for the feel of a narrow silken cord to turn that lustful smile into a death mask. Longingly, he imagined the moment the general, all unsuspecting, felt the first kiss of the cool silk about his throat. In his mind's eye, he saw himself, lithe and strong, come up silently behind his victim, casting his noose, drawing it tight as the general, realising at last, brought up his hands, clawing ineffectually. *Too late, General! Too late!* He savoured the moment that the general, understanding his fate, knew that he had paid the price for defiling precious innocence before a sudden pull, a deft twist, and justice was done: a quick end, quicker than he deserved. But—he would know! And Angelique: safe from him forever! *Now, who is triumphant—eh, mon général?* The air around him positively crackled with menace.

The marquis de Beaulieu, his attention on the precious document in his hands, felt the hair lift on the back of his neck and turned in surprise to the invalid. What he saw made him catch his breath. His father had told him that the marquis was a dangerous man. *Mon Dieu*! He had not told him the half of it. Observing him now, he no longer doubted the story his father had seen fit to impart to him, on the attainment of his majority, about certain past activities of the marquis, rumoured and otherwise. Indeed, until this moment, he had not really credited it, knowing what a gentle idealist his father was. He surveyed him in alarm. Deathly pale, his mouth a grim line, the marquis sat silent, a carven statue—only the eyes were alive: malevolent, burning …

The younger man recoiled, unable to bear to look into their depths. 'Are you all right, Monsieur?' he asked in concern. 'Monsieur?'

The other man sighed and slumped in his chair. 'Oh … yes, my son, yes. Just indulging in might-have-beens, that is all. An unprofitable occupation, I fear. Ring the bell for my man, will you? It must be time I dressed for the day.' He glanced regretfully down at the exotic dressing-gown Angelique had given him for Christmas: black, of course, with sumptuous embroidery. Black market as well, probably, but he had tactfully refrained from enquiry.

He seemed so normal, so much himself, that Etienne, complying with his request, almost thought he had imagined it. But no, everything he had heard about this man was true. He may be on his last prayers, confined to a wheeled chair, but it in no way diminished his extraordinary power. In one masterly stroke, he had smashed the ambition of a very powerful man: one who could not otherwise be stopped. For this was the crux of the matter: during wartime, as a captain of the military, he must obey the orders of a higher ranking officer, and therefore would not be able to interfere with anything the general had in mind. Of course, this was why he had been recalled—but why had not the general realised the powers given by the document? Perhaps he had not read it carefully, believing that a mere captain would naturally obey a superior officer's orders. Well, the marquis du Bois had put paid to that! Yes, General de Langue had met his match today—even if he did not yet know it!

'I say this with all sincerity,' said the young marquis, as he left to supervise his packing. 'It is a great privilege to know you, Monsieur.'

CHAPTER FOURTEEN ~ PLOT AND COUNTERPLOT

15 February 1916

We have to send our darling girl to the Front. Will the nightmare of this war never end? Our only consolation is that Etienne is with her.

General de Langue strode to the Officer's Mess with a sense of great wellbeing, winking at the serving girl as he ordered his coffee. He went to a table and sat down to pass the time of day with several of his cronies.

General le Mesurier, sitting with General LeClerc at a nearby table, remarked under his breath, 'De Langue is looking remarkably pleased with himself this morning. He struts about as if he owns the place.'

'Yes, very cock of the walk, is he not?' replied General LeClerc, understanding his friend's disgruntled attitude since, not so long ago, General de Langue had had a very public and humiliating *affaire de cœur* with his wife. 'I believe we have him to thank for organising our entertainment for tonight.'

'So, that's his latest flirt, is it? No wonder he is crowing like a farmyard cockerel! He should be ashamed of himself: she is hardly more than a child. I wonder that the marquis du Bois has allowed her to come, knowing what he is,' he said, hardly able to contain his disgust.

'I think the general is indulging in dangerous dreams, *mon ami*. But I must correct you: she is not yet his flirt. I believe her to be quite devoted to her fiancé.'

'Huh! Much he would care for that! Especially if said fiancé is a lower-ranking officer!' he replied bitterly. 'You know de Langue: anything in a skirt, as long as it is remotely passable; and if he thinks he can get away with it, he won't take no for an answer, either. *Mon Dieu*, I would not like my daughter to be in such a position!'

No, nor your wife, thought the other with sympathy. He sighed. General de Langue was a great man to have on the battlefield, but an insatiable libertine in the salon. And *les femmes*, they fell for his big cat magnetism; almost fell over themselves to vie for his favours, or so it seemed to his jaundiced eye whenever he went into society.

And lately there had been disturbing rumours that the general, not contenting himself with the services of ladies of the night and disaffected society matrons, had developed a dangerous preference for young virgins, some of them not even out of the schoolroom, which had caused scandals in some very high-stepping families indeed.

Some of these *demoiselles*, once having fallen under the spell of the general's charm, had moved heaven and earth to escape from their schoolrooms and actually went searching for him; whereupon the unscrupulous general could pick them off at his pleasure. He curled his lip. Young girls were inclined to become infatuated with older men, particularly if they wore a uniform. He, in common with all the other men of his acquaintance, felt it was only common decency to repulse them—and sometimes one had to be quite brutal before they got the message. Well, better a broken heart at fifteen than a life of ruin. Pity de

Langue did not think so! He, himself, was not a family man; but thinking of the rabid general, he was, for once, thankful for it.

'One day he will get his just deserts, *mon ami*,' he remarked comfortingly. *One day he would cuckold or ruin the daughter of someone who would not accept it compliantly. Bien sûr, it was only a matter of time.* 'Meanwhile, we will enjoy the fruits of his labours. *Mon Dieu*, I do not know how long it is since I heard the glorious voice of Mademoiselle de Villefontaine! The brutalities of war tend to cast a pall over the arts. It will be good to feel civilised again!'

The other nodded. Even in this great Palace of the Princes de Condé, once the epicentre of all things cultured, the exigencies of war overrode everything; blackening the mood until one could not see a way out of the dreadful impasse of men fighting a debilitating war of attrition in muddy, bloody trenches; reduced to burrowing like animals in the earth for survival.

General LeClerc smiled at him. 'Shall I make your day, *mon ami*? Cheer you up a little, *hein*? What if I tell you that de Langue will have that insufferable smile wiped off his face sooner than he thinks?'

At the other table, General de Langue, idly discussing the news of the day, his mind dwelling obsessively on golden hair and virginal flesh, suddenly paled and shivered.

'A goose has walked over your grave, *mon cher*?'

'So you say. No, I ...' He pulled at his collar, looking ill and uncomfortable. 'I believe I need some air. Excuse me, gentlemen ...' He left the table, reefing at his tie and fumbling with his collar button, refusing assistance with a gesture.

'What is up with him?' asked one of his cronies, glancing over at him as he lurched across to the doorway.

The other smiled cynically. 'Perhaps, *mon ami*, whichever mistress he will discard for Mademoiselle Angelique has made a voodoo doll and stuck a pin in it!'

'No, no, *mon brave*, you have got it wrong! She would

not stick it there!' They laughed, coarsely. 'Perhaps it is a disgruntled husband.'

'Yes, maybe it is old le Mesurier. *He* would like to stick it there!'

'Shh! He is sitting just over there!'

'Oh!' They grimaced, passing on to a more innocuous topic.

General le Mesurier, narrowly watching the beleaguered general's progress to the door, turned to LeClerc. 'De Langue is certainly not smiling now! How did you know that would happen, *mon ami*?'

'I didn't.'

'Then what did you mean: you would make my day?'

'Oh, that? Well, I will tell you.' He lowered his voice. 'Last evening, when I was in Paris, de Langue asked me to witness his signature on a document. I did not think anything of it, and would naturally not have looked at it, except that he asked me to read it and tell him what I thought.'

'And did you read it?'

'I did. It was an agreement drawn up by the marquis du Bois regarding the ward of Mademoiselle Angelique. I even read the final clause at the bottom, which is more than he did.'

'And?'

'It has him trussed up like a turkey, *mon cher*. He will not be able to get his hands on her unless he has permission from the marquis de Beaulieu—and he is not likely to get that! And if he touches her otherwise, he is gone—Pfft!— prosecuted. They can throw the book at him!'

'But ... but, why did he sign it?'

'I am afraid I am to blame for that.' LeClerc smiled reminiscently. 'I told him I thought it was very straightforward. Which it was. Very. You see, he thinks that because the marquis de Beaulieu is only a captain, he will not have to abide by it. But he did not read the last clause, which states that the marquis de Beaulieu is acting in a civilian capacity as guardian of Mademoiselle and no military rank is to be considered above that of ... and it goes on to state his rank. Did you know he is a cousin of the King of England? It also states that he acts as proxy to the marquis du Bois. And you know what kind of pull he has! A clever man, too.' LeClerc almost purred. 'It was a great pleasure to watch de Langue sign away his one chance to have his wicked way with our Angel of Song, I can tell you.'

'Indeed, *mon cher*, indeed!'

'Now, does that make you feel better, dear old friend?'

'Yes, er ... No, dammit, it doesn't!' He slammed his open palm down on the table. 'Nothing will make me feel better until we get those poor men out of the trenches and *les Boches* back in Berlin where they belong!'

'Softly, *mon brave*, it is a good thought and will no doubt happen in time, but meanwhile, we must patiently beaver away.' He put a hand on his shoulder, predicting as he moved off, 'We will both enjoy our soiree tonight, my friend, and forget the war for a couple of hours, at least. The voice of Mademoiselle Angelique will guarantee that for us!'

CHAPTER FIFTEEN ~ A VOICE TO DIE FOR

Late Evening, 15 February 1916

Angel is like a cat on hot bricks this evening, but I have faith in his wisdom. I know he was right to send Angelique to answer the call of her country. But who would have thought that the greatest danger facing our beautiful Angel of Song would not be the bullets and shells of the Enemy, but the treachery of one of our own?

Angelique and her escort were greeted upon arrival at GQG by General de Langue, and nothing could have exceeded his affability. If the marquis de Beaulieu had to grit his teeth at the caressing manner and oily suavity he employed when addressing Angelique, at least he could not find any impropriety in it.

At length, leaving them with his aide, the general strode away, smugly aware of the fine figure he presented in his uniform. The aide, ushering them to Angelique's sumptuous apartment, told Etienne that he was to be housed with the other junior officers on the opposite side of the palace.

'You have made a mistake,' he objected. 'It has been

agreed that I must have a room close to Mademoiselle.'

'The general has given his orders, Captain,' replied the aide, in a bored voice.

'Then you will ask the general to change his orders, or I will roll out my groundsheet across Mademoiselle's doorway, out here in the hall. Since I speak now as the marquis de Beaulieu ... and *not* Captain de Beaulieu, I expect the general to comply.'

He spoke quietly as he showed him the relevant section of the document, but the aide was aware of a cold determination: a certain icy hauteur. In the silence that followed, the aide was also uncomfortably prescient of a latent strength, a coiled-spring, fluid grace about his person that hinted at hidden danger. He hurried to placate the man he had so grossly underestimated.

'Of course, Monsieur. General de Langue has not perfectly understood your requirements. The apartment just across the hall from Mademoiselle shall be prepared at once. If that is suitable to you, Monsieur?' The aide now appeared nervous and worried, anxious to defer. 'It will take a little while, Monsieur ...'

'It will be most suitable, Lieutenant. I am not in a hurry. As long as I have somewhere to dress for the recital ...' The marquis de Beaulieu was all amiability. 'Meanwhile, I shall remain with Mademoiselle. Would it be possible to obtain some refreshment for her, do you think?'

'Certainly, Monsieur. I will send a servant directly. Pray, excuse me.'

Watching him walk away, Etienne silently revelled in the power of the document.

Angelique, sensing the exultant anger in him, said timidly, 'Etienne?'

At once his eyes grew warm, the frightening coldness receding from him as he replied, 'I am here, my sweet. How do you like your apartment?'

'It is magnificent. Come and look,' she giggled, 'there is

even a powder closet, and the bath is positively obscene! One would need a ladder to climb into it. I hope there is plenty of hot water! But I will not show it to you—it puts me to the blush just to be in there on my own. And look! They have made this antechamber into a dressing-room. It is the biggest one I have ever seen!' Chattering happily, she showed him around the apartment; his cynical mind labelling the huge bed with the shell-shaped headboard draped in pink velvet as a lustful creation of the general.

Amèlie, carefully unpacking her evening gown, said she hoped Mademoiselle would not get lost in it during the night, expressing the opinion that it was no wonder the aristocracy had gone the way it had in France. 'Begging your pardon, Monsieur,' she added, flushing as she noticed the presence of the marquis.

He laughed, 'I perfectly understand. But I do not think you can blame the princes for this monstrosity. It is most definitely post-Revolution, most likely even post-beginning of the war ...'

The promised refreshment arrived and soon it was time for Angelique to dress for her performance. The young marquis went off to his own apartment, now made ready for his occupation as relayed by his batman.

The officers gathering in the salon were beginning to congregate in small groups while they waited for their star to arrive.

Another aide, stopping to speak to the aide of General de Langue, clapped him on the shoulder. '*Bonsoir*, Maurice. Your man is looking very blue. I thought he would be as happy as a lark to have such an enchanting celebrity as a guest. What is the matter? Been repulsed by his latest bit of muslin? Or has he had his nose put out of joint by a better looking general?'

The general's aide nodded to him carelessly. 'Oh, a slight tactical reverse, a last-minute hitch: an underestimation of the enemy, one might say. But it is of small moment ... a tiny change of plan and we shall come about.'

'What? You mean you have failed to find a suitable wench to warm the general's bed? Shame on you!' he sniggered behind his hand. 'You could be court-martialled for that!'

'Shut up, you fool! Do you want to get us both court-martialled?' snapped the general's aide, walking jerkily away.

The other stared after him in astonishment. Nervous, that was what he was—nervous! It was not like him to bite at one like that. They often joked between themselves about the libertine propensity and sexual proclivity of de Langue. He shrugged his shoulders and went to sit in the gallery with the other aides de camp. Only the generals got to mingle in the salon with the beautiful soprano—the rest had to watch from the minstrel's gallery—an opposite in kind, when one thought about it.

There was a stir below and Mademoiselle and the marquis de Beaulieu walked into the salon. He smiled dourly as he watched General de Langue take the arm of Mademoiselle Angelique and introduce her to the other generals for all the world as if he were her fiancé and not the handsome young man walking behind them. Bird-like, he noticed everything: the restrained elegance of the marquis de Beaulieu, the way he seemed to reverence Mademoiselle Angelique. And what a lady she was: her golden hair with its glittering ornaments, slender figure enhanced to perfection by her floating white dress, a welcoming smile on her lips. And just look at the general spreading on the smarm, touching her at every opportunity, looking deep into her eyes as he produced each glib compliment. He looked from him to the marquis de Beaulieu, speaking courteously to the raddled wife of a general, and back again. *Yes, I know what you are doing, you old chien, but I wouldn't be surprised if you're caught out!* For his agile mind had interpreted the earlier cryptic comments of his friend.

Then Angelique began to sing, and he forgot everything except the glory of her voice.

Later, finishing the evening with a most electrifying rendition of the *Marseillaise*, she was very touched; for during the final applause, General le Mesurier stood up, motioning for silence. Bowing humbly to her, he said, 'I must thank you, Mademoiselle, on behalf of us all here, but especially for myself. Today I questioned in my heart whether we could win this war. I wondered what the point was of suffering the way we all have, for no apparent gain and many great losses ... But then, tonight, when I heard your beautiful voice, I realised that the Allies have a secret weapon after all; and I knew then that God is on our side, for he has sent his Angel of Song to inspire us in our darkest hour.' He bowed again.

All the officers stood, applauding vigorously.

Angelique returned his bow, tears streaming down her face. 'Thank you, thank you,' she whispered. 'You are too good ...'

§

Later, in her dressing-room, Angelique and Etienne chatted to the generals who, some with their wives, came with bouquets and champagne to toast their Golden Angel. There was conversation and laughter like any post-performance celebration. For just a little while, the horrors of the war receded; and she was a star adulated by her fans.

Etienne, surprised that General de Langue had not joined the group, wondered if knowledge of the clause had been too much for him, perhaps rendering him unable to face them in his disappointment.

As the last of the generals departed, expressing gratitude and compliments, Etienne was approached by General de Langue's aide.

'Monsieur,' he said in a hushed voice. 'There is an urgent telephone call for you, and there is no telephone in here. Can you come to my office to take it? It is your father, the duc de Belvoir.'

'Of course. One moment, if you please.' He went through into the apartment. 'Amèlie.'

'Yes, Monsieur?' Amèlie appeared in the bedroom doorway.

'I have to go to the office of the aide of General de Langue. You must on no account leave Mademoiselle alone! Is that clear? Stay with her until I return. I will not be long.'

'Certainly, Monsieur. I would not leave her.' She hurried out to the dressing-room, putting her head around the outer door as the marquis, ahead of her, accompanied the aide down the corridor. Idly curious, she watched him enter a room at the end of the hall before closing the door and turning to help her mistress out of her evening costume and into a fur-trimmed satin dressing-gown.

Angelique, seated before her mirror, was removing her headdress when she heard the outer door softly open and close. 'In here, Etienne ...' She turned in surprise, for the reflection in the mirror was not the one she had expected. 'General de Langue! I did not think to see you—at this time of night.'

'I am sorry, my little waterlily. I would have come to present my compliments right after your performance, but I was delayed by official business. Thus the burdens of duty, I am afraid. But I am here now to right this terrible wrong, my little dove, for I could not wait any longer to congratulate you on your wonderful performance!' The general, large and handsome, set down his burden of champagne and flowers; his voice and eyes caressing her as he lay one arm about her shoulders, drawing her hand to his lips, letting them linger on her fingers, pressing them to the soft white flesh of her inner wrist. 'You were adorable, my sweet. Utterly adorable!'

Then his attention fell on the maid, returning from her disposal of the evening gown. 'Get out!' he ordered. 'Take these flowers for Mademoiselle, and do what you have to do to them. Mademoiselle will not need you any more tonight, so you can take yourself off!'

'But ——'

'Out!' He practically threw the bouquet at her.

Amèlie was staunchly loyal to her mistress, and she had told the marquis de Beaulieu that she would not leave her; but she knew she could not stand up to a man of the cut of the general. She was aware of Angelique, shrinking and frightened in the circle of the general's arm, and was quick to recognise the signs of what was happening. *Like a bird hypnotised by a snake,* she thought. *Mon Dieu, this general is a fast worker—there won't be much time!*

The only thing left to do was to find the marquis de Beaulieu and let him deal with this debaucher—if he could!

Outside the door, she dropped the flowers onto a settle and ran as fast as she could towards the end of the corridor where she had last seen him.

Taking no more chances, the general strode over to lock the door, pocketing the key.

Returning to place his arm around Angelique's waist, he pulled her to him gently. 'Now, my sweet chicken, let me drink in your loveliness.' With his free hand, he tipped up her face. 'Ah, you are afraid, my dear! Do not be frightened.' His thumb delicately stroked her lips and cheek. 'I would not hurt such beauty. On the contrary,' he chuckled invitingly, 'I have come to take you to a very special party in my apartment to celebrate your first inspirational recital for France.' His hand moved to stroke her throat in the same languorous fashion, moving just a little further down the pearly column each time. His eyes held hers as he murmured endearments and compliments in a soft, intimate monotone, continuing to stroke her gently, awakening sensations in her flesh she did not know she possessed. Her legs turned to jelly, refusing to obey her. She felt hypnotised, afraid … Her mind warned her, but try as she would, she could not move away.

Oh, where was Etienne? Why had he left her? Even in her innocence, she realised the general had a sexual power that made one feel it was impossible to resist him. Too late, she knew that this was what Angelpapa had meant to guard her from, why he had taken the precautions he had.

'No,' she whispered. 'I cannot ... go to a party now. Please, no ... Etienne ...'

'Of course you can, my lovely one! I will not take no for an answer. I promise you that you will enjoy my party. Etienne is just a callow boy. He cannot give the joy that I can give you. Come, my little love, I will show you ecstasies that you have not even dreamt about, I promise you. Ah, sweet innocence ...' he laughed softly at her blushing confusion and moved his hand unobtrusively closer to his goal, holding her to his broad chest. 'Come, let me feel the pulsing of your heart. You will come with me to my party, hmm?' His lips just feathered her brow.

In the room at the end of the corridor, the aide was still trying to make the connection with Belvoir. When he first picked up the telephone, he had tried to get through, shouting into the mouthpiece, repeatedly depressing the cradle.

'Allo. Allo. Is that Belvoir? Allo. Allo. I am sorry, Monsieur, I seem to have lost the line.'

There followed several conversations with the exchange; the marquis drumming his fingers on the desk as, time and time again, he was told, 'Putting you through now, Monsieur' only for the connection to drop out.

Etienne, already uneasy about leaving Angelique and aware of a growing sense of disquiet, felt a strong compulsion to return. Only the knowledge that his father would not have made such a call without sufficient reason kept him where he was. Even so, he was strongly tempted to tell the aide to leave it until morning.

Hearing running footsteps in the hall, he looked out to see Amèlie urgently beckoning and grimacing from about halfway. Acknowledging with a gesture meaning her to return, he turned with one bound, leaning over the desk to grasp the aide by the collar. Dragging him across the polished mahogany, he hissed, 'Tell me quickly! There is no telephone call, is there?' He wrenched the collar tighter. 'Is there?'

The aide, eyes almost starting from their sockets, could not meet his. 'No, Monsieur,' he mouthed miserably, unable to speak.

Etienne flung him away, overturning the chair, running to Amèlie standing before the apartment door.

'It is locked, Monsieur,' she whispered anxiously.

Motioning her to stand aside, he threw himself at it, shoulder first, bursting the lock.

In a cold fury, he saw General de Langue with an arm about Angelique, one hand poised over her décolletage, snatching it away; his face a study in chagrined disappointment as the door burst open and he saw who stood in its frame. For just a second, the marquis looked so dangerous that General de Langue, unaccustomed to fear, stood aside from Angelique to have both hands free, ready to meet whatever was coming.

The younger man surveyed him with contempt. '*Eh bien*, General,' he said. 'Your aide has been looking all over for you. I think it is time you went to him, don't you? A most urgent communication: some kind of strategic failure, I apprehend.' He bowed in mocking condescension, moving aside from the door.

The general, taking the way out he had been given, left silently. Angelique, holding out her arms helplessly, whispered, 'Oh, Etienne.' Moving slowly, languorously, as if she had been drugged, she went into his arms, kissing him passionately, moulding her body to his as if she would meld right into him.

Sensitive to the fact that this abandoned conduct was the result of the powerful seduction technique of the general, a subtle nicety in him would not allow him to take advantage of it. '*Doucement, doucement*, my love,' he murmured, taking her arms from about his neck, kissing her hands and holding them firmly. 'I am sorry to have been fooled by the general's ruse. Did he hurt you, my heart?'

'Hurt me?' She shook her head in bewilderment. 'No, he did not hurt me. I was afraid, but I do not understand … He did not overpower me or … or force me, but it was as if … Oh, as if I had no will of my own. I did not want to obey him, but I could not help it!' She writhed in distress. 'Oh, Etienne, I am so ashamed, for I love you, truly I do! Please, please, believe me!'

Folding her in his arms, he held her close. 'Of course I believe you, my sweet, of course! I know that none of this was your doing.'

She pulled back to look at him. 'But—you do not understand. If you had not come when you did, breaking down the door … I think … I think I would have … gone with him to his apartment.' She clung to him, beginning to weep: her voice rising hysterically, 'Please, please forgive me! Please—do not leave me. Do not let him come near me—ever again! Oh! Say you will forgive me … please!'

He took the smelling salts from his pocket, holding her comfortingly, only thankful that he had not been delayed any longer. 'Oh, there, my poor child, hush,' he murmured. 'I have nothing to forgive, and you have nothing of which to be ashamed, *je vous assure*! These are perfectly natural feelings that you had not yet experienced, and which should have come naturally to you, gradually, through courtship with one you love; so that by the time you are married, you can abandon yourself to them with joy, as is right. But,' his voice hardened, 'the general knows how to arouse these desires in young innocents for his own purposes, none of which have anything to do with love. Only lust. By the time the young girl has sufficient knowledge of what he is about, it is too late and he has had his way. Then, through shame, she allows him to continue from fear that he will tell others what has happened:

blackmail, *en effet.*'

She calmed right down, listening intently. 'But, yes,' she said. 'What you say is true! I would not now—he would not be able to do it to me now—now that I know … And the shame of it! The shame—even though he did not— Yes, what you say is very true: the shame would have been enough … enough to …'

'There, my love, do not even think of it. You must not get upset again; it is not good for you. You must not feel besmirched by this. The general has a prodigious appetite for female flesh, and the resulting knowledge that very few are able to resist his advances if he makes a serious assault upon their senses, especially young innocents who do not know how to guard against such advances. But he is moving perilously close to a prosecution at law.

'Come, my darling, you have had a lucky escape,' he told her. 'And I am seven times a fool not to realise he would try a tactic like this! I see now, baulked by the agreement he signed, this was the only way he could have had you: that once he had seduced you, because of shame and his ruthless form of blackmail, you might have continued to meet him clandestinely. But it was a big risk! His ruse depended on him avoiding discovery before it was too late, and you keeping it a secret. We must be very grateful to Amèlie, my love.'

'Indeed, but …' Her face suffused with colour, she whispered, 'What will she think of me?'

'Why, only that she has saved an innocent maiden from a libertine. What else should she think? I believe Amèlie knows a little more about the world than you do, my dear one. Silly,' he chaffed affectionately. 'She is a witness, too, you know, of the general's attempted crime. *Mon Dieu*! He must have wanted you badly to have run such a risk of public exposure, for the censure of both our families and the marquis du Bois would have finished his career, you know. I have no sympathy for him, for he is a predator, but *du vrai*!' He ran his fingers through her hair. 'I understand why he wanted to make these advances to you, my dear love.'

'I understand he did not love me, that he is a predator, as you say, but he was able to make me feel ...' Unable to find the words to explain the inexplicable, she began again: 'With you, whom I love, will it ...' Blushing and hanging her head, she realised what she was asking him.

He smiled delightfully. 'The general has great skill in these matters, but I most certainly hope so, *Chérie*. Even better, because we love each other, do you not think? But, *alors*, it will be well to wait until we are married!'

He was silent a minute, playing with a curl. 'We should get married,' he said, slowly. 'It would be the answer—for I do not know the extent of his obsession with you. It would make it easier to keep you safe from him.'

'You mean: now?'

'Yes, why not?' he asked. 'As soon as possible, at any rate.'

'But to marry! For such a reason as that!' She drew back against his arm, distressed.

He gave her a little shake. 'Have I not been wanting you to marry me this past age! The general was not in sight then!'

'Oh, of course, dearest Etienne. But I do not want to be married in this terrible war! I do so want a lovely wedding with flowers and decorations and lots of guests and a beautiful, beautiful gown; and I want to come to you in beauty and happiness, and how can one rejoice and be happy in wartime?'

He smiled a little. 'With you at my side, I could give it a shot. You do not need all these trappings to be beautiful to me, my love.'

'It is very sweet of you to say so. How like you! You are always sweet to me. But I have this tour to complete, and it will probably last until the end of the war: It is my duty, Etienne! Please let us wait until the war is over, so that we can be happy—please!'

He sighed, saying with mock severity, 'Very well ... But you had better not kiss me like that again!'

She flushed vividly. 'I am sorry. I do not know what made me do that.'

'Do you not, my darling? Then all is as it should be.' He smiled and kissed her brow gently. 'Do not worry, my love, General de Langue will not come back. Jules and I will see to that. And now you must get some sleep.' He turned his head. 'Amèlie!'

'Yes, Monsieur?' Amèlie appeared, blinking in the light.

'Mademoiselle must go to bed now. You will take good care of her, *hein?*'

'Yes, Monsieur, I shall sleep on the sofa at the foot of the bed with a fire iron ready to hand. Let anyone dare disturb her!' she declared, adding with loathing: 'Men, I hate them. Vile tricksters, only after one thing! Not you, Monsieur,' she hastened to assure him, as she came to Angelique. 'Come, Mademoiselle, you must be exhausted. Let me help you into bed.'

'Carry on, Amèlie. I do not mind what you say. Indeed, you may have cause. You have acquitted yourself well; I thank you.' He did not see her bitter outburst against men as anything out of the ordinary, or realise it was connected to a chain of events that were, in a few short months, to turn the du Bois household upside down.

'Jules and I will sleep here in the antechamber since we cannot any longer lock the door, and we will hope that we all sleep well—with no disturbances. *Bonne nuit!*' He waited until the bedroom door closed behind them before directing his batman to set up two makeshift beds in the antechamber.

'We are going to watch over Mademoiselle tonight,' he told him. 'You will take the first watch and wake me after two hours, and I will do the second watch.' But despite feeling very tired, he mulled over the events of the night so that it was a good while before exhaustion overtook him.

Had they foiled the general's purpose? That was the

burning question. He tried to think of anything he may have overlooked, but could not. His mind wrestled with the problem, twisting and turning. With a little shock, he realised that the marquis had tried to prepare him for the general's ruse. Had he not said as much to him only this morning—no, yesterday, now—when he had warned him to watch her well? What had he said? 'Especially, tonight!' He had known! The conviction grew. He had known! *And I, fool that I was, did not heed the warning!* And it was true! All that was needed was a witness, for once the general's plot became known, it was automatically doomed to failure, depending as it had on secrecy.

Eventually he slept, waking too soon, to keep his lonely vigil, only returning to his bedchamber when daylight came and the servants were up and about.

All the next day, he stayed close to Angelique, who seemed to have recovered from her ordeal remarkably well.

'I am trying to make sure that I remember the words of all the new songs popular with the troops,' she explained. 'It helps to keep me calm.'

'Very well, give me the sheet. Now sing it to me ... Ah, beautiful! Word perfect, my love. I hear our troops are waiting anxiously for you to sing to them tonight. Our military escort will call for us after lunch to take us to the secret location.'

'I wonder where it is?'

'Unless we recognise the landmarks, we shall never find out, my love. They are paranoid about their secrecy—and rightly so. We must keep you safe, you know.'

Despite his precautions, there was no sign of the general; a circumstance for which he was grateful, for it allowed Angelique to set off for her unknown destination with unimpaired equilibrium, and he, himself, an opportunity to relax a little.

Their military escort had been arranged by General le Mesurier, whose aide accompanied them to the convoy.

'After the recital, Monsieur,' he said to Etienne, 'General le Mesurier has suggested we go right through to Paris, returning you home for a few days. Things may be going to get a little hot on the Front, and we want Mademoiselle well away from it.' He studied the decal on the vehicle. 'General de Langue has handed over the organisation of the inspiration of our troops by our Angel of France to General le Mesurier.' His eyes returned to those of the marquis. 'My company will be your military escort from now on. You will be contacted by me before each recital, and you and Mademoiselle will be conveyed to the venue by us. For safety this will be a closely guarded secret; although, you will be able to know which troops she will be singing to, so that she is able to adjust her repertoire accordingly. We shall guard her with our lives, Monsieur. You have my word.' Ushering them into the middle vehicle, he saluted before getting into the car in front.

Seating himself beside Angelique, Etienne took her hand. 'You will not be nervous, singing for the men tonight?'

'Oh, no,' she replied unthinkingly. 'Angelpapa will be with me.'

His eyes questioned her.

'In spirit,' she added. 'He is always with me in spirit when I sing. I think of him, and he is there with me on the stage and I am not nervous any more.'

'It is as simple as that, *hein*?'

'Yes.'

He kissed the hand he was holding. 'Then all is well, my love.'

Smiling, she repeated, 'All is well.'

He sighed and settled his head back against the upholstery. Giving himself up to the swaying motion of the vehicle, he slept, waking as soon as they halted to find Angelique still sleeping; her head on his shoulder.

There at a secret location, in a farmhouse somewhere

north of Amiens, they were given a meal and a room for Angelique to dress. She sang to *Les Poilus* gathered before a makeshift stage in a huge old barn. The French troops saw in her all that was good and sweet and innocent in the world. They saw her as brave and beautiful, and suddenly remembered why it was they spent their lives in grubby mire with death their closest companion; going without food, warmth and the barest of comfort to fight a brutish enemy that without compunction trampled these precious virtues beneath their iron-nailed boots.

In her voice, they heard mercy and justice and honour; they learnt that their lives were not taken by the enemy, but rather, laid down in glorious sacrifice for their loved ones: for greater love hath no man!

Visions came to them of Jeanne d'Arc, of the Winged Victory, of a glorious freedom. They heard anew the rallying cry of their republic: Liberty! Equality! Fraternity! And determined within their hearts that the enemy should not overrun them: no matter what the cost!

Etienne looked around in amazement at the animated faces. He did not know why he should be surprised, for he had many times felt and seen the inspirational effects of Angelique's voice. It was just that these men had been so beaten down, so sunk in gloom when she began that he himself had felt the heavy black burden hovering in the atmosphere around them. There was no doubt that General de Langue, brute beast though he may be, knew exactly what had been needed to inspire his soldiers.

However, it was not General de Langue but General Pétain who climbed onto the makeshift stage to thank her. As he took her hand, she shrank a little, for there was something in his piercing blue eyes a little reminiscent of General de Langue, but instead, he was courteous and grateful, addressing a few words of praise before turning to his men.

'Mademoiselle has shown us what we have been fighting for!' A great cheer arose. 'We will not allow *les*

Boches to take from us all that for which we live!' He raised Angelique's hand in a battle gesture of triumph. 'They shall not get past us!'

The men rose as one. '*Ils ne passeront pas!*' they shouted. '*Ils ne passeront pas!*'

CHAPTER SIXTEEN ~ THE DU BOIS PHANTOM

25 February 1916

Angelique is home for a few days, le bon Dieu merci; and I am proud to say that Angel's perspicacity has been proven. Angelique's presence at the Front has certainly made a miraculous difference to the morale of the troops. Alas, since then, one of the greatest blows to France has occurred. How thankful we are that Etienne was recalled from Verdun to escort Angelique! The Enemy has a new weapon: a femme formidable that is destroying everything in its path, even our greatest fortifications. Great buildings have been pulverised. Incroyable! In the midst of all this horror, Angel is busy designing a beautiful little bird of prey to fight back.

The marquis, learning of the reasons for their sudden return, did not comment but upon hearing that General le Mesurier was now in charge of Angelique's 'military campaign' swiftly drew his own conclusions.

'He tried, did he not?'

Etienne, who had promised Angelique he would not

speak about the general's attempt at seduction, was discomfited.

Eyeing his demeanour, the marquis, drawing even more conclusions, said surprisingly mildly, 'You do not have to say anything. I know that he did. But ...' His gaze was forbidding. 'He did not succeed!'

'No, Monsieur. Thanks only to you, he did not succeed.'

'So, you fell for his ruse, did you?' he asked, interested. 'What was it?'

Embarrassed, the young marquis told him how he had been duped.

'Yes, it was awkward ... I do not see how you could have done anything else. If your father had indeed been calling, it would quite possibly have been a matter of life and death. *Mon Dieu*, I would have liked to have seen the general's face when you burst through that door!'

'He was not pleased.'

'Well for him! You know, if he is not killed in the war, I do not think he will live for long after; if what I have heard about him in the last day or two proves to be true. No gentleman of honour could suffer such an assault on his young daughter without retribution.' He gazed regretfully down at his hands.

The young marquis studied him in meditative silence. With slight misgiving, he wondered if the other was suggesting he should have made away with the general. He did not feel equal to telling him that, in his view, conduct befitting a gentleman of honour did not include creeping up behind another man and choking him to death.

Of course, when he had burst into the room and caught the general with his hands on Angelique, he had experienced an overwhelming desire to put paid to his existence then and there. A scientific chop or two, roughly translated as the rabbit-punch, and pfft! That would have been that. But he had his own ideas on dealing with the general, and as the marquis du Bois obviously regretted, they had nothing to do with murder. He still had contacts in all the important houses and, after the war, meant to put the wheels in motion. He knew a certain highly placed investigator, Levandre, in the *Sûreté* who would be only too pleased to receive certain items of confirmatory evidence, especially since his young wife had been one of the general's earlier conquests.

Meanwhile, there were signs that de Langue would be increasingly ostracised from society until there would be nowhere for him to go except the proper quarter for such adventures: *les filles de joie*, who understood the rules of the game. And if he liked them young, no doubt he would find some backstreet procuress who, for suitable remuneration, would obtain them for him: young girls who had no-one to protect them. The irony of it tugged at his conscience. *Such is the morality of our time*, he thought bitterly. Then: *Perhaps the marquis du Bois has a case, after all.*

He spared a passing regret for women who had been forced into the dishonourable but lucrative profession, not by choice, but in order to feed themselves and their families in these hard times. Even such independent thinkers as Madame Dupont believed that the services of these ladies provided an outlet for the baser passions of gentlemen, thereby making an important contribution to the safety and comfort of their more fortunately placed sisters.

He shrugged. He had never been able to reconcile to himself the double standard in which this occult aspect of society flourished and was inclined, priest-like, to hold himself aloof from it, subduing his passions in the strict disciplinary code and exhaustive training of his martial arts, while he dreamt of the future with his chosen bride.

The other's voice recalled him to the present. 'God will dispose of the general, my son, in his own good time. I have no wish to pre-empt destiny. Now, tell me about the recital for the troops. How did Angelique perform?'

Eyes alight, the marquis de Beaulieu told him of the

amazing transformation of the troops from a motley bunch of defeated looking tramps to a united band of soldiers filled with energy and determined courage.

'Ah, so she *was* needed! The general may be the vilest of rakes, but he knows what is required to inspire his men. I am glad that I let her go; although, for a few hours there …' He fell silent, then he said, 'General le Mesurier is an honourable man. You will not have any more trouble. You have done well, my son.'

Later, Hugh came in with some very bad news. 'Word has been sent from the Front, Sir,' he said in a hushed voice. 'Verdun has fallen. They say the Huns ran all over us, taking Douaumont and at least two other fortifications.'

Etienne went white. 'My God!' he whispered.

Glancing at him, Hugh continued, 'They were not expecting an attack just there. It had been expected farther along the line. Douaumont had only a few old men left there to guard it. And speaking of Douaumont: it has been, to all intents and purposes, reduced to rubble. And by a woman, no less!'

The marquis was staring at him. 'Douaumont, you say … What do you mean: by a woman? What woman?'

'Big Bertha!' Hugh made a wry grimace.

'Ah, *femme formidable* indeed! I believe he named her after his wife. Or was it his daughter?'

'What, old Falkenhayn?'

'No, the Howitzer maker, Krupp.'

'His wife must be *femme formidable*, then. Or his daughter. Whichever it is, I hope I never have to run into *her*.' He shivered. 'Brrr!'

'I do not think so, Hugh,' said the marquis, with a thoughtful furrow in his brow. 'It savours of a certain lack of respect, does it not? She cannot be such a *femme formidable* after all, when one thinks about it. Otherwise he would not dare!'

'Too right, Sir! I mean, would you name our new little

pocket grenade after Madame Dupont?'

'Most certainly not! But this is hardly the time for levity, Hugh.'

The marquis, glancing significantly at Etienne, lapsed into a frowning silence while the young marquis, whispering, 'Douaumont!' stared at the secretary in shocked dismay.

Hugh, looking embarrassed, was about to apologise when he was interrupted by Madame Dupont, who, understanding what made Hugh react in the way he had, tried to explain, 'He is an Australian, Monsieur. Any time is a time for levity with them! Even in the hospital, literally with their dying breath, I have heard them joking about whether they will be greeted by Saint Peter or this ... Old Nick, I think they call him. *Le Diable*, you understand. I think it is their way of dealing with disaster, Monsieur.'

'By Jove, you've put the saddle on the right horse there, Madame. I am sorry, Sir, Captain.' He nodded to both these gentlemen. 'I'll take myself off now, shall I? *À bientôt*, Madame.'

The marquis nodded. 'Get out the new aircraft designs, if you please, Hugh. I have had another idea about them. I will be along presently.'

Etienne, repeating in an agonised whisper, 'Douaumont! Douaumont!' said, 'I should have been there with my men.'

'No, you should not!' Madame Dupont spoke sharply. 'Of what use is your corpse to any of us here, including Angelique? Why should your blood be added to already senseless loss of life? Besides, you are needed to take care of Angelique. Have you forgotten this?'

He shook his head, miserably.

She went on more gently, 'It is not your fault you were spared and others died, my dear. It is because you have not yet fulfilled your destiny. Angelique must inspire our men to hold out against this great wickedness, and your duty is to keep her safe while she does so. Has not your presence already saved her from … from …' Madame Dupont took a breath. 'From a fate even worse than death? Mourn your friends as you must, my dear boy, but do not feel guilty, because God has spared you for a different kind of battle.'

'Madame is right, my son.' The voice of the marquis was strangely comforting, for perhaps it reminded him of his duty to Angelique.

'Yes, I suppose so,' he said slowly. 'It is just that I feel that I have deserted them when they needed me.'

'The only difference one small company of cavalry would have made to heavy mortar fire would have been to increase the casualty rate,' replied the marquis, with brutal frankness. 'We must fight this war in a different way, as the generals are only now beginning to realise. It is a great blessing that you were not needlessly sacrificed, as were those other poor fellows.

'And now, my son, in lieu of your commanding officer, I delegate to you a duty, which I feel you will be able to bear tolerably well, despite the shock you have received. Angelique is waiting with the horses for your escort. Take her for a ride through the Bois and do not hurry back. There will be no singing lesson today.'

Watching him walk out, Madame Dupont's eyes filled with tears of sympathy. 'Poor Etienne,' she said. 'Poor, dear Etienne!'

The marquis stared at her in disbelief. 'What is this?' he thundered. 'Is he not alive? Does he not still have Angelique? I do not know what is wrong with you, Madame! *Du vrai,* you had better pull yourself together or we shall all come unstuck!' He wheeled himself out without looking back.

Madame Dupont stayed where she was, holding a handkerchief to her lips.

Over the design table, the marquis spoke to Hugh further about the news from the Front: 'It is a great blow to lose Verdun, Hugh. It pierces the heart of every Frenchman.'

'The thing is, Sir, that nobody expected it there. All intelligence suggested that it would be farther along the line. That is really why there was nobody there. They were all out in the trenches. Old Falkenhayn can't be the full quid, can he? Wasting all that firepower to shoot up a lot of concrete! And for what gain? The Frogs ... Sorry, Sir, the French, will take Verdun back again next week. Well, maybe not as soon as that but ... you know! General Pétain is taking over the French Command, and he is a very good man.'

The marquis nodded. 'And what about the rest of the Front?'

'It is looking very grim, Sir. Of course, if the Americans come in it will all be over in a shake.'

'A shake?'

'Of a lamb's tail, Sir.'

'Oh ... The Americans, are they likely to join the Allies, do you think?'

'Not at the moment, Sir. Our latest hope for aid was met with refusal by President Wilson to abandon the neutrality of America.'

'It will be difficult for him,' murmured the marquis. 'He has been obsessive about keeping his country out of the war.'

'Yes, Sir. Some say it will take a direct act of war by the enemy on America or her interests before he will consider it.'

'In that case, *les Boches* would be fools to try it,' he murmured, stroking his chin. 'But, on the other hand, perhaps we need not abandon hope after all, Hugh, wisdom not being one of the better known attributes of the Kaiser. Who knows, *mon gar*, perhaps the lambs will shake their tails sooner than we think.'

§

Madame Dupont, drying her eyes, went briskly to the

hospital as was her habit; for there she spent her days helping where she could, and every night in the pages of her diary, often with tears, she chronicled the dreadful progress of the Great War.

One of her lighter entries was concerned with the latest aircraft designed by the marquis and his secretary. Named the du Bois Phantom, it was now ready for its test flight.

They went to the airfield to watch Marcel Devereux, a contemporary of the fighter pilot Roland Garros, test fly the gleaming new aircraft, with its groundbreaking single wing.

The marquis sat in his wheeled chair, Madame Dupont standing on one side of him holding onto her hat, Hugh on the other watching an energetic young ground crew wind the prop to start the engine. Angelique was away with Etienne somewhere close to the Front, singing to the troops.

It is a pity they are missing this, thought Madame Dupont. Her attention refocused as the engine fired; the young man leapt clear; and the pilot, recklessly handsome in his flying gear, brought the engine slowly up to full throttle a couple of times before giving the signal for chocks away.

The little aeroplane, dancing impatiently in place, thus released, tore down the runway and sprang into the air, climbing and diving like an iridescent dragonfly.

Madame Dupont watched, heart in mouth, as the pilot performed the most amazing feats: pointing it straight to earth in a screaming dive, pulling out of it at the very last second to go up at an impossible angle, repeating the process again and again with variations such as spiralling down, side somersault, a *boucle à boucle*, flying upside down, dropping a wing to dart this way and that. Finally, with a salute and a waggle of the wings, he announced the test was over and he was ready to land.

As the plane neatly touched down and the pilot climbed out, the marquis commented, 'I have to give it to him, Madame. He said he would test it, and *Mon Dieu*! He has! Very thoroughly, wouldn't you say, Hugh?'

'Oh, he was very thorough, Sir. Very thorough. I wonder what he thinks of it. Flew it well, didn't he? Wore it like a greatcoat. I'd say if that little effort didn't find any chinks in its armour, nothing would.'

'Yes, very true. We shall soon have the verdict. Here he comes now.'

The pilot came up to them, goggles and flying helmet dangling carelessly from one hand.

'Well, Marcel, what did you think of our little Phantom, *hein*?'

The airman's eyes lit up. 'Beautiful, Monsieur,' he enthused. 'She handles like a dream. And fast, too! *Mon Dieu*! We shall give *Le Diable Rouge* a run for his money with this little bird! How long before she goes into production?'

'That depends on what you say, *mon brave*. If she is up to it or not.'

'Then I say: start tomorrow! No, even better: today! You want to come up for a fly, Monsieur, try her out? See for yourself what she is like? Come on ... *Oui*, Monsieur? *Bon*!'

The combined efforts of Hugh, Marcel and the ground engineer got him into the passenger seat behind the pilot. Madame Dupont, seating herself in his wheeled chair, thought he looked rather dashing in his flying gear as they prepared for take-off. Marcel took him for a joy flight, pointing out in mime the various landmarks, only doing a couple of side somersaults and a *boucle à boucle* before landing.

The marquis returned to the ground very white of face but with spirits unimpaired. 'An exhilarating mode of travel, Madame,' he informed her with a wry grin, removing his helmet and goggles. 'I shall find life very slow after this. I can see I shall have to modify my wheeled chair ...'

CHAPTER SEVENTEEN ~ THE CHAUFFEUR

20 March 1917

It is a sad fact, but it has been brought home to me, that something I have disputed is indeed the truth: the good young men are all at the Front being slaughtered. And those who are left are parasites on society. Or at least one of them is! Perhaps it is wrong to allow one bad apple to colour one's view on the whole barrel.

The war dragged on ... and on ... and on, anxiously monitored by the marquis and the duc. The Western Front moved back and forth across France, never quite reaching Paris: changing by the week, the day, the hour, as men of both sides fought desperately to regain lost ground. Positions lost by the Allies were retaken the next week. The huge loss of life continued, mourned by the world: young men willingly giving up their own lives so that others may have the luxury of freedom and justice.

The marquis acknowledged their valour, 'This generation of young men, Madame, they are God's finest sons. It is the greatest tragedy that their blood waters the earth instead of continuing on to other generations.'

'Indeed, Monsieur, so young, so young,' lamented Madame Dupont. But life must go on. That was what they all said whenever something particularly dreadful happened: life must go on. As if they could find no other reason to continue with the horror of their daily existence.

And still the US President, despite calls from many American citizens and blatant provocation from the German Empire, refused to allow his country to enter the war.

On a grey morning, when the marquis was working at his desk, the sounds of a female in distress provoked him into wheeling his chair over to open the door and look out. Slightly alarmed, he watched Madame Dupont put her arm around Amèlie—Amèlie who should be at Military Headquarters in Chantilly with Angelique!—and lead her into the morning room, firmly shutting the door. Hugh, crossing the hall, detoured around them.

The marquis beckoned to him, speaking first to the butler, 'When Madame comes out of the morning room, Justin, would you ask her to step in here, *s'il vous plaît*? *Bon*.

'Come in here a minute, Hugh. What was that contretemps in the hall, just now? What is going on with Amèlie? Why has she been sent home? And how is Angelique going to manage without her?'

'In the pudding club, I think, Sir,' said Hugh, answering one question at a time. 'Madame le Mesurier is looking after Mademoiselle.'

'What?' exclaimed the marquis, in disgust. 'Do you mean to tell me those incontinent scoundrels up at HQ have been getting at Amèlie?' His face darkened ominously.

'No, Sir. It seems it was the chauffeur.'

'Our chauffeur? Bouvier? I do not believe it! God's teeth, man, he is her father!'

'No, Sir, certainly not! Bouvier retired quite a while ago, about the time of Doctor Martin's arrival. He and Henri pretty much retired together. You were very busy in the hospital then, so perhaps you did not notice. He developed gout, and driving became too painful for him; so we got a new man, and Bouvier trained him. His name is Didier.'

'Didier? I do not know the name. He is not from the du Bois estate?'

'No, Sir.'

'All our servants come from the du Bois estate, Hugh. They are very loyal to us. Who chose him?'

'I did, Sir, but it was Hobson's choice, if you know what I mean, all the young men from the estate having enlisted. All I can tell you is that he was the best of a very bad lot. The good ones are all in the army.'

'I know it. What is he like, this Didier?'

'He is a good driver. Took to it like a duck to water. Looks the part, too: very handsome in his uniform. But,' he added, thoughtfully, 'he's a bit of an oily snake, I reckon. The female staff won't hear a bad word about him—been cutting a swathe through the housemaids, so I hear—all swooning over him and what not.' He shrugged. 'A bit too much of a lounge lizard for my taste. *But* he's always spot-on with the auto: on time and immaculate. As to his private life … I am afraid I don't know anything at all about it.'

'He is a relatively young man?'

Hugh nodded.

'Why then is he not in the army?'

'Well … dicky heart apparently. Although, with what he's been up to …'

'Indeed,' agreed the marquis. 'And I am of the opinion that we do not know the half of it! As to this weakness of the heart, there are ways of faking that: certain drugs, herbs and so on.'

'Yes,' added Hugh. 'And a little bit of something to grease the fist of the MO's clerk doesn't go astray either, unfortunately.'

'Hmm,' said the marquis, meditating. 'But … Amélie is a good girl. I made sure of that when I chose her to be

Angelique's maid. She comes of loyal stock from the château.' He thumped his fist on the arm of his chair. 'She is a good girl, Hugh!'

'Oh, indeed, Sir. Devilish straitlaced. I have heard her repulsing would-be Lotharios. Never takes any nonsense!' He shook his head. 'He must have got at her in some way, either through a confidence trick or got her alone and overpowered her.'

'You mean rape? I'll hang him out to dry!'

'Well, I wouldn't go as far as that, Sir. It is not always rape, you know. You will have to ask her yourself.'

'I intend to, as soon as I have spoken to Madame Dupont. And if it turns out that he has got her into trouble … Very well, he shall marry her,' said the marquis, as if that were to be the finish of the matter. But in the end, it turned out not to be quite as simple as that.

Madame Dupont came in looking very grave.

'Well, Madame? What is all this about Amèlie?' he demanded.

She shook her head. 'Oh, Monsieur, it is very bad. This Didier, he is an utter cad! He told the poor child he loved her, promised to marry her. He even gave her an engagement ring. And what a ring, Monsieur! It is either a very big fake or stolen! I think I have seen it before somewhere, but … I cannot remember …'

'Go on, please, Madame, we can deal with the ring later,' he said, patiently, for him.

'Oh, I am sorry, Monsieur,' she continued, her voice rising in indignation. 'And then, this plausible rogue seduces her, reassures her that if she becomes with child, he will at once marry her—citing the problems of wartime—giving her the old line of taking their happiness where they can because … *You* know, Monsieur! And of course, she becomes *enceinte!* I do not know why her mother did not warn her of this complication … But what do you think he said when she told him of her condition?' She looked from him to Hugh, expectantly.

'I do not know, Madame. We are waiting with bated breath to find out! Continue, if you please.'

'This canaille, he says that he cannot marry her because he is already married with children to support.' She took a deep breath. 'Twice over! Yes, Messieurs! He is already a bigamist! The poor child, she is beside herself!'

Hugh was looking thunderstruck, for once lacking a flippant comment. The face of the marquis reflected his thoughts on the matter, though he said nothing.

Didier, thought Madame Dupont. *At this very moment, twenty years ago, your life would not be worth the half of nothing!*

The marquis broke the silence. 'Bring Amèlie in, Madame. I wish to speak to her.'

'But, Monsieur, she is terribly upset. I do not wish to distress her further.'

'I will treat her gently, my dear. I want to find out just how he managed to overcome her scruples in this way … And there is the rather worrying matter of the ring. I would like to know why it did not sound the alarms for her that it did for you. Go on, bring her in.'

'Do you mind if I take myself off, Sir? It might be better if only you and Madame Dupont are with her.'

'That is very perceptive of you, Hugh. You may go out of sight, but remain within earshot. I wish you to hear what she has to say.'

'Very good, Sir.' Hugh crossed the room to sit behind a handsome Chinese lacquered screen, and not by the slightest change of expression could it be seen how unwilling he was; but as always, the whim of the marquis had a purpose.

'Amèlie, my child,' he said to the shrinking maid, 'I know you are a good girl, and that this has been a very hard lesson for you. I do not seek to add to your woes, but I must know a little more about what happened. Your engagement ring, for instance: may I see it?'

Wordlessly, she took it from the chain around her neck, holding it out to him.

For a moment, he studied the big square-cut diamond mounted in a delicate tracery of gold filigree, inset with diamonds and seed pearls; his lips folded in an uncompromising straight line.

'This is a very beautiful ring, Amèlie,' he said gently.

'Yes, Monsieur.' She gulped back a sob.

'You did not wonder how a chauffeur could afford such a ring?'

'Oh, indeed, I did, Monsieur!' The question seemed to galvanise her, and she answered robustly, much in her normal manner: 'I questioned him very firmly on it! "Jean-Michel," I said, "if you think to pull a trick like that on a poor country girl, you can think again! This ring is too good for the likes of you! I'll have nothing to do with stolen jewellery!" And I shut the door in his face, Monsieur. But he kept on at me until I would talk to him again, and he told me that he wasn't always poor; that his mother had been a Romanian princess who ran away with a lover her father disapproved of. They came onto hard times, and when she died, his mother only had this ring left, having sold all the rest of her jewellery—piece by piece—for them to live. He said he kept it in memory of his so beautiful mother and he said … he said …' She broke down into tears, making it hard to discern her words. '… that I was the only one he had ever loved enough to want … to give it to …'

'There, there, my dear … Hush, little one,' comforted Madame Dupont, putting an arm around her. 'I will take her away now, Monsieur. I think it will be best if I give her a composer and put her to bed.'

'Good. Then come back here as soon as you can. Amèlie, my child, I will have to keep this ring. You understand, do you not?'

'Yes, Monsieur, I do not want it. I realise now that it must be … *stolen*. That it was all … all lies,' she whispered, almost fainting with shock and distress.

The door shut behind them; the click of the latch

echoing in the silence.

'Well, Hugh, what do you think?' asked the marquis, turning his head.

'By the Lord Harry, Sir! If anyone wants dishing up, he does! He's a jewel thief, isn't he? I mean, as well as a bounder and a con-merchant and an out and out dyed-in-the-wool scoundrel! Not to mention a bigamist! Weak heart ... huh!'

The marquis was turning the ring this way and that, examining the stone. 'Hugh, can you remember anything about where he came from when you hired him?' he asked, delicately sliding the faceted edge of the diamond across his watch-glass. 'Look at that!' he added, holding out the watch.

'Not a mark,' said Hugh, squinting at the glass. 'Paste!'

'Yes, the diamond has been removed and replaced by trumpery.'

'Let me go and look in the file, Sir. The fellow had a letter of recommendation from someone or other, but just at the moment I'm blessed if I can lay my tongue to it!'

Madame Dupont returned just as Hugh came back with the letter. The marquis held up the ring. 'The diamond has been removed, Madame. Apart from the value of the setting, this ring is worthless. Ah, Hugh: how did you go?'

'I found it, Sir. The recommendation is from the bailiff of the comtesse de la Roche-Carillac. That is where he came from.'

Madame Dupont gasped, 'Now I remember the ring, Monsieur! It belongs to the comtesse de la Roche-Carillac! It was part of a set she gave to Katarina, only Katarina did not want the ring, preferring her own. And not so long ago, it was stolen, too! But you cannot return it to her, Monsieur! Remember how she came over here—she is gaga, poor old lady—demanding you return her stolen jewellery because of your magic trick with her tiara all those years ago? You remember what you said to her, Monsieur?'

'I do, indeed. I told her to remember that I had returned her tiara immediately and that if I had taken her jewellery, she would find it in her trinket box when she got home.'

'Well, don't you see? If we give it back to her, she will say you were the one who stole it!'

'Yes, and there was a lot of silver that went with it. I do not want to get the blame for that!'

'There is also the matter of that monstrous diamond having been removed from the ring ... and still missing,' added Hugh.

'Good God, yes. I do not want to go to prison at my time of life. You are right. We cannot return it!'

'Well, then, what shall we do with it?' asked Madame Dupont.

'Oh, I don't know!' snapped the marquis, flinging wide his hands.

'Throw it in the river?' suggested Hugh, tongue-in-cheek, vastly entertained.

And that was how it came to pass that a few days later, Madame Dupont, taking a stroll on a bridge over the Seine, suddenly stumbled about midstream, grabbing wildly at the parapet to save herself, a very beautiful ring flew off her finger and disappeared with a tiny splash beneath the water, inciting the sympathy of several good Samaritans coming to her aid.

But for now, there were more important matters to hand for the marquis, thinking of the du Bois jewellery collection he had divided between Madame Dupont and Angelique, he gave instructions, 'Madame, I want you to collect all the du Bois jewellery and any of your own and Angelique's, and take them to Cartier for appraisal. Hugh will go with you and discreetly explain the position. When you come back, we will decide what to do with this ... chauffeur.'

'Monsieur, you do not think ...?' asked Madame Dupont delicately, leaving the question unfinished.

'I do not know what to think, Madame. Hurry, we must know what has been going on.'

'Just as you feared, Sir,' said Hugh grimly, on their return. 'All the large stones have been replaced by paste, but the smaller ones in the settings have not been disturbed. Cartier has said this is not an uncommon occurrence these days, done by the owners themselves now that money is tight. But it is a fairly foolproof way for a thief to operate. It often takes a long time before it is discovered, and by then, the thief and the gems are long gone.'

'And Angelique's beautiful pearls you gave her, Monsieur,' added Madame Dupont, with a tragic moue, 'they are nothing but fish scales and glass!'

The marquis' lips tightened. 'Get Amèlie back here, Madame! *Mon Dieu,* but she has some explaining to do!' he commanded, adding to Hugh as she left, 'I cannot believe I was so far wrong about that girl, Hugh. Think you, she is the accomplice of a jewel thief? I cannot credit such a notion!'

'No, Sir, but she might well have been duped into letting him get his hands on them. Let us see what she has to say for herself.'

But Amèlie, when she stood before the marquis and listened to the charge, denied passionately that she was a jewel thief.

'We know that Didier had in his possession the ring of the comtesse de la Roche-Carillac, which he gave to you after having stolen the diamond and replaced it with paste,' he said sternly, watching her.

'The comtesse …' she whispered, turning pale, 'oh, no!'

'Did you give him or show him any of the jewellery belonging to Madame or Mademoiselle?'

'No! Oh, no!' she wept.

'Think, Amèlie! Is there any way Didier could have got his hands on the du Bois collection?'

She stood a moment, thinking, then her eyes widening,

she clapped a hand to her mouth. 'Oh, Monsieur, there is! I am sorry, so sorry!' she lamented. 'One morning before the tour, I was about to take them to Cartier to be cleaned and the fastenings checked, as I always do before we go. And I was very busy, off my head with chores. And Jean-Michel, he says if I wrap them up well in a parcel so that it cannot be seen what they are—so that nobody hits him over the head for them, Monsieur! Then he will take them to Cartier for me and bring them back when they are ready. And he did. And later he collected them and brought them back to me, and I thought nothing of it, except that I was grateful for his thoughtfulness. Oh, Monsieur … *Je regrette*, so much … But I did not know.' She had grown even paler and began to shake.

The marquis, observing this, replied, 'I will accept that it could be so, Amèlie. Will you allow yourself to be put under hypnosis that I may verify that you are speaking the truth?'

'Of course, Monsieur. I will be glad of it!'

He drew out the gold chain from under his collar. 'Very well, sit down. You see this locket …?'

Dismissing her afterwards, he said to Hugh, 'She is a thoroughly honest girl, that one. You noticed that nothing more came out under hypnosis than what she previously told us? I shall have to do something for her. You go and telephone the *Sûreté*, Hugh, about our enterprising chauffeur.'

The marquis, having sent for his head groom, came straight to the point. 'Ah, Jean. Come in, old friend. I have a favour to ask of you. Amèlie: you know her? She is in trouble. Could we find a young man on the estate willing to marry her, do you think?'

'I do not think so, no, Monsieur.' Jean rubbed his chin thoughtfully. 'Most of them are married or betrothed, and they are all away at the Front. But Bouvier's daughter,' he mused. 'I am sorry to hear it. She is a sweet girl: chirpy.'

'She is not very chirpy now, *mon vieux*. That canaille of a chauffeur has ruined her, unless I can find her a husband.'

'Oh, dear, dear, dear!' tut-tutted the groom, a long time widower. 'No young men ... Would an old one do, Monsieur? One would not like to think of Bouvier's daughter ...'

'An excellent notion, Jean. I will arrange it as soon as possible. Thank you.'

Later, explaining her future to Amèlie, the marquis was unusually gentle. 'I am sorry, Amèlie, we do not always get what we want out of life. This is the best I can do for you. It is not the end of the world, my dear. I wish to thank you for your presence of mind in acting in the way you did to help save Mademoiselle. I am sorry you could not do the same for yourself. Jean will be kind to you. Go, now.'

'Come, my dear, it is for the best. When your baby arrives, that is all you will think about. It will be well, I promise you,' soothed Madame Dupont, leading her away.

When she came back, she said to the marquis, 'You treated her very compassionately, Monsieur, and that was very nice; but you do not usually tolerate fools, and there is no question that she has been most desperately a fool.'

He focused his attention on a bare rosebush in the garden; a muscle clenched in his jaw. She thought he was not going to answer her. Eventually, he spoke, 'She was a fool for love, Madame. How many of us are guilty of that?'

'Monsieur! Monsieur!' The door burst open, and the chauffeur landed in a shivering heap on the carpet at his feet. 'Save me, Monsieur! The Military Police are here!'

Madame Dupont said in a vexed voice, 'Just look at this oily rogue rolling about on our carpet, Monsieur. I shall have to have it re-cleaned!' Making a small disgusted sound like an angry kitten, she left the room.

The marquis looked down upon him with distaste. 'Whatever may be your effect on the other females in this establishment,' he observed, sardonically, 'you do not appear to be cutting any ice with Madame Dupont. And she is a judge of men! And have you not heard of knocking before you enter?' he demanded, suddenly losing patience. 'Get up off the floor and get a hold of yourself! Now, tell me why, in the name of the devil, I should lift a finger to help you!'

The chauffeur, coming to his feet, lifted his head; and over his well-formed features, there came an expression of injured honesty, much as if one had pulled down a blind. The eyes, entreating, were mirrors of a deeply honest soul, as the man prepared to explain to his employer that he had been most dreadfully wronged.

'*Nom de Dieu*!' exclaimed the marquis, adding to himself, *I do not believe it! God's death! It is no wonder he fooled Amèlie! The plausible villain, he should be in the moving pictures.* 'I am listening,' he said, with hauteur.

'I have not done anything, Monsieur,' whimpered the chauffeur. 'It is Amèlie, all Amèlie! She has been using me as a blind, while she and her accomplice have been thieving the jewellery. I am an innocent cat's paw, Monsieur! Oh!' He clapped his hand to his head. 'How could I have been so fooled?'

'A wonder, indeed,' agreed the marquis. 'Tell me about this accomplice. A man or a woman?'

'Oh, a man, Monsieur, a small wiry fellow. He is very athletic. It is whispered that he is a cat-burglar.'

'*Vraiment*?'

'True? Oh, it's true, Monsieur.' The chauffeur nodded with emphasis, throwing wide his arms. 'As true as I stand here.'

The marquis touched the bell. 'I am sorry to have to cut short your performance,' he said, 'but it is time to ring down the curtain.'

'But, Monsieur, I have done nothing! What have I done?' he demanded, the picture of injured innocence.

'It is an impertinence to question your employer. Do you not know this?'

'Please, Monsieur! What have I done?' he reiterated. 'I have done nothing!'

'I am not in a position to know the extent of your iniquity, Fellow,' he replied. 'But since you ask, I will tell you that as far as I am concerned, you have committed the basest, most culpable of crimes: you have not been faithful to your wife!' adding, as the man's face registered genuine surprise, 'I will have no libertines in my establishment!

'One more thing for you to ponder while you rot in prison,' he continued. 'Had you been a faithful husband, it is quite possible that your other nefarious activities would never have come to light. *Adieu*, Monsieur. I will not say it has been a pleasure.

'Ah, in a good hour, Messieurs,' he said as several uniforms appeared in the doorway. 'I have here your criminal, all ready for you.' He looked hard at the Military Police.

'Thank you, Monsieur,' said an officer briskly, turning to his companion. 'Now, is that him? Right: you can leave him to us.' He blew his whistle and several underlings moved forward to remove the snivelling chauffeur who, taking a last desperate chance, made a bid for the window.

'Gotcha, you beggar!' said Hugh, thrusting his walking cane between his legs to send him crashing to the floor, several military personnel diving on top of him.

'Oh, well done, Hugh!' admired the marquis, adding under his breath, '*Bon voyage*, Didier!'

'*Eh bien*, the law has caught up with Didier. I suppose that is not his real name, though?' he said to the officer, as the others took him away.

'No, Monsieur,' agreed the man.

'Perhaps you would like to tell me, Major,' said the marquis, frowning at his uniform. 'Why Military Intelligence have seen fit to involve themselves in a simple criminal offence?'

'The man is a foreign national, Monsieur, a Romanian. It is just routine. Also, he is a notorious jewel thief wanted in several countries. Such criminals become automatically the business of le Deuxième Bureau. Have you lost much to him, Monsieur?'

'Yes, quite a lot of precious stones from the du Bois collection, but I suppose it could be worse, most of the settings are intact. I do not know what you are going to do with this canaille, but he deserves to go to the Front, to no-man's-land as a mine detector,' replied the marquis, only partially jesting.

'Not him,' said the officer. 'I know the type: he would desert straight away. We might as well shoot him before he gets the chance.' He winked at the marquis. 'We shall probably shoot him as a spy. It will give the firing squad a bit of extra practice.'

The marquis raised his brows. 'Not that they need it. *Du vrai*, I think you people have been a trifle trigger-happy of late. And will you not have difficulty with that since he is not a spy? Bigamist, jewel thief, confidence trickster and dishonourable rogue he may be, but—he is not a spy!'

'Oh, there will be no trouble with that, Monsieur,' he brazenly assured him. 'We will just say that he has been stealing military documents en route from you to the War Office, and using your auto to transport them to his contacts.'

Hugh, holding his breath, thought the marquis would explode, but he sat perfectly still.

'No military secrets have gone missing from my office, Sirrah—you may be sure of that!' he said through shut teeth; his voice vibrating with revulsion. 'But I know that the same cannot be said of yours.'

The major flushed darkly, unable to reply to this devastating truth.

His tormentor went on, softly: 'I think the establishment of the marquis du Bois could be said to be doing its bit for the war effort, wouldn't you? What you have suggested is a disgrace!'

The officer's colour deepened further, as the marquis continued, 'It is a disgrace on me and my secretary, but it is an even bigger disgrace on France and our military. As an honourable citizen of the Republic, it is my duty to point out to you that your attitude and that of your office brings dishonour to your country and will come back to bite you. Furthermore, I will tell you that you need not look in this direction for your spy. For, in the new language of electricity, you will be short-circuited there, well and truly!' He shrugged. 'You shoot him if you want, but if you do, it will be as a thief and a bigamist; and you must explain the severity of your punishment to the people. However, if I hear the word "spy" in connection with him, I will not rest until I have overturned your office and had the lot of you court-martialled—personally! Do you understand this, Major? Good!' his voice lashed like a whip. 'Then, your presence here is no longer required.'

The major, swelling up like a toad, took his dismissal badly.

CHAPTER EIGHTEEN ~ POWER CORRUPTS

22 March 1917

It is becoming more and more apparent that our Enemies are not all on the other side. Angel's effort to trap them has taken me back to days gone by. The things we have to do to protect ourselves in these terrible times! However, a new chauffeur and new hope in the battlefield is helping to keep our spirits up.

'They were going to fit him up!' gasped Hugh, when the affronted officer had gone. 'Frame him—an innocent man—well, you know what I mean ...'

'Yes, I know—he is no spy,' replied the marquis, absently. 'But it wouldn't be the first time they have done something like this, Hugh. Not by any means!'

'Alfred Dreyfus,' nodded Hugh. 'I heard about him.'

'Yes. And that silly woman, Mata Hari, languishing in prison for spying when it is patently obvious that she did no such thing. As I have informed Ladoux. More than once.'

'Might as well talk to a tree stump,' said Hugh, shaking his head. 'I don't know about him. I heard the other day that there was no real evidence, the charges trumped up.' he started, 'But good God, Sir: don't you see what this means?'

'*Certainement*. It means that there is an enemy spy in le Deuxième Bureau on the verge of discovery, and he is looking for a scapegoat. What is the matter, Hugh? You think you are about to hear of the marquis du Bois in the same context, *hein*?'

'It crossed my mind, Sir. There is no question that you got up his nose.'

'Got up his nose? Where do you get these charming expressions, Hugh?'

The Australian grinned and lifted his shoulders, remaining silent.

'Well, I don't say it is not apt. I'd get up more than his nose if I could. I would like to turn that office inside out—shoot a few of them! Starting with the minister … It would be a safe bet that we would then get our spy!' He became reflective. 'Le Deuxième Bureau—it stinks with corruption, Hugh. You know, as soon as I saw that officer came from there and not the regular Military Police, I smelled the rotten fish straight away … Poor old Dreyfus,' he added, inconsequently.

'Well, he is going up the ranks now, Sir. I wouldn't be surprised if he makes Lieutenant Colonel soon.'

'*Vraiment?* Then I am glad of it. Although, nothing can make reparation for the way that he was traduced, not to mention all those years in that hellhole, Devil's Island! But you see, the only reason it all came out that the accusation was false is that Alfred Dreyfus is alive and can speak for himself. They have learnt since then—and shoot all those they accuse! Who will be their next victim, I wonder? While the real culprit escapes justice—yet again. It is no surprise we are not winning the war with blackguards like that in positions of trust!'

'Power corrupts,' murmured Hugh.

'Eh, *mon brave,* it gives one to think,' replied the

marquis, sadly. 'When all is played out and history looks back on us, what kind of reputation will we have, think you?'

For a moment, the young Australian soldier looked into the stricken eyes of the older man. 'Sir,' he said. 'As in all great cataclysmic events, men are forced to show their true colours. Some will achieve the status of legend for their courage, brilliance and dedication; some will possess all the same qualities unacknowledged; others will be plodders doing their best; and there will be those who will be what they have always been—sewer rats. This day, Sir, I take my hat off to a legend.' He bowed before striding unevenly over to a chair.

The marquis made a deprecating gesture, lapsing into meditation. After a short while, he said, 'You saw the look on his face, Hugh, when he was telling me what he would do with Didier? He was warning me! He actually had the temerity …'

Hugh shook his head. 'I don't know what the world's coming to, Sir! But you'll have to be careful.'

'So, what do you think, *alors*? There will be a break-in, some important designs will be stolen and in due course turn up in the hands of the enemy? Of course, no-one will believe there has been a robbery; they will think it a cover for my treasonous activities, and you will be implicated, too. Yes, Hugh, we must guard ourselves well. I have an idea, *mon gar*. But first, we must warn Madame Dupont.'

When told of their plans, she listened without comment, saying finally, 'I will tell the servants they are not to come into this wing for the next few days, but are to spring-clean the hospital. They can stay there until next week to give the domestic staff some leave. Will that give you enough time, Messieurs?'

'I think so. I think if anything is going to happen, it will be very soon,' replied the marquis.

'*Bien*, Monsieur.' She hurried away.

'Hugh, do you think it is …?' he gestured

comprehensively.

'The major? No, Sir, I think it is his boss—there is something about him. This man wouldn't have enough imagination to do something like that.'

'Well, don't say it as if it is a fault, Hugh. We must be thankful that at least one of these canailles will be easy to outwit. Now, let us get on with constructing a few little surprises for any would-be burglar!'

'By Crikey, you must have been a bit of a lad, Sir! A holy terror, I'd say,' said Hugh in admiration, obeying his instructions.

'*Peut-être* ...' He smiled. 'You would have to ask Madame Dupont about that. She was the one I tested them on.'

'You must have nearly scared her to death, Sir. Any thief that comes along is going to think that all the devils out of hell have been let loose on him with this little lot we've got here!'

They sat back to wait upon events, which were not long in coming; for the next morning, when they entered the room to check it, they found their villain neatly pocketed in a net suspended from the ceiling and swinging above their heads.

'Ah, a catch!' exclaimed the marquis, observing him, critically. 'But only small fry by the look of it. Let him down, Hugh.'

'Let me out, Monsieur!' The man had begun whimpering as soon as the marquis turned his eyes upon him.

'Of course!' He waited while Hugh undid the ropes. 'This villain,' he said with relish, 'shall tell me all he knows. Tie him up in that chair!'

Hugh put a restraining hand on his arm. 'Sir, you cannot—you must not—torture him!'

'Hugh, Hugh, such a lack of faith!' marvelled the marquis, removing his hand and smoothing his sleeve. 'You are not thinking, *mon brave*. Put him in the chair—so!

'Come, You, look at me. You see this gold locket? Very fine, is it not? Ah, but it makes your eyes glisten. Watch it carefully, now ...

'It is not enough, Hugh,' said the marquis, replacing his locket inside his collar and viewing his comatose subject with profound dissatisfaction. 'He has told us a little, but nothing we can use. They have been careful to employ a go-between. *Eh bien*, you will take him and put him on the train with a ticket to Toulouse—a town very suited to one of his talents, I apprehend—while I write to the Commander-in-chief of France, warning him that there is a very big treasonous fly in the ointment of le Deuxième Bureau.

'Listen, You,' he said to his victim. 'You will accompany Hugh to the station where you will board the next train for Toulouse. You will only awaken when you hear the conductor call the name of the next station: Toulouse. You will not remember where you have been or what you have done. You will only remember that your masters will shoot you for failing them if ever you return to Paris.'

After that, apart from the junior housemaid being frightened out of her wits by the explosive manifestation of a truly terrifying apparition venting the most bloodcurdling screams (even worse than those of the housemaid, said Hugh) when she went to dust the picture hiding the safe (having forgotten Madame Dupont's instructions to keep away from it), nothing further occurred to disrupt the peace.

Madame Dupont, relating the cause and effects of this incident to the marquis—while Hugh, with a running commentary, reset the trap—added that she had found them a chauffeur. 'She is a young Englishwoman who has come to France to look for her husband listed as missing in action—such bravery and devotion, Monsieur!—and what do you think? She has found him in our hospital! The poor young man will be with us a long time: he has many

247

serious injuries. His dog tags are missing, and he has amnesia, which is why he has not been reported as found. But naturally, now she has found him, she wants to stay with him; so, as she was a driver in England, an ambulance driver, I hired her as our chauffeur. Her name is Mary. Mary Kent.'

'I hope she can drive, Madame,' said the marquis. 'At least the hearts of the housemaids should all remain intact.'

'Yes, and she already has a husband, so that's one less thing we'll have to do,' mumbled Hugh; his mouth full of clips and wires as he carefully set up the phosphorescent material to go off when moved.

'She must be a faithful wife, or she would not have come so far alone to find him. He is a lucky man,' the marquis added with approval, watching him work. 'Don't talk, Hugh. You are at a very delicate point. Now, move away very slowly—very, very slowly—that's it. Yes, there it is done: waiting for the next silly housemaid to set it off and fall into hysterics!'

'I think not, Monsieur,' said Madame Dupont with a little grimace and a twinkle in her eye. 'In my experience, one's first encounter with one of your nasty little devices is enough to set one to tread carefully for a very long time, indeed.'

§

Angelique, arriving home unexpectedly, insensibly cheered them up.

'Tell us who you've been singing for lately, my dear,' said the marquis, greeting her fondly.

'I have been singing for the British troops: the Tommies.' She laughed, merrily. 'They were very funny, and we had a good time. They call it "trench humour". They said it was a little like trench foot, only harder to put up with. I learnt some new songs, too, which I will sing for them next time. But General le Mesurier, he said to come home now for a little while. They will call for me in a few days.'

'An offensive?' The marquis turned enquiringly to Etienne.

'Possibly, Monsieur. There is usually something in the wind when General le Mesurier sends us home, but I have not heard anything directly.'

'Hugh? Have you heard anything?'

'Nothing concrete, Sir, but I did hear a rumour that they were planning some sort of an offensive on the Hindenburg Line.'

'I expect we shall soon hear of some more atrocities then,' replied the marquis, morbidly.

'Have you sung for any of our boys yet, Mademoiselle?' Hugh put in brightly. 'The Aussies?'

'There were a few of them with the Tommies, I think,' replied Angelique.

'Whence the joke about trench humour.' Hugh nodded. 'Do you know which regiments they were, Mademoiselle?'

'Erm … yes, I think it was one called the Bedfordshire Regiment, was it not, Etienne?'

'Yes. The Second Battalion of the Bedfordshire Regiment, and one or two others, I think.'

'Oh,' said Hugh, with animation. 'Then you have sung for some Australians, Mademoiselle, some pretty illustrious ones! In fact, that regiment is led by an Australian. He's a quiet sort of a chap—but that's deceptive—as good as a platoon by himself, so they say.' He smiled. 'They are famous, you know, calling themselves "The Old Contemptibles"—and hardly one of them a day over twenty-five!'

'But why?' asked Angelique, bewildered. 'Why do they call themselves a derogatory name like that?'

'It is just their sense of humour, Mademoiselle,' explained Hugh. 'Because they have been on the Western Front since the beginning of the war. I don't know the exact story, but it has its origins in something the Kaiser

once said—or maybe it was General Falkenhayn—
something about them being a contemptible little army.
You remember the Christmas truce of '14?' he asked the
marquis, 'Well, there's a story that they played a football
match with the Germans, until the ball hit an unexploded
incendiary in no-man's-land and went up in smoke!'

'That's right, they had a truce that Christmas, did they
not?' agreed the marquis. 'Everybody thought the war
would be over, "home for Christmas", they said. And even
though, here it is, still grinding on, Christmas or no, I
haven't heard of one since.'

'No, Sir, indeed. The brass have taken good care of
that! Very frightened, they were, that the lads would leave
their rifles down and all go home at the end of the truce;
and they took precious good care that it would not happen
again ... more's the pity. When our boys saw that the
enemy soldiers fighting in the trenches were just like them
and not monsters, it gave them to think somewhat.'

'It is the way of the world, Hugh, for good, honest
fellows to be the pawns of evil men; but I have never seen
the like.' The voice of the marquis vibrated with sadness.
'And I hope I never do again.'

He stirred, seeming to shake off his melancholy, and
addressed Angelique, 'So, my dear, to get back to Hugh's
original question: when are you singing for the Australians,
do you know?'

'I am singing for them next, I think. Is it not, Etienne?'

'What's that, my love?' he asked, still mulling over the
words of the marquis.

'We are singing for the Australians next?'

'Yes. Yes, we are.'

'That's the ticket, Mademoiselle!' said Hugh, heartily.
'Do you know which ones you are singing for?'

'*Mais oui*, it is the ...' she began, looking for help from
the young marquis.

He supplied, 'Ah—the First and Third Battalions of the
AIF.'

'Oh, Good-o!' he exclaimed. 'I have some mates in the third. They will get a real kick out of you singing for them, Mademoiselle. Some of them can sing, too—especially my mate Jack! He is a bit shy about it, but if you can get him to do it, by golly, you're in for a treat!'

'It is thanks to you that I have all their favourite songs, so of course I shall sing to your friends, Hugh.' She gave him her lovely smile. 'It will be my pleasure.'

'Thank you, Mademoiselle, that'll cheer them up no end. If the boss can spare me, I might come, too.'

'Boss, eh?' said the marquis, in resignation. 'Another *bon mot* of yours I have been meaning to ask you about. I only mention it because the last time I heard it, you were using it to describe a great villain. I suppose it is some more of your colonial slang, Hugh?'

'Yes, Sir. It means employer, or man in charge.'

'I am relieved to hear it!' he replied. 'But of course, you may go with them, Hugh. It will be good for you to see your friends.'

'Thank you, Sir.' He limped away, smiling. 'See you later.'

The others all smiled with him. Hugh was a character, almost like one of the family. Without exception, they were all very fond of him.

§

A few days later, Angelique graced the stage of a town hall near the Front, singing to the Australian troops, just as she had promised Hugh.

Towards the end of the recital, as the men sang along with her in the choruses, her ear picked out a fine tenor voice in the second row. It belonged to a fair young man wearing a sergeant's uniform. At the end of the song, she crossed to the edge of the stage and said to the man, 'What is your name, Monsieur?'

'It is Jack, Mademoiselle.'

'What would you like me to sing for you, Jack?'

'Do you know *Roses of Picardy*, Mademoiselle?'

'You wish me to sing it for you? Well, Jack, you have a lovely voice. Will you not come up here and sing this *Roses of Picardy* with me?' She rolled her r's endearingly.

The men cheered.

'I would rather sit here and listen to you, Mademoiselle. You're doing a good job. You don't need me.'

'Oh, come on, Jack! Your friend Hugh said you would be hard to persuade, but that it would be worth it.'

'Hughie, eh? I saw him earlier,' he replied. 'I might have known he would've had something to do with this.'

'Please, Monsieur ...'

The soldier sitting next to him dug him in the ribs with his elbow. 'Go on, Jack! Don't make the lady beg: it's bad manners. Half your luck, Mate!'

'I can hear her better from here, Percy, you numbskull,' he said out of the corner of his mouth. 'Have sense! How do you think I am going to be able to match a voice like that?'

'You'll do it, Mate. Go on!'

Angelique leant towards him, beckoning, 'Oh, come on, Jack. Please ...'

'Acting Sergeant!' roared an uncompromising voice from the back of the room.

'Now I'm in it! Properly!' he mouthed to his mate as he stood up, looking at him in comical dismay.

'In what, Mate?' enquired Percy; a devilish tilt to his eyebrows.

'Don't make me say it, Perce!' he warned, motioning to him to move over and let him out. 'Come on; put your port in the other hand.'

Unwillingly, he climbed onto the stage, crossing to stand with Angelique. He shook hands and bowed to her, nodded to the audience and began to sing, tentatively at first, and then, as their voices matched, becoming stronger.

At the end, under cover of the applause, Angelique said

to him, 'That was very good, Jack. Please, will you sing another?'

He nodded. 'I knew I wouldn't get off that lightly.'

Angelique addressed the men: 'Jack is going to sing another song with me. What shall we have?'

'How about *Mademoiselle from Armentieres*?' yelled a wit from the crowd, provoking a general rumble of protest.

'Oh, naughty!' said Angelique, her eyes sparkling. She assumed a thoughtful stance; head tilted to one side. 'I do not think I know that one ... What do you say, Jack?'

'I think it is your turn to choose, Mademoiselle.'

'Well, then, I choose ... *A Bicycle Built for Two*.'

The choice was approved, each chorus sung with gusto by the audience.

'The last song, Jack.' She smiled, enchantingly. 'What shall we sing?'

'How about *Abide With Me*?'

'Oh, yes: a perfect finale!'

They sang the beautiful old hymn that had brought comfort to so many, so often, in all situations. Tonight it brought even more comfort to those who heard it beautifully sung, for despite his fears, the voice of the Australian soldier blended perfectly with that of France's Angel of Song.

At the end, amid vociferous applause, she shook his hand and bowed. 'Jack,' she said, presenting him to the audience. 'A fine Australian tenor!'

Waiting for the applause to lessen a little, she said to him, 'Thank you, Monsieur. I am enchanted to have met you.'

'And I you, Mademoiselle,' he replied, returning her bow and jumping down from the stage with relief.

'Good on yer, Mate. Put it there!' Percy held out a hand; the first of many to congratulate him and show their appreciation.

The applause went on and on.

Jack caught sight of Hugh. 'I want a word with you,

Mate. There are a few things you need putting-straight on, and I reckon I'm just the bloke to do it.'

'I'll be back as soon as I've seen Mademoiselle and Monsieur to their car, Jack. Want to thank me, do you?'

'That's it,' he replied, a secret smile at the back of his eyes. 'How did you guess?'

§

Returning from his visit to the Front, Hugh went to the War Office, as he did every day, bringing back news to the marquis. 'Brrr. It's cold out there. By the Lord Harry, those Russkies are something else, Sir,' he exclaimed, rubbing his hands together.

'Are they so?' asked the marquis, inviting him with a hand to come closer to the fire. 'What is happening, Hugh?'

'Well, due to censorship and so on, I don't really know much about what's going on, but it seems they have left the Front and have all begun to fight amongst themselves. The proletariat, or whatever they call themselves, appear to be revolting against the Tsar!'

'*Tiens*! Have they gone mad?' Then he answered himself: 'No, they are probably hungry … *and* cold. Their country has very little infrastructure, and the distances are immense. The reckoning for the greed of the tsars has been visited on this generation, Hugh. Without a doubt! It is a great pity that they did not study French history. I hope it does not lose the war for us.'

'Oh, I hope not, Sir! But it is a worry. There's a new offensive being planned, too. An all-out assault by the French. Not sure when, but it is whispered. General Nivelle is the coming man.'

4 April 1917

There has come some wonderful news. A telegram from a country we had despaired of.

Hugh hurried in to tell the marquis the latest from the War Office.

'They've done it, Sir. News just to hand: The American Congress has voted to drop their neutrality. Uncle Sam has agreed to enter the war!'

'Thank you, Hugh. That is the best news I have heard for quite some time.' He was silent a minute, then said, 'I thought when the *Lusitania* was torpedoed in '15, they would have come in then, but no.'

'As far as I understand it, Sir, there was a lot of anti-German feeling over the sinking of the *Lusitania*: a lot of Americans were on that ship. But while the German submarines left their merchant ships alone, Woodrow Wilson would not declare war on Germany.' He made a moue. 'Although, we *did* have his sympathy.'

'A lot of help that was! And there were other ships sunk carrying Americans … *The Sussex* for one. But he is a very stubborn man, Wilson. I suppose one can understand his wish to broker peace. It is just not possible in the current climate. *Mais* … there is nothing like the threat of war over one's back fence to make one rethink one's position.'

'Ah, you mean the Zimmermann telegram, Sir? Yes, that *would* give one to think. That and the unrestricted submarine attacks on their shipping.'

'They have shown remarkable patience, have they not? How many vessels have they lost since January: six or seven?'

'Half-a-dozen or so,' agreed Hugh. 'The Huns have hit them in the hip pocket, Sir. Always a dangerous thing to do to a powerful nation.'

'Indeed, but the German command must have known that this would be a consequence?'

'Doesn't seem to have. Expressly ordered, apparently.'

The marquis raised an eyebrow.

'Because they believe that if they cut off England's supplies, they can starve her into submission!'

'Cretins! Did I not tell you, Hugh, that wisdom is not one of the better known characteristics of the Kaiser?' said the marquis, in triumph.

'Yes, Sir, you did, indeed. And thank God for it, I say. A toast!' he added, with a touch of his reprehensible humour. 'A toast: To the stupidity of the Kaiser. And the guns of Uncle Sam!'

The marquis smiled. 'Propose it at dinner. The trouble will be that it is going to be a while before they can get here, and anything might happen before then.'

CHAPTER NINETEEN ~ THE DARKEST DAY

17 April 1917

Whether queuing for coal at the Opéra Paris, staunching wounds at the hospital, trying to ignore rumours of defeat that spread like wildfire, we are constantly oppressed by the evil that has overrun the world. We, all of us, have suffered loss. So much loss, it is indescribable! And now: Our Darkest Day! Worse even than our worst imaginings. Angel will die, too. I know it!

'*Chemin des Dames,*' whispered Madame Dupont, her eyes anguished. 'No ... Oh, no! How can this be?' General Nivelle's assault was suffering serious reversals. In fact, if the news they'd had from the Front was correct, the battle was a rout from which the French Army might not recover. *More terrible injuries,* she thought. *How can we stand it? Is this how it is to end, after all that we have been through?* Then, she looked up to see a tragic figure swaying in the doorway.

'Xavier!' she exclaimed, dropping the paper to rush to his side. 'Oh my God, whatever is the matter? It is not Philippe?' She put her arm around him. 'Come and sit down, my dear. Tell me what has happened.'

'Philippe has been wounded ... not mortally, thank God. No, Madame ... not Philippe.' He shook his head in disbelief. 'But ... it is ... Katarina. She ... she ...' His words were lost in huge, racking sobs.

Madame Dupont felt a constricting pain in the region of her heart. Katarina: sweet and beautiful? No! It could not be! 'Oh, my dear. She is not ... dead?'

He nodded.

'But where? How? What has happened to her, *mon cher*?'

'I do not ... know. I went to wake her this morning, and I could not. She would not wake up, Madame. She would not ... wake up! Doctor Martin, she thinks it was a stroke.'

'Ah, very probably, since it has happened to her before.' Her calm demeanour concealed the turmoil of grief in her heart. Katarina had been closer to her than her own daughter. *But dead! And so young! Far too young! Oh, my poor, dear child!*

Her heart constricted again into momentary paralysis. *How can I tell Angel? He will be devastated. I am afraid that he will die!* She acknowledged to herself. *If I tell him, he will die!* But she knew that he had to be told.

'Come, Xavier, my dear. We must tell Angel.'

The marquis, seated on his day bed, looked up as they entered. His eyes gleamed with unshed tears, dark with grief. He held out his arms to Xavier. 'Ah, *mon brave*,' he said.

He knows! Thought Madame Dupont, feeling as though she had been kicked in the chest by a mule. *But, nom de Dieu! How does he know?*

Perhaps, one day, he would tell her how Katarina had come to him in his dreams and kissed him lovingly; had melted into his arms, whispering, 'Goodbye, my dearest love'. How he had awoken in grief, knowing she was gone; his empty arms aching for her. Or perhaps he would keep it in his heart and never mention it at all.

For a minute, Madame Dupont stood in the doorway, watching the two men grieving together, arms about each other before going silently away. None knew better than each of them how the other was feeling, and it was possible that no-one could have loved her more than either of them.

Philippe! Xavier had said that he was wounded, but he must be told at some stage depending on the degree of his injuries. She must find out where he was: either still at the Front or, hopefully, in their hospital. *And Angelique! She must be told, as well! Oh dear God, where was she?*

Setting aside her personal grief, Madame Dupont went to her bugbear, the telephone, to try to find the answers to these questions.

Over in the hospital, Matron was issuing her orders for the day, finally saying, 'Nurse de Beaulieu, you will meet the ambulance shortly arriving from the Front, change the soldier's dressings and make him comfortable in bed five, ward two. There is only one patient for us on this one; the rest have been sent to the Paris General. But do not get complacent, for I anticipate being overrun later in the day.'

Elise moved about quietly, collecting dressings, instruments, a bowl of hot water, placing them in readiness on a trolley by the new patient's bed before going out to wait for the ambulance.

'He's just gone in, Nurse. I was a bit early,' said the young Englishwoman driver, closing the rear doors of the van. 'A porter took him in. They went that way.'

'Oh. Thank you,' replied Elise, heading in the direction she had pointed. Ward three. She wouldn't mind betting she would find him in bed five, ward three, if it were not already occupied, someone having misheard Matron.

Sure enough, there he was, fair head drooped and turned to the wall, bandaged shoulder, arm and leg partially covered by the blanket. The bandages were soiled and showed signs of being hastily applied. *Oh, the poor young man!* Soon he would be more comfortable. Her steps were purposeful as she approached. Then he looked up, and her heart bounded wildly into her throat.

'Philippe!' she cried. 'Oh, Philippe, my dear!'

'Elise! By all, that's wonderful! Are you my nurse? Well, what a lucky fellow I am!' He put up his sound arm, drawing her head down to kiss her. 'Oh, my sweet, it is so good to see you. Mmm, you smell so nice.'

She smiled. 'You don't.' *But I love you ... I always have!*

'I know.' He made a moue. 'Mud, blood and mortar fire: a bad combination, my love. But that is your job, is it not: to make me clean and comfortable?'

'Indeed it is. But first, we must get you to your proper bed. I will get the porter.'

'No, wait! Let me look at you.' He detained her by pulling on her apron. 'Please, don't go.' He stroked the side of her face, tucking a tendril of hair under her veil. 'I love you,' he whispered. 'I thought I would never see you again. Please, kiss me once more.'

'I cannot, Philippe. It is not allowed.' She took his hand, bringing it to her lips. 'Oh, I am so thankful you are alive!' She bent towards him.

'Nurse! How dare you! What do you think you are doing?' Matron, whom everyone always felt to be the administrator of the wrath of the Almighty, glared at them in arctic surprise.

Philippe held Elise's hand tightly. '*Doucement*, Matron. You happen to be addressing my fiancée.'

'I beg your pardon, Monsieur, but,' she replied, freezingly, 'since Nurse de Beaulieu is employed in this hospital, I know that to be a lie.'

'Do you, *alors*?' he drawled, tugging Elise's hand to gain her attention, murmuring, 'You will marry me, will you not?' The bright blue eyes both commanded and entreated her. 'Quickly, say yes.'

She nodded.

'There you are, Matron. It is all true. A man must be allowed to kiss his fiancée.'

'Oh, what utter brass-faced cheek!' Matron, rocked off her balance, recovered quickly. 'Not in my hospital, Monsieur, *if* she happens to be his nurse! Nurse de Beaulieu, go to my office, at once!'

Philippe, a previously healthy young man, unused to the absolute autocracy of the matriarch of a hospital, struggled to sit up. 'Now, see here, Matron ...' he began.

Madame Dupont, an astonished witness to the last of this tableau, put out a detaining hand as Elise rushed past her.

'Stay, my dear. You will be needed here. Philippe, dear boy, do not try to sit up. You will only start your wounds bleeding again. Let Elise look after you. Matron, a word in your ear, if you please!' She nodded significantly, taking her aside to whisper a few urgent phrases.

Matron swept the room with one fulminating glance. 'You may attend to your patient, Nurse. Come along, Madame Dupont. We shall speak over coffee in my office.'

She glided regally away, followed a little later by Madame Dupont after she had warmly greeted Philippe, saying she would be back.

'Whew, what a dragon!' said Philippe, laying back on his pillows and submitting to Elise's ministrations. 'It was fortunate that Godmama came along just then. She soon sorted her out!'

'Thank you for saying we were engaged, Monsieur. I know you only did it to get me out of trouble.' Elise kept her attention on the wound she was dressing.

He looked at her. 'Is that what you think? No, I did not! And what is this: Monsieur? You know my name! No, Elise, I want to make it real. Look at me, my love ... Say you want it to be real, too.' He drew in his breath with a grimace. 'Oh! That spot is a little tender!'

'I am sorry.' She loosened the bandage. 'Is that better?'

'Thank you, yes ... But you have not answered me.'

'But ... What about Mademoiselle de Mirabeau?' It had almost broken her heart when, before the war, he had shown a preference for the stately beauty.

'Who? Oh ... her. She was just a passing phase, a forgotten infatuation of callow youth,' he replied, recalling with a twinkle, 'it was the fashion to languish at her feet, you know. Besides, the marquis du Bois set me straight about her, so he did!' He touched her hand. 'I think it has always been you, my darling. Always. Come now, we are still engaged, are we not?'

'Of course, Philippe. I know Papa will approve.'

'Well ...' He studied his bandaged limbs. 'We had better keep it between ourselves until I heal a little more. Your father couldn't, in all conscience, approve a crock like this!'

She laughed. 'Of course, he will! You are a hero! We will tell him as soon as he comes back from Belvoir. There. All done. *Now*, you smell nice,' she said, collecting up the soiled dressings for disposal. 'I must go, for I have to report to Matron,' she added, grimacing as she went to knock timidly on the door of her office.

To her surprise, Matron, still closeted with Madame Dupont, spoke to her kindly, listening attentively to her report. She looked at Madame Dupont, nodding. 'Yes, he will be well enough today to withstand the shock, Madame.'

Elise looked startled. 'Madame?'

'My child ...' Madame Dupont hastened to explain. 'Philippe's mama has passed away unexpectedly during the night, and he must be told of it. I shall tell him, but I need you to stay with him and comfort him. Can you do that?'

'Yes, Madame. But ...' She glanced nervously at Matron.

'All your other duties are suspended, my dear. Your only responsibility until further notice is to Major de Villefontaine,' said Matron, inclining her head sympathetically.

Elise could not believe her eyes and ears: Matron, that dreadful martinet, was actually being kindness itself! 'Th-

thank you, Matron,' she stammered, effacing herself; her only thought for Philippe.

'I shall come with you, my child.' Madame Dupont rose from the table, thanking Matron for her hospitality.

When she had gently broken the sad news, Philippe just said, 'Maman!' and closed his eyes, tears squeezing out from under his lashes.

Madame Dupont touched his hand. 'One day, my son, instead of railing against the fates for the short while we had her with us, we will know that we were privileged to have had her, at all.'

Leaving him to grieve with Elise, she went back to her study. The comte and the marquis had each other, Philippe had Elise; she felt she could safely leave Etienne to tell Angelique, having given him the sad tidings over the telephone. Their respective commanding officers would break the news to the other two boys, and no doubt, if possible, they would be given leave. Who did she, Madame Dupont, have? She sat down with her diary to grieve alone.

A little later, tears suspended, she snapped upright. She had a funeral to arrange.

The duchesse, hearing the news, sent her condolences to the marquis via Madame Dupont and went to visit Philippe. Finding him with Elise in attendance, she glanced from one to the other in bright-eyed comprehension, before taking his hand and speaking to him with great kindness and sympathy over the loss of his mother.

When she took her leave, she said, 'I have no fears about leaving you in the tender care of my daughter. She is a very good nurse.'

'Do you think ——?' asked Philippe, watching her weave her graceful way between the beds.

'Oh, yes.' Elise nodded. 'She only had to look at us. Mother is like that. But she won't say anything.'

'No?'

'You will see: she will leave it to us.'

'We will have to be quiet about it. Because of ...

Maman,' he said, picking at his quilt. 'There is still the funeral, and I will not be able to go.'

'No, I am sorry. But your maman would understand.'

Philippe clasped her hand gratefully and said no more.

The funeral of the comtesse de Villefontaine was a sad and trying occasion for all who loved her. It was almost as if it symbolised the mourning for all those taken too young. When it was over, the comte, having commissioned copies of her portrait for all his children, shut himself away from the world, refusing all contact. Madame Dupont, respecting his right to grieve as he saw fit, went along with his wishes and stayed away.

Believing that the marquis, too, would die now that he had lost Katarina, she waited anxiously for him to show signs of failing. Amazingly, though he seemed to shrink a little and go into a morbid depression for a short time, he maintained his level of health. She realised then that he was trying to stay strong to honour his promise to Angelique that he would be with her when she sang. *Thank God for Angelique*, she thought, *for if it were not for her, he would be dead by now.*

Hugh, making one of his daily reports of the battle was also witness to this fit of *désespoir*. 'They shot up our tanks, Sir. Their heavy artillery was too much for us.'

'But did we not allow for that in our design?'

'*We* did, Sir,' said Hugh, with significant emphasis. 'But Military Engineering used lighter steel plate. They said our specifications made the tanks too heavy and slow.'

The marquis lay his head down on the desk. 'Go away, Hugh,' he said, his voice muffled. 'I cannot deal with this now.'

CHAPTER TWENTY ~ FRAMED

26 June 1917

Today we have had the greatest news. It is hard not to be bitter that it has not happened sooner. At the same time, there is a traitor in le Deuxième Bureau, looking for someone to frame!

Angelique continued to sing for the troops, but she was at home more often now as the Allies mounted increasing offensives against the enemy, gaining strength because, finally, the Americans had arrived at the Western Front. As Hugh, bringing the welcome news to the marquis, explained in his jocular way, 'It has finally happened, Sir: Uncle Sam has put boots on the ground. Their troops are here: in France.'

'Thank you, Hugh. It is about time, *bien sûr*. But will there be enough of them to make a difference?'

'Probably not, at first, Sir. But they have the capacity to keep 'em coming.'

'Indeed, yes.' The marquis smiled. 'Now I want you to go to the hospital and pass on the message to Madame Dupont and the patients. A little good news will work wonders for them.'

He sat for long after Hugh had gone, lost in melancholy. At last, America had troops on French soil; too late for hundreds of thousands of fine young soldiers; too late for Katarina … He put his head down on the desk and wept. As he had not yet been able to do.

Madame Dupont, coming in late, found him sitting in the dark. Lighting a lamp, she saw that he had reached a catharsis and did not probe. 'Dinner will be a little late, tonight, Monsieur, I am sorry. But I must thank you for sending Hugh over to the hospital with the good news. It has given the patients heart.'

He made a deprecating gesture. '*De rien*, Madame! I am not hungry. I thought you would be happy with such tidings. Perhaps it will encourage us all.'

'Indeed, Monsieur. You have heard from Angelique today? Where is she?'

'At GQG. She telephoned to say she will be here tomorrow for a short visit: one night only.'

'This is all so hard on her,' she said. 'It will be good to think the end is in sight, and we can all get back to normal.'

'Normal?' he scoffed. 'What is normal?'

After so many years, it was a good question. Madame Dupont, having no answer, did not reply.

The initial optimism that the advent of the Americans would very quickly end the war was doomed to disappointment as it dragged on in a brutal hand-to-hand combat that went on and on as the Allied Forces slowly flushed the German invaders out of their trenches; although, there was the general feeling that the Germans were now on the back foot.

§

Madame Dupont, entering the gates after having been out shopping, was surprised by a military contingent marching down the carriage drive. She met them at the front door, brows raised in cool enquiry, yet her heart pounding with fear. Just as, all those years ago, she had recognised danger for Angel and had taken the necessary steps to save him, she recognised it today and knew, deep in her heart, that this time she was helpless.

'We have a mandate to arrest the marquis du Bois.'

'What?' she gasped. '*What* did you say, Lieutenant?'

The officer obligingly repeated his statement.

'But ... whatever for?'

'We shall tell that to the marquis du Bois, if you will be so obliging as to move out of the doorway, Madame.'

'No, no. There must be some mistake. The marquis is an invalid in a wheeled chair. He cannot have done anything. You cannot take him away to prison; he needs specialist care!'

'He will be placed under house arrest, Madame. The office of le Deuxième Bureau is fully cognisant of his disabilities.'

'Le Deuxième Bureau? No!' Her eyes dilated. So, this was to be his reward for insulting the major. 'You have made a very big mistake, Monsieur!' The officer stepped back from her regard as she declared, 'The marquis du Bois was never a spy! You cannot do this!' Her eyes condemned all of them, several shifting their feet uncomfortably and all avoiding her glance. 'The marquis du Bois is a patriotic citizen. Perhaps you do not know just how much he has given to our country for the war effort. Oh, you cannot do this!'

'Out of the way, Madame!' Averting his eyes, the lieutenant put her roughly aside and proceeded to enter the hall. His men followed guiltily, hanging their heads.

The marquis du Bois, impelled by some unknown presentiment, awaited them by the door. 'The military has gone down the hill a long way,' he observed, tightly. 'To treat a lady in that fashion, Sirrah. What do you want?'

'Oh, Monsieur,' quavered Madame Dupont. 'They have come to arrest you.'

He made the connection instantly. 'Oh, so I am a spy now, am I? Hah! I thought as much! House arrest?' he jeered. 'What: shall you put hobbles on my wheeled chair?'

The formalities were quickly in place.

'It is not much different to usual, Madame,' he told her after one look at the misery in her eyes. 'It is not as if I ever go anywhere. Just ignore the guard on the door. We shall come about.'

Filled with misgiving, she telephoned Etienne at GQG, informing him of the arrest of the marquis and all that had gone before. They agreed it would be best to keep it from Angelique and not let her come home while the house was under guard. The threat to her guardian would be too much for her fragile constitution, and she would not be able to sing. And France depended on her ability to sing.

Then a day was set for the court martial—only weeks away. Madame Dupont, with a sensation that she was slowly drowning, felt she must do something, anything, and sought an audience with the Commander-in-chief of France. She was persistent, and finally an aide let her in.

'The commander is not in, Madame. He is extremely busy at the moment. You may tell me what your difficulty is, and I will pass it on to him.'

She did her best to explain but felt he had not grasped the import of it. When he had assured her soothingly for the fourth time that the Administrators of France would not allow such a miscarriage of justice, she gave up, only begging him to bring the matter to the attention of the commander, which he assured her he would do.

The afternoon before the court martial, Madame le Mesurier, a very kind, but extremely silly woman, was fussing over Angelique, doing her hair and helping her into her evening gown, speaking to her in soft, motherly tones: 'I am so sorry about what is happening to your guardian, my dear,' she crooned sympathetically. 'I do admire you so. I think it amazing that you can still go out and perform as if nothing has happened, with all that hanging over his head. I know I could not!'

'But what do you mean? All *what* hanging over his head? Has something happened to Angelpapa?' She gripped the other's arms, urgently. 'You must tell me!'

'Gently, my dear, you are hurting me,' gasped Madame le Mesurier.

'Tell me! You must tell me!' The intensity of the amethyst gaze was disconcerting. 'You have to tell me!' Angelique, eyes dilating, began to shake all over.

Frightened, Madame le Mesurier decided she would have to obey. 'I am sorry, my dear. I thought you knew. He has been arrested as a spy, and his trial is tomorrow. But you must not worry, dear child,' she assured her. 'My dear husband is going, and he will very quickly put a stop to it.'

But she spoke to the empty air, for Angelique, shrieking, 'No! He will be shot! No! No! Etienne! Etienne! Oh! Oh! Oh-h-h!' had fainted at her feet.

Madame le Mesurier, staring aghast at the girl on the floor fighting for breath, ordered her maid to fetch the doctor, before collapsing onto the carpet beside her.

The young marquis, entering the room to find the doctor bending over a sedated Angelique on the bed with a glassy-eyed Madame le Mesurier propped up on the chaise longue at the foot, asked an anxious question, smoothing his beloved's hair.

'I do not know, Monsieur,' replied the doctor, tersely. 'But she has received a very deep-seated shock. They both have. Mademoiselle will not sing tonight. You had better tell the general. Leave her: I have given her a sedative, and she will not awaken before morning. We may get something out of Madame le Mesurier in about half an hour. She appears to be coming round. Otherwise it will remain a mystery.'

Etienne, knowing that somehow or other, despite their precautions, Angelique had been told of the trial facing her guardian, went off to relay the bad news to General le

Mesurier; and on the way back, detoured to telephone his father.

CHAPTER TWENTY-ONE ~
KANGAROO COURT

23 July 1917

How can they do this to Angel? After all that he has done for his country! I am so afraid that they will kill him. And all because of a traitorous coward! This trial is a sham! I may have said this before, in the treatment of Alfred Dreyfus, but I cry shame on our so-called justice system!

It was early in the morning. The court of the military echoed now and again with footsteps, as the three accusers, three generals and various members of the military, the court orderlies, and Madame Dupont and Hugh, crossed to their seats.

The marquis du Bois, brought to the court in the back of his redesigned and refurbished ambulance van, was wheeled in by two guards to an empty space near the dock. Two orderlies brought over a small table and placed it in front of him. He let his gaze wander mockingly around the courtroom, travelling past his accusers to fasten on General de Langue, momentarily darkening before moving on to the bench. He lifted a salutatory eyebrow to Madame

Dupont and Hugh before resuming his leisurely scrutiny of his accusers.

Madame Dupont, with a sensation of being in the depths of a particularly miasmic nightmare, felt as if she could hardly breath. Another set of footsteps echoed, and the duc de Belvoir stood at her side, holding her elbow in a sustaining grip. He crossed to shake the hand of the marquis, exchanging a few words with him, before sitting down with her. She was amazed at the comfort his benevolent presence brought to her; an element of surprise that he had come, lifting her momentarily out of her despair. Following the gaze of the marquis to the three generals, she saw that General LeClerc was looking worried, General le Mesurier miserable, but General de Langue sat with a triumphant light in his eye and a little pleasurable smile on his lips.

The court proceeded. The marquis, a frail but imposing presence in his wheeled chair, answered with a quiet dignity and an indefinable air of authority that made those close to him think uneasily of Nemesis, the Goddess of retribution, though they could not have said why: there being nothing feminine in his aspect.

The chief accuser spoke, 'We have evidence, Monsieur, of your complicity in a plot to sell military designs to the enemy. Furthermore, we suspect the complicity of your, er … *companion*, Madame Dupont.'

Tiens, she thought distractedly, *he makes it sound as if I am the veriest harlot!*

'And your secretary, Lieutenant Hugh Watson,' he added smoothly.

The brows of the marquis drew together. 'Messieurs, I hold Madame Dupont, the relict of my greatest friend, in the highest esteem. But as my dependant, she bows to my authority. The same is to be said of all those who are employed in my household, including my secretary. Any charge you wish to aim at me must not include them, for they simply obey my orders since, as you can see, my illness forces me to delegate many things I would once have done myself.'

The presiding judiciary spoke dryly, 'This court will be the judge of that, Monsieur: and if it sees fit, they will both be detained while we determine the evidence for it.'

Madame Dupont fixed her level gaze on his face. He seemed to be alight with some kind of inner excitement. His eyes were bright, mocking. *Secretly laughing at us,* she thought. Her heart jerked. *Mon Dieu, it is him! He is the one! The spy! Oh, the evil beast!*

'You speak of evidence, Monsieur,' replied the marquis. '*Eh bien,* show me this evidence.'

'In good time, Monsieur. The court will proceed. The court has two damning pieces of evidence, which will prove that you, the marquis du Bois, are a spy.' He signed to the chief prosecutor, who picked up a sheet of drawing paper. Rather grubby and slightly tattered, it showed signs of having first been crumpled and then ironed to smooth it out. Handing it over the bench, he bade the court orderly take it to the marquis.

The marquis, first looking at the paper, raised disbelieving eyes to the prosecutor. Astonishment coloured his voice: 'This? … This is your evidence? This piece of drawing paper?'

'Do you deny it is in your hand?'

'No, why should I? It is only a draft of a prosthesis for a patient. I made an error in a measurement and discarded it, starting again on a fresh sheet. It is hardly a damning piece of evidence,' he said, tossing it onto the floor.

The orderly, his face impassive, retrieved it and returned it to the prosecution bench.

'It is a design for a gasmask,' said the prosecutor, sternly, 'that you were going to sell to the Germans to protect them from a deadly gas you had already manufactured for them.'

The marquis' jaw dropped. 'You are jesting, surely! You cannot possibly be serious!' He waved an impatient hand.

'I do not know how you dare to make a statement like that on such a frivolous piece of "evidence". You must see that you, the prosecution, are laying yourselves open to be charged for false arrest on such flimsy pretension.'

'We have other evidence, Monsieur,' said the prosecutor, shortly, flushing a little as he sent it over. 'And this time do not throw it onto the floor.'

The marquis stared at it in fulminating silence. Then he said to the prosecutor, 'No doubt your imagination will be lurid enough to explain in what way this piece of notepaper can possibly be damning to me?'

'Certainly, Monsieur,' purred the prosecutor. 'Both pieces of evidence were found in the pocket of a German spy. Together!' he added with satisfaction. 'Both your formula for your poison gas and its protective mask.'

The marquis snapped. His tolerance for fools, at all times tenuous, had reached its slender limit. 'But what is all this?' he shouted, enraged. 'This is a shopping list of ingredients ordered by my hospital apothecary to make up his medicines! How could that be in the pocket of a German spy? It is not even in my handwriting!'

The prosecutor, beginning to say that the court would arrest the apothecary, also on suspicion of being an accomplice, was drowned out by the marquis.

'Cretins! Dolts!' he raged, banging his fist down on the table in frustration. 'It is the basest fabrication! Liars—this is a travesty of a trial! It has not the barest resemblance to a trial!' His chest heaving, he glared at his tormentors; and so palpable was his fury, that two guards and an orderly shrank unconsciously away from him.

'Order in the court! I will have order!' The chief judiciary struggled to make himself heard.

'Court? Kangaroo court!' said Hugh disparagingly, under his breath. 'I think we are going to cop it, Madame.'

The duc pressed her arm, signalling to General le Mesurier with a lift of his eyebrow, and quietly left the room; the general following in his wake. In a short while, the duc returned. Alone.

Eventually the room regained its quietude.

The marquis, rage spent, holding the notepaper between a fastidious thumb and forefinger, repeated that it was not in his handwriting. Something stopped him from pointing out the obvious: that the drawing and the note were in two different hands. The same thing told him that it was a part of their plan that he should do so. He waited to see what would eventuate when he did not.

After a silence fraught with tension, the prosecutor picked up a letter. 'Do you deny that the War Office has had letters from you, Monsieur?'

'No.' His frown deepened. What were these canaille doing with a letter he had written to General Joffre before the war?'

'I have here one of your letters in this very same handwriting, signed by you,' continued the prosecutor, watching him. 'But you say, it is not in your handwriting?'

Foreseeing where this would lead, the marquis declined to answer.

'You have said the note is not in your handwriting. This letter is in the very same handwriting. If it is not yours, then, whose is it, Monsieur?'

He clamped his lips together, refusing to answer.

'You must answer, Monsieur!' warned the prosecutor.

He remained silent.

'Very well then,' said the prosecutor, sitting back smugly. 'We will assume the note is in your handwriting ... And that you are guilty as charged!'

Still, he did not answer.

'It is in my handwriting, Monsieur.'

All eyes turned to the small woman in black seated between a young Australian soldier and the duc de Belvoir. She rose to her feet. 'I am willing to testify.'

'In good time, Madame. Sit down!' snapped the chief adjudicator. 'You do realise that this may mean you will be charged with espionage, along with the Australian secretary of Monsieur le marquis? This court has ascertained that he spent four years in Berlin before the war, giving him plenty of time to establish a network of contacts.'

'I most strenuously deny that, Sir,' said Hugh, jumping up.

The presiding judiciary, glaring at him, was about to bang his gavel. He subsided, glaring instead at the chief prosecutor for departing from courtroom protocol to bandy words with a suspect.

'Do you deny that you spent four years in Berlin?' he demanded, jaw thrust out.

'No, Sir, I do not! That is because it is the truth. Something that appears to be a very scarce commodity in this court! I was at the university studying engineering. That was before the war, and I went over to England and joined up as soon as the Poms declared war on the Huns. But I categorically deny that I have had any communication with the enemy, except from the business end of a Lewis gun. I am no spy and neither is Madame Dupont or the marquis du Bois!'

'Silence! Sit down! There must be order!' fumed the judiciary officer. 'I call on Madame Dupont to testify.'

Madame Dupont gave her evidence in a calm, straightforward manner. She admitted that the note was in her handwriting, adding that she wrote one like it every week to assist her memory when purchasing the chemicals for the apothecary. She completely denied that it was the coded formula for a new and very dangerous gas, diverging so far as to say that the marquis would never do such a dreadful thing, before adding that, far from giving it to a German spy, she had thrown it in the rubbish bin at the entrance to the apothecary's room, as she always did, once it had been checked off. She had no idea how it had turned up in the pocket of a German spy, if indeed, it had.

This last was said with a straight look that made all of her accusers drop their eyes at once and begin shuffling the papers in front of them.

The marquis, closely watching them, smiled grimly.

When pressed, Madame Dupont agreed that the design with the measurements was in the hand of the marquis, but said it was an incomplete draft of a prosthetic mask for a patient who'd had one side of his face blown off by an enemy shell. (This piece of information was disclosed with a look of such reproach that they all dropped their eyes again). The marquis had not been satisfied with it due to some trifling miscalculation and had thrown it on the floor, from where, she surmised, it would have been picked up by the cleaning staff and put in a hospital rubbish bin.

Finally, she said apologetically, that being only a woman, she did not know much about the paraphernalia of war; but even she would have thought that a gasmask that covered only one half of the face, the nose but not the mouth, and with no provision for eye protection, would be of very little use against any form of deadly gas.

'Would not you, Messieurs?' she asked, gazing at them with wide, earnest eyes.

'The witness may step down,' said the presiding judiciary, as a little ripple went around the room.

The marquis stared at him, eyes glowing with malicious amusement.

Hugh's eyes reflected the devilish humour in those of the marquis, as Madame Dupont negotiated the steps of the witness box. 'Atta girl, Madame!' he whispered, causing the duc, though completely in accord with his sentiments, to frown as he rose to assist her.

Guiding her to her seat, the duc kissed her hand then looked all around the room, daring any to comment. The chief prosecutor, opening his eyes, grew noticeably paler.

§

Meanwhile, a very agitated General le Mesurier was being ushered into the office of the Commander-in-chief of France.

'Come in, General. Why, Hubert,' added the commander, looking up from his work and rising to shake his hand. 'What is it, old friend?'

'Philippe, er … Commander.' He smiled briefly at his gaffe. 'Sorry, I am all at sixes and sevens this morning.'

'So I see, my friend. So I see.' The Commander-in-chief waited patiently for him to explain.

General le Mesurier warmly clasped the proffered hand. 'I do not believe we have spoken since you became Commander-in-chief of France. But it is good to have someone of your calibre in charge.'

'Thank you, my friend.' The commander grimaced. 'Although, between you and me, I must tell you that it is a bit of a poisoned chalice right now.'

'Oh,' groaned the general. 'It is all such a nightmare.'

'An apt description, *mon cher*.' The Commander-in-chief straightened his shoulders. 'And now, you must tell me how I may serve you today.'

'Commander, I crave a great favour. There is a gross injustice about to be perpetrated on an innocent man, and you are the only man in France who can stop it!'

'Indeed, General? So, this is why you are looking so disturbed and "all at sixes and sevens", as you put it. Do you care to unburden yourself and enlighten me, *mon ami*?'

'Commander, I will be blunt. There is some damnable thing going on in le Deuxième Bureau. It has got too hot for someone, and they need a scapegoat to pin it on. And they have chosen, of all people, the marquis du Bois!'

'*Mon Dieu!*' he continued, waving his arms. 'That man is not a traitor! Has he not given most of his earthly possessions, his time and genius, his beautiful ward to the war effort? Not to mention his wonderful hospital! What more can one man do?'

'And I am here to tell you, Commander, that if he is shot as a spy, then our Angel of Song will no longer sing for our troops, and we will lose the war! Already, she is prostrated. I have had to cancel last night's recital, *and* I have had to get a doctor to sedate her.' He strode about the room in agitation, punching a fist into his hand. 'Sir, you must do something! We will have the men mutinying again. As they have not since ———'

The Commander-in-chief held up one hand. An expression of anguish entered his eyes. For just a second he looked like an old man with an intolerable burden. 'Do not ...'

'No, Commander, I am sorry. I know you don't need reminding.' The answering expression in the general's eyes showed understanding as well as distress. 'You know how close it is, what a fine line we tread between victory and defeat!' he finished, shoulders heaving with emotion.

The commander straightened; once more, filled with energy and purpose. 'I do, indeed! And I have personally experienced the effect on our troops of our Angel of Song. Thank you for your brief, old friend. I will go and put a stop to this farce before it goes any further. You're right: there is something rotten in le Deuxième Bureau, but it is so damned deeply entrenched that I have not been able to get to the bottom of it; and if I remember rightly, the marquis du Bois wrote to warn me of it. If this is their way of shutting him up, then they will soon be made to realise their mistake. Let us go!'

§

In the courtroom, a stony silence greeted the testimony of the duc in defence of the character of the accused, since he had very publicly declared himself a biased witness; although, none dared say it to his face.

General de Langue, handsome and plausible when called to the stand, told of how the marquis had refused to give France the design of his airship, reminding the court that London had been battered by bombs carried by similarly designed German airships.

The marquis listened to all this unmoved; his lip curling malevolently as he studied his hands.

Madame Dupont gripped the chair arms, crying inside: *You liar! Perjurer! It was you who refused it! I know who got his airship design! And it was not les Boches!* By the end of the general's testimony, she was shaking with fury. There had been no mention at all of the many other designs and plans he had given to France.

Then, to crown all, the marquis was pronounced guilty as charged.

And as the presiding judiciary, reading out the sentence, reached the part beginning: 'You will be executed at ...' Madame Dupont, leaping to her feet, could contain herself no longer.

'No! No! You shall not! Canaille! *Scélérat!* It is you who are the traitor! *You* ... You!' She pointed straight at the chief judiciary officer.

As the courtroom erupted into pandemonium, Madame Dupont, worn out with emotion, fell against the arm of the chair. The duc, supporting her by the shoulders, gently compelled her back into her seat.

'Well done, Madame!' exclaimed the marquis, regarding her in undisguised admiration.

'Oyez!' echoed Hugh, slapping his thigh.

The judiciary, changing colour, banged his gavel, viciously. 'Order! Order! Evict that woman from the court and charge her with contempt! Put her in a cell! I will throw the book at her!' He was almost foaming at the mouth; his moustaches quivering uncontrollably.

The guards, one each side of the marquis, stepped forward, glancing involuntarily down at him as they did so. His eyes flashed sapphire blue. Before his basilisk stare, they halted, paralysed: barred by an invisible wall.

As they were hesitating between the mounting fury of the presiding judiciary and the malignant power of the marquis, the door opened and into this brouhaha stepped the Commander-in-chief of France. Instantly, all fell silent.

For a moment, he stayed quite still; his eyes ranging over the courtroom. Then deliberately, he strolled forward, taking his time. He paused at the bench of the prosecution, meeting the eyes of each of them before studying the evidence, taking it with him to stand before the presiding judiciary. Staring hard at him, he set it down and picked up the mandate from under his hand. Holding his eyes all the while, he tore it into tiny pieces, dropping them back onto the bench. The sound violated the deep silence like fingernails down a blackboard.

He took up the evidence and crushed it in his hand. 'Case dismissed,' he said, crossing to the fire and tossing into it Madame Dupont's apothecary list and the marquis' drawing. He turned to face the bench. 'Insufficient evidence to support the charge.'

Stabbing an authoritarian forefinger at each of the accusers, he said, with spinechilling sibilance, 'You, you and you will await my pleasure here, for I shall require some pertinent answers.' He made a dismissive gesture. 'The rest of you may go.'

'I am sorry I am late, Monsieur.' He bowed to the marquis. 'You would not otherwise have had to suffer this gross miscarriage of justice. I apologise most humbly.' Lowering his voice, he spoke to him a little longer before moving away.

'Better late ...' breathed Hugh, incorrigible as ever.

The commander smiled at Madame Dupont, bowing over her hand. 'I infinitely regret that I was out when you called, Madame. It would not, then, have taken so long to bring this pack of fools to their senses.'

He bowed to the duc. 'Monsieur.'

Then, jerking his head at the three accusers, he preceded them into an inner chamber.

As the door closed behind them, Hugh expelled a long breath. 'Whew! That was a close run thing. Thank God for the Big Guns. Come on, Sir, Madame, let us get you home.'

The duc turned solicitously to Madame Dupont. 'Allow me, Madame,' he said, rising and taking her arm. 'You are, if I may say so, looking a little peaky.' He led her to where Hugh, congratulating the marquis, was taking charge of his wheeled chair.

'Thank God, *mon brave*!' Madame Dupont put an unsteady hand on the shoulder of the marquis. 'Oh, Angel … my dear!'

'Yes, indeed,' agreed the duc, clasping his hand. 'Justice has been done.'

'Not quite, Monsieur,' he replied. 'Those canaille have not yet answered for their crimes.'

'Quite right, Monsieur,' affirmed the duc. 'Quite right … although, we do not know what the commander is saying to them right now.'

'You may as well join our party, Georges,' said the marquis as they arrived at the back of the van. 'Come along. Tell the chauffeur your direction, and we can drop you on the way or you can come home with us, whatever you wish.'

'Thank you, I will,' replied the duc, preparing to assist Madame Dupont up the ramp behind Hugh, pushing the chair. 'But I believe I will make sure you are safely home, Monsieur, you and Madame, before I leave you. I have an idea …' But he did not say what that idea was; his attention taken by the interior of the van. 'This is very opulent, Angel, very avant-garde,' he approved. 'So, *mon vieux*, I did not think it would happen, but you have finally given in and accepted the automobile, eh?'

'Perhaps, *mon ami*, I got tired of being plagued by my family about my inability to design practical transport for myself,' he said, glancing at Madame Dupont's unresponsive profile. 'And to tell you the truth, I did not fancy being hauled down here by the military in one of their noisy rattletraps!'

He watched the duc look all round the luxuriously upholstered body with a dock for the wheeled chair and open access to the driver's cabin for full communication. 'You like it, Duc? I got the idea from our ambulances, so I obtained one and modified it to fit my chair with comfortable seating for four.'

The duc nodded. 'I do, *mon brave*. It is much quieter, too. *Cette voiture-ci*, she purrs like a kitten instead of growling like *le Tigre*. What did you do to calm it down, *hein*?'

'Oh, nothing much. Just a muffler on the exhaust: a long pipe with a widened section containing baffles. It is not perfect. A crude stopgap only. Perhaps when this war is over, I may find the time to produce a more ... elegant solution,' he said, calling to the chauffeur as Hugh shut the doors. 'That's us, Mary. *En avant*!'

He studied Madame Dupont's white, unsmiling countenance. 'Cheer up, Madame. Far from being indicted as a spy, you will be astonished to know that I am to be awarded *la Légion d'honneur*!'

'So, that is what the commander was saying to you, Monsieur,' she replied. 'It is about time.'

'Well, what do you know?' marvelled Hugh. 'First you're a king, then you're a scarecrow and—hey-presto!— back to a king again! Just like the boss's magic, eh, Madame?'

'Oh, Hugh!' she said, quite crossly for her. 'Is there *nothing* you cannot joke about?'

'Not a lot, Madame, but I must admit a courtroom session like that one quite takes the smile off one's face.'

'Bah! Nincompoops! A set of weaselly rascals, hardly to be given a thought!' said the marquis, brushing aside the whole thing.

The duc, who had been eyeing Madame Dupont in concern since her unprecedented outburst at Hugh, said, 'I think, my dear, you are still in shock. When we get you home, I had better get Doctor Martin to take a look at you.'

Glancing at her sideways, the marquis said, 'I do not

know why you were so worried, Madame. I knew they would not shoot me.'

'Did you?' she replied, completely unamused. 'Then you knew much more than I did.'

'And on what deep truth did you base this knowledge, *mon cher*?' asked the duc, with interest.

'Well, of course they would not shoot me, Georges! Not while they need Angelique to sing for them. We have not yet won the war!'

'*Eh bien*, it is a good thing General le Mesurier pointed it out to them then,' replied the duc rather dryly. 'Otherwise, we would all be in the basket now, would we not?'

CHAPTER TWENTY-TWO ~ A CELEBRATION

23 July 1917

This trial has stressed me beyond imagination. The last minute reprieve of Angel has sent me into a state of lethargy from which it was almost impossible to recover. Something that I don't ever remember happening to me. Our celebration was fleeting but precious, surrounded by the people I love. Dieu merci, I still have Angel.

'What made you come to this unspeakable parody of a trial, Georges?' asked the marquis, in a conversational mood. 'You have travelled a long way.'

'Etienne telephoned me yesterday,' responded the duc, 'telling me of your, er … difficulties. I thought that perhaps you might have needed my help.' He glanced at Madame Dupont who, in her strange, disconnected mood, was unable to voice just how much his presence had helped her; her mind incapable of assimilating the fact that had he not galvanised General le Mesurier into action, right now it might be a very different story.

'It was a long journey,' said the marquis, his eyes

following those of the duc with much the same expression and a curious tone in his voice. 'You must have travelled all night.'

'I did,' confirmed the duc, with a gleam of humour. 'And even with the fastest auto I could hire, and my chauffeur sitting on full throttle all the way, I only just made it, *mon cher*. But you are right: I have never seen such a debacle. What was behind it do you think?'

'Need you ask, duc?'

'Perhaps not. You are so subtle and conciliating in your manner, are you not? Particularly when delivering your own brand of home truth. I expect you offended someone, *mon cher*. It would not be the first time!'

'Indeed. Well, Madame Dupont exposed his … tender side.'

'Yes, indeed,' said the duc, warmly; his eyes drawn to her again. 'A formidable lady.'

'Ah, yes,' agreed the marquis. 'If you have something to hide, you should not come anywhere near Madame Dupont, *cela va sans dire*. But you must be exhausted, *mon vieux*.'

'No, no,' disclaimed the duc. 'I slept along the way, but I must confess I would very much appreciate a cup of coffee on our return, not having had the time for breakfast.'

Madame Dupont's lack of response to this broad hint sent the gentlemen's eyes to her blank face and then to each other's in amazement.

'I am certainly going to fetch Doctor Martin when we get back,' said the duc, shaking his head. 'There can be no doubt: Madame Dupont is in shock!'

'I think you are right, *mon cher*,' replied the marquis after a short silence. He reached over to pat her hand. 'Come, Madame, it is not as bad as all that.' Then looking out the window as they drew up at the front entrance, he exclaimed in pleased tones, 'Angelique! And Etienne! Did you know they were coming, Georges?'

'I had an idea,' replied the duc, preparing to alight. 'How do you disconnect this chair from the vehicle, Monsieur? Oh, I see,' he added as Hugh showed him the mechanism. 'Ingenious, is it not?'

Madame Dupont, ignoring his proffered arm, felt as if she were some insubstantial ghostly being, watching unmoved as Angelique, overcome by her emotions at the sight of the marquis, was snatched up by Etienne just in time to avoid a bad fall on the steps.

A slight irritation filtered through her brain as the girl tore herself away from the support of the young marquis and collapsed over the now frail body of her guardian.

As if we have not enough to bear, she thought hazily. *Who in the world could have been evil enough or stupid enough to have told the poor child of the court martial?* She felt no emotion at the obvious extremis of the marquis or the cry that was forced from his lips.

'Oh, my dear child,' he gasped painfully. 'You have grown a little too much to sit on my knee now, you know.'

And even the sight of the duc and his son, between them, lifting the unconscious beauty off her mentor and their attempts to revive her affected her no more than any other boring scene she wanted nothing to do with.

In fact, she thought dreamily, as she followed them into the salon where they lay Angelique down on the sofa, *the way I feel right now, I might just apply Matron's treatment; if I could only find the energy.* The fact that the child was not actually suffering from a hysterical fit did not seem to weigh with her. However, she was sufficiently herself to acknowledge that such an action would have caused catastrophic turmoil in the breasts of at least three of the four gentlemen present.

Catching her eye, Etienne shrugged helplessly. 'Madame le Mesurier told her. I am sorry, Madame.'

'Oh, that featherheaded flibbertigibbet!' exclaimed Madame Dupont with asperity, suddenly feeling live, tingling anger coursing through her veins. 'Well, of course, she did! When did that stupid woman ever keep a still tongue in her head? Oh, dear, dear!'

Shocked out of her own trauma by her healthy annoyance at the thought of Angelique's unnecessary distress, her compassion once more came to the fore, and she immediately moved to revive her, gently pushing aside the duc whose efforts, though well-meaning, were quite ineffectual.

'Step aside, my dear Georges, I will attend to her. Oh dear, this poor child—she has been quite overcome!'

'Yes,' agreed Etienne, expertly lending his aid. 'It is a good thing we have a happy ending. Imagine how it would have been if ——'

'Do not say it, *mon fils*,' she warned. 'Do not even begin to consider it …' Adding, as the sufferer began to come round, 'Ah: that is better, my dear. Gently, gently, now. Do not try to rise too quickly …'

When Angelique had sufficiently recovered to sit at his feet and wrap her arms around his knees, the marquis reached out a gentle hand and lifted her chin. 'It is wonderful that you are with me, my angel, but there is something more important than either of us. Will you do this one thing for me?' He waited for her confirmation. 'I want you to go and sing to the troops tonight, for me and my acquittal—in joy for us! You will do that, my angel? It is very important. *Bien*,' he added briskly. 'We will have a quick luncheon, and you shall be on your way.' He smoothed her hair, lovingly. 'Do not forget that I will be with you.'

Raising his eyes to look over the top of her head, he said, 'Madame, shall we not bring the duchesse and Elise over from the hospital and make a real party of it?'

'Of course, Monsieur,' said Madame Dupont, her composure reinstated. 'What a good idea! I will get them right away.'

'No, you will not, Madame,' said the duc. 'I shall go. You take a little rest, my dear. I will bring Doctor Martin back with us as well.'

'No, no, it is not necessary …' she began. But she spoke to his unheeding back: the door closing behind him.

'She will attend to Angelique, Madame,' the marquis reminded her with a frown. 'You are not the only one with overstretched nerves, you know.'

'No, you are right, Monsieur. I am sorry; I seem to have lost my perspective.' Having shaken off her strange lethargy, she was beginning to appreciate what kind of hell he and Angelique must have gone through.

'There, there!' He patted her hand. 'None of us have ever seen you like this before, my dear. No wonder Georges thinks you need the doctor! I know I tease you for your optimism, but it is infinitely preferable to your present mood. You do not have to be sorry. Should we not be celebrating, rather?'

'Indeed, Monsieur. I shall go and see the chef at once.'

Wondering how to placate the chef at this last minute influx of luncheon guests, she found him in a complacent frame of mind.

'I do not mind how many unexpected guests you invite to celebrate the freedom of Monsieur le marquis, Madame,' he told her expansively, waving at the kitchen bench with its load of savoury and sweet pies and pastries. 'Monsieur le duc had these sent over from the pâtisserie, so as not to inconvenience the kitchen staff.'

'Oh, but how kind of him!'

'Indeed, Madame. Even we in the kitchen have noticed that he is a very considerate man. Most unusual for one of his consequence, in my experience!'

'Indeed,' said Madame Dupont faintly, overwhelmed alike by the generosity of the duc and the confidentiality imparted by the chef. Recovering, she added, 'Very well, Monsieur, as soon as I am sure of the exact numbers, I shall send to tell you.'

'*De rien*, Madame!' replied the chef, benevolently. 'We shall contrive without effort for at least forty guests.'

'Without a doubt,' she replied, running her eye over the banquet provided by the duc. 'Monsieur le duc has been very generous. But I anticipate no more than ten, Monsieur.'

The duc returned, not only with the duchesse, Elise and Doctor Martin, but Philippe as well, in a wheeled chair.

After the general greetings, the marquis sent Angelique and Madame Dupont to the morning room for a consultation with Doctor Martin, and then turned his attention to the fair young man. 'I have heard that imitation is the sincerest form of flattery, but surely this is taking it to ridiculous lengths, dear boy,' he said, wheeling his chair over to clasp his hand. 'And how do I find you today, *hein*?'

'Oh, fine, fine, but I hope to be flattering you for only one more week, Monsieur. Doctor Martin says I can begin to walk with a stick after that.'

'Very good,' replied the marquis. 'At least you are not spavined like me. How is your father? I have not seen him lately.'

Philippe shrugged. 'No, Monsieur, no-one has. He has become a recluse. Do you know, he has never visited me in hospital? Oh, he sends me letters and gifts such as wine and fruit, but he never visits. I do not understand it!'

Responding to the pathos in his voice, the marquis put a hand out to him. 'Have patience with him, *mon fils*, he is grieving.'

'So are we.' The young man's eyes met his in a blaze of emotion.

'Yes.' For a fraction of a second, the marquis gripped his hand. Looking up, he beckoned to Doctor Martin as the ladies returned: 'Are you pleased with your patients, Doctor?'

'I am,' she said, smiling at Philippe. 'Particularly this one—he is a textbook case. But I know that is not what you have asked me. I have prescribed two days rest for

Madame …'

'Oh-oh,' he said, throwing up his hands. 'Then you will certainly have to tie her down!'

'And for Mademoiselle …'

'Yes?' A shade of anxiety entered his voice.

'A nerve tonic is advisable, Monsieur. She is in a very fragile state, on the verge of neurasthenia. I shall have one made up for her. She is not singing tonight? She is? Then she must take it with her. And I will also prescribe some valerian to help her sleep. I will go and prepare it now. You will excuse me, I hope, if I am late for lunch?'

'Of course, Doctor. Only tell me your favourite dishes, and they shall be saved for you.'

'Oh, I am not an epicure. Any of those exquisite pastries on the sideboard in there will more than suffice, Monsieur,' she replied, hurrying away.

Angelique, meanwhile, fussing over her brother and her best friend, was showing signs of becoming overexcited. The young marquis, excusing himself from a conversation with his parents, moved unobtrusively to her side as soon as he saw her growing breathless. Drawing her arm through his and holding her close to his side, he enquired kindly after Philippe's health and the speed of his recovery.

'Oh, Etienne,' cried Elise. 'It is such an age since I saw you—both of you. Tell me what you have been doing?' she added, including Angelique.

Her brother tried to frown her down, groaning inwardly: *No, Elise. Please do not remind her* … 'Rather, my dear, tell us what you have been doing, apart from looking after Philippe. Have you heard from any of our friends?' he asked, surreptitiously touching her foot with his own.

'Oh,' she said, at first startled and then colouring. 'No, I … I have been very busy in the hospital. Thankfully, none of our friends have come in, and Philippe will officially be a convalescent next week ——'

The timely announcement by the butler that lunch was served halted their conversation, and they all moved into the dining room to seat themselves around the big polished table.

As the various dishes were being passed around, Hugh, graphically describing the courtroom scene to Etienne, concluded, 'Then your dad brought up the heavy artillery, and it was all plain sailing from then on.'

The young marquis, looking bewildered, said, 'Oh, good.'

Smiling a little, the duc explained, 'He means that I asked General le Mesurier to beg the aid of the Commander-in-chief of France, knowing what old friends they are. It was our only chance, but it worked.'

'Yes, indeed,' concurred the marquis, parking his chair at the head of the table and conveniently forgetting his bold statement in the van. 'Very well, too! You are to be congratulated, Georges, on your forethought. Pray accept my heartfelt thanks.'

'*De rien*!' replied the duc, casting an approving glance around the table. 'We are a very nice party, are we not? *Bon appétit*!'

After various joyful toasts to the health of all, they fell into a few minutes of silence while they sampled the culinary efforts of the duc's favourite pâtissier. There was an air of festive reunion, a feeling of relaxation, as they sat and caught up with each other. Angelique and Etienne had been away for weeks, and the duc saw even less of his family with the duchesse and Elise spending their time working in the hospital while he oversaw communications at Belvoir.

Conversations ranged around the table, or were confined to table partners depending on the content; everybody looking up as something Angelique said surprised a little gurgle of laughter from Madame Dupont.

'Oh, Monsieur,' she said in answer to his lifted eyebrow. 'Angelique has just been telling me her followers are calling themselves fans, now.'

'What was that, Madame?' asked the marquis.

'Fans: have you ever heard of followers being called fans, Monsieur?'

'No. What does it stand for: Followers ad nauseum? I like it. A very descriptive term: short, succinct and to the point!' He smiled and raised his glass. 'To Angelique's fans—and freedom! We can never have too many toasts to freedom.'

In a little while, he tapped with his spoon for attention. 'Angelique and Etienne must soon leave us for her, er ... fans at the Front have need of her. But before they go, I believe Monsieur le duc has an announcement he wishes to make to us all. Monsieur?'

'Thank you, *mon cher*. We have a surfeit of good news today, and a very pleasant surprise for me. Philippe, who assures me that he is only looking for sympathy by pretending to be an invalid—a cunning ruse to inveigle my daughter into marrying him! Yes ...' He smiled, holding up his hand for silence at the pleased gasps. 'A little while ago, Philippe asked for the hand of my daughter in marriage, and the duchesse and I are delighted to give them our blessings.'

'Oh!' exclaimed Angelique. 'How wonderful! We really will be sisters, now. I know: let us have a double wedding!' She leapt up and rushed around the table to hug and congratulate her brother and Elise.

'But, Angelique,' said Elise, 'I thought you were not getting married until after the war.'

'Yes, after the war,' she confirmed. 'But ... Are not you?'

'No, little sister,' said Philippe, gently. 'We are only waiting until I can walk again. I refuse to look up to my wife when I plight my troth, and I want to be able to carry her over the threshold. We are getting married in three weeks. Doctor Martin says I should be strong enough by then.'

'But I thought ——' Angelique addressed Elise in agonised undertones. 'What about your wedding plans?

You know … What we used to talk about?'

'Little girls' talk,' said Elise. 'This is real life, my love. We will be married very quietly in the hospital chapel, and I will continue to nurse the patients.'

'Yes, and I shall take very good care you do not succumb to any other wounded fellow looking for sympathy, my girl,' vowed Philippe, kissing her hand.

Angelique, staring huge-eyed from one to the other, flushed and turned her gaze on Etienne. For just a second, guilt and dismay shone in the amethyst depths. 'Oh, no!' she gasped, putting a hand to her mouth. Half a second later, she pushed back her chair and ran out of the room.

There was momentary silence.

'Angelique?' Philippe reddened, bit his lip and lowered his eyes. Elise turned away to hide her tears.

With a murmured apology, Etienne righted the overturned chair and turned to the door. But Madame Dupont was before him.

'*Un moment*, if you please.' The marquis signed to them to return to their seats. 'There is something I need to say.' He turned to the affianced couple with a rueful smile. 'I think that you will find,' he said, in a voice that brooked no argument, 'that Angelique has been overcome with the joy of the occasion, having several times in the last twenty-four hours had unbearable stress placed upon her nerves. I know that you will both be sensible enough to not allow her nervous reaction to colour this felicitous celebration. I shall now propose a toast to the happy couple, and we shall have another when Angelique returns; as I know she will want to add her very best wishes.'

He raised his glass. 'To Philippe and Elise: happiness always!'

Setting it down after the echoing response, his eyes sought those of Madame Dupont.

Nodding slightly, she placed a hand on Etienne's arm as he prepared to leave the table. 'No, my son, let me go. In this instance, I believe it will be best for me to assist her. You stay here with the others,' she said, whisking herself out of the room; her abrupt departure suspending conversation.

Into the uncomfortable silence trod Doctor Martin, carrying her elixir.

'Good gracious me,' she said, looking about her. 'Have you all been turned to stone?'

'Doctor, I hope you are not famished, for there is one small commission I would request of you before you sit down to eat.' The marquis wheeled his chair out of the room beside her as he explained the situation.

Etienne, downcast, met his father's eyes and shrugged.

'My dependence is on Madame Dupont, my son,' said the duc in a low, comforting voice. 'You will see. It is as Monsieur le marquis has said: Angelique has been overcome by the joy of the occasion.' *It is not as if you do not know what she is, alors.*

The others, in an attempt at normality, began to converse lightly, Hugh jokingly asking the newly engaged couple if they were going to change wards for their honeymoon.

'We have not yet decided, Monsieur,' said Philippe, sending him a grateful smile.

§

Madame Dupont found Angelique curled up in a miserable huddle on the sofa in her boudoir. She took her in her arms, saying, 'Come, dear child, surely it cannot be as bad as all that. Tell me what has upset you.'

'It is Elise,' she sobbed. 'She makes me feel as if I am shallow, uncaring, selfish … Oh, guilty! To wish to wait for a special wedding.'

'And what has Elise done to make you feel that way, my dear?' Madame Dupont's voice was gentle.

'She has given up the idea of a romantic wedding. Dismissed it out of hand! All our lovely plans of what we wanted! And now she has made it sound so … childish,' she whispered.

'You are overwrought, my dear, or you would not see it that way. Elise and Philippe's decisions for their lives: how should they affect yours, *hein*?'

Angelique shrugged, biting her lip.

'Oh, your lip is bleeding now! Take this, my dear.' Madame Dupont tenderly placed a folded handkerchief against her lower lip and brought her hand up to hold it. 'There.'

'Now, my dear, we need to be clear about something. It is not Elise who makes you feel this way. It is you. All you. You must be the one to take responsibility for your own thoughts and emotions, my child. For until you do, you will be like a piece of flotsam carried on the waves, wafted about wherever the wind and tide may take you. Etienne can be your anchor, yes. But not your rudder as well. You must be in control of your own life and know yourself where you wish to go before you can safely come home to anchor.

'You must ask yourself why you want what you want, and if you find in your answer a valid reason, then, *eh bien*, hold fast to it.

'Come now, it is Philippe and Elise's day, not yours, and we are spoiling a festive occasion. Is that what you want: to ruin their memories of their betrothal?'

'No! Oh, no, I truly want them to be happy!'

'Of course you do, my dear. We will explain that the excitement of the occasion culminated in an excess of sensibility, which overcame you for a short time.'

'And I *am* overjoyed for them. Despite how it looks. Oh, Godmama, how could I have behaved in such a way? How could I? And Angelpapa, he will be mortified. I have let him down. Oh, how could I?' Angelique was quickly working herself up into a fit of hysteria.

Oh, no! No, no, no! And I thought we were going to avoid this! How on earth am I going to be able to get her back to that lunch table now? Madame Dupont had somehow to nip this in the bud, but helplessness overwhelmed her. Nowhere in her mind was the solution she had so dreamily considered earlier in the day.

'Give me your place, Madame. Quickly!'

She felt herself being pushed away from Angelique.

'Brace yourself, my girl.' The doctor's cool hand was against the young woman's forehead. 'Drink this all at once!' she commanded, tossing the contents of a medicine glass into her open mouth.

Angelique gasped and swallowed, going into a coughing fit. When it was over, there was no sign of hysteria.

'Good girl. Monsieur le marquis sent me to find you and give you your nerve tonic. Now then, can you face the music?—Sorry about the pun—Excellent! I do not wish to hurry you, my dear girl, but I *would* like some lunch.'

§

Touchingly contrite, Angelique made her way around the table, kissing, embracing and charmingly apologising to everyone except Doctor Martin and Hugh.

The doctor, blissfully tucking into a delectable salmon quiche, ignored the whole proceeding; but Hugh, with a diabolical twinkle, said, 'But what about me?'

'I know you for a brave man, Hugh,' commented the duc, sotto voce, 'but you are surely not as foolhardy as all that?'

'Point taken, Sir,' he replied, subsiding with a grin.

'Angelpapa?' suggested Angelique, determined to make amends. 'Since it is a special occasion for Philippe and Elise, and we have had no time to buy them a memento, why do we not sing for them *Éternitie d'amour* as our special gift?'

The marquis nodded, holding out his hand to her. 'Well done, my angel,' he whispered as they prepared for their duet amid cries of 'please!' and 'how wonderful!'

CHAPTER TWENTY-THREE ~ LA LÉGION D'HONNEUR

25 July 1917

Poor Angel; he has tried so hard to save the one who was made the scapegoat instead of him. I suppose I will have to tell him, but I do not know how he will take it. It has certainly made a black dog jump onto my shoulder. The treachery of my own countrymen makes me feel extremely ill.

The perspicacity of the marquis unerringly picked up on a disturbance behind the calm demeanour of Madame Dupont. Observing her closely, he asked, 'You have had some bad news, Madame?'

'It is something I heard in the hospital, Monsieur. I do not know the whole truth of it. The rumour mill, you know ...'

'Take a deep breath, my dear,' he recommended. 'I have all day.'

'Well, it concerns Mata Hari: the exotic dancer who was arrested as a spy.'

'What about her? Is Ladoux still trying to keep her locked up, despite his lack of evidence?'

'Worse than that, Monsieur.'

'Do not tell me!' The marquis got there at once. 'Having lost me as a scapegoat, they are now about to put her on trial?'

'Hugh has gone to try and verify it,' she confirmed. 'But I believe they already have.' Her eyes filled with distress. Back in February, the news of the woman's arrest had rather unnerved her, and she had not known why. *So what?* She had asked herself, shrugging it off. There were courtesans. There were spies. There were courtesans who were spies: why not? It was a reasonable assumption: pillow talk being known throughout history as a handy instrument for the gathering of information, but somehow—she had not known why—the accusation just had not gelled. And not with the marquis, either. She knew that he had taken up Mata Hari's cause with the head of le Deuxième Bureau—and look how he had been repaid! Now in her greater knowledge, she did know why she had been so unnerved and feared with a heavy heart for the dancer who was, in all probability, an innocent pawn.

'No!' he said. 'Those canaille ...'

'Yes, Monsieur,' she continued. 'I have just heard that the very day after your court martial was abandoned—the very day, Monsieur!—those evil beasts took her from her prison cell and put her on trial for espionage!'

He compressed his lips. 'Continue, Madame. This becomes very interesting ...'

'And now, after two days and despite the ... the ...'

'Questionable?' he suggested.

She sent him a grateful glance. 'Yes, despite the questionable nature of the evidence, and indeed strong evidence against it, she has been found guilty!'

'Is this true, Madame?'

'As far as I know, it is. But look, here is Hugh coming now. Perhaps he will be able to substantiate it.'

Hugh, catching Madame Dupont's eye, said, 'Yes, it is all true, Madame.'

'And is this true about the nature of the evidence?' demanded the marquis.

'Oh, the evidence!' groaned Hugh, casting up his eyes. 'It is not quite as blatant as yours, Sir, but very nearly. It was a closed court, so we don't know for sure; but rumour has it that *this* time they admitted to finding it in a bin! It seems that one of our spies, masquerading as a cleaner, found a coded message in a rubbish bin at German Intelligence. It bore the identifying number of the agent,' said Hugh, with dry significance. 'But since nobody knows to whom the number refers, it is only speculation that it is this woman, Mata Hari. And since the message itself is written in a code cracked long ago by our own Intelligence, it is all looking very chancy. Very flimsy, indeed.'

The marquis made an impatient movement. 'God save us, Hugh, they've manufactured the evidence against her. Just as they did to me!'

'Oh, yes, they've stitched her up, Sir. And they'll shoot her, too!'

'Oh, no, Hugh. Surely not!' Madame Dupont wrung her hands.

'They'll shoot her, no question, Madame,' Hugh told her gently. 'They are out for blood, you know. I think it must be fairly obvious to us now that someone in power is looking for a patsy.'

'Patsy? *Mais*, what is that?'

'Scapegoat,' supplied the marquis, in thoughtful tones. 'Yes, they could not get me ... So they got her. If that is their attitude, to defy the Commander-in-chief of France so flagrantly, it is either overpowering conceit or they are very sure of themselves.' He was silent a minute, mulling it over. Then he said, 'The commander has his own troubles and may have too much on his plate to bother with us now. But by God,' he swore, his eyes blazing, 'if she has to go, she will not go without a fight! I will see to that!'

15 August 1917

Here, today, we have a small beacon of joy. A love story within the horrors surrounding us. A precious occasion that must not go unnoticed, however quiet and humble it has to be due to prevailing circumstances. Even Angel has interrupted his particular battle with his enemies in le Deuxième Bureau to take a surprising interest; not least, because he knows that the duc's vital communications work does not allow him to leave Belvoir at this particular time. Such a pity, I feel. But needs must ...

Elise and Philippe, both dressed in their respective uniforms, were married privately in the hospital chapel, with only the duchesse and the marquis to witness the event.

As the groom reverently kissed the bride, the marquis met the eyes of the duchesse. What he saw there made him take her hand and kiss it.

'*Doucement*, Madame,' he murmured. 'I believe we have been privileged to witness the beginning of a very happy union.'

'Yes,' whispered the duchesse. 'I have always thought that they were right for each other.'

'Indeed.' He wheeled his chair over to congratulate the happy couple.

'Thank you, Monsieur,' said Elise. 'I will cherish him.'

'I have no doubt of that, my dear.' The marquis turned to the groom. 'You are a fortunate man, Philippe.'

'I know, Monsieur: the luckiest of men!'

After signing the requisite document, the marquis told them to come over to the house. 'Madame Dupont has a spot of lunch waiting for us. We cannot let the day go entirely unmarked, you know.'

Elise ran her fingers down her snowy apron. 'I am not exactly dressed for celebration in my wedding finery ...'

'Oh, I don't know,' said the marquis. 'It is mostly white. You look very trim.'

'You look perfect,' said her besotted husband.

'So do you.' Elise raised worshipful eyes to his, and in that moment, the others could see that no-one else existed.

The marquis cleared his throat. 'You two may not need sustenance, but the same cannot be said for your witnesses. You may follow at your leisure. Come along, Madame.' As he wheeled away, he said to his companion, 'Do you think they heard me?'

The duchesse, looking back at the couple before the marble altar—arms about each other, lips close, their profiles radiating joy and tenderness—laughed delightedly. 'Do you know, Monsieur, I really don't think they did.'

'*Bon.*' The marquis' lip curved in a little half-smile. 'I was afraid of that.'

§

After this enjoyable interruption, the marquis drew his brows together and went back to his defence of Mata Hari. He continued to lobby the authorities, write letters to the newspapers, point out the spurious nature and discrepancies in the evidence against her, and the strong indications of her innocence. As time went on, there were many who added their voices to his, ranging themselves with him on the side of truth.

To the snide remarks and innuendo published by his enemies, he replied that his only passion was for justice, adding that perhaps her accusers had settled on a woman of her reputation for possibly that very reason: that men would be afraid to come to her aid, thus allowing them to get away with murder.

'For murder it is,' he wrote. 'She may not be an "innocent" woman, but she is not a spy.'

To claims that she had declared herself a spy for France (which had been strenuously denied by the authorities), he countered, 'Guilty of indiscrimination, perhaps, and a penchant for self-aggrandisement. But when, in a civilised country, has the punishment for such a crime ever amounted to a death sentence?'

He urged the women's movement to come to her assistance, deploring outmoded, quasi-virtue that allowed some to hold up their noses and excuse themselves on the grounds that a 'fallen woman' deserved her fate.

He wrote to all the generals he could think of and to the Court of Appeal, engaging a barrister to make application on her behalf; but at the end of it all, he found himself defeated; and as he afterwards found out, at dawn on the fifteenth of October, the day that he received his Légion d'honneur, Margaretha Zelle was executed by firing squad.

Later, Hugh told them in hushed tones of how she had refused a blindfold, going to her death in proud silence, standing tall and fearlessly looking her executioners in the eye.

'She was a brave woman,' said the marquis. 'And she may have been many things, but she was no spy.' He paused; his expression regretful. 'I am sorry that I failed her.'

'You did all that was humanly possible, Monsieur,' Madame Dupont assured him.

'I know,' he sighed. 'But unlike me, she did not have an angel to protect her.' He prodded at the velvet case with a disparaging forefinger. 'I feel like throwing this medal away, Madame. In fact, had I known of her fate this morning, I would never have accepted it!'

'*Doucement*, Monsieur,' she replied. 'I know how you feel, but one bad apple does not ruin the whole orchard. Of course, if I ever hear of a certain *salopard* in le Deuxième Bureau being given one, I shall help you throw it away myself!'

'Madame!' He was shocked. 'In all the years I have known you, I have never heard you use language like that!'

'No,' she replied, walking out with great dignity. 'I have never needed to.'

Hugh, meeting his stunned gaze, shook his head. 'This war is getting to her, Sir.'

The marquis said nothing. Then, in a sudden violent move, he picked up his medal in its velvet case and hurled it against the wall.

CHAPTER TWENTY-FOUR ~ THE GREAT PANDEMIC

27 October 1917

I had thought we had seen the worst of what men can do to each other. But now? The world has gone mad; I am convinced of it! And if I were superstitious, I would believe that the Gods have had enough of the wickedness of man and have decided on vengeance.

The death of the exotic dancer earlier in the month and under such reprehensible circumstances plunged them all into gloom, unrelieved by a run of ill-fortune of which Hugh was the melancholy herald.

'Those bloody Russians,' he swore, when he was alone with the marquis. 'There has been another uprising. This time a rackety bunch known as the Bolsheviks have revolted against the ruling Duma: you know, the lot that a few short months ago revolted against the Tsar! So, of course their Front is in uproar: again! And they've abducted their Royal Family and taken them away somewhere, and "grave fears are held for their safety",' he quoted, adding with feeling, 'I hope they spare them, send them into exile or something. But I am afraid ... And not only are these damned Russkies causing us grief, there is some kind of strange new influenza attacking our troops. It has just struck out of the blue!'

'*Eh bien*, Hugh, as a doomsayer you take the honours. Well for you, it is not my custom to shoot the messenger,' said the marquis, shaking his head over the incomprehensible vagaries of the Russians.

'Sorry, Sir ...' Hugh gave a rueful grin. 'I only wish I could be the bearer of better news.'

'This new influenza: it is not caused by a chemical manufactured by the enemy?'

'I don't know, Sir. It seems to be a type of influenza that hits very suddenly.'

§

The influenza passed quickly without too much collateral damage—or so they thought. The Russians went back to the Front under a flag of a different colour and little changed during another miserable winter of hardship and need.

3 March 1918

The Russians, after fighting each other instead of the enemy, have now surrendered and left us with it. Angel says that it will not be long before we have all the German troops from the Eastern Front gathering here for an all-out battle, having been heartened by their infamous Treaty of Brest-Litovsk.

In the spring, as predicted by the marquis, the Germans launched a powerful offensive on the Western Front, making a push to advance their lines. The Allies, for once having the advantage of not being the ones to come out of the trenches and expose themselves as targets, rained fire upon the enemy, inflicting heavy casualties and driving them back to their trenches in the forests where they dug in, heavily fortified. Stalemate number …? They had all lost count, but all that summer the Allies pushed back hard! For now the Americans had come in their numbers with huge stocks of weapons, and it was beginning to feel as if the end was, finally, in sight. But it did mean a rise in the numbers of wounded rolling up to the doors of the Hospital du Bois and a greater workload on the staff and volunteers.

Bearing all this with fortitude, Madame Dupont very nearly went to pieces when she heard of the massacre of the Russian Royal Family.

The marquis, when Hugh brought him the tragic news, charged him strictly not to tell her.

'Madame Dupont must not know of this! Mind, Hugh, you are not to tell her!'

'Too late, Sir, she already knows. The news is all over the hospital. Ambulance drivers,' he added as a brief explanation.

'*Tiens*, I had better call her,' said the marquis, ringing the bell. He shook his head. 'She cannot take much more, Hugh. She is a very strong woman, but I know when she is at the end of her tether; and the diabolical murder of this family will sorely try her limits.'

'It is particularly nasty, Sir. The children, you know.'

He nodded, saying as Madame Dupont entered the room, 'Madame, you have heard Hugh's sad tidings? I am sorry. I would have kept it from you if I could.'

'Oh, is it not enough that this terrible war began with a massacre? Why does it have to end with one, too?' cried Madame Dupont a little wildly.

The marquis, eyeing her askance, replied in forbidding tones, 'I regret to inform you, Madame, that this war is not yet over.'

'No … And will it ever be?' Madame Dupont was as near to giving way to despair as *she* would ever be. 'Oh, is it not enough that countries must rise up against each other?'

'I wonder: does the duc know of this execrable crime?'

The mention of the duc startled her, and she dried her eyes while she pondered. 'I suppose he would, Monsieur. He has all the new radiotelephonic equipment,' she said. 'Why do you ask?'

'He is related to this poor family, is he not?'

'Oh! Oh, yes, he is, through his relationship to the English King. He is their cousin. Oh, dear, I did not think … Should you telephone him?'

Noting with relief that the imminent signs of a breakdown had been averted and that Madame Dupont had resumed at least some of her composure, he said, 'Perhaps I will, later. Although, it is more than probable that Etienne already knows and will pass it on to him. Yes, that is most likely, I think. Do not you, Hugh?'

'I think so, Sir. Since they are at GQG, the young marquis would have been briefed by old le Mesurier's aide. There is nothing those johnnies don't know. Often more than their bosses.'

'No doubt,' replied the marquis. 'I am sorry, Madame, but it is after the fact, now. There is nothing we can do for the Tsar and his family.'

'No,' she agreed, resolutely blowing her nose. 'I will go back to the hospital until luncheon, Monsieur. I shall see you then.'

He waved her away, already deep in consultation with his secretary.

Madame Dupont set off miserably down the hall, feeling shut-out and alone. All very well for the gentlemen to switch off like that, but as far as she was concerned, it was just one more dreadful event to add to the list of atrocities that characterised this wretched, wicked war. And Hugh's friends, too—some months ago, now—losing most of their company taking out a machine-gun nest, having to fallback because of sustaining such heavy losses. Yes, just one more shocking event in a never-ending litany of courage, sacrifice, treachery, evil … And over it all, a great gloomy cloud of overwhelming sadness.

She straightened her shoulders, detouring to wash her face and press a cool washcloth to her eyes. The patients must not see her like this!

§

Towards the end of autumn, just as there began to be fresh hope of a breakthrough for the Allies, there was more frightening news, as Madame Dupont, returning from the hospital, imparted to the marquis. 'This so-called Spanish flu seems to be running mad again this year, Monsieur. It has hit like last year, but with ten times the virulence. The hospital is full of it, and the young men being brought back from the Front with it are dying in front of us. There is nothing we can do. It is terrible!'

'Yes. The newspapers are censored, of course, but I understand from Hugh that the Military Commanders are very concerned by the heavy losses, especially of apparently healthy young men.' He pondered the irony. 'It would appear to be finishing off those so far not taken by the war.'

'Oh, Monsieur, so many are suffering ill-health owing to the hardships of all these dreadful years of war; and the young men, suffering from deprivation of good food— they are all so terribly, terribly battle weary ... It is only to be expected that these poor, weakened souls should be carried off by it, do you not think?'

'Indeed, Madame, and the way I feel right now, I could be one of them,' he said; his flat tone alerting her.

She asked an anxious question, going to him and putting a hand on his brow.

'My dear Elise.' He removed her hand and kissed it. 'My dearest friend: if I should succumb to this latest plague, I do not want you to mourn me.'

'Angel, *mon cher* ——' she began to protest.

But he stopped her, saying fiercely, 'No, listen!' He

paused, going on in quieter tones, 'Do you think I fear death, Madame? In truth, I welcome it; for death to me is not something to be feared. On the contrary, I embrace it: for it will mean freedom! Freedom from this useless, pain-racked body; freedom to exist in a plane that we as mortals can only dream of; freedom, at last, to be united with my love.'

'Angel, my dear, what is all this?' she asked in jollying tones, for the way he spoke truly frightened her. 'You were not talking that way when they were going to shoot you as a spy!'

'*Sang Dieu!* But you say some silly things sometimes, Madame,' he replied, unresponsive to her attempt at humour. 'Perhaps I did not fancy being shot as a spy: to die without honour: a traitor to my country. In truth, I would prefer to be remembered for the things I have done rather than those I have not!'

'Of course, I was only joking, *mon cher.*'

'*Eh bien*, I did not find it very funny.'

'No, Monsieur. I can see that, and I am sorry. But do not worry: God is not mocked! One day the real traitor will be brought to justice.'

'You really believe that, don't you?'

'Implicitly, Monsieur,' she assured him. 'You do, too— *au fond.*'

'Do I?'

'But of course, my dear Angel, of course. You always had such a burning passion for justice.'

'I?' He raised a quizzical eyebrow. 'You speak of me alone, Madame?'

'Well ... We, then,' she admitted.

'That is better.' He smiled a little. 'Remember how we used to talk when we were young? Plotting the downfall of evildoers. We were passionate, idealistic, ruthless.'

You were ruthless. Me? Not enough, I fear. 'Have we changed, then?'

'Have we? I wonder ...? Less ruthless, perhaps? Age

mellows, so they say.' He lapsed into thoughtful silence.

'Why are we talking like this? You still have the passion. Look how hard you worked to try and save that poor woman, Mata Hari!'

'Another factor of age, perhaps? Back then, my passion for justice, as you call it, would have taken a ... vastly different form,' he said, flexing his fingers.

'Yes, and it would not be Mata Hari who is dead. Well do I know that! But perhaps it is best to leave these matters to *le bon Dieu*—as we have to now.'

'*Le bon Dieu!* Is there a God?'

'Angel!' she gasped. 'You can say such a thing to me? Of course there is a God!'

'Oh, if only I could say that I know Him!'

'Do not fret, my dear. He knows you, and that is what is really important.'

'I seem to remember you telling me something like that a very long time ago.'

'Did I, *mon cher*? Well, truth is truth: it does not change.'

'Somewhere or other, I have heard that before, too.'

'I am sorry if you find it boring, my dear, but ... You will see.' Her dimple came and went. 'It is an ancient truth, *alors*.'

He laughed at that. 'Optimist,' he taunted, though not unkindly. 'Madame Dupont, the optimist.'

'It is true that I have always tried to look on the bright side, Monsieur, to count my blessings. But I will admit that this war has given my outlook a dreadful battering.'

'Endurance, my dear, that is what it is all about. Endurance!'

'Oh, and have we not endured enough?' she cried.

'Indeed, I think so, Madame. Have patience, I believe it will not be much longer now. But I mean what I say: death will be my freedom.' He smiled at her troubled expression. 'You think I am wandering, do you not, my dear? Never mind, perhaps I am. Oh ...' He put a hand to his head. 'I must lie down, I think.'

She helped him from his chair to the day bed, and he sighed, 'That is better. Thank you.'

For a few days, he seemed a little off-colour, suffering extreme fatigue—nothing more—preferring the day bed to his wheeled chair. Madame Dupont left him to rest while she went about her daily regimen, nevertheless checking on him often.

.

CHAPTER TWENTY-FIVE ~ ARMISTICE

11 November 1918

At last, at last! An announcement I thought would never come.

At the Palace of the Princes de Conde in Chantilly, Etienne was roused early by unusual activity and went to investigate.

General le Mesurier's aide, offering him coffee, replied in answer to his question, 'I can hardly take it in myself, *mon cher*, but the war is over: at last! Marshal Foch is meeting the representative of the Kaiser on the Royal Train in about half an hour in the Forest of Compiègne to sign an Armistice.' His eyes shone. 'We will go home, *mon gar*, home! Can you believe it?' He took a sip of his coffee. 'Home to decent coffee and home-cooked meals again. Won't it be wonderful?'

Etienne nodded agreement. *Yes: and I can get married!*

'The silly part is,' confided the aide, 'the Armistice does not come into effect until eleven o'clock: the eleventh hour of the eleventh day of the eleventh month. *Mais, Mon Dieu!* Have they sacrificed practicality for poetry? I mean, what do they expect us to do until then? Keep fighting?'

'Surely not, *mon brave*,' replied Etienne. 'Surely not!'

But as the young marquis would later tell his father: sadly, inexcusably, that is what some of them did.

Effacing himself as soon as possible, Etienne went to find a telephone and an operator who was awake at such an hour. But of course, they all were roused hours earlier by the aides of Marshal Foch to relay messages to the rail staff.

It took some time to get through, but finally, he was speaking to Madame Dupont: 'I am sorry to call you so early, Madame, but I thought you would want to know.' He relayed the information given to him by the general's aide and spoke to her for a few minutes before ringing off. He took out his watch: a little early to disturb Angelique. With his usual placid demeanour, he stayed to telephone his father before going to find some breakfast.

Madame Dupont, throwing on her clothes, ran to the hospital to give them the stupendous news; her heart filled with a kind of incredulous joy. *I hardly dare believe it,* she thought. *What if, at the last minute, something goes horribly wrong and it does not happen?*

On her return, she found the marquis sitting up in bed drinking coffee, still looking pale and tired, but very alert.

'Have you heard the news, Monsieur? The wonderful news that the war is over?'

'No, Madame. You have not been dreaming?' he asked, raising one eyebrow.

'*Pas du tout*, Monsieur, *pas du tout*. Etienne telephoned at some impossible hour this morning to tell me that the Armistice was about to be signed. In our Royal Train, *mon cher*, in the Forest of Compiègne before half past five this morning! What do you think of that, *hein*?'

'It is about time, is it not? But why did you not tell me earlier?'

'You have not been well, Monsieur. I did not want to disturb your sleep.'

'I can sleep at any time, but news like that comes only

once.'

'Yes, Monsieur, and thank God for it. I wonder if *les Boches*, the wives and children, are as happy about it as we are?'

'Who would know, Madame? One would hardly think so. Although, if it means that their bellies will be filled at last, perhaps they will welcome it. Ah, here is Hugh! You have heard the news, *mon brave*?'

'Yes, Sir, an Armistice has been signed. It comes into force at eleven o'clock this morning.'

The marquis sat silent for a moment. 'All over, *hein*? I suppose you will be going home, Hugh?'

'Yes, Sir, I have been recalled to my unit. I expect I will be demobbed in good time. But first, I am going to Calais to see if my little girl will come to Australia with me. If not, I shall stay in England or France with her.'

'We shall miss you, Hugh, my dear. But if you do not go to the Antipodes, you must come back and visit us. Your girl will be welcome, too,' said Madame Dupont.

'Indeed, indeed,' corroborated the marquis. 'Madame Dupont has said it for both of us. Go with God, Hugh, we shall not forget you.' He gripped his hand; his firm clasp saying what words could not.

'Thank you, Sir, nor I you,' replied Hugh, returning his handshake warmly and kissing Madame Dupont, very cheekily, she thought. 'Madame, thank you for your wonderful hospitality. You represent everything good about France and the Frogs.'

'You cannot help yourself, can you?' commented the marquis with a wry smile.

'No, Sir.' Hugh grinned, saluting them both as he went out the door. '*Adieu, mes amis.*'

The room was very quiet after he had gone. It was as if he had taken all the cheer and optimism away with him.

Madame Dupont voiced her thoughts, 'It will be hard for you without him, *mon cher*. He has been a great help to you.'

The marquis did not reply to this, not bothering to state the obvious; however much he enjoyed the company of the bright young Australian, with the war over, there would be nothing to help him with. But to tell the truth, he did not spare much time in thinking of Hugh; for his mind was leaping ahead to a new era: postwar.

'They should execute the Kaiser,' he said slowly. 'He should have to pay for the misery and suffering he has caused.'

'I do not agree with you there!' Madame Dupont took a positive stand. 'He will suffer more left alive. Every day he will writhe at the humiliation he has had to endure with his defeat. Will his miserable life be sufficient reparation for all the honourable young lives he has destroyed? I think not!'

'You may have something there, Madame, but you have not … entirely convinced me.'

'No, Monsieur?'

'No, Madame! Now I think about it, you have strayed onto the wrong track and are about to be derailed.' He smiled, but his eyes were serious. 'The Kaiser must be made to pay for his heinous crime, my dear. You see: if he is allowed to live, he will writhe, as you say, but all his people, who are mostly innocent, will be made to writhe with him. They will still be ruled by him and his warmongering generals with their bad decisions and will suffer accordingly. He and his generals—all those associated with the prosecution of this war—they should all be executed, Madame, to give the German people a fresh start; a new outlook on life. They will not then bear the burden, for justice will have been seen to be done.' He gestured. 'They should be free to devote the brilliance of their science and technology to good, not evil. They, not the Kaiser, should have this chance.' He shook his head. 'He should not be allowed to live. It is not … justice. No, Madame, this is not the answer. As history will no doubt prove.'

'You are probably right, *mon cher*. But we have what we

have ——'

'Listen!' The marquis held up a hand.

They could hear people shouting in the street: 'The war is over!'

Their eyes met. She brought over his wheeled chair to him as the chant became louder.

'The war is over!'

CHAPTER TWENTY-SIX ~ A WEDDING AND A FUNERAL

Early afternoon, 11 November 1918

Our revelling has taken Angel's strength, exhausting him so much that he cannot even lift his arm to take the telephone receiver. We rejoice at all our news today, including one piece that is almost surprising.

'The war is over!' The words still rang in Madame Dupont's head long after the joyful procession had passed along their street and into the distance. The marquis, exhausted by the effort of greeting the revellers from his chair as they passed by his gateway, had retired to his day bed.

Angelique will be able to come home, she thought, tending to his comfort. *So much better for Angel, who spends the greater part of his energy over her. Perhaps a little rest will help him shake off this illness.* The tiny worry that it was the influenza was almost put to rest. This was not how it struck, in her experience. Most definitely, Angelique's return would help him.

At that very moment, overcome with joy, the subject of her thoughts was pushing away a bottle of smelling salts held by the young marquis and wiping away tears with his handkerchief. He held her against him with one practised arm while he dexterously administered the standard method of revival, speaking in gentle tones.

In a little while, she responded: 'Oh, Etienne! It has been so long ... So long. It is hard to believe that it is finally over!'

'Indeed, my love, but it *is* over now. You may believe it! We can go home!' He hugged her closer. 'Home. Think of it!'

'Yes,' she agreed. And as she looked at his kind expression and thought of all the years he had faithfully seen to her comfort and safety while she sang in barns and churches to the soldiers, she was smitten with remorse. He had spent all his time looking after her. What had he gotten in return? Taking a deep breath, she made a supreme effort for calm. 'Etienne, *Chéri*, you have been so faithful, so wonderful to me!'

'But of course, my love. It is nothing! You know how much you mean to me.'

'And you have never asked anything from me, though you have given so much of yourself,' she said in a rush of emotion.

'That is not quite true, my dear. I have asked one thing ...'

'Yes ... And you shall have it. That is ... if you still wish to marry me?'

His overjoyed expression and the tightening of his arms gave her his answer.

'Very well,' she added, returning his embrace. 'If you still want to marry me, then let us do it ... Today!'

'Today?' He held her away to look into her face. 'But, *Chérie*, I thought you wanted a big society wedding: all the trimmings, all the partying? All the years of the war we have waited for it; you shall have it if you want it.'

'No,' she said. 'When I said that, I was a child. It would not be seemly to spend time and money on things that are of no importance; things that are only show. Perhaps I have grown up, for this war has taught me what *is* important in life. I will marry you today: if we can?'

'Oh, we can.' He smiled. 'I have had a special licence in my pocket since the day we came to Chantilly.'

'Oh, Etienne,' she sighed, kissing him tenderly. 'There is just one thing I must do first. You do not mind?'

'Of course not, my dearest one. On the contrary, I would mind if you did not.'

§

Madame Dupont approached the day bed quietly.

'Angel, my dear, can you hear me?' she asked, continuing as he turned his head enquiringly, 'Angelique has telephoned from Chantilly. She says that, unless you object, she and Etienne are getting married today in the notary's office. She wants to speak to you.'

He tried to rise and fell back in a swoon. When his head cleared he said, 'I am sorry … I cannot … Tell her that I approve.'

The effort seemed to be too much for him, and he lay back, looking white and ill.

She took his message to Angelique on the telephone, adding some encouraging words of her own. She brushed over the fact of his illness, but in her heart she realised the worst had happened. Angel had contracted the deadly Spanish flu. And in his weakened condition …

Angelique put down the telephone receiver and dabbed at a tear. 'Godmama says not to hurry back today, that we should have our honeymoon, but … I am so worried, Etienne.'

'*Doucement*, my love,' he comforted. 'I am more than willing to postpone our honeymoon. But since the earliest appointment I could get with the notary is four o'clock, even with the greasing of *several* palms …' He grimaced. 'It would be very late when we got to Paris. Why don't we have the night here and go back in the morning? It will not help the marquis nor Madame Dupont for us to arrive at such an hour. You would not wish to disturb him in the middle of the night?'

'No. Oh no, you are right. It was very kind of the le Mesuriers to offer to be our witnesses, and Madame le Mesurier has promised us a wedding breakfast after the ceremony. I would not wish to insult her by hurrying away, and you know how hard it is to go when she begs us to stay "just a tiny bit longer".'

'Indeed, I can hear her saying it,' said Etienne with a little smile. 'But I must confess that I was hoping you would agree with me, because ...' He paused for effect. 'General le Mesurier has given us a surprise wedding gift.'

'Has he? Oh, Etienne, what is it?'

'It will not be a surprise if I tell you.'

'Oh, Etienne! Do tell me ...' The amethyst eyes pleaded.

But her fiancé, a teasing light in his eye, stood firm against her blandishments to say, with a hint of mystery, 'You will know soon, my dear love.' He kissed her, tenderly. 'And now we both have many things to do before the car arrives at a quarter to four to take us to the notary's office.'

The ceremony passed in a dream for them both. None of it seemed real: not the armistice, nor the fact that they were standing in a dark-panelled room, instead of a cathedral, to take the vows they had fantasised about for years. A slender young man in a captain's uniform and his elegant bride in a dove-grey suit, its severity only relieved by a white lace jabot at her neckline and a crystal-sewn veil swathing her hat.

Surprisingly, Madame le Mesurier did not seem to wish to keep them long, shooing them into the waiting chauffeured car as soon as they had drunk their health and eaten some canapés and a piece of her cake.

When finally, at dusk, after Etienne paid the driver and

instructed him to return in the morning, they stood together at the door of a fairytale building in the depths of the Chantilly Forest, Angelique was beside herself with enchantment. 'But how *quaint*! And charming! Oh, it is just too *sweet*! Is this ———?'

'Yes, the hunting lodge of the duc d'Aumale. Ours for the night, courtesy of General le Mesurier. With a touch from me to add a little romance to our evening. I know how much you gave up to marry me today, and I hope it will not disappoint. And now, Madame la marquise, my beautiful *wife* ...' He swept her up in his arms and carried her over the threshold to set her down in the dimly lit, high-ceilinged hall. Upstairs, despite the fact that they were alone, it was apparent that a considerable amount of preparation had been carried out in the few short hours before their arrival. In the elegant boudoir, where a silk-hung four-poster bed was by no means the dominating feature, chandeliers were glowing either side of the mantel and an inviting fire burned in the grate of a white marble fireplace. A bottle of champagne stood in a silver ice bucket on a low table with two long-stemmed glasses and plates of finger food: savoury vol-au-vents and angels on horseback vying with tiny sweet pastries; and on a matching table, a charger loaded with cheeses, crusty bread and dried fruits sat beside a spirit kettle with the makings of coffee.

Scattered with decadent abandon over the priceless turkey rug in front of the hearth, were piles of satin-covered cushions and pillows embroidered in glowing jewel-colours. They made Angelique laugh with delight. 'But how gorgeous! And *how* "Arabian Nights"!' she exclaimed. 'I adore it: your touch of romance! Or is it a Bacchanalian feast?'

'It is whatever you wish it to be, my heart.' He folded her in his arms. 'With all my love.'

'Oh, Etienne ...' she responded with fervour, then drew back in confusion. 'Should ... will we change into something …?'

'More comfortable? Of course!' He steered her towards a door in a corner of the room. 'There is your dressing-room and mine is through that connecting door, over there. Our luggage has been delivered, I trust.' He kissed her again. 'Back soon, my love.'

When Angelique returned in a white satin peignoir with exquisite self-embroidery making a rich border on the lapels and the hem, golden hair flowing free, Etienne, in long-leg pyjamas and dressing-gown, was engaged in opening the champagne. They glanced at each other a little self-consciously.

'I have never entertained wearing my night attire before,' he said, expertly drawing the cork. 'I don't know what you think …'

Angelique danced over to smooth his collar. 'I love navy silk,' she assured him. 'And the tiny white dots on your pyjamas are very smart. You look *soigné* and handsome and I love you.' She kissed his cheek and whirled around. 'What do you think of my new peignoir?'

'*Ravissante*,' he murmured, seating her on a pile of cushions near the table and lowering himself beside her. 'Words cannot describe your beauty.' He raised her hand to his lips and then put a glass in it. 'My darling, let us make the most important toast of our lives,' he said, pouring the effervescent liquid and raising his glass to her.

'To us,' he toasted.

'To us,' echoed his bride, sipping daintily with him.

'To love forever.'

'Love forever,' she replied dreamily, clinking her glass against his and looking deep into his eyes as they drank.

'To the future.'

'The fu … ture.' Angelique retrieved her hesitation smoothly, but unguarded horror, quickly veiled, shone for an instant in the beautiful eyes before she drained her glass in one convulsive swallow. 'Another,' she demanded, holding it out—stalling him when he would have taken her in his arms—watching the flowing liquid as, without objecting, he filled her glass to the brim and turned away to set down the bottle.

For long moments, Angelique continued to study the champagne as if, in its swirling depths, she might find inspiration. 'But, Etienne ... *mon amour*,' she said, stealing an upward glance from between her lashes. 'Are you not afraid that I will become rather wild and abandoned if I have a second glass?'

Etienne glimpsed the provocative sparkle. 'No,' he replied, with an answering gleam. 'Not tonight ... my wicked one!' He made a little self-deprecating gesture. 'As you can see, I have my eye to the main chance here.' But behind his smiling eyes, tiny alarms were ringing: Angelique had not gulped wine like this since before the war. He relaxed a little when he saw that she was not going to quaff the second as she had the first, but not for nothing had he spent years smoothing her path. She had covered it well, but he had missed neither the slip nor her hunted expression, however fleeting, and knew that he must address whatever was troubling her before their night could unfold as he had dreamt. 'But you are *not* getting a third, and you had better eat something,' he admonished, holding a pastry topped with strawberry preserve to her lips. 'Come, my darling, eat with me the food of love.'

When they'd eaten their fill and finished their champagne, he rose, emptied the coalscuttle on the glowing embers and stirred up the fire, snuffed most of the candles and lay back amongst the cushions. He held out his arms, and Angelique went into them: generous and giving, ardent, pliable.

He kissed her hair, stroking it back from her face, then tilted her chin so that she had to look at him in the flickering light. 'I must ask you a serious question, my love: what is it about the future that frightens you so?'

Everything! Can I live in a future without Angelpapa? A future paved with the bodies of those who have died in this dreadful war?

Feeling guilt forever that I have survived at their expense? That I might even have sent them to their deaths? Always seeing horror whenever I close my eyes … Angelique gazed at him, dumbly. How could she say these things to the one who would share it with her? The one it would hurt so much.

He held her more firmly, looking down into her eyes with love and understanding. 'Is it … tonight? Because you don't have to do anything you don't want. You know that, don't you?'

'Oh, no, it is not tonight. I know you will not hurt me. I *want* us to be … one,' she gasped, pressing the length of her body to his, as if, by doing so, she could meld them together.

'My love … my life,' he murmured, covering her lips with his own; his heart thrilling at her sensuous response. He wanted, more than anything, to abandon himself to the passion that surged against him—a passion that matched his own—but made a supreme effort for control.

This problem, that he had not yet got to the bottom of, was but a tiny dust mote on the glorious fabric of their evening: only a minor detail, but one that he knew he could not afford to ignore. 'Please try to tell me what it is that worries you, *Chérie*. Are you afraid that I will not understand?'

'No. I know you will understand, if only I could tell you what it is. It is just that … Oh, I *cannot* explain.' At his waiting expression, she took a deep breath and tried: 'For years we have lived day to day, not knowing if there was a future; sometimes not believing that there could be … The horrors, the nightmares: How can we forget them? How can we go on and … *live*? When so many have … *died*?' The last words came out as sobs; her tears flowing as if they would never stop. *When I might have killed them? And how can I go on without Angelpapa?*

'I know … I know,' Etienne said, proffering a handkerchief and soothing her with gentle sounds. 'But that is not all, is it?'

'No,' she admitted, but she still could not tell him about Angelpapa. 'I am afraid that my singing ——'

Suddenly, he thought he knew what was worrying her. 'You are afraid that, by inspiring them to go back and fight, you sent our soldiers to their deaths?'

'I ... yes,' she whispered, and turned her head aside.

'But you didn't. You gave them hope, life, inspiration. Look at me, my darling.' He gave her a little shake. 'Don't you see? You did what they did: You gave your all.'

Angelique looked up, arrested. Her new husband had put everything in perspective for her. She'd been doing what she could for her country, just like everyone else. Her voice had not decided any of their fates: the soldiers had made their own decisions. An immense relief flowed over her, dissolving the guilt, washing it away. 'Oh, Etienne. I love you so!' she sobbed. 'I *do* love you so.'

With a passing worry that he didn't have the smelling salts, Etienne soon realised that her tears were not hysterical, but healing, and was content to let her cry herself out in his arms.

'*Doucement, Chérie,*' he said at last, when her tears had abated. 'Those we lost in the war died for us so that we might live. Are we going to squander that for which they fought and died so valiantly? Will we throw away their sacrifice that they knowingly and willingly made for us?'

'No. Oh no. We must not! We must always remember them and what they have done for us.'

'Then let us thank them by living in the moment and savouring every precious second of the time we have together. The time that they have given us. Shall we do that, my dearest love?'

Angelique looked into the golden-hazel eyes and saw, not only a passion and desire that matched hers, but a patient and enduring love: a love that had survived the terrible years of privation and would go on into infinity. And she realised that Etienne, too, had given his all. For her.

Joy sang in her blood, and a great, overmastering love for this man who held her so protectively. This man who had such strength and control that he would not take what she offered until he'd banished her demons; who had given her the means to carry on when darkness overwhelmed; who had transformed their wedding from a drab civil ceremony into a magical world of romance. And suddenly, she could forget what the future might inevitably hold and abandon herself to the present. A present where a surfeit of sensual delights were beginning to overpower rational thought.

The music in her soul soared to a crescendo. Her whole body came alive. 'Oh, yes,' she sighed, against the warm sweetness of his lips. 'Please ...'

§

When the newly married couple returned to the hôtel du Bois the following day, they found that Madame Dupont had already put into operation a twenty-four hour nursing plan: herself, Charles, and a very good English nurse from the hospital bearing the brunt, with Doctor Martin coming and going. For two weeks the marquis fought delirium, then lapsed into unconsciousness.

Angelique wanted to be part of the nursing team, but when both Madame Dupont and Etienne refused to consider it, she came and went, spending many hours holding the marquis' hand and singing softly to him. Sometimes he stirred; his fingers tightening briefly on hers, but he did not awaken. After a few days, he passed into periods of semi-consciousness where he would take sips of barley water, thin gruel or chicken consommé; but he did not know anybody. Christmas passed without the least recognition by any of them, and it was not until the New Year that he showed signs of improvement.

3 January 1919

In the midst of grief, I have been given a small beacon of light: a tiny spark of joy to help me deal with a loss that I could never be prepared for.

And now, Madame Dupont, nursing him carefully with her team and bringing him safely through what she believed was the worst of it, was sitting by his bedside, fairly confident that he was recovering.

'You are looking a little better this morning, Angel. I am very pleased to see it.'

'Indeed, Madame, I am feeling in quite good spirits. But I am as weak as a cat,' he complained, trying to lift one arm. 'Angelique will be home today?'

'Oh, yes.' She nodded. 'She will be here soon. She is singing to the convalescents this afternoon. She has been coming to see you every day, but you have not been well enough to notice.'

'Oh, the dear child. I believe I did sense her presence, even though I could not respond. It will be good to see her. I think I am fully compos mentis this morning.'

'Indeed. Your nurses are very pleased with you, my dear.'

'So … Where is Angelique now, then?'

'She and Etienne have been invited by Monsieur Lafosse to a special New Year exhibition of his work.'

'Who?'

'Monsieur Lafosse. You know, the Dadaist: a pupil of Francis Picabia. It is his first exhibition, and they promised to look in on it.'

'Oh … Long hair?' He nodded at her confirmation. 'I know the one: foppish idiot!'

'But, Monsieur, you said that some of his works had merit.'

He gave the ghost of a smile. 'Did I? Oh, so I did. Dadaism: it is not really my thing.'

'No, Monsieur, it is … unusual. I think it is an expression of rebellion against the privations and

331

anonymity of the war.'

'Probably,' he concurred. 'The name says it all, does it not? Just another word for inconsequential stupidity.'

'Oh, my dear, that is a bit harsh, but I must admit that most people I have spoken to find their art rather shocking and unintelligible.'

'Then the Dadaists have succeeded in their intent, have they not? Not but what such things are a complete waste of time. Exhibitionism at its most crass!' He yawned, dismissing Monsieur Lafosse and his misguided brethren with a slight wave of his hand. 'Tell me: did I dream it, or is it true that Angelique married Etienne in a notary's office?'

'It is true, my dear. They were married in Chantilly on Armistice Day.'

'So. My little one has grown up.' He was silent a minute. 'You know, I would not have expected that of her. She so wanted a wedding with all the trimmings. She would have made the most beautiful bride.'

'I know,' she sighed. 'The war has changed us all.'

'Indeed …' Whatever he was about to say was lost in a coughing fit that battered his weakened frame. Followed by another.

Madame Dupont rushed to support him with an extra pillow behind his back; pressed a handkerchief into his hand; guided it to his lips; watched, in numb horror, as a red froth spread into its snowy folds.

He met her eyes. Understanding passed between them. It was as if he shrugged. She noticed in a kind of abstract haze that the pallor of his skin had taken on a bluish tinge and saw that he was trying to speak. She strained to hear.

'My freedom awaits,' he murmured, with a wry twist, trying without success to thread shaking fingers under the chain of his locket. 'Angelique … Tell her …' His eyes explained what his lips could not say, holding hers until she nodded. Then, they shifted, looked past her with a sudden incredulous joy and welcoming glow. He half-raised himself, stretching out a hand, before falling back onto his pillows.

Silence pounded, thrummed in her ears, held her immobile. She shut her teeth on a soundless cry of denial. Despite her vigilance, all that she had done, the dreadful plague had claimed him. Had she not seen enough of it to know that he was dead?

But stay! Was he, though?

In her mind's eye, she watched him rise from the dried husk on the bed—tall, strong and athletic, his hair shining black—and walk with arms outstretched towards Katarina and Sprite, young and beautiful, so happy to see him, as they entered the room. They went into his embrace together, returning it lovingly; then each taking a hand, began to lead him to the door. There they turned, the three of them, to smile at her. For a moment, or an eternity, she felt the touch of their spirits surrounding her with love.

'*Au revoir*, Elise, my dear. Until we meet again ...' she heard him say clearly with his little quirky half-smile she had loved all her life, before they turned away and went out together, leaving the room unbearably empty and silent. In fact, that was the thing that hit her the hardest— the silence. Unbearable! Inconceivable: life without Angel!

Yet, how could she grieve for him after the vision she had just been granted? He looked so young and happy, reunited with the ones he loved.

So it is true, then: the ones who love you come for you when you die! Through her grief her heart rejoiced. *I shall see him again, God be praised! I shall see them all again!*

She went reverently to close his eyes and lay him out, performing this final service for him. Taking the locket on its fine gold chain from around his neck, she lay it carefully in its velvet case. Her eyes blinded by tears, she removed the thorns from the stem of a red rose, tying it with a black ribbon. Heaven only knew how there came to be a rose at this time of year, the last lingering one, and so perfect. Giving the bow a final twitch into place, she slid it under his folded hands. A dewdrop trembling on a ruby petal caught the light in a tiny, flashing rainbow; a tear, fallen unnoticed: poignant, solitary.

She gently kissed the white, noble brow. 'I shall miss you, dearest Angel. Oh, how I shall miss you, my dear, dear friend.'

She was keeping a vigil by his body when a slender whirlwind erupted into the room. 'Angelpapa! Angelpapa! No-o-o-o-o! No-o!' Angelique prostrated herself over the bed, clutching at his white, cold hands, scattering rose petals heedlessly; her whole body reflecting the agony of her mind. 'Too late! Too late! No-o-o! No-o!'

Madame Dupont knew she must intervene before she became completely hysterical. 'My child, you must calm yourself. It is the way of all humanity, and we must all eventually come to it. But listen, Petite ...' She explained what she had seen, adding, 'You know how you always felt him standing beside you when you sang?'

'Oh, Godmama!' Angelique turned to her impulsively. 'He still does ... Did.' She burst into sobs again.

'Now, listen, Angelique. Remember what he said about the spirit, and what I told you all those years ago? His spirit lives, and he will be beside you when you sing. This you must do for him! Go and sing for him. You will sing better than ever, for his spirit is no longer bound to his body. He will be there with you, stronger than ever. You will see, my child, it will be as I say. But we must get you home, my dear. Where is Etienne?'

'I do not know, Godmama. I left him with Monsieur Lafosse. I just had a feeling about Angelpapa and came straight away. But I was too late!' She put a hand to her mouth to stifle her cries. 'Too late ...'

'There, there, remember what I say. Stay here with him and try not to grieve too much, for he lives—happy at last—happier than he ever was in this world, if I am any judge. Stay, think on these things, while I send for your husband.'

She rang the bell, speaking rapidly to Justin. Then she was back, reaching for the velvet case. 'Take this, my dear. He left it for you. He said you are to wear it always as a reminder of his love.'

'Oh, Godmama!' she cried, opening the box and staring at the oval of beautifully crafted gold and the exquisite cameo in its surrounding wreath of diamond-studded gold leaves with tiny forget-me-nots inset with sapphires. 'Of course, I shall wear it! But I do not need anything to remind me of his love.'

She took it out of the box, holding it by its chain; and Madame Dupont fastened the clasp at the back of her neck.

'I suppose you know that it contains a lock of your mama's hair?'

'Does it?' She turned in astonishment. 'But how did he get it? Did he ——?'

'No.' Madame Dupont shook her head. 'She gave it to him many years ago when they were young. Before she married your father,' she added, seeing the question in her eyes.

'Then she did return his love! Oh, poor Papa! But why ——?'

'No, Angelique, you must not ask these questions in your heart,' she told her gently. 'There are many things in life we do not understand. Your mother did love your papa, in truth most devotedly, having known and loved him since her babyhood. But she fell in love with Angel— her first romantic love, you understand—and he fell immediately in love with her. But he was not in a position to marry her at that stage, so he made her go to Xavier, sacrificing his own happiness for what he believed to be best for her. But there was something so strong, so compelling in the love of Angel that drew her to him ...' She took a troubled breath. 'That she never got over it. And neither did he. You do not have to know how or why: no-one can know this. All you have to know is that this

335

locket is the symbol of love. Possibly the greatest kind of love there is, for he did not look for anything for himself, giving his all for those he loved. His love for you was of this order, and you will wear it for him—and for you—to remind you. He is with your mama and Sprite now, and nothing can hurt him ever again; and he will continue to support you onstage, as always.' Madame Dupont put a hand on her arm. 'And you must be good to Etienne, Petite, for his love is of this order, too.'

'Yes, Godmama, I know. I have learnt to appreciate it. I know that I was infantile and stupid … But I have grown up.'

'Yes and beautifully, too,' said Madame Dupont, softly. 'Angel was proud of you, my dear, very proud. But here is Etienne now. We must pass on the sad tidings to him, and he will take you home.'

Angelique flew into his arms. His eyes went to the still figure on the bed. 'Ah, my darling,' he comforted. 'There, there.'

Madame Dupont met his eyes. 'You knew, then?'

'I guessed, Madame. When she left the way she did, I knew it must be this.'

He looked at her discerningly. 'Will you be all right, Madame, here alone?'

'Thank you, Etienne, yes. I shall sit with him awhile.' She glanced down, straightening the bedcover. 'Perhaps you and Angelique will stay in your suite here until the … funeral, if you don't mind? I will be down later.'

'Of course, Madame, we shall stay with you as long as you want. In truth, you always make us very comfortable.'

§

A week later, Madame Dupont, Etienne and Angelique took the marquis back to the château du Bois to be interred with his ancestors in the vault beneath the chapel. She and Angelique went in Angelique's new automobile;

the earthly remains of the marquis by train, escorted by Etienne, and met by a traditional hearse drawn by four perfectly matched black horses to convey him to his resting place.

Driving along the tree-lined road, Angelique said, 'Godmama, I know that this is in accordance with Angelpapa's wishes, but would it not have been easier to have brought him in his ambulance van straight to the chapel?'

'Perhaps, my dear, but he did hate them so, and he gave these particular orders long before *les voitures* were anything like as advanced as they are now.'

'I do not understand … He was such a forward thinker, and he liked other kinds of mechanical inventions. I mean, he invented so many himself.'

'It is true, he was working on a way to make them quieter, more efficient, and he understood they were the way of the future; but he did, always, love to drive a good pair of horses.'

The chapel was full and people waited outside, lining the road all the way down to the railway station to pay their respects to the last blood descendant of the du Bois, removing hats and bowing heads while the carriage passed; the duc, Etienne and Angelique's brothers heading the group that followed the hearse; the black horses solemnly nodding their plumed heads as they brought him home for the last time.

Angelique sang for him at his Requiem, but it upset her so badly that afterwards she had to be supported to the château by Etienne and the duc. Madame Dupont got through it without breaking down by keeping in her mind the picture of how she had last seen him: the delight on his face as he looked down at his two loving companions.

His will was read publicly and caused a sensation, for aside from the usual bequests, not only did he leave his tenants their homes and farms, he left everything else, including his share in the Opéra Magique, to Angelique—

described in his will as 'Mademoiselle Angelique de Villefontaine, beloved daughter of my spirit'. The terms of the will included an instruction that Madame Dupont remain in her wing of the hôtel du Bois with all care for the rest of her life, after which it also reverted to Angelique. The future of the du Bois Hospital was to be the decision of his heiress.

'There shall be no doubt about it,' said Angelique. 'The Hospital du Bois shall continue whilst ever the injured and disabled soldiers from the Great War have need of it. It shall be Angelpapa's legacy to France.'

CHAPTER TWENTY-SEVEN ~ FEMME FORMIDABLE

11 January 1919

Now that I no longer have Angel to care for, Angelique must be my main priority. I don't know how she will be able to exist without her Angelpapa. Not only has she been given no time to grieve, the poor child has commitments that she must honour. It will be so hard on her.

Now, most important to Madame Dupont was Angelique's state of mind. She had postponed her tour, refusing to leave the marquis in his illness, but now she must honour her contract. More than ever, she would need the presence of her family; for the stress on her would be so much greater. On this tour, only Etienne was to be going with her—but that must change.

The family was gathered in a small salon in the château; the duc and duchesse in the middle of their leave taking.

Angelique held her handkerchief to her mouth. 'I do not know how I can do this ... Go on tour, I mean. Only, I know that I must. People have paid. Everyone has gone to so much trouble making the arrangements. He ... Oh, I know he would say that I must.'

No-one denied it. Etienne regarded her sympathetically. Elise seemed unable to stem her tears. Philippe cleared his throat uncomfortably.

'Somewhere you will find the strength, my dear child,' said the duc, making a gesture that reminded her intolerably of the marquis. 'Chin up, *hein*,' he said kindly, stroking her cheek. 'We are behind you. The duchesse and I must go now, but we will be at your first performance, dear child. It was a wonderful idea to dedicate it to the marquis du Bois. Try not to grieve too much. He would not want that, you know.' He pressed her hand comfortingly, but she could not respond with words, only shaking her head.

Etienne took his mother's arm. 'I will see you to your auto, Maman. We have barely exchanged a word together.'

The duc turned to Madame Dupont, taking the hand she held out to him and patting it. '*Eh bien*, Ma Belle, life goes on.' He sighed.

'Of course, Georges, he would expect it,' she replied, meeting his gaze.

'He would indeed, *ma chère*. To have known him was at once a great privilege of insight into his genius, and a minefield of unforeseen calamity. *Du vrai*, one might almost say it was like living one's life on the *Montagnes Russes!*'

'Exactly, *mon cher*,' she exclaimed, the taut line of her lips softening. 'There was nobody like him.'

'No, my dear, I am aware,' he said, a little dryly, raising the hand he was holding to his lips. '*Au revoir*, now. I shall see you in Paris. Etienne will look after you.' He smiled at them both and turned, a tall, straight figure, accompanied to his car by his daughter and her husband.

For the moment, they were alone: the only ones left who had truly loved Angel; the only ones who understood the pain. Madame Dupont looked at Angelique, at the clouded eyes, the trembling lips. The girl was like a wounded deer. Instantly her compassion was aroused. Putting an arm around her, she asked, 'Would you like me to come with you, my dear?'

'Oh, Godmama,' she cried breathlessly, coming to life. 'Would you? Oh, that would be too marvellous! Thank you!'

Madame Dupont had a sudden idea. 'Shall I try to bring your papa, too?'

'Oh please do, Godmama! But I do not think he will come. He has not left his study since we lost Maman.'

'Then it is time he did, do you not think?' replied Madame Dupont, her dimple peeping out.

Angelique smiled, a little wanly, it is true, but at least it was a smile. 'If anyone can get him to do it, it will be you, will it not? Go get him, Godmama!' she added on a little sob; her attempt at humour ending in pathos.

Etienne returned, folding Angelique lovingly in his arms. He looked at Madame Dupont. 'Shall we go, too, Madame?'

§

Very soon after that, a small, determined *femme formidable* confronted Xavier's intimidating butler.

'Monsieur le comte is not receiving, Madame. He will see no-one. You may leave your card,' he intoned with practised boredom.

She fixed him with an implacable eye. 'You know me, do you not, Marcel?'

'Yes, Madame.' The butler inclined his head majestically.

'Then you know that I am a little more involved with this family than an ordinary visitor, do you not?'

He acquiesced silently, a faint air of unease replacing his previous pomposity.

She eyed him thoughtfully. 'How long have you been in the employ of Monsieur le comte, Marcel?'

'I started as pantry boy over forty years ago, Madame, and I have been butler now for more than twenty-five.'

'You feel you know Monsieur le comte well?'

'Yes, Madame, as well as anyone in my position is able to do, I suppose.'

'Describe him to me.'

'I beg your pardon, Madame?' The butler, startled, began to look uncomfortable.

'Come, Marcel, play a little game of make-believe with me. Just to humour me, you know. Suppose you were not a discreet butler for just a moment, but a friend of the family: how would you describe the character of your master to another friend? Go on, describe him to me.'

The butler, jibbing a little at first, stammered, 'Well, er ... ahem. I suppose ... I ... I would say he is very kind and genial, good-tempered, a loving family man. The only times I have seen him angry is when he feels a loved one is threatened or someone is unfairly treated. A great one to take the part of the underdog is Monsieur le comte. If he has a fault ...' The butler looked embarrassed. 'It is that he is not firm in his decision making, but he gets there eventually. And when he does, there is no fear that he will not stand by his word, Madame, he always stands buff to the end. Very faithful and constant, he is.'

'You speak as a man who thinks highly of him, Marcel. Moreover, you have described to me a very estimable man.'

'Indeed, Madame, he is a good man. All of us here in service esteem him very highly.'

She nodded. Then she was brisk again. 'Very well, then, if it is as you say, if you have any feelings at all for your master, you may take me to him. We must break this cycle before it breaks him.' She held his eye. 'You may be sure that no blame will attach to you. The comte knows that I hold some sway in this matter. There will be no consequences for you; you have my word. Now: announce me.'

The butler, backing before her, led the way to the comte's study. Knocking and opening the door for her, he pronounced in the voice of a doomsayer, 'Madame Dupont.'

Xavier turned his head in surprise; his haunted face forcing a cry from her. 'Xavier, my dear!'

'Madame! Why are you here?' He rose from behind his desk to greet her.

Madame Dupont chose to ignore the ungracious tone, answering the question directly, 'You must not, any longer, shut yourself away like this, *mon cher*. Your daughter has need of you.' She paused. 'As you know, the marquis du Bois has passed away, and I am no longer needed to care for him. But now, Angelique has need of us to support her on her tour; for she is bereft without him.' At the expression on his face, she became severe. 'He was always there for her, Monsieur.'

'I know, Madame.' He looked at the floor. 'Indeed, I am sorry for your loss.'

'I thank you, Monsieur,' she said, waiting for him to reply to her statement. When he didn't, she reminded him, 'And now, your daughter has need of her papa ...'

Still he did not reply.

'When you first shut yourself away, I went along with it, telling myself that you had the right to grieve in the way you saw fit ———'

'Madame,' he bowed ironically. 'You were correct in your assumption. How is it that you no longer respect my wishes? And override my orders to my own servants?'

'My dear,' she said gently, ignoring the peevish sarcasm, 'you are doing yourself no good by this ... self-incarceration. Life does—it must—go on. You have children. Soon, you will have grandchildren. Don't you want to see them grow up?'

'No, my life ... ended with Katarina's,' he mumbled, shaking his head like a bull beset by a stinging fly. 'Who says I want to do myself good?'

'Perhaps you do not. But I will not believe that you have changed so much, become so selfish, that you do not want the best for your daughter!'

He seemed unable to respond, opening and closing his mouth, negating with his hands.

'Are you telling me you will not come?' she asked incredulously; once more the indomitable *femme formidable*.

For the space of five seconds, he was silent, swallowing a lump. Then he groaned, 'I will come.'

'Good.' Her tone was bracing. 'The rheumatism: how is it?'

'Not too bad at the moment, Madame. It comes and goes.'

'Indeed.' She looked at his wheeled chair parked in the corner of the room. 'I will send over the wheeled chair of the marquis for you. It is a much better design and will be easier to travel—to get you in and out of trains, that sort of thing—than that *passé* model.' She made a dismissive gesture. 'The tour begins in two weeks at the Opéra Magique as a tribute to the marquis. Then we go to Vienna.' She cast her eye over the still slim, upright figure in his old-fashioned morning dress. 'You had better see a tailor, Xavier. You must be dressed *à la mode* as the father of the diva, you know.'

CHAPTER TWENTY-EIGHT ~ ÉTERNITÉ D'AMOUR

26 January 1919

I am very proud of my abilities, having managed to get Xavier out of his self-imposed solitude. I foresee that I will be extremely busy taking care of both him and his daughter.

Madame Dupont was glad to get away from the du Bois mansion. She could not believe how lonely it was without the marquis or how much she missed him. Two weeks: it seemed to take forever to pass, even though she was busy with the wardrobes of herself, Angelique and Xavier; and becoming familiar with details of the tour—like who the new tour manager was, for instance. Everything had changed through the years of the war, and while the marquis had been so ill. She felt empty, boring, as if she knew nothing. Then, to crown all, the day before the performance at the Opéra Magique, Angelique suffered a fit of nerves that took the form of an extreme loss of confidence in herself and her singing. So much so, that Madame Dupont was beginning to doubt that they would get her as far as her dressing-room, and even Etienne's eternal calm was beginning to be disturbed. Wondering how she could turn the tide, she was relieved to find Angelique prepared to talk about it.

Confiding her fears to Madame Dupont, she said, 'We are supposed to be going to Vienna in a spirit of reconciliation, but I do not know … You will still come with me?' Her anxiety was patent. 'You won't just leave after the recital at the Opéra Magique?'

'Of course I will come with you to Vienna, Child. What darkness has come over you that you would doubt it? And your papa is coming with us, too.'

'*Is* he?' she asked, diverted for the moment. 'But, Godmama, how did you convince him?'

'Never mind that, now. The important thing is that he is coming. Oh, and there is an eminent specialist physician in rheumatics in Vienna. We must try to get him an appointment. Now, tell me why you are suffering such a revulsion of feeling about this tour to which you have agreed, and indeed, which you had been all ready to start?'

'I cannot explain it, Godmama. I am worried about singing for those who, only a short while ago, we regarded as our enemies.'

'Indeed, it will be strange, my dear. We must do our best to forgive, even if we are unable to forget. And, too, most of their population wanted the war as little as we did, you know.'

'Yes, I have been told that. I must try to remember it. Oh, Godmama,' she cried, wringing her hands. 'I wish I did not feel so excessively nervous! I have not felt like this since before we did *Le Perdu* for the first time.'

'Oh, you were a child then!' exclaimed Madame Dupont. 'It seems a whole lifetime ago, now. But once you get onstage, dear child, the familiarity of it will ease your panic. And Monsieur Merignac will be with you. *Du vrai*, age has not seemed to slow him down!'

'No, indeed, he is as spry as a cricket,' agreed Angelique, apathetically.

'Then what, my dear? You know who else you will have, don't you?' said Madame Dupont, beginning to feel that she had put her finger on it.

'Will I?' The girl turned a ravaged face to her. 'I am afraid he will not be there any more.'

'Oh, my dear, of course he will! Did you not feel his presence when you sang for him in the chapel?'

'Yes, that was why it was too much for me; for he wasn't there, was he? He was already gone!'

'No, he was not already gone. If you felt his presence, then he was there with you.'

'But you said he went away with Maman and another …' Angelique bit her lip.

'Yes, his assistant, Sprite, who died tragically … young. Please, Angelique, do not bite your lip. You are singing tomorrow!'

'Well, what if he has gone and does not come back?' wailed Angelique, disregarding her plea.

'He will come back! Of course he will! He did not say to me, "Goodbye forever", but, "Until we meet again". Do you remember he told you that he would be with you when you need him? That you have only to call?'

She nodded. 'Yes, I suppose.'

'Then you must have faith in that!' Madame Dupont took her by the shoulders. 'And now, you do understand that there is no need for nerves, *hein*?'

For the first time, Angelique smiled, relief transforming her lovely features. 'Yes, thank you, Godmama. I must believe, for if I do not, it is the end of my career.' Her smile went awry as she whispered, 'And my life.'

It was hardly the answer Madame Dupont wanted, and it took her aback considerably; but it had to suffice, for she was astute enough not to pursue it. Needless to say, she and Etienne kept a close eye on her, never leaving her alone; and all would have been well had not a certain set of circumstances all coincided with evil consequences. But that was for later.

For now, all appeared to progress with comparative ease as Angelique dressed and prepared her voice for her tribute to her guardian, not allowing herself to even think of what might happen if he failed her.

Even so, their first night of the tour at the Opéra Magique was a trauma for all three of them: Xavier and Madame Dupont in the de Villefontaine box without Katarina, Angelique onstage without the marquis.

This theatre is full of ghosts, thought Madame Dupont, seated next to Xavier in front of the empty stage. She glanced at him to see how he was taking it, but she could not tell; for his expression gave no clue to his thoughts.

The curtain rose on a slender, solitary figure in the spotlight. The crowd went mad. Angelique, smiling her thanks around the auditorium, held up a hand for silence.

Thank God, she seems composed, thought Madame Dupont, as the young diva began to speak.

'The songs that I will sing for you tonight are dedicated to my beloved teacher, guardian angel and spiritual father: the marquis du Bois,' she told her audience. 'Without him, I would not be here tonight.' Bowing her head, she waited some minutes for the acclaim to cease; for he was acknowledged as the Master and many regretted his passing.

Now at the height of her fame, she stood at centrestage; her hair reflecting and shining an aureole of light about her head. Dressed, as always, in floating, filmy white, she was still the beautiful angel of their dreams, preparing to stun them with the unparalleled magnificence of her voice. She flung up her head, stretched out her arms; the crowd falling silent before her electrifying persona. In this, her first performance since the marquis passed into spiritual realms, she held the audience in the palm of her hand; her deep amethyst eyes sparkling with a presence and power hereto only hinted at.

As she began to sing, her soaring golden notes resonating all around them, an amazing thing happened to

Madame Dupont. In an instant, for precious moments, she saw that Angelique was not alone. Angel and Katarina stood on either side of her, each with a hand on her shoulder, singing with her as she produced every sweet, achingly pure note with a power and brightness, a vibrant mystery she had never shown before. While there, coming from behind, dancing around them with spellbinding beauty was Sprite: ethereal and graceful as ever.

Her eyes glued to the stage, Madame Dupont could hardly credit them, as golden rivers of sound filled the theatre: rolling, tumbling, cascading in sunlight; trickling sweetly into droplets; rising triumphantly into a great tidal wave; finally leaving the auditors stranded on the shore with the glory of it still ringing in their ears. It was over. She blinked. Angelique stood alone on the stage, receiving her just acclaim. Turning to Xavier, Madame Dupont realised that, incredibly, he had not seen anyone other than Angelique. Smiling and applauding his daughter, he said, 'I am glad I came, Madame. I had forgotten what a magnificent voice my daughter has. Thank you.'

Later, in her dressing-room, Angelique turned away from Etienne to Madame Dupont with a blinding smile, throwing her arms around her ecstatically. 'Godmama, did you see? Did you see Angelpapa? He was there with me on the stage, singing with me, as he promised! Did you see?'

'I did, my darling, I did see him. Did I not tell you how it would be?' Madame Dupont returned her hug warmly.

Etienne stood back a little from these transports; a slight frown in his eyes. He met those of the comte—a glance and an indulgent shrug passing between them. *Les femmes and their imagination,* it seemed to say. *Well, if it helps them to cope ...*

Xavier quietly left the room, returning in a short while. Later, one of his attendants handed him a velvet case. Embracing his daughter, he presented her with it. 'I have been meaning to give you these for a long time, my daughter, but I have found it extraordinarily difficult to part with them,' he explained, opening the box to reveal a delicate pearl and diamond tiara and necklace. 'Your mother would want you to have them.'

'Oh, exquisite!' she breathed, turning for him to put them on her. 'I thank you, Papa. Their value is beyond price. I will wear them at every performance,' she vowed, kissing him fondly, and then dashing tears from her eyes as she saw herself in the mirror. 'Oh, I remember so *vividly* ... Maman wearing these at ——'

The comte, shaken, rushed out of the room. Madame Dupont put a hand on Angelique's arm as she was about to follow him. 'No, leave him alone. It will be best. He needs to be able to release his emotions. He has been too long in a frozen wasteland. We will see him later ... Just to check on him.'

Although she successfully hid it from Angelique, she had a horrible feeling that the comte was about to go back to his study and stay there.

§

The comte, though he did not back out of the journey as Madame Dupont had feared, was a morose travelling companion, speaking only when spoken to and spending most of the journey looking mournfully out of the window. Once in Vienna, however, he was a courteous and amiable guest, acceding graciously to whatever entertainment was offered by his hosts.

Madame Dupont had faithfully made the appointment with the great specialist physician in rheumatics; the only problem being that it coincided with the day of Angelique's first performance in the city. And here was the difficulty: an urgent business complication had come up, which Etienne had perforce to deal with. And this would culminate in a situation they had so far most carefully avoided: Angelique left on her own, without one of them. Recipe for disaster? They hoped not.

The marquis explained his problem: 'For Madame, if I do not go now, there will be no money to pay our entourage.' He shrugged. 'There has been some mix-up with the bank, which requires my signature before any transactions can proceed. I sold some bonds with instructions that the proceeds be sent to the bank here in Vienna. Now it seems there has been such a cock-up that they have continued to sell the bonds, but none know where the money has gone. And to stop this madness and track down the funds, they need my signature on the order. I only hope they have not done something stupid with the monies that I wired ahead, or things will begin to be extremely difficult.'

'Oh dear,' she sighed. 'I see your point. This is a problem that must be unravelled, for we must have funds. That is elementary. I shall try to postpone the comte's appointment until another day.'

However, an attempt to postpone brought the intelligence that this was the only available appointment. The comte would not be able to see the professor on any other day, for he was going out of the country. What would Madame wish to do?

Madame Dupont had misgivings, but she confirmed the appointment. She could not miss this chance of help for the comte. Turning to Etienne, she said, 'Oh, I really do not like to leave Angelique without one of us here, my dear. I believe it is just asking for trouble.'

Tapping his teeth, thoughtfully, the marquis replied, 'You must not abandon this chance for relief for the comte, Madame, and it would be impossible to send a servant to look after him. You know what he is ...'

'I know, I know. None better, *mon fils*. He would very likely go into a fit of apathy at the sight of someone or something that reminded him of Katarina and not even turn-up. A servant would not have any influence over him in that event. And it would be more than a possibility, you know. Katarina loved Vienna.'

'It is an unfortunate coincidence, but I must go to the Exchange and sort out this dreadful misunderstanding; for it is imperative that I track down these funds that have gone missing. I only hope it does not leave us without a feather to fly with.' He smiled at his witticism, for Angelique's fame ensured that it was not even a probability; nevertheless, it would be awkward. Temporary, but awkward. 'I think we shall do, Madame, for I should only be away for an hour or two at the most; and if I time it for Angelique's rest period in the afternoon, there should be no difficulty.'

And so, Madame Dupont set off early with the comte to make sure he kept his appointment; and after a leisurely lunch, having settled Angelique to rest after rehearsal and sent the maid to press her gown and make everything ready for the recital, the young marquis sallied forth to attend to this particularly annoying piece of business, with no premonition or sense of déjà vu.

CHAPTER TWENTY-NINE ~ ANGELS OR SPIRITS

8 February 1919

I have wished before that I could be in two places at the same time, but never with more fervour than today!

'Monsieur Clement! Monsieur Clement!' The agitated tones and running footsteps of his assistant disturbed the tour manager working quietly at his desk. He knotted his brow. It was his job to make sure all was running smoothly, and in the financial department things were just not adding up.

'Oh, what now?' he mouthed, taking a deep breath and putting on his professional face.

'In here, André. Come in. What is your trouble?'

'Monsieur, you had better come at once,' gasped the young man, quite breathless. 'Madame la marquise has gone into alt!'

'Whatever do you mean?' enquired the manager, frowning a little.

'She's having hysterics all over ... A right old tantrum!'

'That's the opposite of alt, you fool!' declared Monsieur

Clement. 'For what reason is she exhibiting these, er ... transports?'

'W-what do you mean?'

The manager cast up his eyes. 'Perhaps if I rephrase the question: why is she so upset?'

'Oh, yes, yes, of course! Well, it seems that when the maid was ironing her dress—the one she wants to wear tonight—she burnt a hole in it.'

His superior looked him over. 'So?' he said, with dangerous calm.

'Well, that's it, Monsieur,' replied André, aware of the undercurrents and at a loss to understand them. He shrugged, eyeing his superior, warily.

'Then why—I only ask because I am amazed you have not thought of it yourself—did you not get her another one? Why have you not attended to this *bêtise* yourself, instead of annoying me with it?'

André flushed at the unmistakable sarcasm. 'Well I did, Monsieur, but apparently it doesn't suit her. "I do not like it!",' he mimicked, adding in exasperation, 'So, of course that set her off again!'

'Then get her another one! One she does like!' shouted the manager, upsetting his books as he leapt to his feet. 'Why do I have to tell you this? Do I have to think for you as well as myself? You are employed to assist me, not ruin my day! You know how highly strung she is!'

'Highly strung? Oh, that's a nice one. I'd like to give her highly strung! An excuse to ride roughshod over everybody! Why do we have to waste our time with her tantrums?'

Monsieur Clement's eyebrows shot up in astonishment. 'Are you mad?' he asked, on a rising inflection.

'No, but she is!' said the assistant, picking up the books and returning them to the desk.

'Thank —— What do you mean?' asked the manager, distracted.

The assistant took a deep breath. 'Well ... When I went

to the dressing-room to see what all the screeching was about, she was talking to someone; so I waited outside to avoid disturbing them.' He eyed the manager, apprehensively. 'She told him all about it: how she couldn't go on stage like that, wailing and crying that she could not possibly sing unless she wore a gown that suited her, one she felt good in, that she was so nervous about singing for the enemy—that was the way she put it—you understand.'

'God's life!' muttered the manager. 'And?'

'Eventually she stopped crying, answering the man in docile tones; and then all was quiet, and I hadn't heard anything for awhile; but nobody came out, and I did not like to intrude, so I waited and waited, but time was getting away and something had to be done. So I knocked, and she told me to come in. But, Monsieur,' he whispered. 'That was the funny thing, because I looked all around and—even though nobody had come out—there was no-one with her …'

'Talking to a ghost, was she?' asked Monsieur Clement, lifting a sardonic brow.

'Well, perhaps,' acknowledged the assistant. 'Whoever it was, she called him Angelpapa.'

The tour manager lowered his eyes, hiding the flash of fear that leapt into them. 'The marquis du Bois!' he exclaimed under his breath. 'Then she *was* talking to a ghost!'

'I beg your pardon, Monsieur?'

'It does not matter,' he said, adding fiercely, 'Mad or not, she must be placated. You know how fragile her nerves are, and how much her fans adore her!' He smiled ironically, without mirth. 'The goose that lays the golden eggs must be most carefully nurtured. I thought you would know that! Where is her husband, the marquis de Beaulieu? He seems to be the only one who can soothe her when she gets like this.'

'He was called away urgently on some business. He said he will be back before the performance.'

'A lot of help, that is!' replied the manager, wondering fleetingly if the business of the marquis had anything to do with the deficiency he had noticed in the books. 'What about Madame Dupont? She is the only other person likely to have some influence with Madame la marquise. Go and find her,' he ordered, returning to his accounts.

'Madame Dupont has also gone out,' said the assistant, shaking his head. 'She has taken the comte to see a specialist physician about his rheumatism. I understand it was the only available appointment. They have been gone for a number of hours. She should not be much longer.'

'What a cursed misfortune it is for something like this to have happened when they are both away,' groaned Monsieur Clement. 'Surely, you can hold it together until one of them returns! Send for the best couturière in Vienna with every white gown she has! I do not know why you cannot attend to a simple thing like that! Give her what she wants! Is that so hard? And pray that the marquis de Beaulieu is not long delayed.' He waved his hand, irritably. 'Go on, go on!'

'Yes, Monsieur, of course,' replied André, discreetly biting back an acid comment to the effect that it was extremely difficult to give someone what she wanted when she did not appear to be at all certain of it herself. He took a reluctant step towards the door, turning back at the sound of Monsieur Clement's voice.

'Oh, before you go: one question.' The manager lifted his head. 'Did you hear his voice?'

'Who?' asked the assistant, momentarily confused.

'The one she was talking to, Imbecile!'

The manager sat back, watching in malicious amusement as his assistant went white, mouth opening and closing like a beached fish.

Madame Dupont, knocking and entering, looked from one to the other. 'Trouble, Messieurs? I had a message at the door. You wanted to see me, Monsieur Clement?'

'Madame, thank God you are here!' The manager sent

her a grateful glance.

The assistant, head down, mumbled an excuse, almost bolting out of the room.

'What is the matter with him?' asked Madame Dupont, turning her head to watch his departure.

'Ah, Madame, I do not know where to begin to tell you,' replied the manager, diplomatically, steering her off to Angelique's dressing-room, explaining volubly the latest fracas to impinge upon the sensibilities of their star.

'Oh dear,' she sighed. 'I knew I should not have left her alone today.' But one glance at the girl's face made her put an arm around her. 'Come, my dear child, do not take on so. We shall contrive. Now, let us look at your gown and see what we can salvage.'

Angelique pointed wordlessly to the ethereal confection hanging on the wall, her eyes welling with fresh tears. Madame Dupont handed her the smelling salts, and she and the manager went over to inspect the gown. At first glance, it appeared as if nothing marred its shimmering perfection; the translucent fabric falling in graceful folds from its hanger.

'I do not see ...' began the manager, viewing the pristine layers. A slender arm reached past him, pulling aside a section of the skirt to reveal a large hole with singed and crumpled edges. 'Oh!' he gasped.

'*Dieu me sauve!*' said Madame Dupont, clicking her tongue. 'How in the world did this happen?'

'Ask Mimi,' replied Angelique in brittle tones. 'She will tell you!'

Madame Dupont turned to the shrinking figure in the doorway, saying in a shocked voice, 'Mimi? You have not been careless?'

'Oh, no, Madame, I have not! It is all the fault of this—this *merde* of an iron!'

'Mimi! Watch your language, *s'il vous plaît*!'

'I am sorry, Madame, but it is enough to make a saint swear! Truly it is!' replied the maid. 'It is all the fault of this new patent iron they sold us—guaranteed not to overheat, Madame! I particularly made sure of that, but they did not mention that the spirit was likely to overflow and catch fire, did they?' she cried. 'But it did, and all over my hand—just look at it, Madame!—and onto the silk, burning a great hole in it before I could put it out! And all in the wink of an eye, Madame! Oh, it is too bad! Madame's beautiful gown!'

'Let me see your hand, Mimi,' said Madame Dupont, concerned. 'Hmm, you will need some salve on that. Bring me the small basket with the lid from my room. You must have that bandaged at once.

'And now, my dear,' she said to Angelique, having attended to Mimi's injured hand and resuming her perusal of the gown. 'This robe of yours: I have been looking at it carefully. There is plenty of fabric in this skirt, Petite, and we do not really need that floating panel; in fact, I thought it a little too much when you bought it. We will remove the section with the burnt patch—you see how we can do that, do you not?—the skirt is in gores. Nothing will be simpler; we will unpick it and replace it with the floating panel, suitably cut, and no-one will be any the wiser. If the skirt width is reduced, it will be only very marginally—it will not be noticed. You can wear it.'

'Quickly, Monsieur!' She turned to the tour manager. 'A couple of good seamstresses, *tout de suite*, and we shall do.'

He went out, calling to his assistant, as Madame Dupont, comforting Angelique, said, 'You may be easy now, my child. Do not worry; your gown will be ready for you to wear tonight. Ah, here is Etienne! *À la bonne heure, mon brave!*'

'So I understand, Madame. We do not seem to be able to leave these fools for a second without something going wrong,' he replied, tight-lipped.

'No, indeed, but all is in train now.'

'How did your errand go, Madame? Did you manage to keep my father-in-law to his task?'

'Yes, indeed. The comte has been given some hope with a new treatment: a special diet and a course of baths. So that was worthwhile, *Dieu merci*. And how did your business progress? Have we averted disaster, *mon fils*?'

'I believe so, Madame. But not without a cost, *hein*?' he said, looking at his wife. 'Come here, my angel. Softly, softly, all will be well. Madame will mend your gown, and you shall come with me to visit one of your greatest fans.'

'Oh, Etienne,' she sighed, pouting. 'I do not want to go anywhere. I am too worried about my gown.'

Interpreting the look Madame Dupont shot at him, he said, 'You must come with me, my dear. It has been arranged specially. This fan and his friends are very cultured, very talented, and they are putting on a performance just for you. Come, you will regret it if you do not.'

'What fan and his friends?' she asked, intrigued in spite of herself.

He shrugged, teasing her. 'I do not tell any more. You will have to come with me to find out. Ready?'

'Oh, I don't know,' she replied ungraciously. Then she smiled. 'Oh, Etienne, I am sorry to be a grump. It is just … Oh, it is all so dire here. Tell me, Dearest, who is this fan?'

'I shan't tell you any more than that he is a dancer.'

'A dancer? Ballet, you mean?'

'You could say that—yes, you could say that! Classical, at all events! Will you come?'

'Well, perhaps, I will come. You have piqued my curiosity now.'

'Oh, I didn't mean to do that!' he said, looking shocked.

This was a familiar game: one she enjoyed. Smiling at him provocatively, she asked, 'Did you not? What: not even just a tiny, *teeny*, little bit?'

Waiting for his usual response of 'Well, perhaps just a *leetle* …' she was alarmed when he turned his head haughtily and headed for the door.

'Etienne! Where are you going?' she cried anxiously. This was not how the game went!

'Oh, nowhere important,' he replied in a bored voice. 'Only to tell your fan that you cannot be bothered with him and his dancing white horses.'

'Dancing white horses?' she shrieked. 'Do you—Oh, you cannot mean: The Spanish Riding School? Truly? Oh, you have to take me there at once! I have wanted all my life to see the white stallions of Vienna!'

'Are you sure you will not find it too fatiguing after all that has happened today?' he drawled, eyelids drooping.

'Etienne! Oh, come on, you—you—jokester!' she said through shut teeth, pushing him out the door.

He winked at Madame Dupont over his shoulder as he allowed himself to be propelled along.

Shaking her head at him, Madame Dupont turned away to take down the ruined gown, smiling as she lay it on the table. Trust Etienne to be able to take Angelique out of herself. He knew exactly what to do to lighten her mood and whet her curiosity. And now she was the one hurrying them away, which was exactly what they all wanted. Two busy seamstresses and Madame Dupont would be enough people in the room without an anxious diva looking over them. *Etienne*, she mused. *There is more to that young man than meets the eye*, adding as a pious afterthought: *Thank God.*

§

The assistant hurriedly brought the seamstresses to the manager. He felt he had better try and ingratiate himself with Monsieur Clement, who had looked at him in such a way. He had made him feel quite nervous, as well as shouting at him in a most unusual manner. He felt queasy when he thought of some of the events of the afternoon, but his instincts told him that if he wanted to keep his job, he would need to get back into his good graces—fast! He followed as the manager brought the seamstresses to Madame Dupont.

'Ah, Madame,' said Monsieur Clement, introducing the ladies. 'And how is our beautiful diva? Has she settled down?'

The two seamstresses, clicking their tongues, went straight to work. Madame Dupont, realising she could leave them with it, turned her attention to the manager. 'Oh, yes, Monsieur, thank you.'

'She is here, now?'

'No, the marquis de Beaulieu has her in his charge. I think, but I am not sure from his cryptic conversation, that he is taking her to the Spanish Riding School.'

'Oh, yes, the director is a great fan of hers. I am told he has her on a pedestal, only one rung lower than his stallion; and that, I may tell you, is several rungs higher than any other human being, including the Emperor! Understandably, I might add, since the Emperor is a little persona non grata now with most of his countrymen, but ... She will have a lovely time. I mean, where else does one go in Vienna for a classical experience—if one has been fortunate enough to have been invited—except to the concert hall, of course!' Monsieur Clement laughed at his witticism.

'I can think of better places,' sniggered the assistant, rolling a lecherous eye.

'Get out of here!' shouted the manager, suddenly, hurling at him the nearest thing to hand: a small Venus on a side table. Watching André duck and the ornament smash against the wall, he stood, looking bewildered, as if he couldn't imagine having done such a thing.

Madame Dupont stepped back, startled. 'Oh, Monsieur,' she faltered, 'for a moment, I thought you were someone else ...'

Monsieur Clement straightened and looked her in the eye with a sudden change of expression. 'Seeing spectres now, are we, Madame?' he jeered, a little half-smile on his lips. 'Angels or spirits?' His expression was sardonic, amused, slightly cruel.

Madame Dupont jumped, even more startled; her eyes searching his face. 'Monsieur?' she questioned, shakily.

He sighed, passing a hand over his brow. 'I am sorry, Madame,' he said, huskily, but in his own voice. 'I cannot think what has come over me.'

'It is of no moment, Monsieur, we are all under pressure. Do not give it another thought.' Her eyes assumed a faraway expression as she murmured, 'He always did have a wicked sense of humour.'

Are we all mad? Wondered Monsieur Clement, staring at her. Retreating with as much haste as was seemly, his mind was in turmoil. What had just happened to him in there? Had he understood her correctly? Who was it she had referred to? *Is there something in the water of Vienna?* He asked himself, despairingly. And when it came to looking in the mirror to adjust one's tie, or some such thing, to be confronted by the mocking blue eyes of a stranger looking back at him, it was so creepy as to give him a dislike of the place, and well—it was the outside of enough! One thing was certain: he would sack his worse-than-useless assistant before he got much older! This contretemps—all of it— was his fault!

CHAPTER THIRTY ~ DANCING WHITE HORSES

Afternoon, 8 February 1919

Who could have known that a day that began so dreadfully would end so well? The sights and treasures of Vienna are breathtaking, but none so beautiful as the living treasures that now belong to the people.

Observing Angelique's wrinkled brow as she went to the wardrobe (Mimi having been seconded to Madame Dupont and the seamstresses), her husband asked: 'You have another problem, Sweetest?'

'I don't know what to wear,' she explained. 'What does one wear to the Spanish Riding School? Day wear or evening? It is a performance, after all. And I do not want to insult them by dressing down.'

'Put on your riding habit,' he advised. 'You never know …'

She turned an incredulous face. 'What: do you really think I would be allowed to ride one of the stallions?' she scoffed. 'It has never been heard of!'

'Probably not, my love,' he admitted. 'I cannot imagine

we would be allowed to ride a trained stallion. They are priceless, you know. But we have been asked to wear riding dress, so perhaps a young remount or a hired horse? Who knows what the director has in mind.'

'The director? The director is this fan you have been talking about? Oh!' There was a silence while she digested this. 'Then I suppose we must do as he asks,' she said, scrabbling in her wardrobe, fully absorbed in the anticipation of the moment. Etienne, observing her shining eyes and curving lips as she emerged with her riding habit, was satisfied.

§

Upon their arrival at the wonderful old building that housed the Spanish Riding School, a young rider in the distinctive uniform came to lead them to their seats in the great Riding Hall. They saw that they were the only guests.

'The director has said to please make yourselves comfortable and wait, Madame and Monsieur,' the young man said courteously, before he left them. 'The stallions will not be long.'

There was a slight stir as the horses and riders entered in single file, arranging themselves around the walls. As one they began their exercises, imperceptibly building into an electrifying performance. There was no orchestra, things were tight after the war; but Angelique only had eyes for the breathtaking white stallions floating over the soft surface with little muffled swishing sounds; the quiet jingling of the bits the only background music she desired. *They are treading the air*, she thought, watching their hooves touch the earth so lightly in the collected trot, amazed to see them actually slow down as, paradoxically, their strides lengthened into extended trot and then, in one stride, into the proud suspension of passage. She drew in a breath at the dramatic zigzag patterns they made as they crossed and re-crossed the arena: first in half pass and then extended trot—the stallions barely missing each other as they crossed from the opposite diagonals—each striving for longer and longer strides, never varying in the beautiful, supple rhythm that had sent them into legend. It was all too beautiful, so far beyond description as to make the heart sing.

As an artist, she recognised in *Haute École* a high art form, the greatest discipline of not just one artist, but two acting as one; and as no mean rider herself, she could appreciate that these men rode with a flair and feel high above the ordinary, and out of the league of other horsemen, sitting so still as to be a part of their horse. Over three-hundred-and-fifty years of tradition, and a lifetime of training; of secrets handed down from the Chief Riders to their pupils, both equine and human; a dedication to the excellence of their principles and the wellbeing of their horses made this wonderful place unique, and she knew she was blessed to have had a glimpse of it.

'*Haute École*! Oh, it is like a fairytale!' she whispered. 'Have you ever seen anything more beautiful?'

'Frequently,' murmured Etienne, smiling at her sideways.

'Oh,' she said impatiently, 'you are always funning. Can you not be serious? This is so ... special!'

'Of course, my love,' he replied soothingly. 'Can you see Monsieur le Directeur Herold? I do not.'

'I have not yet met him,' she reminded him, making a shooshing gesture as the horses, all-in-shoulder-in down the centre, diverted to either side to make their dramatic finale in a glorious extended trot.

As if in homage, the stallions spaced themselves around the hall, facing the centre as a great white stallion with the presence of a monarch entered at a sober walk; his rider, not on his back, but walking beside his near hind leg, holding long reins against his glistening hindquarter.

'Ah, here he is,' said Etienne. 'I wonder what he has in

mind for us?'

Approaching the centre of the hall, the stallion reared high, standing on his hind legs for a second, before beginning a series of amazing bounds; the director running to keep up.

'He is doing one of the famous airs above the ground,' gasped Angelique, quite astounded. 'Look, is it not magnificent?'

'It is the courbette: a battle move designed to protect the rider,' whispered Etienne. 'It is indeed magnificent. I have only seen it in photographs and paintings and they do *not* do it justice!'

They fell silent for, as if of his own accord, the stallion began to make a series of spectacular leaps; the director standing aside to give him plenty of room. On the apex of the last bound, the mighty stallion lashed out wickedly with both hind legs. He brought all four legs back to earth simultaneously, standing like a rock to receive their applause.

'Ooh!' gasped Angelique, quite wordless.

'Ah,' sighed Etienne. 'I do not pretend to be a judge, but I understand the capriole to be the specialty of the director's stallion. It is another battle move, for if you find yourself surrounded by the enemy, the idea is that your horse performs the capriole to scatter those behind, then spins around and gallops through the breach, leaving you to fight another day. Not bad, *n'est-ce pas?*'

Angelique, watching the stallions and their riders file out after this memorable performance, felt that she was glad it was over; for what could surpass that which they had just seen?

The director bowed to them, beckoned and followed the others to the door, as the same young rider came to tell them that his master requested their presence, taking them to an area just inside the doorway to the Riding Hall where the director waited with his horse. He greeted them with a diffident smile, bowing and shaking hands.

Angelique rushed into speech: 'The Riding Hall is magnificent, Monsieur, and the horses so beautiful and talented, and so immaculately conditioned and groomed. I suppose it is not *comme il faut* to ask you how you managed to keep these dear creatures so beautifully during the war?'

Etienne closed his eyes. *Oh, my love, you are never gauche—why now?*

But the director answered seriously, because to him it was a valid question. 'It was very hard, Madame. Yes, it was hard. But do you know that now, it is much, much harder? Yes, it is so.'

'Indeed, Monsieur? I am sorry to hear it. But how so?'

'You see, the Spanish Riding School has always been the private property of our Emperor; and even in the worst times, he was able to make provision for the care of the stallions. The performances have always been only for him and his guests. And, of course, you would have been one of them, Madame, without question, had our two countries not been ... at war,' he assured her, lest she be offended.

But Angelique, not in the least offended, said, 'Do go on, Monsieur. The war was not your fault.'

'No, indeed not. But now, in the aftermath of defeat ...' He smiled a little wryly. 'You see, we did not have an Angel of Song to help us win our war—but we are greatly privileged that she has had the forgiveness to come and heal our hearts, too.'

'Oh, Monsieur, that is very kind of you to say such a lovely thing.'

He made a gesture. 'No, no, not at all, Madame, but now that Austria is part of a republic, the State and not the Emperor is the owner of the school. And do you know that even in the worst of the war, the Emperor had more funds for us than the State does now? Yes, it is true, though I writhe to admit it; they do not give us enough money even to buy brooms with which to sweep our stables! At the moment, we are having postcards printed to try and raise money, and we are working towards public performances in the near future to help pay for its upkeep. But until we have some brooms to clean up ...' He shrugged his shoulders. 'And now, these beautiful stallions—by birthright deserving to live in luxury—have to beg like paupers for their very existence. Heaven forbid that we should be the generation to allow this great tradition to be destroyed through apathy! ... But enough of this! I did not invite you here to complain, but to entertain you with a gift fitting for such a great artist as yourself, Madame. I hope I may take it that you both have enjoyed our performance?' he said; his eyes on Angelique.

'I have never seen anything more beautiful! Never!' she assured him, and he could not doubt that her words came straight from her heart. 'I shall never forget it, as long as I live! I do not know how you do it! Such skill! Such talent!' She stopped.

At the admiration in her voice, the stallion stretched out his neck to blow softly on her cheek; his eyes full of friendly curiosity.

'Oh, you sweet thing!' she exclaimed, as he gazed at her in gentle enquiry. 'So, you want to be introduced, do you? Are you going to tell me who you are, then?'

'He is my dearest friend, Madame.' She heard pride and love in the director's voice. 'He has a very long and proud name, which of course, we always use officially; but just between ourselves, man to man, you understand, I call him "Arni", and I allow him to call me "Mori".'

'And does he take the liberty?' she asked.

He shook his head. 'He never takes liberties, Madame. He is too much the gentleman.'

'Are you then, you beauty,' she cooed. 'Of course one can see that he is a very great gentleman ... What is his official name, if you please?'

The director obligingly told her.

'Neapolitano Mont ——' she repeated. 'Oh, I have forgotten it already! Arni it must be then, your name is too impressive! Very well, Arni, I am enchanted to meet you, dear sir,' she cried gaily, bowing to him.

Astonished, she watched the stallion, his lovely dark eyes alight with intelligence, drop onto one knee and bow right back.

'Oh, you clever thing! You have a sense of humour. I can see you are secretly laughing at me.'

'Not at: with,' corrected the director, smiling. 'I speak for us both, Madame, when I say that we shall be most honoured if you would consent to mount him.'

'Really?' she gasped. 'You would let me ride your wonderful horse? But I thought ... in the tradition of the school that women are not allowed to ride the stallions?'

'That is quite true, Madame,' agreed the director, gravely. 'But since I have taken the precaution of closing the front doors and sending everyone out to the field for some cross-country exercise—a treat the stallions enjoy—there will be no witnesses; so I am fairly confident that tradition will continue to be preserved.' Eyes twinkling, he went on, 'For even if it is whispered that the director was so besotted with France's Angel of Song that he allowed her to ride his stallion, it will never be believed, because as everyone knows, I do not allow even my best rider on his back. No-one rides him but me. And now, Madame, allow me to mount you. You must sit very still and do nothing. I will direct him. Have no fear; he is completely under my command—by his own will, of course. No stallion here is ever coerced. Each retains his own personality and his *amour-propre*. Anything else would be a sin and contrary to our tradition. I would have no control over him had he not the magnanimity to allow it. Eh, old friend?' he finished, running a loving hand over his stallion's crest and handing the reins to Angelique.

'She has a light hand and a good seat,' he commented approvingly to Etienne, as he watched her settle herself in the saddle and take a feel of the horse's mouth. 'I could almost wish they did allow women to train here.'

But I do not, most emphatically, thought Etienne, nodding politely at his words.

The director went on, 'I purposely did not do these airs in the performance. I have kept them for Madame ... You are ready, yes? Good,' he said to Angelique, and turned his attention to his horse.

In answer to an infinitesimal signal, the stallion began to pace majestically from one diagonal to the other—a slow, cadenced, dancing trot, perfectly in place— going nowhere with grace and energy in the magnificence of piaffe.

Angelique gave a gasp of pure joy, revelling in the power of the rippling muscles beneath her; conscious of the curved neck with its flowing silvery mane and sculpted, listening ears; aware that the entire attention of the horse was focused, not with her, but the man who stood, not close by his shoulder, but at some little distance. Her spirit soared, thrilling to the power and freedom. Could anything be better than this?

'Sit very still, Madame. You may lean a little forward,' said the director softly, making another invisible signal.

She felt the great stallion settle both hind hooves well under him, felt the surge of strength in his haunches as he lowered them, gently lifting both front legs off the ground to tuck them neatly against his body. There he sat, the ultimate in grace and controlled power, for what seemed an age.

'This is levade: the highest collection possible,' said the director, proudly. 'There are not many who can do it ...'

For a few seconds the horse maintained his noble pose. Then, with a little snort, he unfurled his forelegs and brought them gracefully back to earth where he stood, rock still; his eye on his master.

He knows he has done well. I can feel it, thought Angelique, stroking his neck.

Arni had not moved from his original position by more than half-a-hoof length, and yet he had given her the ride of her life, leaving her in a state of euphoria, with a sense of awe at the memory of such grace and power and energy as she hardly thought could exist. His grace was that of a classical dancer, and his obedience was not an abject subservience, but a willing disposal of his entire being to the will of another. It made one feel humble to think of it: the dear, wonderful, *glorious* creature!

Even at the performance, seated at a distance, she had noticed that the stallion seemed to wish to give his all to the invisible cues of his trainer, performing the difficult airs with spirit and gaiety, as if of his own free will. He even seemed to be enjoying himself—showing off his prowess! Particularly the capriole: she would swear he loved it!

'Thank you, you dear thing,' she whispered to the horse, quite overcome as she dismounted with the help of the director. 'And thank you, Monsieur, for your wonderful generosity in sharing your horse. It is an experience I shall never forget. And you,' she said to the stallion, rubbing him under one big eye with a gentle forefinger. 'You beautiful, beautiful, *darling* thing; I will treasure your memory always … Oh, until I die.' Her voice broke on the last word with the intensity of her emotion, and she dissolved into tears, gesturing helplessly to Etienne.

Upon seeing the director's expression change from happy pride to consternation, Etienne hastened to ease the situation and explain his lady's affliction. 'I pray that you will excuse my wife, Monsieur, she has great sensibility, and a great love for the horse. It is a combination that can sometimes seem contradictory, but as in many other things in life, it is not what it seems. I hope your concern will be relieved when I tell you that it is when she is at her happiest that her emotions are most likely to spill over and overcome her for a short period. So, you see, you have made her extremely happy, you and your horse, I do assure you of that. It is the intensity of her delight at the great honour you have accorded her, which has caused this lapse. Her nerves are not strong, you know. It is a problem that sometimes makes it difficult for her to perform onstage.'

'I see,' said the director, embarrassed. 'I am sorry; I had no idea.' He looked as if he wished in that moment that he had never had the idea of inviting her to sit on his horse, either. For a little moment, the pedestal rocked.

Etienne, divining his discomfort, said, 'Please, do not regret it, Monsieur. She will recover presently and remember this occasion always with a special joy—as will I,' he added courteously.

'Oh, it was so beautiful, so ... *fantastically* gorgeous! Oh, I cannot find words to do it justice, Monsieur. It was so *heavenly* that it has made me cry,' sobbed Angelique, emerging from Etienne's handkerchief for long enough to right the pedestal. Her lovely eyes, fringed with long, tear-drenched lashes, glowing into the director's, overflowed with sincerity. 'Please, please, forgive me. It is an affliction that I cannot help.'

'Madame,' said the director, gallantly; his heart wrenched by her sweetness. 'If these are tears of joy, then we count ourselves greatly honoured, do we not, my friend?'

The stallion's big dark eyes surveyed them with gentle wisdom. He lifted one front hoof decisively and pawed the ground once.

'So,' said the director, smiling at Angelique. 'We are in complete accord, you see!'

She tried to smile, looking to her husband.

Etienne, appreciating the director's attempt to make them comfortable, replied, 'I assure you, you should do so! What Angelique wishes to convey to you is that while she feels her performance cannot possibly be the equal of yours, we would also be honoured if you and your party would grace us with your presence at her recital,' he said, presenting him with tickets. 'I know she would wish to invite your noble companion, also, but I believe he will be happier in his warm stable with his oats and carrots.'

'Yes, he is easily satisfied,' agreed the director. 'I wish it were so for man ... And now, if you will excuse me, I must put him away. It is all the reward he asks.' He smiled at Angelique, taking her hand. 'I am greatly complimented to have so moved you, Madame, and I know it shall be at least as moving for me to listen to you tonight. It is a treat I look forward to with great anticipation. I shall not forget you, either, and I thank you for gracing our school and my horse,' he said, bowing to them in farewell.

For a moment or two, they stood watching the man and the horse walk away together to the stable: a great man and a great horse; a man with intense, visionary eyes, who had devoted his life to these glorious creatures in his charge; and a fabulous horse, a real 'professor'. Somehow, in some way they did not understand, there was a pathos to it. They both felt a rush of emotion. As Etienne put his arm around her, Angelique looked up at him, tears springing afresh.

'They must not be lost, Etienne,' she whispered, 'these wonderful horses.'

'No, my love, they must not. And we can help a little.'

'You put it in?'

'Of course, dear love. Come on,' he said, with sudden decision. 'Let us go back. You must rest before your performance.'

Madame Dupont was waiting for them. She looked at Angelique and was content. There was no need to ask whether she had enjoyed her outing.

'Come and see your gown, Petite. You, too, Etienne,' she said, shepherding them over to the filmy creation hanging in its place. 'Look,' she commanded, taking it down and drawing out the skirt to its full width, swirling it in the light. 'What do you think? Is it not better without that floating panel? More elegant! And—I think—you will see its lines better.'

They had to agree with her, Angelique exclaiming, 'Oh, it is perfect, Godmama! Thank you! Oh, what a perfect afternoon I have had!' An outburst that caused Etienne to grin wryly at Madame Dupont, before adding his own approving sentiments.

Later, observing the gown critically as Angelique stepped into it in response to her demand that he tell her how it looked on her, he said, 'Madame was right, as always, dear love. It does look much better without that floating panel. I know Monsieur Poiret said it looked like angel's wings when he designed it, but I think he missed the mark. In truth, Mimi did you a favour by causing its removal! You look—breathtaking!' He stood back, admiring her slender beauty. 'Monsieur le Directeur will be dazzled, my dear, as is your humble husband.'

Perhaps because of her experience, or because she knew there were people in her audience she felt she could regard as friends rather than the anonymous enemy she had feared, Angelique's voice had even more expression; and her performance was simply astounding, winning over more hearts and confirming her in the adoration of those already of her following; and the director, his immediate worries eased, was able to relax and enjoy the recital even more than he thought. A circumstance possibly due to an envelope labelled 'Brooms and Carrots', which fell out when he had taken out his tickets. This innocuous packet, containing a bank draft generous enough to allow him to purchase these items and much, much more, was to make his life a tiny bit easier; his gratitude overflowing into devotion for his favourite singer.

Neither Angelique nor Madame Dupont mentioned the spirit of the marquis du Bois, who had already declared his presence in more ways than one and was in the consciousness of both of them. He was, of course, right there onstage with her, noticed only by themselves and those few souls blessed (or cursed) with the 'sight'; not many of whom were wont to attend a recital (and even fewer to comment on it). But one day, one of them would. Madame Dupont had no doubt of it. It was only a matter of time.

CHAPTER THIRTY-ONE ~ THE MEDIUM

16 September 1919

It had to happen one day. How long have I known it?

It happened in Italy.

But first, they went to England for Angelique to sing in the Royal Albert Hall as she had promised the King so many years ago. After the performance, Their Majesties were pleased to speak privately with them.

'So, my dear, at long last we hear your glorious voice again,' said the King, taking her hand and speaking to her for a few minutes before moving on to Madame Dupont.

'Ah, Madame Dupont. How lovely to renew our acquaintance. My condolences at the loss of the marquis du Bois; a most remarkable man. You approved of what we did with his invention? Good. Yes, a great man, sadly missed.

'Etienne, dear boy.' King George wrung his hand. 'I am delighted to see you. I must congratulate you on your excellent taste. The Queen and I were very happy to hear of your nuptials, weren't we, my dear? And how is your dear father? He has not graced us with his presence this time? It is a pity. I was quite looking forward to seeing him.' He dissolved into a coughing fit, reaching for his handkerchief. The Queen pressed one into his hand. 'Thank you, my dear. I need to visit Belvoir again, breathe in the warm air and sunshine. You were saying?'

'Only that my mother is ill again: too ill to travel. My father felt he could not leave her.'

'What a dreadful coincidence,' said the Queen, breathing in so that her jewellery flashed in the candlelight. 'She was too ill to travel last time you came, too.'

Yes, but this time it is real. 'They were terribly disappointed, Ma'am.'

'No doubt,' responded the King, answering for both of them. 'As are we. Is it serious, do you think?'

'Yes, but the doctors say she will make a full recovery if she rests.'

'Excellent,' he said, stopping before Xavier; the enquiry in his eyes quickly answered by Etienne.

'Allow me to present to Your Majesties my father-in-law, the comte de Villefontaine.'

'I am very pleased to meet the father of an angel, Monsieur. You are to be congratulated on your extraordinarily talented daughter. And you must be comforted by the fact that she has an excellent protector in the person of the marquis de Beaulieu.'

'Indeed, Your Majesty, I am a proud father and father-in-law.' Xavier bowed stiffly.

'Ah, you suffer from the rheumatism, Monsieur. No doubt you will wish for warmer climes. English weather is very unkind to painful joints.'

'Indeed, Your Majesty. But I assure you, the warmth of English hearts more than makes up for it.'

Their Majesties, pleased with the gracious compliment, bowed and moved on.

§

In the Palazzo Farnese, the elite of Roman and French society were mingling in the largest reception room where Angelique had given her recital. A stage had been placed at one end and guests were served by uniformed waiters in between songs. It was one of the least stressful of her appearances on tour—and it was to be the last, for that very morning, she had made a discovery that was to change her life; a secret she had shared with no-one.

Late in the evening, a woman came up to her. 'Perhaps you do not remember me, Madame? We were introduced earlier. I am the ambassador's mother.'

'Of course,' murmured Angelique. 'I am sorry. I have met so many people. Do you know Madame Dupont?'

'*Enchanté*,' said the woman, looking from one to the other with bright, inquisitive eyes. She focused on Angelique. 'You are a dark horse, Madame. Such a handsome man, so *épris*, such address!'

'Pardon?' replied Angelique, bewildered.

The woman's eyes twinkled. 'Very good, Madame, but you cannot fool me. The tenor who accompanies you onstage—he is very good looking, and he loves you very much—one can see that. I have seen him with you everywhere. It is obvious that he cannot bear to be away from me for a second. Ah, such devotion ...' she sighed, clasping her hands. 'I wish I had it. And such a distinguished air. That is why I say you are a dark horse. So young and already a beautiful young husband, and a *soigné* lover, *hein*? So naughty, but so clever of you to manage them both so skilfully, my dear.' She stood back, regarding her in admiration.

Angelique looked distressed. 'But I don't know what you are talking about,' she said. 'I do not have a lover, no. The very idea ...'

Madame Dupont spoke for the first time. 'This man you have described, Madame—do you see him, now?'

Now it was the woman's turn to look distressed, eyes widening in comprehension. 'Oh, I am sorry, sorry, sorry.

Sometimes, I cannot tell the difference between the physical beings and the spiritual; they all look the same to me: the living and the dead. And when I see them I do not realise they are dead, that no-one else can see them. He is dead, isn't he?' She rattled on, 'He is your father? No, your father is here. He is someone you love very much, I know. Oh, I really have made a *faux pas*, have I not?'

Yes, and not the first, either, thought Madame Dupont. *Talk first; think later—that is you.*

Angelique burst into sobs.

'Do not be distressed, my dear,' said the woman kindly. 'The dead live on, you know. They are here amongst us.' She spoke surreal words normally, as if it were an everyday conversation for her; but it was too much for Angelique.

Once more, Madame Dupont quietly intervened: 'Madame, please—the child is still suffering the recent loss of her guardian and teacher, the marquis du Bois. It will not do to remind her.'

'Ah, poor child. So that is who he is—such presence, such polish—no wonder you are a spectacular singer.'

Will she never stop? How much more can this poor child take?

The woman met Madame Dupont's significant glance and chattered on, trying with more words to negate unfortunate ones. 'But you should be happy, my dear, truly you should. You have not lost him, no—he is with you still—and your mother and another. You are very, very lucky.'

'Maman? And another?' She turned to Madame Dupont. 'But, Godmama, who could it be?'

'She is a ballerina, very dainty, very graceful,' said the woman.

'It is his assistant, Sprite. Remember, I told you about her?' Madame Dupont put an arm about her. 'What a wonderful dancer and magician she was!'

'Your godmother is right. It was a most moving performance. You are fortunate, my dear, to have so many who love and support you. After all, this is a very special time for you.' On this cryptic utterance, she finally bowed and turned away.

'Godmama, this is too much. Too much!' Angelique dissolved into tears. 'All the time Angelpapa has been with me, no-one has ever before seen him—or if they did, they have not mentioned it. And how could she say Maman and … and … Sprite are here, too?'

'Hush, my dear, it was inevitable. I think she thought you would want to know, and perhaps, as she said, she cannot tell the difference between a physical and a spiritual body. I acquit her of malice, but not foolish curiosity. She may have been unwise to approach you in that fashion, but is there not some reason she was compelled to speak to you?' Madame Dupont regarded her with a calm, questioning gaze.

Angelique shrugged her shoulders. 'Can you get Etienne, please, Godmama? I would like to go now.'

'Of course, dear child.' She caught Etienne's eye, and he came at once. On the alert, as ever. 'I will go and collect your papa and join you later.'

She found the comte sitting with an old acquaintance, but he was plainly glad to see her. 'We are going, Madame? Very good.' He suppressed a groan as he struggled to his feet. 'It was wonderful to catch up with you, *mon cher*, after all these years. Fancy it being in Rome!'

Fancy, thought Madame Dupont. *It would never have been in Paris; that is certain.* But with a bit of luck, it would be different now. The comte would really not be able to shut his doors as a recluse again. She smiled. That was one thing she *could* see to.

When they reached their hotel, Etienne and Angelique were waiting, an arm about each other.

'Angelique has something to tell us,' said Etienne; a proud smile touching his lips.

'Godmama, Papa, there is a child coming. There will be no more tours until he or she is weaned. I have promised Etienne.'

The comte became emotional, kissing his daughter and gazing into her face, a hand either side. 'A grandchild for me? Oh, how Katarina ——' He broke up, reaching for his handkerchief.

At a sign from Madame Dupont, Etienne took him off to his rooms.

The comte calmed under his gentle attention, apologising for his lapse.

'Believe me, Monsieur; I am honoured by your tears. They have meaning … Especially since,' he added, somewhat dryly, 'you have another grandchild you have not even seen.'

'Yes, I must remedy that when we return to Paris. Thank you … for reminding me.'

'*De rien*, Monsieur! Now, we must pray for a healthy infant.'

'Indeed, my son, no-one shall pray harder, I promise you.'

'Thank you, Monsieur. Sleep well.' He left him with a smile.

Madame Dupont raised an enquiring eyebrow as the marquis returned.

'He is settled,' replied Etienne. 'Nothing to worry about. Indeed, he is planning to meet his first grandchild.'

'Oh, very good, Etienne. *Parfait!*' She turned to Angelique. 'Your papa has decided to live again, my dear. Is it not wonderful? Philippe has been so hurt that he would not see his child. And now, to think that he will …'

'Yes, indeed! And all because of our news. This child is special, Godmama. I can feel it.'

'Of course, my dear. There can be no doubt. But what about your singing? You need to sing, you know.'

'I know.'

'Why do you not make a record? It will not matter then if you are *enceinte*; no-one will see you in the recording studio.'

'Yes, why not? That may be an idea, Angelique.'

Etienne drummed his fingers thoughtfully. 'It will keep your fans in touch with you while you are away from the stage.'

'Perhaps I will. But it will be all right, Godmama, it truly will. I will practise every day, as usual, and I shall sing in the evenings for my family; and when he or she comes, I shall sing to my baby.'

'Of course, my dear child. The answer is really so simple, is it not?' Smiling mistily, she wished them goodnight.

Angelique and Etienne held each other in silence, still taking in the enormity of the changes about to be wrought in their lives.

She leant back to look at him, freeing herself. 'We will go back to Paris, Etienne?'

'For now, my darling. You must see a specialist physician to make sure everything is well with our baby.'

'We shall stay on in our apartment in the hôtel du Bois? But I thought you would wish your child to be born at Belvoir?'

'I will, of course, but your wellbeing comes a long way before that, you know. We will see what Madame Dupont has to say: wherever is best for your health. We will continue to spend time in both Paris and Belvoir, but it must be as you wish, my love. We will take it a day at a time.'

'We will go to Belvoir for Christmas as usual, and then … we will see.'

'Very well, my love. Now, the mother of my child must get her beauty sleep.'

'So now I am not Angelique any more, but the mother of your child?' She pouted. 'I have lost my identity!'

Laughing, he took her in his arms. 'There are several thousand fans out there who will attest to your identity, my dear love. Come on: bed.'

CHAPTER THIRTY-TWO ~ RETRIBUTION

23 September 1919

A desire for justice transcends everything, even death.

Back in the hôtel du Bois, about to follow Angelique upstairs to their apartment, Etienne hesitated, one foot on the bottom step. Catching the eye of the butler on his way across the hall, he said, 'You have somebody waiting in the salon, Justin? I thought I heard a noise.'

The butler shook his head. 'No, Monsieur.'

'Madame Dupont?' suggested Etienne.

'No, Monsieur. Madame Dupont went up to her studio half an hour ago.'

'Her studio?' His brows rose in surprise.

'Yes, Monsieur. She has plans to turn it into a nursery.'

'Oh, I see.' Smiling, the young marquis glanced upwards. Madame Dupont, she would run your life if you let her. But somehow it was easier to give her full rein—at least she had some sensitivity about it—rather than be the cause of reproach or distress in those big, kind eyes. *I know I am a coward, but—no.*

'Shall I take a look in the salon, Monsieur?'

'No, no, you carry on. I will go.' Turning as he spoke, he trod softly to the door, pushing it open by slow degrees.

At the new cocktail cabinet, pouring himself a whiskey, was a scarecrow figure. He wore a torn, faded and filthy uniform, and down at heel, scuffed top-boots. From the back view, which was all that was available to Etienne, his white, wispy, over-long hair resembled a bird's nest; the skull horrifically shining through it. The bottle clattered against the rim of the glass as the unkempt creature poured a liberal measure, continuing to pour until the glass overflowed.

'Hey! Don't you know when to stop, Monsieur?' called Etienne, constrained to speak out at this.

'Uh,' he grunted, swinging around, spilling whiskey in a wide circle from the mouth of the decanter.

'Put the bottle down, you inebriate!' commanded the young marquis, thinking of an appropriate phrase of Hugh's: *Pissed to the eyeballs, is what he would have said. And he would have been right*, he decided, observing the unshaven face, rotting teeth and ragged clothing. *An old tramp*, he thought. 'How did you get in? I cannot believe Justin has so far forgotten himself to allow someone in your condition into my house.'

'Your house? Is this not the house of the marquis du Bois?'

'Never mind that. How did you get in?'

'This *is* the house of the marquis du Bois!' stated the drunk, abruptly setting down the decanter.

'All right, then, it is. How did you get in? It comes to something, so it does, when the *sans-culottes* can come in off the streets and help themselves to a gentleman's liquor.

The disreputable creature drew himself to his full, not unimposing height. 'Who are you calling a *sans-culotte*?'

'That's something I would like to know myself,' said the young marquis, puzzled at his arrogance, yet finding nothing he could recognise in the dissolute countenance.

'How did you get in?'

The *vieillard* tapped the side of his nose. 'Du Bois may have a trained butler to throw out those whom he has no wish to entertain, but his security is not as good from the other side.' He jerked a thumb over his shoulder; a tremor shaking the tattered ends of his sleeve.

'The hospital? You have come from the hospital? No—you were never in there, looking like that! They would, at least, have cleaned you up.'

The drunk assumed a soldierly bearing, curiously at odds with his appearance. 'I have been,' he asserted. 'Several times.'

'Get out.' Etienne jerked his head towards the door.

The man glared, holding himself erect. 'You will have manners in my presence, and you will speak only when you are spoken to, young man,' he ordered, some long forgotten authority re-emerging.

Something about him reminded Etienne of someone, but as the *vieillard* slumped, it eluded him.

Taking a long pull at his whiskey, the inebriate smacked his lips. 'I have come for what is mine,' he announced. 'I have come to have it out with that swine, the marquis du Bois and take back what is mine.'

The young marquis, completely mystified, said, 'I have no idea what is in that addled brain of yours, but let me rest it about one thing. You cannot have it out with the marquis du Bois, unless you chance to be a medium, because the marquis du Bois is dead.'

'Dead?' The dreadful creature began to laugh hysterically. 'Dead? Dead? Ha, ha, ha. Ding dong bell, the pussy's in the well; the marquis is dead and gone straight to hell.'

'Oh! You disgusting, *vile* creature. How dare you? Oh, how dare you?' shrieked Angelique from the doorway, as the young marquis began to stride purposefully towards him. A hand to her mouth, she stood staring in distress.

The intruder, a maniacal light in his eye, threw back his

head. 'The marquis is dead,' he said, with relish. 'I can do anything I like. Come here, my lovely.' In two bounds, he had crossed the room and was upon Angelique, grabbing at her jacket as she turned to flee in panic.

'My God, it is de Langue,' said Etienne, as he went after him, reaching the general just as the jacket slid from her shoulders. Angelique made good her escape, as her husband, frustrating his attempt, pulled him off her and threw him in one of his oriental manoeuvres into the unlit fireplace. It had taken much more effort than he expected, leaving him gasping.

The general, mumbling, 'Think you have fooled me, eh? You shall not get away, my dove', leapt nimbly to his feet, taking hold of the mantel while he grabbed for the poker.

Nobody who was drunk could move so swiftly, or have such a devilish light in his eye, or such strength. In the same instant as Etienne realised he was not drunk but mad, the huge, carved overmantel came crashing down off the wall onto his head, scattering photographs, ornaments and pieces of its broken mirrors all over the floor. The general went down without a sound, buried beneath the smashed remains.

Pulling it aside gingerly, Etienne looked down on the unconscious man and then up towards the ceiling; a strange expression on his face. 'Thank you,' he said. 'But did you not think I could have handled this myself?

'*Mon Dieu!*' he told himself. 'I am getting as bad as Madame and Angelique. I mean, how do I know this was not just a happy accident?'

The words were hardly out of his mouth when a small ginger jar from China, the only thing not swept off the shelf by the overmantel, began rattling its lid and teetering on the edge. Rushing to save it, the young marquis stretched out a hand. Just as he touched it, he felt a blow jog his arm, dislodging the jar with such force that it shattered against the opposite wall.

He felt pinpricks all over. How had his hand made such a move?

Not by my decision, he thought. Then, as the portrait of the marquis on the same wall suddenly dipped one corner, he said, 'Enough, enough. There is no need to smash the room up completely. I am sorry that I doubted you.'

Madame Dupont, casting a cool glance around from the doorway, came in. She walked over and looked down at the general. 'If you were talking to him, I don't think he is going to answer you, *mon cher.*'

'I wasn't.'

'Oh,' she said, casting another glance around the room. 'Then it is just as well. I doubt if he will be able to answer sensibly for quite a while, if at all,' she added, looking at him straightly. 'Why are you laughing?'

He met her steady gaze; his own uneasy. 'God knows, Madame. In truth, I do not find it funny.'

She studied the supine figure. 'One would never recognise in him the same dapper gentleman who played such havoc with feminine hearts.'

'No, indeed, Madame. It is not possible that it should be him. And yet, it is.'

'Since the war, I have never heard of him again, have you?'

'Not since I gave Levandre the evidence he needed, no. But it is not an impossibility that we should not have heard of him, is it?'

'No, I suppose not. I was too busy caring for Angel and afterwards ... we have been touring since the war. But perhaps we should call an ambulance, *mon cher,* and have this monster taken away before he comes to?'

'I suppose it would be more charitable than tossing him out on the street, which was my first thought. I will do it. If you would go and make sure Angelique has taken no hurt because of this?'

'She is fine, my dear, absolutely fine. Upon hearing her scream, I came down and caught her on the stairs. After I had the story from her of an old drunk trying to molest her, I told her the best thing she could do was to come up with me to the nursery and tell the decorators what she wants. Of course, when she said it was General de Langue, I told her I would come down and see what has happened. But I knew you would have dealt with him. I will go back and tell her the general has been dispatched.'

'There is no doubt that he has been dispatched,' he agreed. 'But, strictly speaking, not by me.'

'Was it not? The overmantel?'

He shrugged. 'Just fell down on him, right there.'

'Oh, I see. And the ginger jar, over there?'

'That's the queer thing, Madame. It was the only ornament not swept off the mantel by that thing.' He pointed to the debris surrounding the general. 'But later it started to fall, and when I went to catch it … I still do not know what happened, but just as I got my hand under it, something seemed to jostle my arm. I did try to save it but … it landed over there, where you see it.'

She went over and straightened the portrait, apparently addressing the painted countenance, 'I hated the overmantel, but I did rather like that ginger jar.'

'Oh well, it cannot be helped,' said Etienne, after a short silence. 'Though it is, in some ways, my fault. I dare say we may find another. I will look out for one. Do you think you might go back to Angelique now, Madame? I am feeling a little nervous about her. I want to be here in the unlikely event that this madman wakes up and decides to have another try.'

'You must not worry about Angelique, my dear. She has Mimi, the gardener, six workmen and the footman— all engaged in moving furniture, holding up assorted wallpapers and spreading carpets for her choice. She is quite safe. But perhaps you had better stay,' she said, walking out. 'One cannot be too careful.' She looked back; a slight smile on her face. 'On second thoughts, I do not know why we are worried. There are plenty of missiles in here. I doubt he will be allowed to escape.'

The young marquis collapsed into a chair and laughed until he felt sick.

The butler, eyeing him askance, bridled as he saw the state of the room. 'The ambulance is here, Monsieur, for the body of the general. The medical personnel are at the door.'

'He is not dead, Justin.'

'Is he not? Indeed?' The butler's tone said, *more's the pity.*

'Send the medics in, and when they have gone you may tidy the room.'

'I should think so, Monsieur. Shall I call the carpenters, or will we have a new overmantel?'

'Consult with Madame Dupont over that. Just take away the, er ... debris.'

'*Mais certainement,* Monsieur.'

Etienne, greeting the two white-coated men, pointed them to the still figure amongst the chaos.

'Good God,' said one of the medics, dropping the stretcher. 'Oh, damn—it is, too.'

'Come on,' said the other, rubbing thumb and fingers. 'Hand over the dibs.'

Watching in astonishment as the first medic put a hand in his pocket to pull out five silver coins, the young marquis said, 'Is this a figment of my imagination, or are you both as mad as the general?'

Pocketing the cash, the second one said, 'I apologise, Monsieur, for our unprofessional conduct; but one would not credit it! You see, I got the idea that we would find it was General de Langue, and Jacques, here—well, he called me an imbecile. So, I bet him five silver francs ... Monsieur, you would not believe how many times we have been called to come and get him and take him off to the lunatic asylum; and it is always out of the house of one of the gentry.'

'Indeed? I have not seen him since the war. I must

confess; I did not recognise him. How did he get to this state, do you know?'

'Well, Monsieur, we were called to a house on Armistice Day, in the evening. There were great celebrations and much drinking. And General de Langue, he went up to the schoolroom and seduced a young girl of about fourteen: the daughter of the house. The governess caught him at it and hit him over the head with a warming pan, knocking him unconscious. Then we were called to take him away. After that, even though it was a police matter, the family did not press charges—to keep the young girl's name out of it. Of course there were whispers, as always, and he was ostracised by society.

'So then, and this is very unpleasant hearing, Monsieur, for some unknown reason, he took to the streets in the lower-class quarter and began assaulting the prostitutes and streetwalkers. Any old hag—so they say.'

'Assaulting them? But did not the police intervene?'

'No, Monsieur. You know how it is—the prostitutes cry rape when a client refuses to pay them and the police do not appear to think it possible that a streetwalker can be raped.' He shrugged. 'But they have had their revenge upon him: a number of times.'

'The pox?'

'Yes, Monsieur—and those trollops are riddled with it. There is not a man in his right mind who would have truck with any of them.'

'So why did the general, do you think?'

The medic pointed a forefinger to his head, making a winding gesture. 'He is *fou*, Monsieur. You see, he has had to have the mercury treatment so many times to cure him of syphilis that he has gone out of his mind. And now, look at the pitiful wreck that he is.' His face worked. 'It is a shame. He was a very courageous man, you know. He did many, many brave things during the war.' The men had, by this time, bound up the general's head wound and laid him on the stretcher.

Etienne accompanied them to the ambulance. 'Yes, that is true,' he said. 'But he was always a bit that way inclined, you know. The difference was, that back then, many *les femmes* came to him willingly.'

'I have heard that, Monsieur. I am not a woman, but I doubt if any would do anything but scream in horror now.'

'No, he is not very prepossessing. Strange how all the good things about him have gone, and only his vice remains to obsess him. What will you do with him?'

'He will be locked up in the mental institution, *if* he recovers. That was quite a blow he took—may have been fractured. But don't worry: they will not let him out again. The gentle people of Paris object to having their salons invaded by such as him.'

'And quite rightly, too,' said the other, shutting the door of the ambulance. 'Good day, Monsieur. Thank you.'

Returning their salute, Etienne went thoughtfully back indoors. All the plans he had made to bring General de Langue to justice, long forgotten in the hurly-burly of touring, were as nothing to the justice wrought upon him by his own profligate nature.

CHAPTER THIRTY-THREE ~ NICOLAS

16 March 1920

There is a new chapter about to be written: a new generation. How unspeakably wonderful it is to hold a newborn baby in my arms and know the future is embodied in him.

Nicolas de Beaulieu entered the world on a cold, blustery March afternoon under the experienced eye of Doctor Martin, in the great carved bed of the marquis du Bois.

Doctor Martin, having lost her husband on the Russian Front, now devoted her life to the wounded soldiers of the Great War: improving the lot of those she could, and making as comfortable as possible the lives of those whose injuries left them in the hospice.

Angelique's pregnancy had been trouble free until the last few weeks when she had become very uncomfortable. And so, the decision had been made. Her child would be born, not at the château de Belvoir as tradition demanded, but here in the hôtel du Bois: none of them being blind to the advantages of a physician of the calibre of Doctor Martin within call and hospital facilities at the length of a corridor.

The bedchamber of the late marquis had been made ready for birthing, Angelique having expressed the wish for her baby to be born there. Somehow, they all knew it would be a boy.

'Have you not chosen a girl's name?' asked Madame Dupont when Angelique showed her the list.

She had shaken her head. 'No. I know it is a boy. I shall call him Nicolas after Angelpapa. You see the names? Anton, after Monsieur Dupont ——'

'But you did not know him ...'

'There is a reason, besides the fact that I loved his photograph. Now, where was I? Nicolas after Angelpapa, Georges after *mon beau-père* and Etienne for his papa. But you see, Godmama, if I write his names one under another for his initials to make an acronym, you see what name it makes? It will be my pet name for him.'

'*Ange*,' she read. 'You are calling him Angel?'

'He will be my little angel, just as Angelpapa called me his little angel.'

The infant was large and the labour protracted, and when, at last, he arrived, the mother was exhausted, the father a nervous wreck, and Madame Dupont and the doctor considerably relieved.

'You have done well, my dear,' said Doctor Martin, placing a wrapped bundle into her arms. She touched the cap of fluffy dark hair with gentle fingers. 'A lovely, healthy boy.'

'Oh, he is beautiful, is he not, Godmama?' Angelique lay contentedly, nursing her baby, almost asleep.

'Indeed, he is, my dear. Very beautiful.' Madame Dupont took him from her, and he opened his eyes: dark, unfathomable, like all the newly born. *Is he a blank page? Or has it already been written?*

'Oh, I miss him already, my little angel.' Angelique stirred. 'What day is it?'

'It is the sixteenth.'

'Godmama ... Do you realise ...?'

'Yes.' She nodded. 'It is the birthday of the marquis du Bois. Fitting, is it not?'

'Angelpapa's birthday ... Very fitting.' The new mother sighed and yawned.

'You must sleep now, my dear. I will take your little angel to meet his papa and bring them both back when it is time for his next feed.'

§

Nicolas de Beaulieu sat on the floor of the picture gallery, hugging his furry toy, *Lapin*; his adoring gaze fixed unerringly on a portrait: the one he always went to.

He looked into the lovely eyes and imagined that the beautiful lady in the portrait was telling him she loved him. He wanted to touch the chestnut curls that rested so lightly on her shoulder, cascading down almost to her waist. He wanted to nestle in her arms and have her sweetly smiling lips kiss his brow like Mama did. He wanted to snuggle his face into her warm, creamy neck and stay there forever. He did not know who she was, or why he felt this way; but deep inside himself, he knew he loved her.

Nicolas grew up between his nurseries in the hôtel du Bois and the château de Belvoir. He was a beautiful child with silky dark hair and enormous sapphire-blue eyes. His skin was fine; his cheeks were pink; and he had the most adorable and beguiling smile; and a very subtle and foolproof method of getting his own way: a melting gaze, combined with the former, made him irresistible.

So besotted were his parents, it was not until he was nearly three years old that Angelique felt that she could tear herself away from him on a short tour for the sake of her fans. Because it was summer, which they now always spent at Belvoir, and because Madame Dupont was unaccountably unwell, they left him with his grandparents.

Today, as always, when Mimi's eye was off him (which was reprehensibly often), he came to sit here and bask in the warmth radiating from the beautiful, smiling lady. Beside him, in complete agreement, stood his secret friend. Someone he'd gradually become aware of and now almost took for granted.

Mimi, eventually missing Nicolas, came running. 'Ah, there you are, Petit! I always know where to find you, do I not? Like a moth to a flame, you are.'

As she scooped him up, he pointed to the portrait. 'Belle! Belle!'

'Indeed, she is. You've good taste; I'll say that for you. Come along, *mon chou.*' And she bundled him off to the nursery where he patiently awaited his next opportunity to escape.

Mama and Papa were away a very long time. He began to miss them terribly, even though Grandmama came every day to read to him, and every night to kiss him goodnight and put him to bed. Most mornings, Grandpapa put him up before him on his horse and took him for a little canter down the road. Even the visits from his secret friend cheered him for only a little while. They were bright spots in a very miserable time, but the brightest times were those stolen moments he spent in the picture gallery.

When Mama came back, she hugged him as if she would never let him go and refused to be parted from him ever again. No matter what the difficulties, her little angel must accompany her on the next tour.

Mimi was excited, he could tell, Mama having asked her to come with them, distracted by the packing for herself and her nursling. Consequently, he found lots of opportunities to run away to the picture gallery and be with the beautiful lady he loved.

He spent exciting days with Mama, Papa and Mimi on a huge ship, endlessly fascinated by the waves and patterns on the water as he leant out over the gunwale, held safely in Papa's strong arms. Godmama, recovering from her illness, came, too; but she spent most of her time in her stateroom, dealing with *le mal de mer.* Poor Godmama, she was usually good for hours of entertainment, but not at the moment, it seemed.

Now in The Metropolitan, he awoke to strange sighs and whisperings near at hand; and afar off, beautiful, trilling notes.

'Mama!' He sat up. Whenever he heard Mama sing, he felt a compulsion to go and join her. Where was Mimi? Nowhere to be seen. *Good.* Carefully stretching down from the crib set up for him in a little room off Mama's dressing-room, his sturdy legs reached the floor, carrying him to the open door of the private room where Mama rested between performances.

No, she was not here. Of course, she was onstage. But someone was. He put his head around the door. It was Mimi and someone else. Whatever was she doing? His brow knit in astonishment. She was cuddling a gentleman on Mama's chaise longue. Oh, dear, they did look funny: legs and arms all tangled together. He held back a chuckle, frowning in concern as she moaned softly. Her eyes were closed. Was she in pain? Perhaps he'd better leave.

Suddenly opening her eyes, she turned her head and stared at him. He froze; although, it seemed a little while before she saw him.

'Go back to bed, little cabbage,' she said, gently. 'I will be along in a minute to tuck you in.'

He found his voice, accusing her, 'What are you doing with that man, Mimi?'

'I am comforting this poor gentleman because he is unhappy. Go along; I won't be long. *Go on …*' This, as he stood, staring.

Turning away, he went back to his little cupboard; then, seeing she wasn't watching, edged around to the dressing-room. Hearing his mother's voice reach its glorious heights, he was drawn to the outer door. It was closed, but he knew how to open it. Encouraged by his secret friend, he dragged a footstool over. Just as he got up on it, he heard a whispered argument between Mimi and the gentleman. She wanted to go and see to him now, but the gentleman begged her to stay … just a little longer. Their voices stifled into sighs.

'Go, go!' urged his friend. Quick as a flash, he twisted the knob, opened the door and was away, little legs pumping along the corridor to the stage. Now it was serious. He must put enough distance between himself and Mimi so that he could make the stage before she realised he was missing and drag him back. He had tried to bolt several times but had never before made it this far. Ah, there was the stage. He hid himself in the curtain, edging along until he could see his mother. She was taking a bow. Papa, just inside the wings, had his eyes on Mama, as always. Creeping past, in a fold of the curtain, he erupted into the glare of the footlights.

'Mama!'

The audience roared with delight.

'Nicolas? Etienne!' cried Angelique, in disbelief at the former, and a cry for help to the latter.

The little boy held up his arms to her. 'Nicolas sing with Mama!'

'Yes!' answered the crowd. 'Yes!'

'Oh, but he is so-o-o cute!' cooed a woman in the front row with a twangy New York accent.

His father was on the stage, swinging him up into his arms, facing him to the patrons to introduce him with a smile. 'This is Nicolas, our son. He knows how to make an entrance, does he not?' He waited for the applause to finish. 'Perfect timing, *hein*?'

While the audience registered agreement, Etienne communicated wordlessly with Angelique. She held out a hand to the little boy. 'Nicolas wants to sing with Mama?'

He nodded and clapped. 'Sing,' he declared. 'Nicolas sing.'

The captivated audience took up the chant. 'Sing, Nicolas, sing!'

And so, at just three years of age, and in his nightgown,

Nicolas de Beaulieu made his debut before his first audience—the elite of New York—and his fame was assured.

It was a simple little French nursery rondeau, *Sur le Pont d'Avignon,* and the crowd clapped and sang along with him as, sitting on the shoulder of his papa, he performed his duet with Mama in a pure, silvery soprano, holding her hand.

Afterwards, Papa took him back to the dressing-room, even though he wanted to stay and sing some more with Mama.

'Come along, back to bed, *mon enfant. Tout de suite!* Wave goodbye to your audience.'

'No! Sing with Mama!'

'You have sung with Mama, and now you must go back to bed.'

After a long standing ovation, during which Nicolas further enslaved his audience by his antics, he was carried offstage: his father striding rapidly along the corridor.

'Don't you know that when Mimi puts you to bed at night you're supposed to stay there?'

'Forgot.'

'You forgot? No! I don't believe it. Not a clever boy like you.'

'Silly ol' Nic'las forgot!'

'Hmm … How did you make your escape, *mon fils, hein?*'

'Me open the door.'

'You opened the door? By yourself? Truly? How did you reach the handle?'

'Stool.'

'I said you were a clever boy! And where was Mimi while you were doing all this?'

'Not there.'

'Not there? Then, where?'

'On Mama's chaise longue.'

'Oh? She was sleeping?'

'No, she was comf … comf'ting *un monsieur*.'

'Comforting a gentleman?' Papa looked as if he could not believe his ears.

He nodded. 'The poor gentleman was unhappy. Then me hear Mama sing; so me come here to sing with Mama.' He peered at him anxiously, sensing a tension in his father's demeanour.

'I see.'

Nicolas watched his lips tighten. 'Papa is cross?'

'No, my son. Perhaps it was destiny. I hope you are serious about singing onstage, because it looks as though your audience is serious about you. Come, now, into bed. And no more getting up.' He carried the little boy through both rooms into his crib, ignoring the apologies of the white, shaking nurse, staying beside him until the child slept; and he went out, closing the door.

In the dressing-room, he surveyed the hapless girl.

'I am sorry, Monsieur,' she muttered, unable to meet his eyes.

'Mimi, you have thirty seconds to explain to me why you were "comforting" a gentleman instead of taking care of my son. And do not dare say it was because he was unhappy.'

'I am sorry, Monsieur. I thought Nicolas was asleep.'

There was an incredulous silence, then: 'Is that supposed to be an excuse?'

'Monsieur, it was Alain, my fiancé. It has been so long …'

'What? Alain from Belvoir? What is he doing here?'

'He could not bear to be without me, Monsieur. He was jealous. He could not stop thinking of me with someone else, so he raised enough money to buy a passage to New York.'

'Oh, did he, indeed? This becomes more and more inexcusable. Right on harvest, too.'

'His cousin came back from Italy to help with the harvest in his place, Monsieur. Alain would not be irresponsible.'

'No? You are irresponsible enough for the both of you, are you not? I am very disappointed in you, Mimi. I thought I could trust you with my son. In the morning, you and Alain will take yourselves back to Belvoir. You had best get married. You can have one of the courtyard cottages for the time being. I hope you take better care of your own children, when they come, than you have with mine. Both of you will present yourselves to my secretary at nine in the morning. He will furnish you with tickets and funds to return home. Now, go.'

'But, who will look after Nicolas?'

'What? You dare to ask me that? Not you; that is certain.' He rounded on her. 'Go, I said. Get out of my sight!' For possibly only the second time in his life, the marquis de Beaulieu was near to losing his temper, and the frightened girl lost no time in making her departure.

Madame Dupont spoke from the doorway. 'So, Mimi found another distraction, did she?' She came farther into the room. 'She will not go home, you know. I think she and Alain will stay in America ... Angelique needs you, *mon cher*. You had better go back to her. I will stay with *le petit*.'

'Thank you, Madame.' He shook his head. 'I could not believe it when I saw him run across the stage. You guessed what had happened?'

'Well, she is a featherheaded girl, is she not? And easily distracted, even though good natured and sweet to the child. Perhaps a family of her own will be what she needs to ground her.'

The marquis shrugged. 'She was very good to Nicolas, kind and motherly. He liked her much more than any of the others we tried.'

'Yes, she was very accommodating. Perhaps, in hindsight, a little too much so.'

'True enough. You are right in what you say there, Madame.'

'Nicolas is very intelligent, Monsieur. Perhaps he liked her because she did, now and again, take her mind off him.'

He looked up at that. 'Why do you say that, Madame? This has not happened before?'

She nodded. 'Oh, yes, I think it has happened quite often at Belvoir. I remember Mimi telling me on the ship that she always knew where to find him, for there was only one place he went.'

'Did she, indeed? And where was that, Madame?'

'I understand it is Angelique's copy of the portrait of her mother that draws him. It is a lovely painting.'

'*Vraiment?* Of course, she was a great beauty. But ... he is just a little child.'

'Who knows what draws a child to someone? She was a very sweet person, you know, and that quality shines out of her portrait.'

'Yes, yes, you are right. I only met her as a small child before she became, er ... ill; but I do remember. Of course, Nicolas was not born until long after her death.'

'No, it was a great pity, that. She was a good mother, and she would have been a loving grandmother. But *c'est la vie, hein?* Now, we must deal with what is. Of course, now that Nicolas has begun his career, he will sing every night, will he not?'

He shrugged. 'If we try to keep him away from his fans they will eat us.'

Her eyes sparkled. 'We shall dress him in a tiny formal suit and have him sing *Brahms' Lullaby*. He knows it, and American audiences are delightfully sentimental. He is a hit, my dear, and he loves it. It is his medium, without doubt.'

'I think you are right, Madame. He certainly was not intimidated by the audience. In fact, he seemed to treat them as if he expected adulation from them. As if it was his right.'

'You have it, my dear. I noticed it, too. He briefly

reminded me of someone, but it was gone before I could remember. While he feels that way, it cannot do any harm to let him perform once or twice per night—as long as it is not too late in the evening. Do not look for another nurse at this point. I shall take care of him for the rest of the tour.'

'But, Madame, you came with us to New York to find your daughter. I am most grateful for your offer, but you will be very limited if you take on the care of Nicolas.'

'It does not matter, dear boy—needs must. I do not think Cèline would see me, anyway. But I will hire a private detective, and at least, I will know how she is.'

'You are very good, Madame. Leave the private detective to me. If your daughter is in New York, I will make sure that you see her.'

'Thank you, my dear. Meanwhile, I shall arrange everything for Nicolas: his stage apparel and so on. We can teach him some more songs and a few little dance steps—a simple routine. I can do that. Then he will have his own little repertoire.' She smiled happily.

Watching in silence, Etienne said finally, 'Madame, you terrify me. Have I not always said you are *femme formidable*? Shall I appoint you as his manager?'

Her dimple came and went. 'There will be no need, *mon cher.* I think, from what we have seen of him so far, he will manage his own career quite well, without any interference from the rest of us.'

He was laughing as he left her to return to Angelique. Somewhere between the dressing-room and the stage, he felt a great weight lift from his shoulders, which he knew was due entirely to Madame Dupont: at this moment, totally involved in planning dance lessons to further the stage career of child prodigy, Nicolas de Beaulieu, who, the next night, was named by his ecstatic followers 'Beau Nicolas'.

§

In due course, a discreet Pinkerton's man sent up his card to Madame Dupont in her suite in the Waldorf, and she met him in the private lounge.

'Madame, I have traced your daughter, Cèline Morelli. You know that she has recently divorced her husband, Alberto Morelli?'

Madame Dupont nodded. 'I knew that they were separated, Monsieur. It does not surprise me.'

'She is, at present, touring Australia with the New York Dance Company. They will be away for some months. Do you require us to send a man out there to contact her?'

She made a negating gesture. 'No, Monsieur, *pas du tout*. I think I must now leave it up to Cèline, or fate, to make contact. I only want to know that she is well and happy.'

'I think I may be able to reassure you on that head, Madame, as far as anyone other than herself is able to know. She is certainly well, or she could not hold the high position in the dance company that she does; and I understand she plans to marry her fiancé, an operatic baritone, at the completion of the tour. I have enclosed his name and details, including a photograph, in this folder. He is a count, but I am sorry: I find his name unpronounceable …'

'Oh, a Georgian, I see; and handsome, too. Thank you, Monsieur, for all your trouble. You have been entirely helpful in easing my mind about my daughter.'

'It has been a great pleasure, Madame. Oh, and that French couple you asked about? Mimi Duval and Alain Poisson? You were right. They did not board the ship. They appear to have sold their tickets and headed west on the train.'

CHAPTER THIRTY-FOUR ~ THE SECRET FRIEND

12 October 1925

Nicolas has found himself a real life version of his favourite portrait, and at five years of age has fallen in love and announced that he wants to marry her. It is so sweet that we have all had a chuckle, and the girl has taken it in such good part and gone along with him. What a sweet, warm personality she is. Just the right person not to make fun of a little boy's dreams. They are now firm friends and each other's fan. She says she finds him adorable and is only waiting for him to grow up enough to put the ring on her finger!

But there is something else I have discovered about Nicolas that is intriguing.

There was an air of anticipation and excitement at the Opéra Magique. A talented new dancer had been engaged to replace the understudy to the current prima donna, and it was her first performance. At the end, there was a great roar from the audience and many curtain calls.

Nicolas was waiting in the wings with his parents when the ballerinas filed offstage. The new ballerina was at the head. She was petite and slender, elegant in a waltz-length tutu and satin *pointe* slippers. Under a little jewelled headdress, she had a wealth of chestnut hair plaited into a coronet.

'*Belle dame*!' said Nicolas, clapping his hands.

The ballerina smiled widely, her blue eyes twinkling. 'That is the best curtain call I've had tonight, *mon brave*. And you are ...' She stood back. 'No, let me guess: Beau Nicolas!'

'How did you know?' The solemn eyes quizzed her.

'Your fame has gone before you, *Chéri*. And *I* am your biggest fan.' She turned to his parents. 'How do you do? Lisette: I am so pleased to meet you. Congratulations on such a beautiful child!'

'Thank you. He is such a handful!' laughed Angelique, clasping the proffered hand.

'He keeps us all on our toes,' murmured Etienne, bowing.

'Sette? Settie! Will you marry me, one day?' The little boy gazed up at her—his eyes wide and serious—the most adorable expression on his face.

The ballerina gave a delightful chuckle. 'Oho, I see what you mean!' She looked down at him. 'Here's a Prince Charming for you, then. Nothing backward about this one, eh?'

'Will you?' He took her hand and pressed a kiss on the back of it.

'Of course, *mon brave*! I would be honoured.' She knelt down, put her hands on his shoulders and looked into his eyes. 'When you are big enough.'

'But I am big now.'

'Indeed you are. Big and handsome.' She smoothed his hair and stood up. 'But a little bigger, I think, don't you?'

He shook his head. 'When, then?'

The ballerina raised her arm high and waggled her

fingers. 'See my hand up there? When you are as tall as that, we will speak again, *n'est-ce pas? Bien.*' Her smile, mischievous and conspiratorial, lit up her face, enveloping him in warmth.

Nicolas did not return her smile, but he basked in its sunshine. 'Will you sign my autograph book, then, Sette?'

'With pleasure, *mon chou*. But only on the condition that you do the same for me, *hein*? But we must do it another time. Your audience is waiting for you.'

'Can we not do it now, Mama?' he begged.

'I'm sorry, *mon ange*,' said Angelique. 'We must go onstage. Monsieur Merignac is beckoning us.' She glanced at the ballerina, her eyes brimful of laughter. 'You can continue your flirtation some other time, *hein*?'

Nicolas' gaze followed his mother's. 'Sette?' The big eyes beguiled. 'If you please, can we do it after the show?'

'But of course, *mon chou*. If your parents will permit?'

'*Mais certainement*,' said Etienne. 'Please come to our dressing-room after the performance. When we are at the Opéra Magique, we always hold a little champagne party. Do come. If you are sure it won't be an inconvenience?'

'Not at all. *Merci*,' laughed the ballerina, blowing Nicolas a kiss. 'He is, without question, the most adorable suitor I have ever had!'

§

Lisette, now wrapped in a shawl over her costume, entered the dressing-room to find the party in full swing. Her hosts were circulating amongst artists and celebrities who were eating, drinking and all talking together in a confused babble. She was welcomed by Etienne with a glass of champagne and a plate of canapés, introduced to countless people whose names she forgot at once.

Nicolas was drinking blackcurrant juice, but put it down when he saw her, losing no time in presenting her with a pen and his autograph book. 'Here in the centre,' he said. 'A double page, just for you, Settie.'

'Thank you, what shall I write?' *To my darling Beau Nicolas: a singer sans pareil.* She signed with a flourish and handed it back. 'I heard you sing tonight. You have a voice, Maestro. *Bien sûr*, you have a voice! What are you going to write in mine?'

With a little quirk to her mobile lips, she watched him run over to his father, dictate a message and then sit up at the dressing table, laboriously writing something.

He ran back, handing it to her with a rueful grin. 'I *did* sign it myself. See? I can only write my name yet.' The message read: *To a belle dame sans pareil, with love from* and under it in large uneven letters: *Nicolas.*

'How beautiful! Thank you, I will treasure this.' Lisette felt tears rush into her eyes as she stooped to give him a hug. She laughed as she brushed them away. 'You, my child, are set to be a heartbreaker!'

Later, when signatures, messages and compliments had been exchanged, Angelique explained to Lisette about the portrait and its effect on Nicolas.

'But, how sweet!' she exclaimed. 'And what a coincidence! He is one of a kind, this one, eh? And what was her name: the lady in the portrait? Katarina? I will remember it.'

Soon, Lisette took her leave. '*Au revoir*, how lovely to meet you. *Au revoir*, my soldier.'

Nicolas held out his arms. 'Sette? May I kiss you?'

'Ooh, forward!' She held hers wide and Nicolas flew into them. 'Goodbye, then, my charmer. See you soon.' She thanked Angelique and Etienne and wended her graceful way to the door.

'*Belle dame*,' said Nicolas, watching her progress. He looked at his grandfather, who had come to stand with his family, and pointed. 'I love her: Sette.'

The duc put out a hand and lightly stroked the boy's hair. 'You have good taste, *mon fils*,' he sighed. 'One cannot help but fall in love with a beautiful ballerina.'

'She has a much livelier disposition than Mama, but somehow, she is like her, don't you think?' asked Angelique. 'The portrait, I mean. Before ...'

'Oh, yes, very much like her,' replied the duc. 'On first impression, remarkable: hair and eye colour, face shape. Although, she is not nearly as tall. The personalities are different, I think. Katarina did not have the mischief that is in her smile, but the same sweet kindness radiates from her face.' He put an arm around Nicolas, drawing him closer. 'I do see where my grandson is coming from. I do, indeed!'

From that moment, Nicolas felt a great, indefinable affinity with his grandfather.

3 January 1926

This child is beautiful, inside and out: Angel, without the darkness. Besides, all children have at least one secret friend. Why should I be surprised?

One day, Nicolas was visiting Madame Dupont, as he often did when his Mama and Papa were socialising, and as usual, climbed up to tinker at the piano. But this time it was different. A tune emerged. The child, less than six years old, was actually composing.

And then, something about the way he turned his head, listening as he touched the keys, got through to her, shocking her into speech. 'Angel?' she whispered. 'Angel ...? *Mon Dieu*, it is Angel!'

The little boy climbed down from the piano stool and came to stand beside her chair. 'What did you say, Godmama?'

'Nothing, Child. You just reminded me of someone. You are a clever boy. You are composing?'

'Yes. But I am not clever. I have a friend who helps me. He tells me the notes.'

'Oh, indeed? This friend, he was with you just now?'

'Yes, Godmama. He says he will be with me always.'

'Does he? And what does he look like, your friend?'

'I don't know. He says it is best if he remains unseen. That way he can be with me all the time. Less comp … complicated, he says.'

'But you have never spoken of him before?'

'No, because it is a secret. He said he is my secret friend, and I am not to tell anybody. But just now when you said something, he told me to tell you. He said you would understand.'

'Did he?' She was white, shaken. 'Of course I understand. Every child has a secret friend, *n'est-ce pas*?' Almost, she could not ask it: 'And did he tell you his name?'

'Yes, Godmama,' he said, with the sweetest of smiles. 'He said his name is Angel. It is odd, isn't it? Mama calls me her angel.'

She stared at him. It could not be … Yet it explained something else. Since Nicolas had begun to sing with his mother as a three-year-old, Angel had not been seen at Angelique's side onstage. Had Angelique missed him? Or was she, too, aware of him as an invisible presence? When she had a chance, she would ask her. Stunned, Madame Dupont could find nothing to say to the little boy in reply.

'Godmama? Who is that?' Nicolas pointed to a photograph on her bureau.

'That is Monsieur Dupont, my dear. He died long before you were born, before your mama was born, even. He was a very kind man. He had a loving spirit.'

'Do you know, Godmama? I feel as if I know him. Strange, isn't it?'

'Indeed, my dear, it is very strange. And how do you feel about him?'

'I love him. May I have a hug, Godmama?'

'Of course, my darling. Hop up on my knee … Mmm, you're a good hugger!'

'I know. I love you, Godmama.'

8 February 1926

This week has been a nightmare. First, I lost an old and dear friend. And now, with him hardly cold in the ground, I have received a message that another has been killed in an automobile accident.

Madame Dupont was saddened and touched to hear that Gaston had been found dead at his desk on Monday by a maid bringing his midmorning coffee. He'd refused to retire, never giving in to the chest pain he described as indigestion.

'Poor Gaston,' she said to Mathilde. 'Always so devoted to his work and the Opéra Magique.'

'No, Madame,' replied Mathilde, thanking her for the flowers she had brought. 'It was *you* he was devoted to. His whole life. You.'

Suddenly, she felt uncomfortable at the blunt, almost accusatory words, remembering the times when she thought Gaston had betrayed her and reacted accordingly. She should have known he would never willingly do such a thing. Misguided, yes. Clumsy, certainly. But all his life, he had devoted himself to her and her causes.

She couldn't meet his wife's piercing gaze. 'I am sorry, Mathilde,' she murmured. 'He was a very faithful man. And a faithful friend. I, we, will miss him.'

'Very much, Madame.'

'Indeed. And you, Mathilde? How will you manage without him?'

'It will be hard, Madame. You see, both of us have been here so long. It is home to me.'

'You must stay as long as you wish. You know that, don't you?'

'It is like you to say so, Madame. But I would not stay without being of use to you.'

'That is of no moment. Do not give it a thought,' she replied. Then, perceiving that the woman still had something she wanted to say, added, 'What do you have in mind?'

'Gaston taught me all the running of the house, in case something happened to him. I have spoken to Monsieur Merignac and Jeanne, and we believe that we can carry on with some hired help for the heavy work and the accounting.'

Madame Dupont's brow cleared. 'But of course, hire who you like. You three are in charge.' She rose. 'Mathilde, you are sure about this? That you can do this?'

'Yes, Madame. In a funny way, I will feel that Gaston is still here, and I wish to stay so that I can be with him.'

'You may be right.' *This opera house is full of ghosts.* 'Yes, you may be right,' she sighed and took her leave.

Before the week was out, Madame Dupont received a visit from Philippe, to tell her that Xavier's car had been hit on a crossroad by a runaway van, killing him instantly. He had been on his way back to Villefontaine after visiting his grandchildren in Paris. While he was with her, Philippe dropped another bombshell: he had joined the diplomatic corps. He and Elise and their family were waiting for the call to see where in the world they would be sent. Philippe thought they would be leaving soon after his father's funeral.

A melancholy descended on her. There were so few of her friends left, now. And there was the difficulty that she had not properly mourned for Gaston before Xavier had been taken. She felt it deeply. *Poor Xavier,* she thought. *At least he lived a little at the last. I hope he is happy now. And dear, faithful Gaston.* Then, as always: *But how will Angelique take the news?*

15 September 1926

This is a day when I could think of 'what ifs' and 'might have beens', if I allowed myself the luxury. There is also the added pain of having another letter to my daughter returned, unopened. There

*is something particularly anonymous and hurtful about a letter
stamped 'Return to Sender'. I have put it with all the other letters
I have sent to Céline over the years. All of them have been
returned in this way. They make quite a packet: all tied up with
pink ribbon. Perhaps she will read them, one day.*

On the morning of the fiftieth wedding anniversary of the
duc and duchesse de Belvoir, Madame Dupont came
downstairs to find her salon filled with the heady fragrance
of masses and masses of flowers; the centrepiece of which
was a huge bouquet of red roses. On a whim, she counted
them. There were fifty-one. Gathering them up, she held
them to her, heedless of the thorns, burying her face in the
petals, weeping into their velvet fragrance. All the tears
that she had held within for so long, crowding into her
eyes, fighting to get out.

She cried for Angel, herself, Katarina, the duc, the
duchesse, Xavier, Gaston, all the beautiful young men lost
in the war, all their vanished dreams, her rift with her
daughter. She cried for them all, and at the end felt flat and
drained.

Then she picked up the letter marked 'Return to
Sender' and slowly made her way upstairs. *No more tears,*
she thought. *I do not have any left ...*

15 January 1929

*Today I went to the Gare Saint-Lazare to farewell Nicolas,
Angelique and Etienne; and I am missing them already. This
time, fate has decided that I don't go with them to New York. I
have a pain that I have been ignoring for a long time, but now it is
too insistent to neglect any longer. As I waved them goodbye, I had
a strange premonition that this would be the last time I would see
them. In this life, anyway.*

When Nicolas was almost nine years old and sailing on a

big ocean liner to perform with his mother, yet again, in New York, Madame Dupont, declining for the first time to accompany them, made an appointment with her doctor, who sent her for a second opinion.

After that, there was the dark day that the physician diagnosed a condition that she could not even bring herself to name in her diary, but which, nevertheless, set the limit to her earthly life.

The physician spoke kindly, 'I cannot tell you exactly how much time you have left, Madame. I am not God. He is the only one who knows this.'

She inclined her head. 'Yes, Monsieur.'

'I will just say this: If I were you, I would get my affairs in order. As soon as possible.'

'Can you be more specific, Monsieur, if you please?'

'I am afraid not, Madame, everyone is different. But most patients I have seen at your stage have a matter of weeks, possibly a few months, but not usually more than a few weeks. I am sorry, Madame.'

'Do not be sorry, Monsieur. I have already outlived most of my friends. I am ready to go whenever *le bon Dieu* calls me.'

The physician nodded. 'Indeed, Madame. But until that day, you will need someone with you. I will send two nurses for you. They are very good. They will take care of you, between them, twenty-four hours a day. They will know what to do to keep you comfortable.'

She thanked the physician composedly, facing her own mortality with the same calm fortitude with which she had approached almost every other crisis of adversity in her life.

And so, Nurses Jacques and LeFevre moved into her home. Capable and kind, they unobtrusively took care of every aspect of her life, seeming to know without being told when she was in pain and dealing with it competently. She approved their brisk efficiency and no fuss, common sense attitude—it was something to which she could relate.

Uncannily, they seemed to be able to anticipate her every need, and there was always one there with her at night, bringing her something to help her sleep, quietly checking on her from time to time, speaking soothingly if she were awake. She found their presence comforting.

A private person, she decided it would be best to keep the knowledge of her condition to herself. Angelique was on tour again, and she did not want anything to disturb her equilibrium.

The duc, having his own manifold means of keeping himself informed of her welfare, learnt of her illness, making an urgent visit to her.

Receiving him on her day bed in her sitting room next to her bedchamber, she said, 'It is a great pleasure to receive this visit from you, Monsieur. I am sorry I cannot rise to greet you.'

Greeting her with loving concern, he kissed her hand, retaining it in his. 'Ma Belle, I am desolated to find you in such poor health.' He reached for a chair and drawing it up, sat close to her.

Just then, Nurse Jacques knocked on the door and came in with a gigantic vase of flowers.

'Thank you, Nurse. You found a vase big enough, then?'

'Only just, Monsieur.'

'Very good. Put them over there on that table where Madame Dupont can see them.'

The nurse obeyed and went out, smiling.

Madame Dupont was very touched. 'I thank you, Monsieur. They are beautiful.'

'I shall not state the obvious, Ma Belle,' he replied, kissing her hand again. 'I only wish I could restore your health to you.'

'*Anno Domini,* Monsieur. *Anno Domini.* It is a fact of life.'

'Ah, Ma Belle, you are still the same delightfully composed and tranquil lady you have always been.

Nothing will change that.'

'*Que sera,* Monsieur, I have always believed it. *Le bon Dieu* does not call us before our time. And I am ready. There comes a time when it becomes harder to live than it is to die, *mon cher,*' she replied with a twinkle.

'Oh, Ma Belle—so brave!' He cradled her hand to his face. 'Does Angelique know of this: your illness, my dear?'

'No, Monsieur. I do not want her told until she finishes her tour. If I am still here, *très bien.* If not ...' She shrugged. 'I do not want to interrupt her tour and cause more stress on her already fragile nerves.'

'Do you not think she would wish to see you, Ma Belle?' he asked, gently.

'Perhaps,' she acknowledged. 'I would spare her grief if I could. Once I am gone, she will get used to it. And she has Etienne and Nicolas with her and the support of you and your family.' *And Angel.*

'You may rest assured that we will take very great care of her, Ma Belle,' he said, tenderly. 'And her great talent shall be nurtured the way you would wish. I promise you that. She is a precious member of my family, you know.'

'I know, *mon cher,* and I am grateful.'

'You know that she has taken to calling me Papa-duc?'

'Has she? The sweet child! But how is the duchesse? Etienne said, before he left, that she has not been well and that you were all very worried about her.'

'The duchesse has dementia, my love. Her condition has deteriorated to the point where she knows none of us.' He shrugged his hurt. 'She is but ... an empty shell.'

'Oh, my dear, I am *so* sorry.'

He tightened his grip on her hand. 'I have already lost her, and now I am about to lose you.'

His pain caught at her heart. 'Georges, dearest ...'

He met her eyes. 'I know ...'

'*Cher* Georges, I know that you will be lonely without your dearest friend, but you must not worry about me; for I have been shown a wonderful vision.' Her eyes beginning to shine, she gave him her other hand, which he held with rapt attention, indulgently observing the wonder in her face. 'It is true, Monsieur, that when you die, the ones who love you come for you. It is indeed true. Indeed, indeed, it is. I have seen it.'

'Then, of a surety, my love, one of us will come for the other,' he answered, transferring both her hands to one of his and stroking her cheek with the other.

She looked at him, how well and good-looking he still was in his seventies, with the health and vigour many a man of fifty would envy.

'My dear,' she said, folding her hands primly in her lap, her dimple appearing. 'Of course. But there is little doubt that I shall be the one to come for you, for I know I have not long left to me.'

I know who will be coming for me. In her mind's eye, she saw them: Sprite, Katarina and Angel, coming towards her, holding out their hands.

She held hers out now to the duc. 'My dear faithful one, even though I did not know it, you have always been there for me, have you not? I thank you most sincerely for the support you gave me in my need.'

'Ma Belle, it has been my greatest pleasure in life to render to you whatever service was in my power,' he said huskily, gathering her hands in his. 'I only wish it could have been more. My greatest regret is that our paths in life did not allow us to fulfil our dreams of each other.' He tried to smile. 'Perhaps, in the next life, we shall do so, eh?'

'Undoubtedly, dearest Georges! Love lasts forever, and yours has lasted a lifetime, already. When we die, love is the only thing we can take with us. Of a certainty, we shall be happy together, *mon cher.*' Her eyes glowed with tender emotion.

He kissed her gently, tears in his. '*Au revoir*, Ma Belle. Until we meet again.' He rose and left the room: a tall, lonely figure, turning at the door to give her a small salute. She acknowledged it with a little gesture of her own.

Until we meet again, my love …

Her eyes remained on the empty doorway long after he had gone; his final words to her reminding her of her last goodbye with Angel before he went away with Sprite and Katarina.

There was nothing she could change about her life now. It was, to all intents and purposes, over. Would she have changed it if she could? There was one thing she would have done differently. The guilt poured over her as it had at every thought of it. *Angel and Katarina …* She'd never have interfered if she had known then what she knew now. So often had she regretted that she had not seen their love for each other. And if she had? Would their lives have turned out any better?

And there was one other thing … But no, she would not then have had Cèline: Cèline, who had kept her word and never spoken to her again. She closed her eyes.

'*Que … sera,*' she murmured to the empty air.

CHAPTER THIRTY-FIVE ~ REUNITED

21 May 1929

My dear duc has promised to take care of Angelique, so that is a great weight off my mind. And she has Etienne and Nicolas, who is astoundingly like Angel: Angel without the darkness, as I like to say. Of a truth, as I wait in the antechamber of le bon Dieu, I grow weary and pray for the day when I, too, shall be with the angels; and I shall see my dear friend again. I cannot wait for he and Katarina and Sprite to come for me the way they came for him, and I shall be young and happy: carefree like them, forever. I

...

Hearing a slight rustle, as if of angels' wings, Madame Dupont looked up and gave a glad cry; the pencil rolling unheeded from her fingers.

The nurses, feet up, enjoying tea in the sitting room, looked at each other half-guiltily and with one accord, sprang up, rushing into the room.

'Oh, she's gone, poor thing,' said Nurse Jacques, checking for vital signs and closing the weary eyes.

The other, Nurse LeFevre, taking the diary from under her slack hand and bending to pick up the pencil, opened the top drawer of the bureau. 'Oh, my Lord! Look at all these diaries! I wonder what's in them?' she exclaimed, dropping it in on top of the others and closing the drawer.

'They're not for your eyes; that's certain,' commented Nurse Jacques. 'She was always scribbling away in them.'

'An old lady like her? Bedridden! What would she have to write about?'

'You might be surprised,' said Nurse Jacques, with a little smile. 'She lived a long time, and she had some pretty high-up friends. She was quite a famous ballerina herself, I believe. And she lived here with the marquis du Bois. She wasn't always old, you know! And if that wasn't the duc de Belvoir that came in the other morning with all those flowers, I'll eat my hat.' Her lips curved. 'Like a young beau with his first love, he was; and he must be seventy-five, if he's a day. Oh, yes, she would have had a story to tell, that's certain.'

'Ah, well,' said the other, 'it's a funny old world.'

'Indeed, it is. By the way, she called out to someone just before we came in. Did you hear who it was? Was it to us, do you think?' she asked doubtfully, remembering the joyous note in her voice.

Turning the key in the lock and putting it with the pencil on top of the bureau, Nurse LeFevre moved back to look down with compassion on the crumpled grey figure on the bed. She had not seen the beautiful young ballerina dancing gaily towards the one who had come for her. 'I thought she said "Monsieur Dupont",' she replied, smoothing the cover carefully under the folded, timeworn hands.

§

Late in the day, a woman came to the door. Nurse LeFevre let her in. 'I am sorry, Madame, you are too late. She died this morning. So sad! She was always hoping you'd come …'

'But ... you cannot know who I am?'

'She kept a photograph of you beside her bed.' Nurse LeFevre looked her over kindly, leading her to the bedchamber. The lips were marginally thinner; the masterful nose a little more prominent; the wheat-gold hair tinged with silver; but her dancer's figure was still supple and elegant: still recognisable as the young ballerina in the photograph on Madame Dupont's bedside table.

'I was such a terrible child. My jealousy was such that it made me—*evil*. I did something, once. Something terrible. I don't know if she knew ... I wanted to come back and apologise, make amends, but I was always too proud. And now, I never can.' Her mouth worked. 'She looks so peaceful ...' She turned to the nurse. 'I know nothing of her life. I haven't seen her since I was fifteen. Oh, Maman, Maman, *je regrette* ... so much ...' She knelt by the bed, overcome by tears.

Nurse LeFevre took the key and opened the drawer containing the diaries. She touched the weeping Cèline on the shoulder. 'You want to know about her life? Look your fill. You shall know all ...'

Cèline rose, wiped her eyes and thanked Nurse LeFevre gushingly for taking such good care of her mother. She took the armful of books and a packet of letters tied with pink ribbon, with a sob.

The nurse did not see the slight triumphant smile as she walked out the door.

§

On a stage in New York, Angelique and Nicolas were receiving a standing ovation; Nicolas scanning the audience, as usual. 'Look, Mama. Godmama is here.'

'No, she cannot be ... Where?'

'Look over there, in that seat in the front row on the aisle. See? With that dear old gentleman with the wavy white hair. You know, Monsieur Dupont. The one in the photograph on Godmama's bureau.'

'You are talking nonsense, my angel. She cannot be here, and neither can Monsieur Dupont.'

'Yes, she is,' he asserted, waving in their direction. 'Oh, no, she is not there now. Where has she gone?'

'Perhaps it is someone who looks like her. Smile, darling. Get ready for this bow. Give me your hand. One ... Two ... Three ... Now. There are many people who look like others. *Par exemple*, even though you look like your papa, you remind me very much of my Angelpapa, the marquis du Bois.'

Nicolas gave her an unreadable glance as his fingers entwined in hers. His right hand stretched out to his invisible friend. They took another bow.

EPILOGUE

6 December 1929

The publisher tapped the last page with a forefinger. He went back and re-read a couple of pages for clarification, then sat staring pensively into space. There would be no more diaries; that was certain. How, then, was he to find out?

This young lad, Nicolas, would bear watching. His nose told him there was a story here. Odd, the inferences made by Madame Dupont, and the last entry in the book. As if …? He shivered and straightened up decisively.

Of course, as promised, he now knew who the author was. He should have thought of the daughter. But she would be of no further use to him. She may have had knowledge of the early life of Angel and Madame Dupont, but she would know nothing about the person who now aroused his journalistic instincts. No, any research must now be done by him—or his delegate—and he knew just who to set onto it.

His son, the youngest subeditor, would be given the task of researching the biography of Nicolas, only son of the marquis de Beaulieu, heir of the duc de Belvoir. This would give him something to do. Already the Crash was beginning to be felt by many, including publishing houses. But perhaps in time, he would obtain the answer to the puzzle he had found in the last few pages of a diary.

Can it be possible, he asked himself, *that one might live on into eternity, as Madame Dupont had implied?*

Can it possibly be that Angel: Master of Illusion and marquis du Bois, might remain the Master forever?

MASTER OF ILLUSION BOOK ONE

Murder. Magic. Music. Obsession.

Master of Illusion follows the lives of childhood comrades, Angel and Elise, as they run hand in hand from a history of treachery, heartache and crippling abuse. Under the mask of exceptional talent and in the name of justice, they each grapple with their own damaged version of love and loyalty, while fiercely protecting their terrible secrets.

Set in the operatic era of 19th century France, talented dancer Elise is discovered by the eminent Opéra Français and is whisked away from a simple life to fulfil her dreams of becoming prima ballerina. Her path is forever changed the day she rescues the disfigured, amnesic genius— Angel—from a life of abandonment and mistreatment. Angel's obsessions define him: his emulation of the Phantom of the Opera coupled with a latent dark side develop into a fervent passion for a young soprano. Cast under Angel's charming spell, Elise assumes the role of his protector and nurturer—only to discover that she, too, wields powers of her own: persuasion and contrivance.

In their efforts to reach the pinnacle of operatic success, Angel and Elise are faced with the challenge of defining justice, love and self-acceptance. Through abandonment, Angel knows only one form of love— obsession; and Elise, whose purity lies in ruins at the hands of evil, is raped of her capacity for romantic love.

Can they fulfil their childhood dreams without blood on their hands?

MASTER OF ILLUSION BOOK TWO

Secrets, Tragedy, Courage, Love.

Master of Illusion Book Two continues the story of the tormented genius, Angel, and his childhood friend, Elise, the prima ballerina who once graced the stage as La Belle and now directs their own opera house, the Opéra Magique. Their lives ensue in an entanglement of secrets, subterfuge, tragedy and love through which they battle their fated hand. Though the skeletons of the past continue to haunt, the veil concealing the truth begins to fall.

It is Paris, 1892, and the Opéra Magique is riding a wave of unparalleled success, with the help of Sprite, the Master's popular, fairy-like assistant. Walking the fine line required to keep in abeyance the mutual passions of her star, the volatile magician known as the Master of Illusion, and her goddaughter, the beautiful comtesse de Villefontaine, Madame Dupont needs all her ingenuity to divert the jealous rage of the comte and the suspicions of Police Chief Captain Moreau.

Few people know the truth behind the Master's identity, yet one of them is about to give him away. But as their opera house and lives are plunged, yet again, into unthinkable tragedy, fate thrusts Angel and Elise—the Master and Madame—onto a new path of discovery: a path that holds both alluring revelations and nightmares of untold suffering.

Angel and Elise battle choices of life and death, of courage and sacrifice, as they finally discover the answers they've so longed for. But, in discovering the truth of the past, the truth about Angel and the truth about love, do they find the solace they so crave?

ABOUT ANNE ROUEN

Anne Rouen is an award-winning historical fiction author from Australia, who is inspired by the opulent operatic age of 19th century France, the classic Belle Époque era and the dark times of the Great War. This passion was ignited from her own heritage, combined with a lifelong love of historical fiction writing, particularly those of a similar ilk to Georgette Heyer.

This is where inspiration for the *Master of Illusion* series was born.

Anne Rouen is the alter ego of Lynn Newberry: a country woman from the New South Wales New England region, who breeds Brangus cattle by day and is a dedicated, passionate horsewoman.

The lady behind Anne Rouen has completed a specialist teaching degree in the Rural Sciences department of the University of New England, and has spent most of her life involved in the agricultural industry—twenty of them as an educator.

Throughout her career, Lynn has escaped the everyday demands of work through the hand of Anne Rouen. *Master of Illusion—Book One* was her first published novel, and it, along with its sequel, *Master of Illusion—Book Two*, has been nominated in several award programs, most notably, the *Global Ebook Awards* where it won the Silver Medal for *Modern Historical Literature Fiction* in 2014.

Lynn has also seen success with her short story writing, achieving a Highly Commended in the *Rolf Boldrewood Literary Awards* (2011) for *The Scent of a Criminal*.

With a broad range of interests, Anne Rouen writes a regular blog, where she chats about her firsthand experience beating breast cancer, her love of horses and other current issues that are close to her heart.

You can keep up with the latest information about Anne Rouen on social media and through her website at www.annerouen.com.